Louise Penny is the Number One *New York Times* bestselling author of the Inspector Gamache series, including *Still Life*, which won the CWA John Creasey Dagger in 2006. Recipient of virtually every existing award for crime fiction, Louise was also granted the Order of Canada in 2014 and received an honorary doctorate of literature from Carleton University and the Ordre Nationale du Québec in 2017. She lives in a small village south of Montreal.

Praise for Louise Penny and the series:

'Louise Penny is one of the greatest crime writers of our times' Denise Mina

'She makes most of her competitors seem like wannabes' *The Times*

'A cracking storyteller, who can create fascinating characters, a twisty plot and wonderful surprise endings' Ann Cleeves

'Outstanding . . . a constantly surprising series that deepens and darkens as it evolves' *The New York Times*

'No one does atmospheric quite like Louise Penny . . . a fantastic series' Elly Griffiths

'Louise Penny's writing is intricate, beautiful and compelling. She is an original voice, a distillation of both PD James and Barbara Vine at their peaks and a worthy successor to both' Peter James

'[An] atmospheric, distinctive series' Kate Mosse

'Penny is an absolute joy' *Irish Times*

'The series is deep and grand and altogether extraordinary . . . Miraculous' *Washington Post*

The Gamache series

LOUISE PENNY

Glass Houses

HODDER

First published in the United States in 2017 by Minotaur,
a division of St Martin's Press
First published in Great Britain in 2017 by Sphere
This edition published in 2021 by Hodder & Stoughton
An Hachette UK company

1

Map by Rhys Davies

A CIP catalogue record for this title is available from the British Library

B format ISBN 978 1 529 38659 2
eBook ISBN 978 1 529 38660 8

Printed and bound in Great Britain by Clays Ltd, Elcograf S.p.A.

Hodder & Stoughton policy is to use papers that are natural, renewable
and recyclable products and made from wood grown in sustainable
forests. The logging and manufacturing processes are expected to
conform to the environmental regulations of the country of origin.

Hodder & Stoughton Ltd
Carmelite House
50 Victoria Embankment
London EC4Y 0DZ

www.hodder.co.uk

A LETTER FROM LOUISE

When I was thirty-five, I thought the best was behind me.

I was lonely, and tired, and empty. Plodding through life.

At thirty-five.

By the time I was forty-five, I was married to the love of my life, and my first book was about to be published.

And now I'm sixty. Living in a beautiful Québec village, surrounded by friends, with thirteen books to my name. And counting.

This milestone birthday gives me a chance to look back in wonderment. And gratitude. And amazement. That I should be here, happy, joyous, and free.

No one quite appreciates, and recognises, the light like those who've lived in darkness. That awareness is what I try to bring to the books. The duality of our lives. The power of perception. The staggering weight of despair, and the amazement when it is lifted.

The gap between how we appear and how we really feel.

Those are foundations of the Gamache books.

Initially they were called the Three Pines books, which, of course, they are. Three Pines is the tiny hidden village in Québec. Not on any map, it is only ever found by those who are lost.

But, once found, never forgotten.

At their core, though, these books are about the profound decency of Armand Gamache, and the struggles he has to remain a good person. When 'good' is subjective, and 'decent' is a matter of judgement.

These books might appear, superficially, as traditional crime novels. But they are, I believe, more about life than death. About choices. About the price of freedom. About the struggle for peace.

Armand Gamache, of the Sûreté du Québec, is inspired by my husband, Michael Whitehead. A doctor who treated children with cancer. Who spent his life searching for cures. Who saved countless young lives, boys and girls who now have children of their own.

Despite the dreadful deaths and broken hearts all around him, Michael was the happiest man alive. Because he understood the great gift that life is.

Michael gave that perception to Armand.

Michael died of dementia. And it broke my heart. But I still have Armand. And Clara, and Jean-Guy. Myrna and Gabri and Olivier. And crazy old Ruth.

At thirty-five, I thought the best was behind me.

As I celebrate my sixtieth birthday, I can hardly wait to see what happens next.

> *Ring the bells that still can ring*
> *Forget your perfect offering*
> *There's a crack in everything.*
> *That's how the light gets in.*

Welcome to the very cracked world of Armand Gamache and Three Pines. I am overjoyed to be able to share it with you.

Meet you in the bistro …

Louise Penny
March 2018

To Lise Desrosiers, whom I found in my garden,
and who now lives in my heart

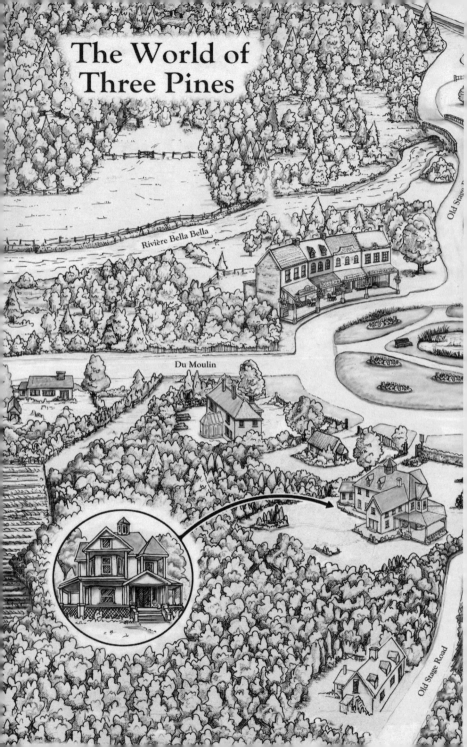

The World of Three Pines

Rivière Bella Bella

Du Moulin

Old Stage Road

St. Road

HADLEY MILL

Du Moulin

CHAPTER 1

———

'State your name, please.'

'Armand Gamache.'

'And you are the head of the Sûreté du Québec?'

'The Chief Superintendent, *oui*.'

Gamache sat upright on the wooden chair. It was hot. Sweltering, really, on this July morning. He could taste perspiration from his upper lip and it was only just ten o'clock. It was only just starting.

The witness box was not his favorite place in the world. And far from his favorite thing to do. To testify against another human being. There were only a few times in his career when he'd gotten satisfaction, even pleasure, from that and this wasn't one of them.

Sitting uncomfortably on the hard chair, under oath, Armand Gamache admitted to himself that while he believed in the law, had spent his career working within the justice system, what he really had to answer to was his conscience.

And that was proving to be a pretty harsh judge.

'I believe you were also the arresting officer.'

'I was.'

1

'Is that unusual, for the Chief Superintendent to actually be making arrests?'

'I've only been in the position a little while, as you know. Everything is unusual to me. But this particular case was hard to miss.'

The Chief Crown Prosecutor smiled. His back to the rest of the court and the jury, no one else saw. Except perhaps the judge, who missed little.

And what Judge Corriveau saw was a not particularly pleasant smile. More a sneer, really. Which surprised her, given the Chief Crown and the Chief Superintendent were apparently on the same side.

Though that didn't mean, she knew, that they had to like or respect each other. She had some colleagues she didn't respect, though she doubted she'd ever looked at them with exactly that expression.

While she was assessing them, Gamache had been assessing her. Trying to get a read.

Which judge was drawn for any trial was vital. It could affect the outcome. And it had never been more critical than in this case. It wasn't simply about the interpretation of the law, but the atmosphere in a courtroom. How strict would they be? How much leeway would be allowed?

Was the judge alert? Semi-retired? Biding her time until the cocktail hour? Or, occasionally, not so much biding as imbibing.

But not this one.

Maureen Corriveau was new to the bench. Her first homicide case, Gamache knew. He felt sympathy for her. She could have absolutely no idea that she'd drawn the short straw. That a whole lot of unpleasantness was about to come her way.

She was middle-aged, with hair she was allowing to go gray.

As a sign, perhaps, of authority, or maturity. Or because she didn't have to impress anymore. She'd been a powerful litigator, a partner in her Montréal law firm. She'd been blond. Before she'd ascended. Taken silk, as they said in Britain.

Interestingly, it was not unlike how parachutists described jumping out of a plane.

Judge Corriveau looked back at him. Her eyes were sharp. Intelligent. But Gamache wondered how much she was actually seeing. And how much she was actually missing.

Judge Corriveau looked at ease. But that meant nothing. He probably looked at ease too.

He glanced out at the crowded courtroom in the Palais de Justice in Old Montréal. Most of the people who might have been there had decided to stay home. Some, like Myrna and Clara and Reine-Marie, would be called as witnesses and didn't want to come in until they absolutely had to. Other villagers – Olivier, Gabri, Ruth – simply didn't want to leave Three Pines to come all the way into the stifling city to relive this tragedy.

But Gamache's second-in-command, Jean-Guy Beauvoir, was there, as was Chief Inspector Isabelle Lacoste. The head of homicide.

It would be their turn to testify, soon enough. Or perhaps, he thought, it would never come to that.

He shifted his eyes back to the Crown, Barry Zalmanowitz. But on its way there, his gaze had brushed by Judge Corriveau. To his chagrin, she tilted her head, very slightly. And her eyes narrowed, very slightly.

What had she seen, in his eyes? Had the rookie judge caught the very thing he was trying to conceal? Was desperate to conceal?

But if she did see it, he knew she would misinterpret it. She'd assume he was troubled about the defendant's guilt.

But Armand Gamache had no doubt about that. He knew perfectly well who the murderer was. He was just a little afraid that something would go wrong. And a particularly cunning killer would go free.

He watched the Crown Prosecutor walk deliberately to his desk, put on his glasses and carefully, one might even say dramatically, read a piece of paper.

It was probably blank, Gamache thought. Or a shopping list. Almost certainly a prop. A wisp of smoke. A shard of mirror.

Trials, like Masses, were theatrics. He could almost smell the incense and hear a tinny, tiny bell.

The jury, not yet wilted from the heat, followed the skilled Crown's every move. As they were meant to. But he was not the lead in this drama. That role was taken by someone off-stage, who would almost certainly never utter a word.

The Chief Crown took off his glasses and Gamache heard the slight rustle of the judge's silk robes as she reacted with impatience barely concealed. The jury might be taken in, but this judge was not. And the jury wouldn't be taken in for long. They were too smart for that.

'I understand the defendant actually confessed, is that right?' the prosecutor asked, looking over his glasses in a professorial manner wasted on the head of the Sûreté.

'There was a confession, yes.'

'Under questioning, Chief Superintendent?'

Gamache noticed that he repeated his rank, as though someone so lofty could not possibly make a mistake.

'No. The defendant came to my home and confessed. Willingly.'

'Objection.' The defense attorney leapt to his feet, a little late, Gamache thought. 'Irrelevant. The defendant never confessed to the murder.'

4

'True. The confession I'm talking about wasn't to the murder,' said the Crown. 'But it led directly to the charge, is that right, Chief Superintendent?'

Gamache looked at Judge Corriveau. Waiting for her to rule on the objection.

She hesitated.

'Denied,' she said. 'You may answer.'

'The defendant came willingly,' said Gamache. 'And yes, the confession was the key to laying the charges at that moment.'

'Did it surprise you that the defendant came to your home?'

'Your Honor,' said the defense, getting to his feet again. 'Objection. Subjective and irrelevant. How could it possibly matter if Monsieur Gamache was surprised?'

'Sustained.' Judge Corriveau turned to Gamache. 'Don't answer that.'

Gamache had no intention of answering the question. The judge was right to sustain. It was subjective. But he didn't think it was altogether irrelevant.

Had he been surprised?

Certainly when he'd seen who was standing on the porch of his home in the small Québec village, he'd been surprised. It had been hard to tell at first exactly who was in the heavy coat, with the hood up over the head. Man, woman? Young, old? Gamache could still hear the ice pellets striking his home, as the bitter November rain had changed over to sleet.

Just thinking about it now, in the July heat, he felt a chill.

Yes. It had been a surprise. He hadn't expected the visit.

As for what happened next, surprise didn't begin to cover it.

'I don't want my first homicide case to end up in the appeals court,' Judge Corriveau said quietly, so that only Gamache could hear.

'I think it's too late for that, Your Honor. This case began in a higher court, and it's going to end there.'

Judge Corriveau shifted in her chair. Trying to get comfortable again. But something had changed. In that odd and private exchange.

She was used to words, cryptic or otherwise. It was the look in his eyes that threw her. And she wondered if he knew it was there.

Though Judge Corriveau couldn't really say what it was, she did know the Chief Superintendent of the Sûreté should not look like that. While sitting in the witness box. At a murder trial.

Maureen Corriveau did not know Armand Gamache well at all. Only by reputation. They'd passed each other in the halls of the Palais de Justice many times over the years.

She'd been prepared to dislike the man. A hunter of other humans. A man who owed his living to death. Not actually meting it out, but profiting from it.

No murder, no Gamache.

She remembered one chance meeting, when he was still head of homicide for the Sûreté, and she was still a defense attorney. They'd passed in the hall, and again she'd caught his eyes. Sharp, alert, thoughtful. But again, she'd caught something else there.

And then he was gone, bending his head slightly to listen to his companion. A younger man she knew was his second-in-command. A man in the courtroom now.

A very slight scent of sandalwood and rose had lingered. Barely there.

Maureen Corriveau had gone home and told her wife about it.

'I followed him and sat in on the trial for a few minutes this afternoon, to listen to his testimony.'

'Why?'

'I was curious. I've never been up against him, but I thought if I was I should do some homework. And I had some time to kill.'

'So? What was he like? Wait, let me guess.' Joan shoved the tip of her nose to one side and said, 'Yeah, da punk offed da guy. Why're we wastin' time wid a trial, ya yella-bellied, flea-infested cowards. Hang him!'

'That's uncanny,' said Maureen. 'Were you there? Yes, he turned into Edward G. Robinson.'

Joan laughed. 'Still, Jimmy Stewart and Gregory Peck never got to be head of homicide.'

'Good point. He paraphrased Sister Prejean.'

Joan put down her book. 'In a trial?'

'In his testimony.'

Gamache had sat in the witness box, composed, relaxed but not casual. He was distinguished looking, though not perhaps, at first glance, handsome. A large man in a well-tailored suit. He sat upright, alert. Respectful.

His hair, mostly gray, was trimmed. His face clean-shaven. Even from the gallery, Maureen Corriveau could see the deep scar by his temple.

And then he'd said it.

'No man is as bad as the worst thing he's done.'

'Why would he quote a death-row nun?' asked Joan. 'And those words especially?'

'I think it was a subtle plea for leniency.'

'Huh,' said Joan, and thought for a moment. 'Of course the opposite is also true. No one is as good as the best thing.'

And now Judge Corriveau sat on the bench, in her robes, in judgment. And tried to figure out what Chief Superintendent Gamache was up to.

This was closer than she'd ever been to him, and for a more sustained length of time. The deep scar at his temple was still

7

there, and always would be, of course. As though his job had branded him. Close up, she could see the lines radiating from his mouth. And eyes. Life lines. Laugh lines, she knew. She had them too.

A man at the height of his career. At ease. At peace with what he'd done and must now do.

But in those eyes?

The look she'd caught a long time ago, in the halls, had been so unexpected that Maureen Corriveau had followed him, and listened to his testimony.

It was kindness.

But what she saw today wasn't that. It was worry. Not doubt, she thought. But he was worried.

And now she was too, though Judge Corriveau couldn't say why.

She turned away and they both returned their attention to the Crown attorney. He was playing with a pen, and when he made to lean against his desk, Judge Corriveau gave him a look so stern he immediately straightened up. And put down the pen.

'Let me rephrase the question,' he said. 'When did you first have your suspicions?'

'Like most murders,' said Gamache, 'it began long before the actual act.'

'So you knew a murder would happen, even before the death?'

'*Non*. Not really.'

No? Gamache asked himself. As he had asked himself every day since the body was found. But really what he asked himself was how he could not have known.

'So again, I ask you, Chief Superintendent, when did you know?'

There was an edge of impatience in Zalmanowitz's voice now.

'I knew there was something wrong when the figure in the black robe appeared on the village green.'

That caused a commotion in the courtroom. The reporters, off to the side, bent over their electronic notebooks. He could hear the tapping from across the room. A modern Morse code, signaling urgent news.

'By "village", you mean Three Pines,' said the prosecutor, looking at the journalists as though the Chief Crown knowing the name of the village where Gamache lived, and the victim died, should be noteworthy. 'South of Montréal, by the Vermont border, is that correct?'

'*Oui.*'

'It's quite small, I believe.'

'*Oui.*'

'Pretty? Tranquil even?'

Zalmanowitz managed to make 'pretty' sound lackluster and 'tranquil' sound tedious. But Three Pines was far from either.

Gamache nodded. 'Yes. It's very pretty.'

'And remote.'

The Crown made 'remote' sound disagreeable, as though the further one got from a major city, the less civilized life became. Which might be true, thought Gamache. But he'd seen the results of so-called civilization and he knew that as many beasts lived in cities as in forests.

'Not so much remote as off the path,' explained Gamache. 'People mostly come upon Three Pines because they're lost. It's not the sort of place you drive through on the way to somewhere else.'

'It's on the road to nowhere?'

Gamache almost smiled. It was probably meant as an insult, but it was actually apt.

He and Reine-Marie had chosen to live in Three Pines

primarily because it was pretty, and hard to find. It was a haven, a buffer, from the cares and cruelty of the world he dealt with every day. The world beyond the forest.

They'd found a home there. Made a home there. Among the pines, and perennials, the village shops, and villagers. Who had become friends, and then family.

So that when the dark thing appeared on the pretty, tranquil village green, displacing the playing children, it had felt like more than an oddity. More than an intruder. It was a violation.

Gamache knew his sense of unease had really begun the night before. When the black-robed creature first appeared at the annual Halloween party in the bistro.

Though real alarms didn't go off until he'd looked out his bedroom window the next morning and seen him still there. Standing on the village green. Staring at the bistro.

Just staring.

Now, many months later, Armand Gamache looked at the Chief Crown. In his black robes. Then over to the defense table. In their black robes. And the judge, just above and beside him, in her black robes.

Staring. At him.

There seemed, thought Gamache, no escape from black-robed figures.

'It really began,' he amended his testimony, 'the night before. At the Halloween party.'

'Everyone was dressed up?'

'Not everyone. It was optional.'

'And you?' asked the Crown.

Gamache glared at him. It was not a pertinent question. But it was one designed to slightly humiliate.

'We decided to go as each other.'

'You and your wife? You went in drag, Chief Superintendent?'

'Not exactly. We pulled names from a hat. I got Gabri Dubeau, who runs the local B&B with his partner, Olivier.'

Armand had, with Olivier's help, borrowed Gabri's signature bright pink fluffy slippers and a kimono. It was an easy, and extremely comfortable, costume.

Reine-Marie had gone as their neighbor, Clara Morrow. Clara was a hugely successful portrait artist, though it seemed she mostly painted herself.

Reine-Marie had teased her hair until it was almost on end, and put cookies and a peanut butter sandwich in it. Then she'd dabbed paint all over herself.

For her part, Clara had gone as her best friend, Myrna Landers. They were all slightly concerned she'd show up in blackface, though Myrna had said she wouldn't take offense as long as Clara painted her entire body black.

Clara had not painted herself, for once. Instead, she wore a caftan made from the dust jackets of old books.

Myrna was a retired psychologist from Montréal, who now ran the shop right next to the bistro, Myrna's New and Used Bookstore. Clara had a theory that villagers manufactured problems, just to go sit with Myrna.

'Manufacture them?' the old poet Ruth had said, glaring at Clara. 'You have a whole warehouse full of them. You've cornered the market on problems.'

'I have not,' said Clara.

'Really? You've got a huge solo show coming up and all you've got is crap. If that's not a problem, I don't know what is.'

'It's not crap.' Though none of her friends backed her up.

Gabri had gone to the Halloween party as Ruth. He'd put on a gray wig and made up his face until he looked like a fiend from a horror show. He'd worn a pilled, moth-eaten sweater and carried a stuffed duck.

All night long he'd swilled Scotch and muttered poetry.

> '*With doors ajar the cottage stands*
> *Deserted on the hill—*
> *No welcome bark, no thudding hoof,*
> *And the voice of the pig is still.*'

'That's not mine, you sack of shit,' said Ruth. She wore a pilled, moth-eaten sweater and carried a real duck.

'*A little blade of grass I see,*' said Gabri. '*Its banner waving wild and free.*'

'Stop it,' said Ruth, trying to cover her ears. 'You'll murder my muse.'

'*And I wonder if in time to come,*' Gabri pressed ahead. '*"Twill be a great big onion.*'

The last word he pronounced *un-ee-yun*.

Even Ruth had to laugh, while in her arms Rosa the duck muttered, 'Fuck, fuck, fuck.'

'I worked all day on that,' said Gabri. 'This poetry stuff isn't so hard.'

'So this was October thirty-first of last year,' asked the Crown attorney.

'*Non.* It was November first. We all stayed home on the actual Halloween night, to give out candy to the trick or treaters. This party is always the next night.'

'November first. Who else was there besides the villagers?' asked the Crown.

'Matheo Bissonette and his wife, Lea Roux.'

'Madame Roux, the politician,' said the Crown. 'A rising star in her party, I believe.'

Behind him, Monsieur Zalmanowitz heard the renewed tapping on the tablets. A siren song. Proof he'd make the news.

'Yes,' said Gamache.

'Friends of yours? Staying with you?'

Of course the Crown knew the answer to all these questions. This was for the sake of the judge and jury. And reporters.

'*Non*. I didn't know them well. They were there with their friends Katie and Patrick Evans.'

'Ahh, yes. The Evanses.' The Crown looked over at the defense table, then back at Gamache. 'The contractor and his architect wife. They built glass houses, I believe. Also friends of yours?'

'Also acquaintances,' Gamache corrected, his voice firm. He did not like the insinuation.

'Of course,' said Zalmanowitz. 'And why were they in the village?'

'It was an annual reunion. They're school friends. They were in the same class at the Université de Montréal.'

'They're all in their early thirties now?'

'*Oui*.'

'How long have they been coming to Three Pines?'

'Four years. Always the same week in late summer.'

'Except this year, they came in late October.'

'*Oui*.'

'Strange time to visit. No fall colors left and no snow yet for skiing. It's pretty dreary, isn't it?'

'Perhaps they got a better rate at the B&B,' said Gamache, with an expression of trying to be helpful. 'It's a very nice place.'

When he'd left Three Pines early that morning to drive into Montréal, Gabri, the owner of the bed and breakfast, had run over with a brown paper bag and a travel mug.

'If you have to mention the B&B, can you say something like "the beautiful B&B"? Or you could call it lovely.'

He had gestured behind him. It wouldn't be a lie. The old stagecoach inn across from the village green, with its wide verandah and gables, was lovely. Especially in summer. Like the rest of the village, the B&B had a front garden of old perennials. Roses and lavender, and spires of digitalis and fragrant phlox.

'Just don't say "stunning",' Gabri advised. 'Sounds forced.'

'And we wouldn't want that,' said Gamache. 'You do know this is a murder trial.'

'I do,' said Gabri, serious as he handed over the coffee and croissants.

And now Gamache sat in the trial and listened to the Chief Crown.

'What took the classmates to Three Pines initially?' Monsieur Zalmanowitz asked. 'Were they lost?'

'No. Lea Roux and Dr Landers knew each other of old. Myrna Landers used to babysit her. Lea and Matheo had visited Myrna a few times and came to like the village. They mentioned it to their friends and it became the site of their annual reunion.'

'I see. So Lea Roux and her husband were the ones who instigated it.' He made it sound somehow suspicious. 'With the help of Madame Landers.'

'Dr Landers, and there was no "instigation". It was a perfectly normal reunion.'

'Really? You call what happened perfectly normal?'

'Up until last November, yes.'

The Chief Crown nodded in a manner that was meant to look sage, as though he didn't quite believe Chief Superintendent Gamache.

14

It was, thought Judge Corriveau, ridiculous. But she could see the jury taking it all in.

And again, she wondered why he would imply such a thing, with his own witness. The head of the Sûreté, for God's sake.

The day was heating up, and so was the courtroom. She looked at the old air conditioners slumped in the windows. Turned off, of course. Too noisy. It would be distracting.

But the heat was becoming distracting too. And it wasn't yet noon.

'When did it all, finally, strike you, Chief Superintendent, as abnormal?' asked Zalmanowitz.

Gamache's rank was emphasized again, but now the Crown's tone suggested a degree of incompetence.

'It really began during that Halloween party in the bistro,' said Gamache, ignoring the provocation. 'Some of the guests wore masks, though most were recognizable, especially when they spoke. But one was not. One guest wore heavy black robes down to the floor, and a black mask. Gloves, boots. A hood was pulled up over his head.'

'Sounds like Darth Vader,' said the Crown, and there were chuckles in the gallery.

'We thought that, at first. But it wasn't a Star Wars costume.'

'Then who did you think it was supposed to be?'

'Reine-Marie ...' – Gamache turned to the jury to clarify – 'my wife ...' They nodded. 'wondered if it was the father from the film *Amadeus*. But he wore a specific hat. This person just had the hood. Myrna thought he might be dressed as a Jesuit priest, but there wasn't a cross.'

And then there was his manner. While around him people partied, this figure stood absolutely still.

Soon people stopped speaking to him. Asking about his costume. Trying to work out who it was. Before long, people stopped approaching him. And a space opened up around the dark figure. It was as though he occupied his own world. His own universe. Where there was no Halloween party. No revelers. No laughter. No friendship.

'What did you think?'

'I thought it was Death,' said Armand Gamache.

There was silence now, in the courtroom.

'And what did you do?'

'Nothing.'

'Really? Death comes to visit and the head of the Sûreté, the former Chief Inspector of homicide, does nothing?'

'It was a person in a costume,' said Gamache with patience.

'That's what you told yourself that night, perhaps,' said the Crown. 'When did you realize it really was Death? Let me guess. When you were standing over the body?'

CHAPTER 2

⌒

No. The figure at the Halloween party was disconcerting, but Gamache had really begun to think something was very wrong the next morning, as he'd looked out their bedroom window into the damp November day.

'What're you looking at, Armand?' asked Reine-Marie, coming out of the shower and walking over to him.

Her brow dropped as she looked out the window. 'What's he doing there?' she asked, her voice low.

Where everyone else had gone home, gone to sleep, the figure in the dark cloak had not. He'd stayed behind. Stayed there. And was still there. Standing on the village green in his wool robes. And hood. Staring.

Gamache couldn't see from that angle, but he suspected the mask was also in place.

'I don't know,' said Armand.

It was Saturday morning, and he put on his casual clothes. Cords and shirt and a heavy fall sweater. It was the beginning of November and the weather wasn't letting them forget it.

The day had dawned gray, as November often did, after the bright sunshine and bright autumn leaves of October.

November was the transition month. A sort of purgatory. It

was the cold damp breath between dying and death. Between fall and the dead of winter.

It was no one's favorite month.

Gamache put on his rubber boots and went outside, leaving their German shepherd Henri and the little creature Gracie to stare after him in bewilderment. Unused to being left behind.

It was colder than he'd expected. Colder even than the night before.

His hands were icy before he'd even reached the green, and he regretted leaving his gloves and cap behind.

Gamache placed himself right in front of the dark figure.

The mask was in place. Nothing visible except the eyes. And even those were obscured by a sort of gauze.

'Who are you?' he asked.

His voice was calm, almost friendly. As though this were a cordial conversation. A perfectly reasonable situation.

No need to antagonize. Time enough for that later, if need be.

But the figure remained silent. Not exactly at attention, it wasn't that wooden. There was about it a sense of confidence, of authority even. It was as if it not only belonged on that spot, but owned it.

Though Gamache suspected that impression came more from the robes and the silence than the man.

It always struck him how much more effective silence was than words. If the effect you were after was to disconcert. But he didn't have the luxury of silence himself.

'Why are you here?' Gamache asked. First in French, then in English.

Then waited. Ten seconds. Twenty. Forty-five seconds.

*

In the bistro, Myrna and Gabri watched through the leaded-glass window.

Two men, staring at each other.

'Good,' said Gabri. 'Armand'll get rid of him.'

'Who is he?' Myrna asked. 'He was at your party last night.'

'I know, but I have no idea who he is. Neither does Olivier.'

'Finished with that?' asked Anton, the dishwasher and morning busboy.

He reached for Myrna's plate, now just crumbs. But his hand stopped. And, like the other two, he stared.

Myrna looked up at him. He was fairly new to the place but had fit in quickly. Olivier had hired him to do the dishes and bus, but Anton had made it clear he hoped to be head chef.

'There is only one chef,' Anton had confided in Myrna one day while buying vintage cookbooks at her shop. 'But Olivier likes to make it sound like there's a fleet of them.'

Myrna laughed. Sounded like Olivier. Always trying to impress, even people who knew him too well for that.

'Do you have a specialty?' she asked as she rang up the total on her old cash register.

'I like Canadian cuisine.'

She'd paused to look at him. In his mid-thirties, she thought. Surely too old, and too ambitious, to be a busboy. He sounded well educated, and was well turned out. Lean and athletic. With dark brown hair trimmed on the sides and longer on top so that it flopped over his forehead in a way that made him look more boyish than he actually was.

He was certainly handsome. And an aspiring chef.

Had she been twenty years younger . . .

A gal can dream. And she did.

'Canadian cuisine. What's that?'

'Exactly,' Anton had said, smiling. 'No one really knows. I think it's anything that's native to the land. And rivers. And there's so much out there. I like to forage.'

He'd said it with a deliberate leer, as a voyeur might have said, 'I like to watch.'

Myrna had laughed, blushed slightly, and charged him a dollar for both cookbooks.

Now Anton, stooping over their table at the bistro, stared out the window.

'What is that?' he asked in a whisper.

'Weren't you at the party last night?' Gabri asked.

'Yes, but I was in the kitchen all night. I didn't come out.'

Myrna looked from the thing on the village green to this young man. A party just through the swinging doors, and he'd been stuck doing dishes. It sounded like something out of a Victorian melodrama.

He seemed to know what she was thinking and turned to smile at her.

'I could've come out, but I'm not big on parties. Being in the kitchen suits me.'

Myrna nodded. She understood. We all have, she knew, a place where we're not only most comfortable, but most competent. Hers was her bookstore. Olivier's was the bistro. Clara's was her studio.

Sarah's, the bakery. And Anton's was the kitchen.

But sometimes that comfort was an illusion. Masquerading as protecting, while actually imprisoning.

'What's he saying?' Anton asked, taking a seat and gesturing toward Gamache and the robed figure.

'Is there something I can help you with?' Armand asked. 'Someone you'd like to speak to?'

There was no answer. No movement. Though he could see steam coming from where the mouth would be.

Evidence of life.

It was steady. Like the long, easy plume of a train moving forward.

'My name is Gamache. Armand Gamache.' He let that rest there for a moment. 'I'm the head of the Sûreté du Québec.'

Was there a slight shift in the eyes? Had the man glanced at him, then away?

'It's cold,' said Armand, rubbing his frigid hands together. 'Let's go inside. Have a coffee and maybe some bacon and eggs. I live just over there.'

He gestured toward his home. He wondered if he should have identified his home, but realized this person probably already knew where he lived. He'd just come from there, after all. It was hardly a secret.

He waited for the robed figure to respond to his breakfast invitation, wondering briefly what Reine-Marie might think when he brought home his new friend.

When there was no response, Armand reached out to take hold of his arm. And coax him along.

All conversation had stopped in the bistro, the morning service grinding to a halt.

Everyone, patrons and servers alike, was staring out at the two men on the village green.

'He's going to drag the guy away,' said Olivier, joining them.

Anton made to get up, but Olivier waved him back down. There was no rush anymore.

They watched as Armand lowered his hand, without touching the man.

*

Armand Gamache stood perfectly still himself now. And while the robed figure stared at the bistro, the bookstore, the boulangerie, and Monsieur Béliveau's general store, Gamache stared at him.

'Be careful,' Armand finally whispered.

And then he turned, and returned home.

The robed figure was still there in the afternoon.

Armand and Reine-Marie passed him on their way to Clara's home, on the other side of the village green.

An invisible moat had formed around the man. The village had slowly ventured out and gone about its business. Though a wide circle was circumscribed around him, beyond which no one went.

No children played on the grass and people walked faster than usual, averting their eyes as they passed by.

Henri, on his leash, gave a low growl and moved to the far side of Armand. His hackles up. His huge ears were forward, then he laid them back on his large and, it must be admitted, slightly vacuous head.

Henri kept everything important in his heart. He mostly kept cookies in his head.

But the shepherd was smart enough to keep his distance from the robed figure.

Gracie, who'd been found in a garbage can months earlier, along with her brother Leo, was also on a leash.

She stared, as though mesmerized by the figure, and refused to move. Reine-Marie had to pick her up.

'Should we say something?' Reine-Marie asked.

'Let's leave him be,' said Armand. 'It's possible he wants attention. Maybe he'll go away when we don't give it to him.'

But she suspected that wasn't the reason Armand wanted

to ignore it. Reine-Marie thought Armand didn't want her to get that close to it. And truthfully, neither did she.

As the morning had progressed, she'd found herself drawn to the window. Hoping it would be gone. But the dark figure remained on the village green. Unmoving. Immovable.

Reine-Marie wasn't sure when it had happened, but at some point she'd stopped thinking of him as 'him'. Any humanity it had had drained away. And the figure had become 'it'. No longer human.

'Come on in,' said Clara. 'I see our visitor is still there.'

She tried to make it light, but it was clearly upsetting her. As it was them.

'Any idea who he is, Armand?'

'None. I wish I had. But I doubt he'll stay much longer. It's probably a joke.'

'Probably.' She turned to Reine-Marie. 'I've put the new boxes in the living room by the fireplace. I thought we could go through them there.'

'New' wasn't completely accurate.

Clara was helping Reine-Marie with what was becoming the endless task of sorting the so-called archives of the historical society. They were actually boxes, and boxes, and boxes, of photographs, documents, clothing. Collected over a hundred years or more, from attics and cellars. Retrieved from yard sales and church basements.

So Reine-Marie had volunteered to sort through it. It was a crapshoot of crap. But she loved it. Reine-Marie's career had been as a senior librarian and archivist with the Bibliothèque et Archives nationales du Québec and, like her husband, she had a passion for history. Québec history in particular.

'Join us for lunch, Armand?' asked Clara. The scent of

soup filled the kitchen. 'I picked up a baguette from the boulangerie.'

'*Non, merci*. I'm heading over to the bistro.' He lifted the book in his hand. His Saturday afternoon ritual. Lunch, a beer, and a book, in front of the fireplace at the bistro.

'Not one of Jacqueline's,' said Reine-Marie, pointing to the baguette.

'No. Sarah's. I made sure of that. Though I did get some of Jacqueline's brownies. How important is it?' asked Clara, cutting the crispy baguette. 'That a baker knows how to make a baguette?'

'Here?' asked Reine-Marie. 'Vital.'

'Yeah,' said Clara. 'I think so too. Poor Sarah. She wants to pass the bakery on to Jacqueline, but I don't know ...'

'Well, maybe brownies are enough,' said Armand. 'I think I could learn to spread brie on a brownie.'

Clara winced, and then thought about it. Maybe ...

'Jacqueline's only been here a few months,' Reine-Marie pointed out. 'Maybe she'll catch on.'

'Sarah says with baguette you either have it or you don't,' said Clara. 'Something to do with touch, but also the temperature of your hands.'

'Hot or cold?' asked Armand.

'I don't know,' said Clara. 'It was already too much information. I want to believe baguettes are magic, not some accident of birth.' She put down the bread knife. 'Soup's almost ready. While it warms up, would you like to see my latest work?'

It was unlike Clara to offer to show her work, especially those in progress. At least, as Armand and Reine-Marie reluctantly walked across the kitchen to her studio, they hoped there'd been progress.

Normally they'd have leapt at the rare chance to see Clara's work, as she painted her astonishing portraits. But just recently it had become clear that her idea of 'finished' and everyone else's were very different.

Armand wondered what she saw that they did not.

The studio was in darkness, the windows only letting in the north light, and on a cloudy November day there was precious little of that.

'Those are done,' she said, waving into the gloom at the canvases leaning against one wall. She switched on the light.

It was all Reine-Marie could do not to ask, 'Are you sure?'

Some of the portraits looked close, but the hair was just a pencil outline. Or the hands were blotches, blobs.

The portraits, for the most part, were recognizable. Myrna. Olivier.

Armand went up to Sarah, the baker, lounging against the wall.

She was the most complete. Her lined face filled with that desire to help that Armand recognized. A dignity, almost standoffish. And yet Clara had managed to capture the baker's vulnerability. As though she feared the viewer would ask for something she didn't have.

Yes, her face, her hands, her attitude, all so finely realized. And yet. Her smock was dashed on, missing all detail. It was as though Clara had lost interest.

Gracie and her littermate, Leo, were wrestling on the concrete floor, and Reine-Marie stooped to pet them.

'What is that?' Everyone spasmed a little on hearing the querulous voice.

Ruth stood there, holding Rosa and pointing into the studio.

'Jesus, it's awful,' said the old poet. 'What a mess. Ugly doesn't begin to describe it.'

'Ruth,' said Reine-Marie. 'You of all people should know that creation is a process.'

'And not always a successful one. I'm serious. What is it?'

'It's called art,' said Armand. 'And you don't have to like it.'

'Art?' Ruth looked dubious. 'Really?' She bent down and said, 'Come here, Art. Come here.'

They looked at each other. Even for demented old Ruth, this was odd.

And then Clara began to laugh. 'She means Gracie.'

She pointed to the little thing, rolling on the floor with Leo.

Though they'd been found together, in the garbage, Clara's Leo was growing into a very handsome dog. Golden, with short hair on his lean body, and slightly longer hair around his neck. Leo was tall and gangly right now, but already regal.

Gracie was not. She was, not to put too fine a point on it, the runt of the litter. Literally. And perhaps not even a dog.

No one had been quite sure when Reine-Marie had brought her home months earlier. And time had not proven helpful.

Almost completely hairless, except for tufts of different colors here and there. One ear stood boldly up, the other flopped. Her head seemed to be evolving daily and she had grown very little. Some days, to Reine-Marie's eyes, Gracie seemed to have shrunk.

But her eyes were bright. And she seemed to know she'd been saved. Her adoration of Reine-Marie knew no bounds.

'Come here, Art,' Ruth tried again, then stood up. 'Not only ugly but stupid. Doesn't know its name.'

'Gracie,' said Armand. 'Her name's Gracie.'

'For Christ's sake, why did you say it was Art?' She looked at him as though he were the demented one.

They returned to the kitchen, where Clara stirred the soup and Armand kissed Reine-Marie and walked to the door.

'Not so fast, Tintin,' said Ruth. 'You haven't told us about that thing in the middle of the village. I saw you speaking to him. What did he say?'

'Nothing.'

'Nothing?'

Clearly for Ruth the concept of keeping the mouth shut was completely foreign.

'But why's he still here?' asked Clara, all pretense of not caring gone. 'What does he want? Did he stand there all night? Can't you do something?'

'Why's the sky blue?' asked Ruth. 'Is pizza really Italian? Have you ever eaten a crayon?'

They looked at her.

'Aren't we tossing out stupid questions? For what it's worth, the answers to your questions are, don't know, don't know, and Edmonton.'

'The guy's wearing a mask,' Clara said to Armand, ignoring Ruth. 'That can't be right. He can't be right. In the head.'

She spun her finger at her temple.

'There's nothing I can do,' he said. 'It's not against the law in Québec to cover your face.'

'That isn't a burka,' said Clara.

'For heaven's sake,' said Ruth. 'What's the big deal? Haven't you seen *Phantom of the Opera*? He might burst into song at any moment and we have front row seats.'

'You're not taking this seriously,' said Clara.

'But I am. I'm just not afraid. Though ignorance scares me.'

'I beg your pardon?' said Clara.

'Ignorance,' Ruth repeated, either missing or pretending to miss the warning in Clara's voice. 'Anything different, anything you don't understand, you immediately believe is threatening.'

'And you're the poster child for tolerance?' asked Clara.

'Come on,' said Ruth. 'There's a difference between scary and threatening. He might be frightening, I'll give you that. But he hasn't actually done anything. If he was going to, he probably would've by now.'

Ruth turned to Gamache to back her up, but he didn't respond.

'Someone puts on a Halloween costume as a joke,' she continued. 'In broad daylight, and you get all scared. *Puh*. You'd have done well in Salem.'

'You got closer than any of us,' Reine-Marie said to her husband. 'What do you think it is?'

He looked down at the dogs, intertwined on the floor, sprawled against Henri, who snored and muttered. More than once Armand had envied Henri. Until Henri's kibble was lowered next to his water bowl. There the envy ended.

'It doesn't matter what I think,' he said. 'I'm sure he'll be gone soon.'

'Don't patronize us,' said Clara, her smile only slightly softening the annoyance in her tone. 'I showed you mine' – she pointed toward her studio – 'now you show me yours.'

'It's just an impression,' he said. 'Meaningless. I have no real idea who or what he is.'

'Armand,' Clara warned.

And he relented.

'Death,' he said, and looked over at Reine-Marie. 'That's what I thought.'

'The Grim Reaper?' asked Ruth with a hoot. 'Did he point a crooked finger?'

She lifted her own bony finger and pointed it at Armand.

'I'm not saying it's actually, literally Death,' he said. 'But I do think whoever's in that costume wants us to make the connection. He wants us to be afraid.'

28

'Guess what,' said Clara.

'Well, you're all wrong,' said Ruth. 'Death doesn't look at all like that.'

'How would you know?' asked Clara.

'Because we're old friends. He visits most nights. We sit in the kitchen and talk. His name's Michael.'

'The archangel?' asked Reine-Marie.

'Yes. Everyone thinks Death is this horrible creature, but in the Bible it's Michael who visits the dying and helps them in their last hour. He's beautiful, with wings he folds tight to his back so he doesn't knock over the furniture.'

'Let me get this straight. The Archangel Michael visits you?' asked Reine-Marie.

'Let me get this straight,' said Clara. 'You read the Bible?'

'I read everything,' Ruth said to Clara, then turned to Reine-Marie. 'And he does. But he doesn't stay long. He's very busy. But he pops in for a drink and gossips about the other angels. That Raphael is a piece of work, I tell you. Nasty, embittered old thing.'

A *hmmm* escaped one of them.

'And what do you say to him?' asked Armand.

'Armand,' said Reine-Marie, warning him not to goad the old woman. But that wasn't his intention. He was genuinely curious.

'I tell him about all of you. Point out your homes and make some suggestions. Sometimes I read him a poem. *From the public school to the private hell / of the family masquerade,*' she quoted, tipping her face to the ceiling in an effort to remember, *'Where could a boy on a bicycle go / when the straight road splayed?'*

They stared for a moment, taking in the words that had taken their breaths away.

'One of yours?' asked Clara.

Ruth nodded and smiled. 'I do know it's a process. To be honest, Michael's not very helpful. He prefers limericks.'

There was an involuntary guffaw from Armand.

'And then, before dawn, he leaves,' said Ruth.

'And leaves you behind?' asked Clara. 'That doesn't sound right.'

'Think about it,' murmured Reine-Marie.

'It's not my time. Not even close. He likes my company because I'm not afraid.'

'We're all afraid of something,' said Armand.

'I meant I'm not afraid of Death,' said Ruth.

'I wonder if Death's afraid of her,' said Clara.

'I'll take two of those, please,' said Katie Evans, pointing to the chocolate brownies. With melted marshmallows on top.

The sort she remembered from years ago.

'And you, madame?'

Jacqueline turned to the other woman. Lea Roux.

She recognized her, but then, most would. She was a member of the National Assembly, and in the news often. Interviewed on French and English talk shows, across the province, for her opinions on politics. She was articulate without being pompous. Funny without being sarcastic. Warm without being cloying. She was the new darling of the media.

And now here she was. In the bakery. Large as life.

In fact, both women were large. Really, more tall than big. But they certainly were a presence. Easily overshadowing the tiny baker. But while the women might have presence, Jacqueline had baked goods. And, she suspected, at that moment that made her the more powerful.

'I think,' said Lea, surveying the bank of patisserie behind the glass, 'I'll take a lemon tart and a mille-feuille.'

'Pretty strange,' said Katie, going up to Sarah, who owned the boulangerie and was restocking the shelves with biscotti.

There was no need to ask what Katie meant.

Sarah wiped her hands on her apron and nodded, glancing out the window.

'I wish it would go away,' said the baker.

'Anyone know what it is?' Lea asked, first Sarah, who shook her head, then Jacqueline, who shook her head and looked away.

'It's very upsetting,' said Sarah. 'I don't know why someone doesn't do something. Armand should do something.'

'I doubt there's much that can be done. Even by Monsieur Gamache.'

Lea Roux had sat on the committee that had confirmed Gamache as head of the Sûreté. She'd disclosed that she knew him, casually. They'd met a few times.

But then, almost everyone on the bipartisan committee knew Armand Gamache. He'd been a high-profile officer in the Sûreté for years and was involved in uncovering all that corruption.

There had been very little discussion, and less debate.

And two months ago, Armand Gamache had been sworn in as Chief Superintendent of the most powerful police force in Québec. Perhaps the most powerful in Canada.

But even with all that power, Lea Roux knew there was absolutely nothing he could do about the creature on the village green.

'You know you can order those in the bistro,' said Sarah as they left, pointing to the small boxes in their hands. 'We supply Olivier and Gabri.'

'*Merci*,' said Katie. 'We're taking these to the bookstore, to share with Myrna.'

'She does like brownies,' said Sarah. 'They've been a big hit since Jacqueline arrived.'

She looked at the much younger woman, as a proud mother might a daughter.

Except for the baguette thing, Jacqueline's arrival was pretty much the answer to Sarah's prayers. She was in her late sixties now, and getting up at five every morning to make bread, then on her feet all day, was getting too much.

Closing the boulangerie wasn't an option. And she didn't want to retire completely. But she did want to hand over the day-to-day operations to someone.

And then Jacqueline had arrived three months ago.

If she could only just learn how to make baguette.

'Oh, that looks good,' said Myrna, as she poured the tea and Lea put out the pastries.

Then the three of them sat around the woodstove in Myrna's bookstore, on the sofa and armchairs in the bay window. Where they could see the robed figure.

After discussing it for a few minutes and getting nowhere, they turned to Katie's latest project. A glass house on the Magdalen Islands.

'Really?' said Myrna, though her surprise was muffled by the mouthful of brownie. 'The Maggies?'

'Yes, there seems quite a bit of money there now. Lobster business must be good.'

Lea raised her brow but didn't say anything.

There was a whole other commodity that was creating wealth where once there had been hardworking poverty.

'A glass house on the islands must be a challenge,' said Myrna.

And for the next half hour they discussed weather, geography, design, and homes. The issue of home, rather than house, fascinated Myrna and she listened with admiration to these younger women.

She was interested in Katie. Liked her. But it was Lea she felt a bond with, having been her babysitter all those years ago.

Myrna had been twenty-six, just finishing her degree and scraping together whatever money she could to pay off student debt. Lea had been six. Tiny, like a gerbil. Her parents were divorcing, and Lea, an only child, had become almost housebound with terror. Uncertainty.

Myrna had become her big sister, her mother, her friend. Her protector and mentor. And Lea had become her little sister, daughter, friend.

'You should meet Anton,' said Myrna, watching with pleasure as Lea gobbled the pastries.

'Anton?'

'He's Olivier's new dishwasher.'

'He names his dishwashers?' said Katie with a smile. 'I call mine Bosch.'

'Really?' said Lea. 'Mine's Gustav. He's a dirty, dirty boy.'

'Har har,' said Myrna. 'Anton's a person, as you know very well. Wants to be a chef. He's particularly interested in developing a cuisine based solely on things native to this area.'

'Trees,' said Katie. 'Grass.'

'Anglos,' said Lea. 'Yum. I'd like to meet him. I think there're some programs that might be able to help.'

'I'm sorry,' said Myrna. 'You must be asked that all the time.'

'I like to help,' said Lea. 'And if it means a free meal, even better.'

'Great. How about tonight?'

'I can't tonight. We're going in to Knowlton for dinner. But we'll work something out before we leave.'

'When's that?'

'Couple of days,' said Katie.

It was, thought Myrna, oddly vague for people who surely had rigid schedules.

When the bakery was finally empty, and the cookies were in the oven, Jacqueline set the timer.

'Do you mind if I—'

'No, go,' said Sarah.

Jacqueline didn't have to say where she was going. Sarah knew. And wished her well. If she and the dishwasher got married, and he became the chef, then Jacqueline would also stay.

Sarah wasn't proud of these selfish thoughts, but at least she wasn't wishing Jacqueline harm. There would be far worse things, Sarah knew, than marrying Anton.

If only Anton felt the same way about Jacqueline. Maybe if she could bake baguettes, thought Sarah, scrubbing down the counters. Yes. That might do it.

In Sarah's world, a good baguette was a magic wand that solved all problems.

Jacqueline scooted next door to the bistro kitchen. It was midafternoon. They'd be preparing for the dinner service, but it was a fairly quiet time of day for a dishwasher.

'I was just going to come over to see you,' said Anton. 'Did you see it?'

'Hard to miss.'

She kissed him on both cheeks, and he returned the kiss, but the way he might kiss Sarah.

'Should we say something?' Jacqueline asked.

'Say what?' he said, trying to keep his voice down. 'To who?'

'To Monsieur Gamache, of course,' she said.

'No,' said Anton firmly. 'Promise me you won't. We don't know what it is—'

'We have a pretty good idea,' she said.

'But we don't know.' He lowered his voice when the chef looked over. 'It'll probably go away.'

Jacqueline had her own reasons to worry, but for the moment she was focused on Anton's reaction to the thing.

Armand sat in the bistro, reading.

He could feel eyes on him. All with the same message.

Do something about that thing on the village green.

Make it go away.

What good was it to have the head of the entire Sûreté as a neighbor, if he couldn't protect them?

He crossed his legs, and heard the mutter of the open fire. He felt the warmth, smelled the maple wood smoke, and sensed the eyes of his neighbors drilling into him.

While there'd been a comfortable armchair right by the open hearth, he'd placed himself in the window. Where he could see the thing.

Like Reine-Marie, Armand had noticed that as the day went by, he'd slowly stopped thinking of the figure on the green as 'he'. It had become an 'it'.

And Gamache, more than any of them, knew how dangerous that was. To dehumanize a person. Because no matter how strange the behavior, it was a person beneath those robes.

It also interested him to see his own reactions. He wanted it to go away. He wanted to go out there and arrest it. Him.

For what?

For disturbing his personal peace.

It wasn't useful to tell everyone that there was no threat. Because he didn't know if that was true. What he did know was that there was nothing he could do. The very fact he was head of the Sûreté made it less possible, not more, for him to act.

Reine-Marie had stood at his side at his swearing-in. Gamache in his dress uniform, with the gold epaulets and gold braid and gold belt. And the medals he wore reluctantly. Each reminding him of an event he wished hadn't happened. But had.

He'd stood resolute, determined.

His son and daughter watching. His grandchildren there too, as he'd raised his hand and sworn to uphold Service, Integrity, Justice.

Their friends and neighbors were in the audience, packed into the grand room at the National Assembly.

Jean-Guy Beauvoir, his longtime second-in-command and now his son-in-law, held his own son. And watched.

Gamache had asked Beauvoir to join him in the Chief Super-intendent's department. Once again as second-in-command.

'Nepotism?' Beauvoir had asked. 'A grand Québec tradition.'

'You know how much I value tradition,' said Gamache. 'But you're forcing me to admit that you're the very best person for the job, Jean-Guy, and the ethics committee agrees.'

'Awkward for you.'

'*Oui.* The Sûreté is now a meritocracy. So don't—'

'Fuck up?'

'I was going to say, don't forget the croissants, but the other works too.'

And Jean-Guy had said *oui. Merci.* And watched as Chief Superintendent Gamache shook hands with the Chief Justice of Québec, then turned to face the crowded auditorium.

He stood at the head of a force of thousands charged with protecting a province Armand Gamache loved. A populace he saw not as either victim or threat, but as brothers and sisters. Equals, to be respected and protected. And sometimes arrested.

'Apparently there's more to the job,' he'd said to Myrna, during one of their quiet conversations, 'than cocktail parties and luncheon clubs.'

He had, in fact, spent the past couple of months holding intense meetings with the heads of various departments, getting up to speed on dossiers from organized crime, drug trafficking, homicide, cyber crime, money laundering, arson and a dozen other files.

It was immediately obvious that the degree of crime was far worse than even he had imagined. And getting worse. And what drove the gathering chaos was the drug trade.

The cartels.

From there sprang most of the other ills. The murders, the assaults. Money laundering. Extortion.

The robberies, the sexual assaults. The purposeless violence committed by young men and women in despair. The inner cities were already infected. But it wasn't confined there. The rot was spreading into the countryside.

Gamache had known there was a growing problem, but he'd had no idea of the scope of it.

Until now.

Chief Superintendent Gamache spent his days immersed in the vile, the profane, the tragic, the terrifying. And then he went home. To Three Pines. To sanctuary. To sit by the fire in the bistro with friends, or in the privacy of his living room with Reine-Marie. Henri and funny little Gracie at their feet.

Safe and sound.

Until the dark thing had appeared. And refused to disappear.

'Did you speak to him again?' the Crown attorney asked.

'And say what?' asked Chief Superintendent Gamache, in the witness box. From there he could see people in the gallery fanning themselves with sheets of paper, desperate to create even the slightest of breezes to cut the stifling heat.

'Well, you might've asked what he was doing there.'

'I already had. And in any other circumstance, you'd be asking me why I, a police officer, was harassing a citizen who was just standing in a park, minding his own business.'

'A masked citizen,' said the Crown.

'Again,' said Gamache. 'Being masked is not a crime. It's strange, absolutely. And I'm not going to tell you I was happy about it. I wasn't. But there was nothing I could do.'

That brought a murmur from those listening. Some in agreement. Some feeling that they'd have acted differently. And certainly the head of the Sûreté should have done something.

Gamache recognized the censure in the mumbling, and understood where it came from. But they were sitting in a courtroom now, with full knowledge of what had happened.

And still he knew there was nothing he could have done to stop it.

It was very hard to stop Death, once that Horseman had left the stables.

'What did you do that night?'

'We had dinner, stayed up and watched television, then Madame Gamache went to bed.'

'And you?'

'I poured a coffee and took it into my study.'

'To work?'

'I didn't turn on the lights. I sat in the darkness, and watched.'

One dark figure watching another.

As he'd sat there, Armand Gamache had the impression something had changed.

The dark figure had moved, shifted slightly.

And was now watching him.

'How long did you stay there?'

'An hour, maybe more. It was difficult to see. He was a dark figure in the darkness. When I took the dogs out for a last walk, he was gone.'

'So he could have left at any time? Even shortly after you sat down. You didn't actually see him leave?'

'No.'

'Is it possible you drifted off to sleep?'

'It's possible, but I'm used to surveillance.'

'Watching others. You and he had that in common,' said Zalmanowitz.

The comment surprised Chief Superintendent Gamache and he raised his brows, but nodded. 'I suppose so.'

'And the next morning?'

'He was back.'

CHAPTER 3

—

J udge Corriveau decided it was a good time to break for lunch.

The Chief Superintendent would be in the witness box for many days. Being examined and cross-examined.

It was now stifling in the courtroom, and as she left she asked the guard to turn the AC on, just for the break.

When she'd sat down that morning, Maureen Corriveau had been grateful that her first murder case as a judge would be fairly straightforward. But now she was beginning to wonder.

Not that she couldn't follow the law involved. That was easy. Even the appearance of the robed figure in the village, while strange, was easily covered by clear laws.

What was making her perspire even more than just the overbearing heat was the inexplicable antagonism that had so quickly developed between the Crown and his own witness.

And not just any witness. Not just any arresting officer. The head of the whole damned Sûreté.

The Chief Crown wasn't just getting in the Chief Superintendent's face, he was getting up the man's nose. And Monsieur Gamache did not like it.

She wasn't an experienced judge, but as a defense attorney she was an experienced judge of human actions and reactions. And nature.

There was something else happening in her courtroom, and Judge Corriveau was determined to figure it out.

'Is it just me, or is this trial going a bit off the rails already?' asked Jean-Guy Beauvoir as he joined his boss in the corridor of the Palais de Justice.

'Not at all,' said Gamache, wiping his face with his handkerchief. 'Everything's perfect.'

Beauvoir laughed. 'And by that you mean everything's *merde*.'

'Exactly. Where's Isabelle?'

'She's gone ahead,' said Beauvoir. 'Organizing things back at the office.'

'Good.'

Isabelle Lacoste was the head of homicide, personally selected for the job by Gamache when he'd left. There'd been grumbles when the announcement of Gamache's successor had been made. Complaints of favoritism.

They all knew the story. Gamache had hired Lacoste a few years earlier, at the very moment she was about to be let go from the Sûreté. For being different. For not taking part in the bravado of crime scenes. For trying to understand suspects and not just break them.

For kneeling down beside the corpse of a recently dead woman and promising, within earshot of other agents, to help her find peace.

Agent Lacoste had been ridiculed, pilloried, subtly disciplined, and finally called into her supervisor's office, where she came face-to-face with Chief Inspector Gamache. He'd heard of the odd young agent everyone was laughing at, and had gone there to meet her.

Instead of being thrown away, she was taken away by Gamache and placed in the most prestigious division in the Sûreté du Québec. Much to the chagrin of her former colleagues.

And that rancor had only escalated when she'd risen through the ranks to become Chief Inspector. But instead of responding to the critics, as some within her division had begged her to do, Lacoste had simply gone about her job.

And that job, she knew with crystalline clarity, was indeed simple though not easy.

Find murderers.

The rest was just noise.

When the day was done, Chief Inspector Lacoste went home to her husband and young children. But she always took part of her job with her, worrying about the victims and the killers still out there. Just as she always took part of her family with her when she went to work. Worrying about what sort of community, society, they would find when they left the safety of home.

'I just got a text,' said Beauvoir. 'Isabelle has everyone in the conference room. She's ordered sandwiches.'

He seemed to give both pieces of information equal importance.

'*Merci,*' said Gamache.

The corridors were crowded with clerks and witnesses and spectators, as the courtrooms in the Palais de Justice emptied for the lunch break.

Every now and then there appeared a figure in black robes.

Barristers, Gamache knew. Or judges. Also hurrying to grab something to eat.

But still, a sight that should have been familiar now gave him a start.

Inspector Beauvoir said nothing else about the morning's testimony. The frozen look of efficiency on his boss's face told him all he needed to know about whether it was going according to plan. Or not.

Chief Superintendent Gamache's guard was up. A tall, thick wall of civility that even his son-in-law couldn't penetrate.

Beauvoir knew exactly what was behind that wall, clawing to get out. And he also knew the Crown Prosecutor would not want it to actually get out.

They walked swiftly along the familiar cobblestoned streets of Old Montréal, a well-traveled route between their office and the courthouse. Past low-ceilinged, beamed restaurants full of the lunch crowd.

Jean-Guy glanced in, but kept going.

Up ahead was Sûreté headquarters, rising from the old city. Towering over it.

Not, Beauvoir thought, an attractive building. But an efficient one. It, at least, would have air-conditioning.

The two men emerged from the narrow street into the open square in front of Notre-Dame Basilica, weaving around tourists taking photographs of themselves in front of the cathedral.

When looked at years from now, they'd see the magnificent structure, and a whole lot of sweaty people in shorts and sundresses wilting in the scorching heat as the sun throbbed down on the cobblestones.

As soon as they entered Sûreté headquarters, they were hit by the air-conditioning. What should have felt good, refreshing, a relief, actually felt like someone had thrown a snowball into their faces.

The agents in the lobby saluted the chief, and the two men took the elevator. By the time they reached the top floor, they were drenched in sweat. Perversely, the AC opened the floodgates of perspiration.

Gamache and Beauvoir entered the chief's office, with its floor-to-ceiling windows overlooking Montréal, and from there across the St Lawrence River to the fertile flatlands and the mountains on the horizon. Beyond which lay Vermont.

The gateway into the United States.

Gamache paused for a moment, staring at the wall of mountains. More porous than they appeared from a distance.

Then he opened a drawer and offered Beauvoir a clean, dry shirt.

Beauvoir declined. 'I'm good. I wasn't on the witness stand.' He walked to the door. 'I'll be in the conference room.'

Gamache quickly changed into the new shirt, then joined Beauvoir, Lacoste and the others.

They stood as he entered, but he waved them to be seated before taking his own chair.

'Tell me what you know.'

For the next half hour he listened and nodded. Asking few questions. Taking it all in.

These men and women, pulled from various departments, had been specially, carefully chosen. And they knew it.

This was a new era. A new Sûreté. His job, Gamache knew, wasn't to keep the status quo. Nor was it to fix what was wrong.

His job was to build afresh. And while institutional memory and experience were important, it was vastly more important to have a solid foundation.

The officers in that room were the foundation upon which a whole new Sûreté du Québec was rising. Strong. Transparent. Answerable. Decent.

He was the architect and much more involved than his predecessors, some of whom had engineered the corruption of the past, and some of whom simply let it happen, by not paying attention. Or being afraid to say something.

Gamache was paying attention. And he insisted his senior officers did too.

And he insisted that they not be afraid to question. Him. The plans. Each other. Themselves. And indeed, many had questioned the new chief, ferociously, when shortly after taking over and immersing himself in their dossiers and briefings, he'd presented them with the reality.

'Things are getting worse,' he'd said. 'Far worse.'

This had been almost a year earlier. In this same conference room.

They'd looked at him as he detailed what 'far worse' meant. Some not comprehending. Some understanding perfectly well what he was saying. Their faces going from disbelieving to shocked.

He'd listened to their protests, their arguments. And then he said something he'd hoped wouldn't be necessary. He didn't want to shatter their confidence, or drain their energy. Or undermine their commitment.

But he could see now that they needed to know. They deserved to know.

'We've lost.'

They looked at him blankly. And then some, those who'd followed his report most clearly, blanched.

'We've lost,' he repeated, his voice even. Calm. Certain. 'The war on drugs was lost a long time ago. That was bad enough, but what's happened is the knock-on effect. If drugs are out of control, it isn't long before we lose our grip on all crime. We aren't there yet. But we will be. At the rate things are going, growing, we'll be overwhelmed in just a few years.'

They'd argued, of course. Not wanting to see it. To accept it. And neither had he, when he'd first compiled the information. Put it all together. In the past, the departments had competed, been territorial. Had been reluctant to share information, statistics. Especially those that might make them look bad.

It appeared to Gamache that he was the first one to meld all the information. To put it all together.

He wondered if this was how the captain of a great ship felt when he alone knew it was sinking. To everyone else, it still looked fine. Moving along as it always had.

But he knew the cold waters, unseen, were rising.

At first he'd been in denial too. Going over and over the files. The figures. The projections.

And then one day in early autumn, at home in Three Pines, he'd laid his hand on the last dossier, gotten up from his seat by the fire, and gone for a walk.

Alone. No Reine-Marie. No Gracie. No Henri, who'd stood perplexed and hurt by the door. His ball in his mouth.

Gamache had walked, and walked. He'd sat on the bench above the village and looked out over the valley. The forests. To the mountains, some of which were in Québec. And some in Vermont.

The border, the boundary, impossible to see from there.

Then he'd lowered his head. Into his hands. And he'd kept it there, shutting out the world. The knowledge.

And then he'd gotten back up, and walked some more. For hours.

Trying to find a solution.

Suppose they got a larger budget? Hired more agents? Threw more resources at the crisis?

Surely there was something that could be done. The situation couldn't possibly be hopeless.

He only stopped when he'd met himself again. The Armand who'd been standing on the side of the quiet road, in the middle of nowhere, waiting. At the intersection of truth and wishful thinking.

Where the straight road splayed.

And he knew then. They were all going down. Not just the Sûreté, but the entire province. And not necessarily his generation. But the next. And the next. His grandchildren.

He was up to his neck in crime. They'd be over their heads.

And he knew something else. Something he wished he didn't know, but could not now deny.

There was nothing that could be done. They'd reached and passed the point of no return. Without even a lifeboat in sight. The corruption of decades within government and police forces had seen to that.

'So what do we do?' asked one of the older officers in the meeting. 'Give up?'

'*Non.* I don't have a solution. Not yet. So we bear down, do our jobs, communicate. Gather information and share it.'

He looked at each of them, sternly.

'And we try to come up with creative solutions. Come to me with anything, everything. No matter how crazy it sounds.'

What he felt in that room, as he left, wasn't despair, not quite yet. Not yet panic, but panic adjacent.

*

And now, many months later, they sat in the same conference room.

All had looked so bleak back then. Now they were close, so close to their first major victory.

But it depended on this trial. The outcome, but also the path of it.

Perversely, when things had been at their worst, everything had appeared just fine. Québec, the Sûreté, functioning as it should.

Now that there was a glimmer of hope, things appeared to be spinning out of control.

Senior politicians and some media outlets had lately noticed what appeared to be a certain sleight of hand on the part of the head of the Sûreté.

Arrests were up. And for a while that had caused outright celebration on the part of politicians and their electorate.

Until the Radio-Canada television show, *Enquête*, had investigated and discovered that the arrests were mostly for small to medium-size crimes.

'Explain this,' the Premier Ministre du Québec had demanded, having called Chief Superintendent Gamache into his office in Québec City the day after the program aired.

The Premier had slapped a thick file onto his desk. Even from across the room, Gamache could see what it was.

The printout of the latest monthly report on Sûreté activities.

'I've checked. Fucking *Enquête* is right, Armand. Yes, arrests are up, and thank God you're still managing to arrest murderers, but what about the rest? There hasn't been a significant arrest in other divisions since you took over. No biker gang member, no organized crime figure. No drug arrests or even seizures. Minor trafficking, but nothing more. What the hell are you doing over there?'

'You of all people should know that statistics,' Gamache nodded toward the file, 'don't tell the whole story.'

'Are you saying all this,' the Premier put his hand on the file, 'is a lie?'

'*Non*, not a lie. But not the complete truth.'

'Are you running for office? What sort of gibberish is that? I've never heard you so evasive.'

He glared at Gamache, who stared back. But said nothing more.

'What are you up to, Armand? Dear God, don't tell me *Enquête* was right.'

In the TV program they'd intimated, but never crossed the line of actual slander, that Gamache was either incompetent or, like his predecessors, in the employ of organized crime.

'No,' said Gamache. 'I can see how they might come to that conclusion, or have that suspicion. But *Enquête* was not right.'

'Then what is? I'm begging you for an answer. Give me something. Anything. Other than this pile of shit.' He shoved the papers across his desk with such force they cascaded over the edge. 'You're deliberately putting up this mist of arrests that looks good, until someone realizes they're minor. Until fucking *Enquête* realized that.'

'We are arresting murderers.'

'Well, congratulations on that,' said the Premier.

They'd known each other a long time. Since Gamache had been a junior agent and the Premier was articling in the legal aid office.

'They're calling you the worst Chief Superintendent of the Sûreté in a very long time. And that's some bar to squeeze under.'

'It certainly is,' said Gamache. 'But believe me, I am doing something. I really am.'

The Premier had held his gaze, searching for the lie.

Then Gamache bent down and picked the report off the floor. He handed it back to the Premier, who held the pile, which was heavy on statistics, and light on actual action.

'My own party is circling, smelling blood,' said the Premier. 'Yours or mine. They don't really care. But they want action, or a sacrifice. You have to do something, Armand. Give them what they want. What they deserve. A significant arrest.'

'I am doing something.'

'This' – the Premier laid his hand, with surprising gentleness, on top of the retrieved pages – 'is not "something". Not even close. Please. I'm begging you.'

'And I'm begging you. Trust me,' said Armand quietly. 'You have to get me across the finish line.'

'What does that mean?' the Premier had asked, also whispering.

'You know.'

And the Premier, who loved Québec but also loved power, blanched. Knowing he might have to give up one to preserve the other.

Armand Gamache looked at the good man in front of him and wondered which of them would survive the next few months. Weeks. Days. When the St-Jean-Baptiste fireworks went off at the end of June, which of them would be standing there to see the skies lit up?

Which of them would still be standing?

Chief Superintendent Gamache had taken the train back to Montréal, walking from the station through the old city, to his office. A few heads turned as he passed, recognizing him from the unfortunately popular TV show that had aired the night before.

Or maybe they knew him from past appearances in the media.

Even before he was the most senior officer in the Sûreté, Armand Gamache had been the most recognizable police officer in Québec.

But what had once been glances of recognition and even respect were now tinged, tainted, with suspicion. Even amusement. He was on the verge of becoming a joke.

But Armand Gamache could see beyond those looks, to the finish line.

That had been mid-June. A month earlier, almost to the day. Now Gamache glanced at the clock and stood.

'Time to get back to court.'

'How's it going, *patron*?' asked Madeleine Toussaint, the head of Serious Crimes.

'As expected.'

'That bad?'

Gamache smiled. 'That good.'

They locked eyes, and then she nodded.

'You have that report coming in from an informant on the Magdalen Islands,' he said. Trying not to sound too hopeful. Or was the word 'desperate'?

She'd mentioned this in the meeting. There'd been interest, but nothing unusual. Only a handful of them understood just what that report might mean.

'Will you hear in time for the meeting at the end of the day?' Beauvoir asked.

'I hope. It all sorta depends on what happens at the trial, doesn't it?' said Toussaint.

Gamache nodded. Yes. It did.

After Superintendent Toussaint returned to her office, Beauvoir and Chief Inspector Lacoste remained with Gamache.

'Speaking of the trial,' said Lacoste, gathering up her papers, 'I'm not sure I've seen a prosecutor go after his own witness in such a way. And the judge sure hasn't. She's new to the bench, but not to be underestimated.'

'*Non*,' said Gamache, who'd noticed the sharp look in Judge Corriveau's eye.

They walked the length of the corridor and the elevator arrived. Lacoste got off at her floor.

'Good luck,' she said to Gamache.

'Good luck to you,' he said.

'Almost there, *patron*,' said Isabelle, as the doors closed.

Almost there, thought Gamache. But he knew that most accidents occurred within sight of home.

'Chief Superintendent Gamache, you testified this morning that the figure on the village green in Three Pines returned the next day. How did that make you feel?'

'Objection. Irrelevant.'

Judge Corriveau considered. 'I'm going to allow it. The trial is about facts, but feelings are also a fact.'

Chief Superintendent Gamache thought before he answered.

'I felt angry, that the peace of our little village was being violated. Our lives disrupted.'

'And yet, he was just standing there.'

'True. You asked how I felt, and that's the answer.'

'Were you afraid of him?'

'Maybe a little. Our myths are so deeply ingrained. He

52

looked like Death. Rationally I knew he wasn't that, but inside, I could feel the chill. It was' – he searched for the word – 'instinctive.'

'And still, you did nothing.'

'As I told you before the break, there was nothing that I could do, beyond speaking with him. If I could have done something more, I would have.'

'Really? Judging by the Sûreté track record of late, that's not exactly true.'

That brought outright laughter from the courtroom.

'Enough,' said Judge Corriveau. 'Approach the bench.'

The Chief Crown did.

'You will not treat anyone like that in my courtroom, do you understand? That was a disgrace – to you, to your office, and to this court. You will apologize to the Chief Superintendent.'

'I'm sorry,' said the Crown, then turned to Gamache. 'I apologize. I let my astonishment get the better of me.'

The judge gave a small sigh of annoyance but let it stand.

'*Merci*. I accept your apology,' said Gamache.

But still, Gamache glared at the Crown attorney with such focus, the man took a step back. Neither the jury nor the audience could fail to see both the look and the reaction.

In the gallery, Beauvoir nodded approval.

'So you did speak to him again, that next morning?' asked Zalmanowitz. 'What did you say?'

'I told him again to be careful.'

'Clearly not of you,' said the Crown.

'No. Of whoever he'd targeted.'

'So you no longer thought it was a joke?'

'If it had been, I don't think he'd have returned. He'd spooked the village with his first appearance. That would have been enough, had it been a joke, or even vindictive. No, this went deeper. There was commitment. There was a purpose.'

'Did you think he meant to do harm?' asked the Crown.

That was a more difficult question, and Chief Superintendent Gamache considered it. And slowly shook his head.

'I didn't really know what he intended. Harm of some sort, it seemed. He was intentionally threatening. But did he have an act of violence in mind? If he did, why warn the person? Why wear that getup? Why not just do it, under cover of darkness? Hurt, even kill the person? Why just stand there for everyone to see?'

Gamache stared ahead of him, deep in thought.

The Crown seemed at a loss. So unusual was it for someone to actually think on the witness stand. They answered clear questions by telling the rehearsed truth, or a preplanned lie.

But they rarely actually thought.

'Of course, there are different ways of hurting, aren't there?' said Gamache, as much to himself as the Crown.

'But whatever the original intention,' said Monsieur Zalmanowitz, 'it led to murder.'

Now Gamache did focus, but not on the prosecution. He turned to the defense desk, and looked at the person accused of that murder.

'Yes, it did.'

Maybe, he thought, but didn't say, it wasn't enough to just kill. Maybe the point was to first terrify. Like the Scots and their shrieking bagpipes as they marched into battle, or the Maori and their haka.

It is death. It is death, they chant. To terrify, to petrify.

The dark thing wasn't a warning, it was a prediction.

'You took a picture of him, I believe,' said the Crown,

stepping in front of his witness, placing himself between Gamache and the defendant. Intentionally breaking that contact.

'Yes,' said Gamache, refocusing on the prosecution. 'I sent it off to my second-in-command. Inspector Beauvoir.'

The Crown turned to the clerk.

'Exhibit A.'

An image appeared on the large screen.

If the Crown was expecting gasps behind him as those in the courtroom saw the photograph, he was disappointed.

Behind him there was complete and utter silence, as though the entire gallery had disappeared. So profound was the silence, he turned around to make sure they were indeed still there.

To a person they were staring, dumbfounded. Some openmouthed.

There on the screen was a quiet little village. The leaves were off the trees, leaving them skeletal. Three huge pines rose from the village green.

In contrast to the bright, sunny summer day beyond the courtroom window, the day in this photo was overcast. Gray and damp. Which made the fieldstone and clapboard and rose brick homes, with their cheery lights at the windows, all the more inviting.

It would have been an image of extreme peace. Sanctuary even. Would have been, but wasn't.

In the center of the photo there was a black hole. Like something cut out of the picture. Out of the world.

Behind the Crown attorney there was a sigh. Long, prolonged, as life drained from the courtroom.

It was the first look most of them had had of the dark thing.

CHAPTER 4

———

'Now?' asked Matheo Bissonette, turning from the window to look at Lea. They'd finished breakfast at the B&B and now sat in the living room in front of the fireplace.

Despite the fire in the grate, and the sweater he wore, he still felt chilled.

'He just took a photo of the thing,' said Matheo. 'If we wait much longer, it looks bad.'

'Bad?' said Lea. 'Don't you mean worse?'

'We should've said something yesterday,' said Patrick. His voice, slightly whiny at the best of times, was now almost infantile. 'They'll wonder why we didn't.'

'Okay,' said Matheo, trying not to snap at Patrick. 'Then we're agreed. Now's the time.'

It wasn't what Patrick said that was so annoying, it was how he said it. He'd always been the weakest of them, and yet, somehow, Patrick always got his way. Maybe they just wanted the whining to stop, thought Matheo. It was like nails on a blackboard. So they gave in to him.

And, with age, it was getting worse. Matheo now felt like

not just yelling at the guy, but also giving him a swift kick in the pants.

Gabri had brought in a fresh French press of coffee and asked, 'Where's Katie?'

'There's a glass house nearby,' said Patrick. 'Not a classic one, like we make, but interesting. She wants to see it. Might work for the one we're building on the Magdalen Islands.'

Gabri, who'd asked just to be polite, drifted, uninterested, back to the kitchen.

Matheo looked from his wife, Lea, to his friend Patrick. They were both exactly his age, thirty-three, but they appeared older, surely, than he did. The lines. The hint of gray. Had they always looked like that, or just since the robes and mask had appeared?

Lea, tall, willowy, when they'd met at university, was less willowy. She was now more like a maple. Rounded. Solid. He liked that. Felt more substantial. Less likely to weep.

They had two children, both at home with Lea's parents. He knew that when they returned, it would be like walking into a ferret's den. The kids, under the questionable influence of Lea's mother, would have gone feral.

To be fair, it didn't take much.

'Gamache's in the bistro with his wife. Everyone'll hear,' said Patrick. 'Maybe we should wait.'

'But everyone should hear,' said Lea, getting up. 'Right? Isn't that the point?'

The friends weren't looking at each other as they spoke. Or even at the mesmerizing fire in the grate. All three stared out the window of the B&B. At the village green. Deserted. Except for ...

'Why don't you stay here?' she said to Patrick. 'We'll go.'

Patrick nodded. He'd caught a chill yesterday, and his

bones still felt it. He pulled his chair closer to the fire and poured a strong, hot coffee.

Armand Gamache wasn't looking at the mesmerizing fire in the large open hearth of the bistro. He was staring out the leaded-glass window, with its flaws and slight distortions. At the cold November day and the thing on the village green.

It was as though a bell jar, like those put around dead and stuffed animals, had been placed over it. The robed figure stood completely alone, isolated, while around him the villagers went about their lives. Their movements circumscribed, dictated by the dark thing.

The villagers were pushed to the edge. Edgy. Glancing toward it and away.

Gamache shifted his gaze and saw Lea Roux and her husband, Matheo Bissonette, leaving the B&B, walking quickly through the chilly morning. Their breaths coming in puffs.

They arrived with a small commotion, rubbing their hands and arms. They hadn't brought the right clothing, not expecting weather that was cold even for November.

'Bonjour,' said Lea, walking up to the Gamaches' table.

Armand rose while Reine-Marie nodded and smiled.

'Mind if we join you?' asked Matheo.

'Please do.' Reine-Marie indicated the empty chairs.

'Actually,' said Lea, a little embarrassed, 'I wonder if Myrna would mind if we talked in the bookstore? Would that be okay?'

Armand looked at Reine-Marie, both of them surprised by the suggestion. She got up.

'If it's all right with Myrna, it's fine with me,' she said. 'Unless—'

She waved toward Armand, indicating perhaps they meant

they just wanted to speak with him. She was used to that. Sometimes people had things they wanted to say to a cop, and did not want Madame Cop to hear.

'*Non, non*,' said Lea. 'Please come. We'd like you to hear this too. See what you make of it.'

Picking up their coffees, and curious, the Gamaches followed Lea and Matheo into the bookstore.

Myrna didn't mind at all.

'It's a quiet morning,' she said. 'Apparently Death standing vigil in the middle of the village isn't good for business. I'll alert the Chamber of Commerce.'

'Don't leave,' said Lea. 'We'd like your opinion too. Right, Matheo?'

It really wasn't a question. Though he looked less sure, he recovered quickly and nodded.

'About what?' asked Myrna.

Lea waved them to take seats on the sofa and in the armchairs, as though it were her place. Far from taking offense, Myrna liked that Lea felt so at home. And there was nothing officious about the gesture. She made it feel inclusive rather than demanding.

When they were settled, Matheo put a bunch of papers on the pine coffee table.

Gamache looked at the pages, mostly articles from Spanish newspapers, in Spanish.

'Can you tell me what they're about?'

'Sorry.' Matheo sorted through the pages. 'I meant to put this one on top.'

It was pink and unmistakable. The *Financial Times*.

The front page article had the byline *Matheo Bissonette*. Gamache noted the date.

Eighteen months ago.

A photograph accompanied the article. It showed a man in a top hat and tails, carrying a briefcase with writing on it. The man looked both dapper and seedy.

Gamache put his glasses on and, along with Reine-Marie and Myrna, he leaned over the picture.

'What does it say on the briefcase?' asked Myrna.

'Cobrador del Frac,' said Matheo. 'It means debt collector.'

Gamache was reading the article, but stopped and looked up over his half-moon glasses.

'Go on.'

'My parents live in Madrid. About a year and a half ago, my father emailed this article.' Matheo shuffled the printouts and found an article from another newspaper. 'He's always looking for things that might interest me. I'm a freelance journalist, as you know.'

Gamache nodded, his attention taken by the Spanish article, which also had a photo of the top-hat-and-tails debt collector.

'I pitched it to various papers and the *Financial Times* bought the story from me. So I went to Spain and did some research. The cobrador del frac is a particularly Spanish phenomenon, and with the financial crisis they've grown.'

'This man is a debt collector?' asked Reine-Marie.

'*Oui.*'

'Well, they sure look nicer than the debt collectors in North America,' said Myrna.

'They're not what they appear,' said Matheo. 'They're not at all civilized or genteel. That's more a disguise than a costume.'

'And what are they disguising?' asked Gamache.

'What it is they're collecting,' said Matheo. 'A collection agency here will repossess a car or a home or furniture. A cobrador del frac takes away something else entirely.'

'What?' asked Armand.

'Your reputation. Your good name.'

'How does he do that?' asked Reine-Marie.

'He's hired to follow the debtor. Always keeping a distance, never speaking to the person, but always there.'

'Always?' she asked, while Armand listened, his eyebrows drawing together in unease.

'Always,' said Lea. 'He stands outside your home, follows you to work. Stands outside your business. If you go to a restaurant or a party, he's there.'

'But why? Surely there're easier ways to collect on a bad debt?' said Reine-Marie. 'A lawyer's letter? The courts?'

'Those take time, and the Spanish courts are clogged with cases since the meltdown,' said Matheo. 'It could be years, if ever, before someone pays up. People were getting away with terrible things, taking clients and partners and spouses for all they were worth, knowing they'd almost certainly never be made to pay it back. Scams were proliferating. Until someone remembered—'

He looked down at the photograph. Of a man in a top hat and tails. Only now did the Gamaches notice the man in the crowd, a distance ahead, hurrying forward but glancing back. A look of dread dawning.

And the cobrador del frac following. His face rigid, expressionless. Remorseless.

A corridor was opening through the crowd to let him pass.

'He shames people into paying their debts,' said Matheo. 'It's a terrible thing to see. At first it looks comical, but then it becomes chilling. I was in a restaurant in Madrid recently with my parents. A very nice one. Linens and silverware. Hushed tones. A place where high-level business is discreetly conducted. And a cobrador was standing out front. First the maître d' then the owner went out and tried to shoo him away. Even tried to shove him. But he just stood his ground. Holding that briefcase. Staring through the window.'

'Did you know who he was staring at?' Reine-Marie asked.

'Not at first, but the man eventually gave himself away. Got all flustered and angry. He went outside and screamed at him. But the cobrador didn't react. And when the man stomped off, he just turned and quietly followed. I can't tell you exactly why, but it was terrifying. I almost felt sorry for the man.'

'Don't,' said Lea. 'They deserve what they get. A cobrador del frac is only used in the most extreme cases. You'd have to have done something particularly bad to bring that on yourself.'

'Can anyone hire a cobrador?' asked Myrna. 'I mean, how do they know there is a legitimate debt? Maybe they just want to humiliate.'

'The company screens,' said Matheo. 'I'm sure there're some abuses, but for the most part if you're being followed by a cobrador, there's good reason.'

'Armand?' Reine-Marie asked.

He was shaking his head, his eyes narrow.

'It feels like vigilante action,' he said. 'Taking justice into their own hands. Condemning someone.'

'But there's no violence,' said Lea.

'Oh, there's violence,' said Gamache. And put his finger on the face of the terrified man. 'Just not physical.'

Matheo was nodding.

'The thing is,' he said, 'it's very effective. The people almost always pay up, and quickly. And you have to remember, innocent people aren't targeted. This isn't the first action, it's the last. It's what people resort to when all else fails.'

'So,' said Gamache, looking at Matheo. 'Are you consider-ing bringing the cobrador del frac to Québec? Are you asking me if it would be legal?'

Matheo and Lea stared at Gamache, then Matheo laughed.

'Good God, no. I'm showing you this because Lea and I think that that' – he pointed out the window – 'is a cobrador del frac.'

'A debt collector?' asked Gamache, and felt a slight frisson. Like the warning before a quake.

Lea was all eyes now, glancing swiftly from Armand to Reine-Marie to Myrna and back. Examining them for any hint of amusement. Or agreement. Or anything. But they were almost entirely expressionless. Their faces as blank as the thing on the village green.

Armand sat back in his chair and opened his mouth, before closing it again, while Reine-Marie turned and looked at Myrna.

Finally Armand leaned forward, toward Matheo, who leaned toward him.

'You do know that that' – he inclined his head toward the village green – 'doesn't look anything like this.' He nodded at the photograph.

'I know,' said Matheo. 'When I was researching the article, I heard rumors of something else. Something older. Dating back centuries.' He also glanced over, then looked away, as though it was folly to stare at the thing too long. 'The ancestor of the current cobrador. I'd hear whispers that the thing was still alive, in remote villages. In the mountains. But I could never find one, or find anyone who admitted hiring one.'

'And that original cobrador is different?' asked Reine-Marie.

'It's still a collector, but the debt is different.'

'Degree of debt?' asked Gamache.

'Type of debt. One is financial, often ruinous,' said Matheo, looking at the photo on the table.

'The other is moral,' said Lea.

Matheo nodded. 'An elderly man I spoke with in a village outside Granada had seen one, but only once, as a boy, and in the distance. It was following an old woman. They disappeared around a corner and he never saw either again. He wouldn't speak on the record, but he did show me this.'

From his pocket, Matheo pulled a blurry photocopy of a blurry photograph.

'He took this with his Brownie camera.'

The image was grainy. Black and white.

It showed a steep, narrow street and stone walls that came right to the road. There was a horse and cart. And in the distance, at a corner, something else.

Gamache put his glasses back on and brought the paper up so that it almost touched his nose. Then he lowered it and handed it to Reine-Marie.

Removing his glasses, quietly, he folded them. All the while staring at Matheo.

The photo showed a robed, masked figure. Hood up. And in front of the dark figure there was a gray blur. A gray ghost, hurrying to get away.

'Taken near the end of the Spanish Civil War,' said Matheo. 'I hate to think . . .'

There was no mistaking it. In the photo, almost a hundred years old, was the thing that now stood in the center of Three Pines.

'And did you believe it, Chief Superintendent?' asked the Crown.

His rank now seemed more a mockery in the mouth of the Crown than an advantage.

'It was hard to know, at that moment, what to believe. It seemed not only extraordinary but, frankly, incredible. That some sort of ancient Spanish debt collector had appeared in a small village in Québec. And I wouldn't have believed it, had I not seen it for myself. The photograph and the real thing.'

'I understand you took that piece of paper Matheo Bissonette showed you.'

'I took a copy of it, yes.'

The Crown turned to the clerk.

'Exhibit B.'

The photograph of Three Pines that gray November morning was replaced by what looked, at first, like a Rorschach test. Blots of black and gray, the borders bleeding, uncertain.

And then it coalesced into an image.

'Is that it?'

'It is,' said Gamache.

'And is that what was on your village green?'

Gamache stared at the image, the collector of moral debts, and felt again that frisson.

'It is.'

CHAPTER 5

⁓

Jacqueline kneaded the dough, leaning into it. Feeling it both soft and firm beneath her hands. It was meditative and sensual, as she rocked gently back and forth, back and forth.

Her eyes closed.

She kneaded and rocked. Kneaded and rocked.

Other hands, older, colder, plump, were laid on top of hers.

'I think that's enough, *ma belle*,' said Sarah.

'*Oui, madam.*'

Jacqueline blushed, realizing she'd overworked the baguette yet again.

If she didn't get this right, she'd lose her job. No matter how well she baked brownies and pies and mille-feuilles, if you couldn't do a baguette in Québec, you were useless to a small boulangerie. Sarah wouldn't want to let her go, but she'd have no choice.

All depended on this. And she was blowing it.

'You'll get the hang of it,' said Sarah, her voice reassuring. 'Why don't you finish your petits fours? Madame Morrow has ordered two dozen. She says they're for guests, but . . .'

Sarah laughed. It was full-bodied and wholehearted. An antidote to Jacqueline's fears.

She wondered if Anton was next door, cooking. Trying to come up with a dish to impress Olivier. To convince the bistro owner to elevate him to chef. Or even sous chef. Or to a prep station even.

Anything other than dishwasher.

But she suspected his heart wasn't in cooking anymore. Not since the robed figure appeared.

If she lived to be a hundred, Jacqueline would not forget the look on Anton's face when they'd discussed the thing on the village green. When she'd suggested approaching Gamache. Telling the Sûreté officer that they both knew what it was.

'Are you all right?' asked Sarah.

'I was just thinking,' said Jacqueline.

'Maybe that's the problem. When you make baguette, you should clear your mind. Open your mind. You'd be surprised, all the beautiful things that appear when you let your mind go.'

'When you go out of your mind, you mean?' asked Jacqueline.

Sarah looked at her for a moment. Then laughed again.

It wasn't often the serious, almost glum young woman made a joke.

Maybe she wasn't so serious after all, thought Sarah. There were glimmers almost of giddiness. And she also wasn't all that young. Young compared to Sarah, but her young apprentice would be in her mid-thirties.

Still, the beauty of baking. You only got better as you got older. More patient.

'You certainly have to be out of your mind to run a

bakery,' Sarah agreed. 'If you need any help, *ma belle*, just ask Tante Sarah.'

And Sarah headed off to check on the pies in the ovens.

Jacqueline couldn't help but smile.

Sarah wasn't really her aunt, of course. It had become a thing between the older woman and the younger. A joke, but not really. Both had discovered they quite liked the idea that they were family.

In that laugh, in that moment, no dark thing existed. But then the mist of laughter dissipated and it reappeared.

And her mind went to Anton.

Tante or not, if she didn't learn to make baguette, Sarah would eventually have to fire her ass. Replace her with someone who could.

And then she'd lose Anton.

Jacqueline threw out the overworked dough and started again. Her fourth try that day, and it wasn't yet noon.

Armand and Reine-Marie had returned home.

She was in the living room, going through a box from the archives.

Armand had fed the photocopy he'd made of the original cobrador into the scanner and emailed it off to Jean-Guy. He'd received a slightly rude reply, asking if he was bored. Or drunk.

Gamache had picked up the phone and called. Getting his daughter Annie first, who handed the phone off to Jean-Guy.

'What's with the weird photos, *patron*?' he asked.

Gamache could hear chewing and imagined Jean-Guy with a huge sandwich, like Dagwood. A reference that would be lost on his son-in-law.

When he'd explained, Jean-Guy, his mouth no longer clogged with food, said, 'I'll get right back to you.'

And Gamache knew he meant it.

He'd known Jean-Guy long before he'd become his son-in-law, having hired Agent Beauvoir away from a dead-end job guarding evidence. He'd taken a young man no one else wanted and made him an inspector in homicide, to every-one's surprise.

But it had seemed natural, to Gamache. He barely had to think about it.

They were chief and agent. *Patron* and protégé. They were the head and the heart. Now father-in-law and son-in-law. Father and son.

They had been thrown together, joined together, it seemed, for this lifetime, and many past.

One evening, during a dinner at Clara's, they'd all got to talking about life. And death. And the afterlife.

'There's a theory,' said Myrna. 'Not sure if it's Buddhist or Taoist or what, that says that there are certain people we meet time and again, in different lifetimes.'

'I believe it's ridiculous-ist,' said Ruth.

'The same dozen or so people,' Myrna continued, running over the verbal speed bump that was the old poet. 'But in different relationships. In this life you might be partners,' she looked at Gabri and Olivier, 'but in another life you were brothers, or husband and wife, or father and son.'

'Wait a minute,' said Gabri. 'Are you saying that Olivier might've once been my father?'

'Or your mother.'

The two men grimaced.

'We change roles, but what stays the same is the love,' said Myrna. 'That is absolute and infinite.'

'Fucking nuts,' said Ruth, stroking Rosa.

Fuck, fuck, fuck, agreed the duck.

There was a growing resemblance between Ruth and Rosa. Both had scrawny necks. Their heads white. Their eyes beady. They waddled when they walked. They shared a vocabulary.

If it wasn't for Ruth's cane they'd be almost indistinguishable.

Armand had looked across at Reine-Marie, her face glowing in the light from the log fire. She was listening, smiling. Taking it in.

If what Myrna said was true, then he'd known all these people before. It would explain his almost immediate attraction to them, and the village. The trust and comfort he felt in their company. Even mad old Ruth. With her doppelgänger. The duck who might have been her child, in a past life.

Or the other way around.

But Reine-Marie. His daughter, or mother, or brother?

Non.

She had always been his wife. He'd known that the first moment he'd seen her. He knew her, that first moment.

Through the ages. Through the lifetimes. Every other relationship might change, flow, morph into another guise, but his relationship with Reine-Marie was absolute and eternal.

She was his wife. And he was her husband. Forever.

Now, Jean-Guy was another matter. Armand had long felt there was something ancient there too. A very old camaraderie. A tie that didn't bind, but strengthened. And Reine-Marie could see it as well. Which is why she'd put only one proviso on his becoming the top cop in Québec.

Jean-Guy Beauvoir must join him. As he had through time.

And now Armand, reflecting on that, waited for a response from Jean-Guy and looked out his window at something that seemed to have also stepped from time.

And he wondered, if love followed them through lifetimes, did hate also follow?

'Anton?'

There was no reply.

'Anton!'

Olivier turned off the water. Suds had cascaded out of the deep sink onto the floor.

'People are ordering the soup special,' said Olivier. 'And we need more pans. You okay?'

'*Désolé, patron.* I was just thinking.'

He wondered if Olivier, or anyone, understood what had appeared on their pretty village green.

'Please,' said Olivier, and circled his hand in the signal to hurry up. 'And when you've finished that, can you take a couple bowls out to table three?'

'*Oui.*'

The pans were washed, quickly dried, handed to the chef. Anton ladled out two bowls of celeriac and quince soup, topping them with crème fraîche and dill, and took them out to table three.

'*Merci,*' said the woman.

'*Un plaisir, madame,*' said Anton, glancing at her politely before shifting his eyes out the window.

He had the vague impression he knew this woman. Had seen her before. Not a villager. A visitor. But his attention was now totally focused on the green.

As he watched, the thing moved. Very, very slightly. Perhaps just an inch. A millimeter.

Toward him.

'Did it just move?' Reine-Marie asked.

She'd come into the study to find a book, and now stood behind Armand's chair, looking out the window.

'It was slight,' said Armand. 'But I think so. Might've been just the breeze ruffling his robes.'

But they both knew the dark thing had indeed moved. Just a little. It was almost imperceptible, except to someone who happened to be looking, and who had been watching it for a while.

The thing had turned, slightly. Toward the bistro.

'Did you know then,' the Crown asked, 'who it was looking at?'

'*Non*. It could have been any one of a dozen people. Or more.'

'But most likely someone at a table in the window, *non*?'

'Objection, leading the witness.'

'Sustained.'

'What happened then?' asked the Crown.

CHAPTER 6

⌒

'Who else have you told about your cobrador theory?' Armand asked Matheo.

It was early afternoon and the visitors had invited some of the villagers to the B&B for tea. Gamache had taken the journalist into a corner where they could have a quiet word.

'No one. I wanted to run it by you first.'

'*Bon*. Please keep it that way.'

'Why?'

'No real reason. I just like to confirm things before rumors get out of control.'

'It is confirmed,' said Matheo, getting slightly annoyed. 'I told you.'

'Unfortunately, monsieur, your word alone, like mine alone, still needs to be verified.'

'And how do you do that?'

'One of my agents is looking into what you told us. I scanned the photograph to him. We'll have the confirmation soon. Then we can talk about it.'

'Fine.'

'*Merci.*'

'Hurry up,' called Ruth from the sofa. 'I'm dry.'

'You haven't been dry since 1968,' said Gabri, who was pouring her Scotch into a fine bone china teacup.

'Nixon's election,' said Ruth. 'Very sobering.'

'Have you noticed that the thing now has birds all over it?' asked Clara.

'Looks like a statue,' said Reine-Marie.

'Hope they shit on it,' said Matheo.

With the birds perching on its head and shoulders, the robed figure should have been comical, and yet the sparrows simply added to the sense of the macabre. He looked like a black marble statue in a cemetery.

'You okay?' Reine-Marie asked.

Like everyone else, Armand was staring at the figure on the green. He'd gone into a sort of trance.

'I just had the oddest feeling,' he whispered. 'For a moment I wondered if we had it all wrong, and he wasn't here to hurt, but to help.'

'You're not the first to think the cobrador's heroic,' said Matheo, who was standing beside them and had heard. 'A sort of Robin Hood. Righting a wrong. But that' – he inclined his head toward the window – 'is something else. You can almost smell the rot.'

'That's manure,' said Gabri, refreshing Matheo's wine. 'Monsieur Legault is spreading it on his fields.' He took a deep, satisfied breath and exhaled. 'Ahhhh. Smells like shit. What did you call it? A cobrador?'

'It's just a word,' said Matheo. 'A nickname.'

He walked away before Gabri could question him further.

'He gave the thing a nickname?' Gabri asked the Gamaches.

Armand shrugged and watched Matheo, now chatting with

Clara. And wondered if Matheo had called it a cobrador, in front of Gabri of all people, on purpose. Right after Gamache had asked him to keep it quiet.

Was it an honest mistake? Willful? Strategic?

'Where's Katie?' asked Myrna.

'She was here a few minutes ago,' said Patrick, looking around.

'She said she was heading to the microbrewery in Sutton to get more beer,' said Lea, raising her glass. 'Proof that God loves us and wants us to be happy. Benjamin Franklin.'

Gamache watched Lea Roux and wondered if one day in the not-too-distant future he'd be working for her. The next Première Ministre du Québec.

Gabri, following Ruth with the Scotch bottle like some Victorian retainer, said, 'I hate beer. Won't have it in the house. Brings the whole tone down.'

'And the duck doesn't?' asked Patrick, eyeing Rosa.

'We make exceptions,' said Gabri. 'Both the duck and the fuck are family.'

'Actually, we like having Ruth and Rosa around. They make the rest of us look sane,' Clara explained.

'Well . . .' said Lea.

'Glass houses,' said Ruth, clutching Rosa to her and glaring at Lea.

She absently laid a veined hand on Rosa's wings, folded tight to her back. Like a very small archangel. Rosa was nothing if not arch.

Lea took a breath and smiled. 'Quite right. My apologies.'

'And you are quite wrong.'

'Sorry?'

'Benjamin Franklin didn't say that about beer,' said Ruth.

'Who did?' asked Myrna.

'Franklin,' said Ruth.

'But you just said—' Patrick began.

'It's not about beer,' said Ruth. 'He was writing to a friend about wine. The quote got hijacked by people who felt it was better to paint the intellectual and diplomat as a man of the people. A lover of beer, rather than wine. Such is politics, *non*?' She turned back to Lea. 'Illusion.'

'You got that right,' said Lea, and toasted the elderly woman with her beer.

But there was no amusement in her eyes anymore.

Yes, thought Gamache, holding the Scotch Gabri had poured him, but not drinking it, there was definitely more here than, well, met the eye.

'Does he look familiar?' asked Reine-Marie.

No one had to ask who she meant.

'Well, he's been standing there for more than a day now, so yes, he does,' said Clara.

'No, look again.'

In silence they contemplated the robed figure standing alone on the gray November day.

The quiet seemed to extend beyond the room. Beyond the B&B. Into the entire village. It was as though the bell jar was growing. Taking over more and more of Three Pines.

Two days earlier, children had been playing, laughing and shouting on the village green. Now there was nothing. No commotion. No motion. Not even the birds on its shoulders moved. It was as though in touching the thing, they'd turned to stone.

'He looks like Saint Francis of Assisi,' said Clara.

'That's what I was thinking,' said Reine-Marie. 'All those birds.'

'Don't kid yourself,' said Lea. 'That's no saint.'

'Did you ask the Archangel Michael about our visitor?' Gamache asked.

Reine-Marie turned to him, surprised by the question. And yet curious to hear the answer.

No one believed an archangel actually visited the mad old poet. Not really. They didn't even believe she believed it. Not really.

But they were curious.

'I did.'

'And?'

Just then a car appeared at the top of the hill into Three Pines.

'Must be Katie,' said Patrick. 'Nope. Not our car.'

The vehicle stopped level with the creature. The stone birds took flight, but the robed figure did not.

Finally, the car moved forward.

It was Jean-Guy, bringing news.

'What had Inspector Beauvoir found out?' asked the Crown attorney.

It was nearing the end of the day and he was pushing, hurrying the Chief Superintendent along. Wanting to get this piece of information in before the judge broke for the day.

Wanting to leave the men and women of the jury with this as the last thing planted in their heads, before they headed to the *terrasses* and brasseries for a beer on this hot summer afternoon.

The Crown nodded to the clerk. 'Exhibit A again, *s'il vous plaît.*'

And up came the village and the dark mark in the middle. This time, instead of silence, or that long sigh, there was a murmur of recognition, of excitement even.

Their shock had turned to familiarity, titillation. The alarm was gone. They felt almost comfortable with it, and proud of themselves for adjusting to so odd a sight.

Of course, it was just a picture. Not the real thing.

And their bravado was false. Not the real thing.

It was a mistake, Gamache knew, and suspected they did too, to get comfortable with such a creature. Even in a photograph.

'So?' the Crown prodded Gamache forward.

But while Gamache agreed with the strategy to hurry, he knew from years of testifying in this high court that it was a terrible mistake to rush along and leave questions unanswered. Leave loopholes for the defense to tear wide, through which a guilty person could escape.

Now Armand Gamache found himself performing that high-wire act of clarity and speed.

And there were things even the Crown didn't know. And must not find out.

'Inspector Beauvoir had spent his Saturday researching the cobrador del frac. When he had what he considered enough information, he drove down.'

'But why drive down? Why not just call or email?'

'He wanted to see the thing for himself. To be sure. He was going on just the photograph I'd sent. He needed to see it in person.'

What Gamache didn't say was that Jean-Guy also felt the need to give him the information face-to-face. To judge the reaction.

'And?'

'How much do you know, *patron*?' Beauvoir asked.

They sat in the living room of the Gamaches' home in

Three Pines. Jean-Guy, Reine-Marie and himself.

'Just what Bissonette told us, and I passed along to you,' said Armand. 'The cobrador del frac.'

'The debt collector,' said Beauvoir. '*Oui*. But not the original.'

He put aside his hot chocolate and brought a file folder from his satchel. From the file he withdrew a few pages, mostly photographs, and spread them on the coffee table, reorganizing them slightly, so that he looked like a street shill playing a shell game.

When he finished, there was a fan of photos in front of the Gamaches.

'This' – Beauvoir picked up the outlier – 'is a cobrador del frac.'

It showed the now familiar image of a man in top hat and tails. White gloves. Briefcase. With *Cobrador del Frac* writ large.

'But this's what I want to show you,' said Jean-Guy.

He moved the first photo in his lineup closer to Gamache.

'This is from 1841. A village in the Pyrenees. It's one of the earliest surviving photographs. A daguerreotype.'

The image was gray, blurry. It showed a narrow cobbled street winding between rugged stone buildings. Off in the distance it was possible to make out mountains.

'The people and animals don't show up,' Beauvoir explained. 'The film had to be exposed for ten minutes. Anything that moved in that time disappeared.'

Armand put on his glasses and leaned over the photograph. He grew even more still. Had Monsieur Daguerre photographed him, Armand Gamache would have shown up.

And then he looked up, over his glasses, at Jean-Guy.

And Beauvoir nodded.

'It's called a cobrador,' said Jean-Guy, almost in a whisper. 'The del frac was added much later by some clever marketer. But this is the real thing. The original.'

Reine-Marie leaned in. She could see the buildings, the street, the landscape beyond. But nothing else. Her eyes scanned, moving quickly over the photograph.

Only when she slowed down did she see it.

It came to her, emerging from the image. Slowly. Resolving. Becoming clearer and clearer.

Darker and darker.

Until it was unmistakable.

There, against one of the walls, stood a man. So still that an exposure of ten minutes or more had captured him. And only him.

All other living things, the horses, dogs, cats, people, had disappeared, as though they'd abandoned their village. Leaving just the thing in the dark cape and hood, with the black expressionless face.

It looked like one of those horrific images from the bombing of Hiroshima, where people were vaporized, but their essence was seared onto a wall. A permanent shadow. But no longer a human.

There, in this small Spanish village, a shadow stood. There was no anger, or sorrow, no joy, or pity, or triumph. No judging. The judgment had already been passed.

A collector. There to collect.

'It was only recently, when an exhibition in Paris was being put together of Louis Daguerre's work, that someone noticed the image,' said Beauvoir. 'This one' – he pointed to the next photograph, somewhat clearer – 'is from the 1920s, and this' – he picked up the next one – 'is from 1945. The week after the war in Europe ended.'

It showed the robed figure standing in front of a middle-aged man, who was vehemently protesting while others looked on.

'The man was dragged away and hanged as a collaborator,' said Jean-Guy. 'He'd informed on friends and neighbors. Offering hiding places to Jews, then turned them in in exchange for favors from the Nazis.'

Looking at the terror in the man's face, his hollow, unshaven cheeks, pleading eyes, his wild hair and disheveled clothes, it was hard not to feel some sympathy for him. Until they thought of his victims. The men and women, boys and girls, who'd gone to their deaths. Because of him.

The cobrador had found him. And followed him. Hounding him. To his death.

'Did the cobrador hang him?' asked Reine-Marie.

'No. He just pointed the finger,' said Jean-Guy. 'The others did the rest.'

A crooked finger, thought Gamache. Maybe Ruth was right.

'There was an uptick in cobrador sightings in Spain after the war,' said Jean-Guy. 'And then nothing for a long time.'

'Matheo said when he did his research he couldn't find anyone who'd actually seen one of the original cobradors,' said Armand. 'And he didn't find these photos.'

'He probably wasn't looking very hard,' said Reine-Marie. 'In my experience in the national archives, freelance journalists have tight schedules and are very focused. His article was on the modern cobrador del frac. Not the old one.'

'That's probably it,' said Armand.

'But there have been some more recent sightings,' said Beauvoir. 'Of the original.'

'Like here,' said Reine-Marie.

81

The Old World cobrador had crossed into the New World. Into their world. And they could almost smell the decay. The rot. Though Gamache was beginning to wonder if the smell wasn't from the cobrador at all. But someone else. Nearby. Whoever the creature had come for.

'So all this started back in the 1800s,' said Reine-Marie, looking again at the daguerreotype. 'I wonder why.'

'*Non*,' said Beauvoir. '*Non, non, non*. Not the 1800s but the 1300s.'

'Seven hundred years ago?' asked Reine-Marie.

'Yes. You must have an atlas.'

Armand went to one of the shelves in the living room and brought back a large book.

'There's an island off the coast of Spain, between Spain and Morocco,' said Beauvoir, flipping through the pages until he found what he was looking for. 'It was called Cobrador.'

Gamache leaned in. 'But it doesn't say Cobrador.'

'No, the name's been changed. But that was the name back then. It's where plague victims were sent. And not just plague, but lepers, the insane, babies who were born with deformities. Those suspected of being witches were taken there by the Inquisition. Being put on La Isla del Cobrador was considered worse than being burned at the stake. At least that only lasted a few minutes. These people were damned by the Church for eternity. And this' – Jean-Guy tapped the island in the atlas – 'was hell.'

Gamache's brows drew together. 'Except—'

Jean-Guy nodded. 'Except not everyone read the fine print. Inconveniently, they didn't all die. The Church and the authorities assumed either the plague would kill them or they'd kill each other. There was some of that, of course. But then something happened. It started with the women. Some of them began caring for the babies. Nursing them to health. Raising them.'

'The witches performed a mitzvah,' said Armand.

'That would drive the Inquisition crazy,' said Reine-Marie.

'The infighting stopped and they began helping each other,' said Jean-Guy. 'They built homes, planted crops. Away from the shit-hole cities, many of the plague victims recovered.'

'Remarkable,' said Gamache. 'Beautiful, really. In its own way. But what does that have to do with the cobrador?'

He gestured outside.

It had been there for almost forty-eight hours, and the villagers, far from growing used to it, were growing more and more stressed. Nerves had begun to fray. Arguments were breaking out. Quarrels between long-standing friends could be heard in the bistro. Over trivial matters.

The short tempers could have been blamed on the fact that they hadn't seen the sun in days. Felt like weeks. Felt like forever. The November skies remained cloudy. Occasionally dropping rain, sleet. That seemed to seep right through clothing, skin, and pool in the bones.

But the core of the problem stood on the dying grass of the village green.

A long, long way from an island in fourteenth-century Spain. A long way from home.

The bell jar had expanded again, the cobrador's world was swelling, his dominion growing, while theirs seemed to be collapsing into itself.

Armand was wondering how much longer they had before something terrible happened.

'Some of those who were strong enough returned to the mainland,' said Jean-Guy. 'But they were disfigured by disease, so they wore masks and gloves. And long cloaks with hoods.'

'Why return?' asked Reine-Marie.

'Revenge,' said Gamache. It was, he knew, a powerful force. Often overwhelming good sense.

'That's what I thought too,' said Jean-Guy, turning to him. 'But no. They went looking for the people who banished them. Damned them. Mostly priests, senior church officials. Magistrates. Even princes. But incredibly, when they found them, they did nothing. Just followed them. Which, of course, turned out to be quite something.'

'What happened?' Gamache asked.

'I think you know. I think they knew,' said Beauvoir. He didn't need to consult his research. He doubted he'd ever forget what he'd read. 'The first ones were beaten to death by mobs, who believed they were the embodiment of the Black Death. But as one died, another appeared. Little by little, the mobs noticed that the guys in the black robes and masks weren't doing harm. There was even, it seems, a sort of dignity about them. Even when they knew they were going to die, they just stood still. They didn't try to defend themselves. They didn't fight back. They just kept staring at the person they were following until they were beaten to the ground.'

Gamache shifted in his seat and glanced over his shoulder, toward the village green.

Such devotion to a cause was admirable. But it was also, perhaps, insane.

'The priests and authorities couldn't allow this to continue,' said Beauvoir. 'They figured out who these people were, and where they came from. Soldiers were sent to La Isla del Cobrador, and every man, woman and child was to be slaughtered.'

Gamache inhaled sharply. Even from a distance, over time and territory, he could feel the outrage, the pain.

'When the population heard about that, there was a shit storm,' said Beauvoir.

Gamache glanced down at the printouts, fairly certain 'shit storm' was not how it was described there.

'The robed figures became part of the mythology,' said Jean-Guy. 'They were called cobradors, after the island. But it was a sideshow to all the other crap happening in Europe at the time. The cobradors were quickly forgotten.'

'But they didn't disappear completely,' said Reine-Marie.

'*Non.* It seems not everyone from La Isla del Cobrador was killed. Some escaped. The theory was that they were helped by soldiers who couldn't bring themselves to follow orders. Every now and then one would be spotted, mostly in the mountain villages.'

'And they continued to follow people who had done something terrible?' asked Gamache. 'Something for which they had not been held accountable?'

'That's what it looks like.'

'And that's how cobrador became debt collector.'

'No, that's just it. That's a modern interpretation. *Cobrador* translates, literally, into "collector". And there is that about them. The debt. But in the villages, they became known as something else. A conscience.'

The courtroom clock ticked past five.

All other cases had been adjourned for the day. They could hear footsteps in the hallway and voices murmuring and occasionally calling. Barristers who'd been pounding away at each other minutes before in court now invited each other for drinks on the *terrasse* of the nearby brasserie.

Inside Judge Corriveau's courtroom, the atmosphere was close. The heat stifling. Everyone yearned to get out into the fresh air and sunshine. Get away from both the atmosphere and the increasingly claustrophobic story.

But there was one more question to be asked and answered.

'Chief Superintendent Gamache,' said the Crown. For once he didn't sound self-important or pompous. For the first time all day he wasn't preening or acting. His voice was quiet, grave. 'From what Inspector Beauvoir found out about the cobrador, did you come to any conclusion?'

'I did.'

'And what was that?'

'That someone in the village had done something so horrific that a conscience had been called.'

CHAPTER 7

~

'Not coming home tonight?' Reine-Marie asked Armand when he called that evening.

'Afraid not. I'll stay in the Montréal apartment. Too much to do here and court starts early.'

'Would you like me to drive in? I can bring something from the bistro.'

'No, that's okay. I'm not much company, I'm afraid. And I have to work.'

'The trial?'

'*Oui.*'

'Are things going your way?'

He rubbed his forehead and considered the question. 'It's hard to tell. So many things have to come together just right. There seems such a fine line between falling into place and falling apart.'

Reine-Marie had seen him worried about court cases, the testimony of certain witnesses especially. But in this case, he was the only witness so far. What could worry him so soon?

'Will you get a conviction?'

'Yes.'

But his answer was too swift, too certain, for a man usually so measured and thoughtful.

'What are you doing for dinner?' she asked.

'Grabbing something here at the office.'

'Alone?'

Armand glanced through the crack in the door into the conference room, where Jean-Guy, Isabelle and the other officers were bent over maps. Mugs of coffee and platters of sandwiches from the local brasserie sat on the long table, along with jugs of water, laptops and papers. Beyond all that, he saw the lights of Montréal.

'*Oui.*'

Chief Superintendent Gamache rejoined the team and, putting his glasses back on, he bent over the large map of Québec.

Transparencies were layered on top of it. Each with different patterns, in different colors.

Bold slashes. Of red. Of blue. Of green. Of black Magic Marker. Though hardly, Gamache thought, examining the patterns, magic.

Held up on their own, the bright lines on the transparencies were meaningless. But once laid on top of each other, and then on top of the map of Québec, the lines coalesced. A casual observer might think it was a subway route map. A very large subway and an extremely busy route.

And they wouldn't be far wrong.

It was, in effect, a map of the underworld.

Lines snaked down the St Lawrence River. Others came down from the north. Many branched from Montréal and Québec City. But they all made for the border with the United States.

Superintendent Toussaint, the new head of Serious Crimes, picked up a blue marker from the cup on the conference table.

It was, for some of the younger members of this inner circle, like picking up a hammer and chisel, so crude was this method of mapping. They were used to laptops and more precise, more powerful, tools.

But the map, and those transparencies, had a great advantage. No one could hack them. And, when separated, no one could decode what they meant.

And that was vital.

'Here's the latest information,' said Madeleine Toussaint. 'Our informant on the Magdalen Islands says a shipment arrived two days ago on board a cargo ship from China.'

'Two days?' asked an agent. 'Why's it taken so long to get the information?'

'We're lucky to get it at all,' said Toussaint. 'We all know what'll happen if they find our informant. And he knows too.'

She lowered the pen until a blue blotch appeared on the islands, hanging out in the Gulf of St Lawrence.

'Do we know how much?' asked Beauvoir.

'Eighty kilos.'

They looked at her in silence.

'Of fentanyl?' asked Isabelle Lacoste.

'*Oui.*' Toussaint lifted the marker. Blue for fentanyl.

They looked at each other. Eighty kilograms.

It would be the largest shipment in North America. By almost double. Certainly the largest they knew of.

The cartels were growing bolder and bolder.

And why not? They went almost unchallenged.

Everyone in that room turned to Chief Superintendent Gamache, who was staring at the tiny group of islands floating in the salt water between Gaspé and Newfoundland. A prettier spot would be hard to find. Or a more perfect place for trafficking.

Windswept, isolated, sparsely populated. And yet on a major trade route for cargo vessels from, and to, the whole wide world.

It was a port of entry into Québec. Into Canada. A kind of back door. A revolving door. Given short shrift by authorities who were busy investigating the major ports, air and sea.

But the tiny, achingly beautiful Magdalen Islands were the sweet spot.

And from there?

Gamache looked at the various bold lines in different colored marker. Originating in different points of Québec, but all heading in the same direction.

The border. *La frontière.*

The United States.

Almost all the lines, all the colors converged, and went straight through a tiny village not even on the map. Gamache had had to pencil it in.

Three Pines.

But it was now obliterated by the Magic Markers making for the border.

Drugs flowed into the United States through that hole in the border, and money flowed back.

Tons of cocaine, methamphetamines, heroin had moved across the border there. For years.

When Gamache assumed the leadership of the Sûreté and realized the extent of the drug problem in and through Québec, he realized something else. Only a fraction of the trafficking could be accounted for through the traditional routes.

So how was the rest getting across?

Armand Gamache, the new Chief Superintendent of the Sûreté du Québec, had assigned teams to investigate those drugs made in Québec, and those imported. Those consumed here, and those destined for a more lucrative market.

He set up teams. Scientists, hackers, ex-cons, informants, marine and aviation experts, biker gang infiltrators, dock workers, union officials, packagers, and even marketers were recruited. Most had no real idea what the end goal was, or even who they were working for. Each formed a small cell, with a single problem to solve.

And while the drugs were funneled to one point, so was all this information.

Chief Superintendent Gamache.

A decisive blow had to be landed. Not a series of small irritants, but a hard, fast, effective strike. At the heart.

After almost a year of intense investigation, the lines on the transparencies had grown. Intersected. Entwined. And a pattern had appeared.

But still Chief Superintendent Gamache didn't act.

Despite pleading by some of his senior officers, Armand Gamache waited, and waited. Bearing the brunt of increasing private and professional and political criticism, from a public and colleagues who saw only a growth in crime and inaction on the part of the Sûreté.

Then, finally, the team had found what they were looking for. The person at the head of all this.

The break had come through collaboration, intelligence, courage on the part of undercover agents and informants.

And the appearance of a dark figure on a sleet-slashed village green.

Though few people knew that was the pivot point, and Gamache was desperate to keep it that way.

The officers looked at Chief Superintendent Gamache. Waiting for him to say something. To do something.

Superintendent Toussaint lowered the bright blue Magic Marker and drew a line on the transparency, from the harbor on the Magdalen Islands, around the curve of the Gaspé Peninsula. The marker squealed as it slowly traveled down the great St Lawrence River. Finally turning inland. And down, down.

Until the blue line hit the border.

There Toussaint's hand stopped.

She looked at Gamache. Who stared at the map. At the mark.

Then he looked up, over his glasses. Past his officers to the wall, and the schematic.

A map of a different sort. It showed not how the drugs, and money, and violence flowed, but how the power flowed.

Photographs were affixed to the chart. Some mug shots, most clandestine photos taken by a high-powered lens.

Men and women going about their lives. Apparently quite normal. On the outside. Their skin stretched across the void inside.

And at the top, where all the lines and images converged, was simply a dark silhouette. No picture.

Faceless. Featureless. Not quite human.

Armand Gamache knew who it was. Could indeed have placed a face there. But chose not to. In case. He stared for a moment into that dark, blank visage, then shifted his attention back to Superintendent Toussaint. And nodded.

She hesitated, perhaps to allow him time to change his mind.

There was utter silence in the room.

'You can't,' said Toussaint quietly. 'Eighty kilos, sir. It

might be on the move already. I haven't heard back from our informant. At least let us put people in place.'

Chief Superintendent Gamache took the marker from her hand, and without hesitation he drew one final line.

A slash across the border, as the opioid poured out of Québec and into the United States.

Armand Gamache put the cap back on the marker with a firm click and looked up into the faces of his most trusted officers and saw the same expression there.

They were appalled.

'You have to stop it,' said Toussaint, her voice rising before she was able to modulate it. 'You can't let it cross the border. Eighty kilos,' she repeated, her outrage threatening to break free again. 'If you don't—'

Gamache stood up straight. 'Go on.'

But she fell silent.

He scanned the other faces and didn't have to ask who agreed with her. Clearly it was the majority opinion.

But that didn't make it the right one.

'We stay the course,' he said. 'I made it clear when we set up this operation almost a year ago. We have a plan and we stick to it.'

'No matter the consequences?' demanded another of the officers. 'Yes, we have a plan. But we have to be responsive. Things change. It's crazy to stick to a plan just because we have it.'

Gamache raised his brows, but said nothing.

'I'm sorry, *patron*,' said the officer. 'I didn't mean crazy.'

'I know what you meant,' said Gamache. 'The plan was made before we had all the information.' The officer nodded. 'It was made in a cold, clinical, logical environment.' More nods.

'Why are we bothering to risk lives to get this information?' Another officer waved at the map. 'If we aren't going to act on it?'

'We are acting,' said Gamache. 'Simply not in a way the cartels expect. Believe me, I want to stop the shipment. But this entire operation is about the long view. We hold firm. *D'accord?*'

He looked at each of them, one at a time. Handpicked. Not because they'd bend to his will, conform, but because they were smart and experienced, ingenious and creative. And courageous enough to speak their minds.

And speak they did. But now it was his turn.

Gamache considered before speaking. 'When we go on a raid and bullets are flying and chaos threatens, what do we do?'

He looked at all of them, each of whom had been in that situation. As had Gamache.

'We keep our heads and we keep our nerve. And we keep control of the situation. We focus. We do not give in to distractions.'

'Distractions?' said Toussaint. 'You make this sound like a noise off to the left.'

'I'm not trivializing this shipment, the decision or the consequences, Superintendent.'

He glanced over, briefly, at the schematic on the wall. Drawn to the dark face.

'Never lose sight of the goal,' he said, returning his gaze to his subordinates. 'Never.' He paused to let that sink in. 'Never.'

They shifted, but began to stand a little straighter.

'Every other officer in your position has abandoned the strategy,' continued Gamache. 'They've bailed. Not because they were weak, but because the consequences were so great. There was a screaming need for action. And it is screaming.' He put his finger on the fresh mark. 'And it is a need. Eighty kilos of fentanyl. We need to stop it.'

They nodded.

'But we can't.'

He took a long, deep breath and focused briefly on the lights of the city behind them. And beyond that, in the long view, the mountains. And the valley. And the village.

And the goal.

Then he brought his eyes, and his thoughts, back to the conference room.

'We monitor,' said Chief Superintendent Gamache, his voice brisk now. 'From a distance. We do not interfere. We do not stop the shipment. *D'accord?*'

There was just a moment's hesitation before first one, then another said, '*D'accord.*'

Agreed. It was grudging, but it was given.

Gamache turned to Superintendent Toussaint, who had been silent. She looked down at the map. Then over at the chart on the wall. Then back to her boss.

'*D'accord, patron.*'

Gamache gave a curt nod, then turned to Beauvoir. 'A word?'

Once back in his office, with the door firmly closed, he turned square to Beauvoir.

'Sir?' said the younger man.

'You agree with Superintendent Toussaint, don't you.'

It was not a question.

'I think there must be a way to stop the shipment without letting them know that we've worked it out.'

'There might be,' agreed Gamache.

'We've seized smaller shipments,' said Beauvoir, taking

advantage of what he saw as an opening, a softening of his boss's position.

'That's true. But they were headed through the traditional routes, crossing the border at a predictable place. If all seizures stopped, the cartels would know something was up. This one is huge and almost certainly headed right to the place they think we don't know about. If they trust the route with this much fentanyl, it means they feel it's safe, Jean-Guy. But it only works if we allow them to believe it.'

'You're not saying this is good news.'

'It's what we hoped would happen. You know that. Look, I know this is particularly difficult for you—'

'Why does it always come down to that?' demanded Beauvoir.

'Because we can't separate our personal experiences from our professional choices,' said Gamache. 'If we think we can, we're deluding ourselves. We have to admit it, examine our motives, and then make a rational decision.'

'You think I'm being irrational? You're the one who's always accusing me of not trusting my instincts. Well, you know what they're telling me now? Not just my instincts, but yes, my experience?'

Beauvoir was all but shouting at Gamache.

'This is a huge mistake,' said Beauvoir, lowering his voice to a growl. 'Allowing that much fentanyl into the US could change the course of a generation. You want to know about my personal stake? Here it is. You've never been addicted,' he said. 'You have no idea what it's like. And opioids? Designer drugs? They get right into you. Change you. Turn you into something horrible. Everyone keeps repeating, "eighty kilos".' He waved toward the door and the conference room across the hall. 'What's heading for the border isn't a weight, isn't a number. There's no measure for the misery that's heading our way. A slow and wretched death. And not just for the addicts you're about to create, but how about all the other lives that'll be ruined? How many people, alive today, healthy today, will die, sir, or kill? Because of your "rational" decision?'

'You're right,' said Gamache. 'You're absolutely right.'

He waved toward the sitting area of his office. After a moment's hesitation, as though weighing if it was a trap, Jean-Guy took his usual chair, sitting stiffly on the edge.

Gamache sat back, trying to get comfortable. Abandoning that, he too sat forward.

'There's a theory that Winston Churchill knew about the German bombing of the English city of Coventry before it happened,' he said. 'And he did nothing to stop it. The bombing killed hundreds of men and women and children.'

Beauvoir's tense face slackened. But he said nothing.

'The British had cracked the German code,' Gamache explained. 'But to act would've meant letting them know that. Coventry would have been saved. Hundreds of lives would've been saved. But the Germans would've changed the code and the Allies would have lost a huge advantage.'

'How many were saved because of that decision?' Beauvoir asked.

It was a terrible calculus.

Gamache opened his mouth, then closed it. And looked down at his hands.

'I don't know.'

Then he raised his gaze to Beauvoir's steady eyes. 'There's some suggestion the English never did use their knowledge, for fear of losing their advantage.'

'You're kidding, right?'

Though it was clear he was not.

'What good's an advantage if you're not going to use it?' Beauvoir asked. More astonished than angry. 'And if they allowed the bombing of that city—'

'Coventry.'

'—what else did they allow?'

Gamache shook his head. 'It's a good question. When do you use up all your currency? When are you being strategic, and when are you being a miser, hoarding it? And the longer you hold it, the harder it is to give up. If you have only one shot, Jean-Guy, when do you take it? And how do you know when that time comes?'

'Or maybe when you finally do take that shot, it's too late. You've waited too long,' said Beauvoir. 'The damage done is way more than any good you could do.'

All of Beauvoir's rage had dissipated as he looked at Chief Superintendent Gamache. Struggling with that question.

'People will die, Jean-Guy, when that fentanyl hits the streets. Young people. Older people. Children, perhaps. It will be a firestorm.'

Gamache thought of his visit to Coventry with Reine-Marie, many years after the bombing. The city had been rebuilt, but they'd kept the shell of the cathedral. It had become a symbol.

He and Reine-Marie had stood a long time in front of the altar of the ruined cathedral.

Just days after the bombing, someone had etched words into one of the walls.

Father Forgive.

But forgive whom? The Luftwaffe? Goering, who unleashed the bombers, or Churchill, who chose not to stop them?

Was it courage or a terrible misjudgment on the part of the British leaders, safe in their homes and offices and bunkers hundreds of miles away?

As he was safe, high above the streets of Montréal. Far from the firestorm he was about to unleash. Saint Michael, he remembered. Coventry Cathedral had been dedicated to the archangel. The gentle one who came for the souls of the dying.

He glanced down at his index finger and was surprised to see a bright blue line. As though the eighty kilos of fentanyl would be traveling straight through him on its way south.

Armand Gamache stood astride the route from the Magdalen Islands to the US border. A line that passed through an insignificant little village in a valley.

He had a chance, now, the power to stop it.

Gamache knew he would be marked for the rest of his life by the decision he was making this night.

'Isn't there something you can do?' asked Jean-Guy, his voice hushed.

Gamache remained silent.

'Have a quiet word with the DEA? Warn them?' Jean-Guy suggested.

But he knew that wouldn't happen.

Gamache's jaw was tight, and he swallowed, but said nothing. His deep brown eyes remained on his second-in-command. His son-in-law.

'How long do you think it will take the fentanyl to reach the border?' Gamache asked.

'If it left immediately? It should cross tomorrow night. Maybe sooner. It might already be on its way.'

Gamache nodded.

'But there's probably still time to intercept,' said Beauvoir, though he knew what he really meant was that there was time for Gamache to change his mind.

But he also knew that would not happen. And deep down, Jean-Guy Beauvoir knew it should not happen.

The fentanyl had to cross the border. Their secret had to be protected.

To be used later. In the final *coup de grâce*.

Armand Gamache nodded and, getting up, he headed to the door. And he wondered if, when he left his office that night to return to the small apartment he and Reine-Marie kept in Montréal, a dark figure would detach itself from the shadows and follow him.

Come to collect a debt Chief Superintendent Gamache knew he could never repay.

All he could really hope for was forgiveness.

CHAPTER 8

— ⸱ —

'I thought you said this was going to be a fast trial,' said Judge Corriveau's wife, Joan. 'Will we be able to go away this weekend?'

Maureen Corriveau moaned. 'I don't know. Can we get out of the reservations if we have to?'

'I'll call the inn and see. Don't worry, we can always go away another weekend. Vermont will be there.'

Maureen grabbed a piece of toast, kissed Joan, and whispered, 'Thank you.'

'Off you go, and play nice,' said Joan.

'It's my sandbox. I don't have to play nice.'

She looked outside. It was barely seven in the morning and already the sun was beating down.

Getting in her car, she yelped and lifted her bottom off the scorching seat.

'Shit, shit,' she muttered, throwing on the AC and lowering herself slowly.

She could see heat distorting the air above the hood and wondered what the courtroom would be like.

But Judge Corriveau knew that, even without the heat wave, it would be suffocating.

*

'All rise,' she heard.

The door was opened by the guard, and Judge Corriveau stepped across the threshold.

There was a hubbub as all rose. Then sat, as she sat.

Everyone looked slightly disheveled. Already.

She nodded to the Crown, who recalled his witness from the day before.

As Chief Superintendent Gamache walked up to the witness box, Judge Corriveau noticed he seemed composed, wearing a tailored suit that might not look quite so good by the end of the day.

The AC had been turned off and already the room was close.

She also noticed, as he took his seat, that very slight scent of sandalwood.

The gentle aroma sat with her for just a moment before dissipating. Then Judge Corriveau turned her attention to the defendant, who was watching the Chief Superintendent.

There was a sharp focus, and a plea in the eyes. Aimed at Gamache.

It was intense. And only two people in the courtroom could see it. Herself. And the Chief Superintendent.

But what was the defendant pleading for? Mercy? No, that was not Gamache's to give.

The defendant wanted something from Gamache, was desperate for it.

Forgiveness? But again, surely, that wasn't his to give either.

What could the Chief Superintendent offer the defendant, a person he himself had arrested, at this point?

Only one thing, Judge Corriveau knew.

Silence.

He could keep some secret.

Judge Corriveau looked from the defendant to the Chief Superintendent. And wondered if a deal had been struck. Something she knew nothing about.

Again, the photo of the cobrador on the village green was put up on the screen. And there it would stay, throughout the trial.

It appeared to be watching them.

'You understand you're still under oath, Chief Superintendent?' she asked.

'I do understand, Your Honor.'

'Bon,' said the Crown. 'You told us yesterday afternoon, before we broke for the day, that you'd concluded someone in the village of Three Pines had done something so hideous that that thing' – the Crown pointed to the cobrador – 'had to be called. Who did you think it was?'

'I honestly didn't know.'

'I know you didn't know, I asked who you thought it might be. Did you have any suspicions?'

'Objection,' said the defense attorney.

Judge Corriveau sustained it, with regret. She'd have loved to hear the answer.

'A conscience?' said Ruth. Behind her on this dreary November evening, cold rain hit the window and slid down, not quite liquid, not quite solid. 'So that's what it is. I wonder who he's come for.'

She surveyed them from her seat in one of the deep armchairs in the Gamaches' living room. Once in, she couldn't possibly get out without help. It was how her neighbors preferred her. Comfortable and confined.

Rosa sat on her lap, her head swiveling toward whoever was speaking. Like a duck possessed.

'Who made this?' asked Olivier, standing at the door between their kitchen and the living room. Holding a baguette.

'Jacqueline,' said Clara. 'Sorry. It was all that was left at the bakery. She hasn't improved?'

In his other hand, Olivier lifted the bread knife, its teeth askew. He went to the back door and tossed the baton of bread out, for some beaver to sharpen its teeth on. Though he suspected it would still be lying there when some future archeologist found it. It would become like Stonehenge. A mystery.

Myrna got up and, taking her red wine to the window, looked out into the dusk.

'*A peace above all earthly dignities,*' she quoted. Then turned back to the room. '*A still and quiet conscience.*'

'Shakespeare,' said Reine-Marie. 'But it doesn't feel very peaceful.'

'That's because we're not there yet,' said Myrna. 'That thing is here because someone in the village doesn't have a quiet conscience.'

'It's just a man in a costume,' said Armand. 'He's playing a mind game with someone.'

'But not us,' said Gabri.

'Really?' asked Ruth. 'Not us? We're immune? Is your conscience really so still and quiet?'

Gabri squirmed.

'Is anyone's?' Ruth asked, looking at them all before coming to rest on Armand.

In that instant he found himself standing before the door he kept closed, deep in his memory.

He reached out. A very slight tremor in his right hand.

And opened it.

It wasn't locked. He couldn't lock it though, God help him, he'd tried. Sometimes it swung open on its own, revealing the thing inside.

Not some fetid, sordid shame.

Before him stood a young man, barely more than a boy. Smiling. Filled with hope, and laughter, with ambition tempered by kindness. He was slender, spindly even, so that his Sûreté uniform looked like a costume.

'He'll grow into it,' Chief Inspector Gamache had assured his mother at a reception honoring new recruits.

But, of course, he hadn't.

The boy stood there now, smiling at Armand. Awaiting the day's orders. Trusting him, completely.

I'll find you. It'll be all right.

But, of course, it wasn't.

Go away, was what Armand wanted to say. Leave me in peace. I'm so sorry about what happened, but I can't undo it.

But he never said it. And Armand Gamache knew that if the young man ever did leave, he'd miss him. Not the almost unbearable pain he always felt when that door swung open, but his company.

This was one special young man.

And Armand had killed him.

It had been an honest mistake, he'd told himself. A wrong decision made in a crisis.

It had not been deliberate.

But it was a stupid mistake. Avoidable.

Had he turned right instead of left, in that horrible moment, the young man would be alive. Married. Children probably, by now.

May your days be good and long upon this earth.

But, of course, they weren't.

Armand's conscience rose up now. Not a dark thing at all, but a skinny young man who never accused, he just smiled.

Armand brought his hand to his temple and absently followed the line of the scar. Like a mark of Cain.

Ruth tilted her head, watching Armand. Knowing, as they all probably did, what he was thinking about. Who he was thinking about.

The old woman looked at her empty glass of Scotch, then down at Rosa, as though accusing the duck of drinking it.

It would not be the first time. Rosa was a mean drunk. But then, she was pretty mean sober as well. It was very hard to tell, they'd realized, if a duck was drunk.

'Or maybe he's here for me,' said Ruth. 'Seems more likely, doesn't it?'

She smiled at Armand. In much the same way the boy smiled at him. There was tenderness there.

'Some of the things I've done you know about,' she said. 'I've admitted them and made amends.'

Clara looked at Gabri and mouthed, 'Amends?'

'But there is one thing . . .'

'You don't have to tell us,' said Reine-Marie, laying her hand on Ruth's.

'And have that thing' – she lifted her empty glass toward the village green – 'follow me for the rest of my life? No, thank you.'

'You think it's here for you?'

'It might be. Do you know why we moved to Three Pines when I was a child?'

'Your father got a job at the mill, didn't he?' asked Gabri.

'He did. But do you know why he applied? He had a good job in Montréal with Canada Steamship Lines. A job he loved.'

Ruth stroked Rosa, who was bending her elegant neck in what was either pleasure or a drunken stupor.

The old poet took a breath, as a cliff diver might before the plunge.

'I was skating on the pond on Mount Royal. It was late March and my mother had warned me not to, but I did anyway. My cousin was with me. He didn't want to do it, but I made him. I'm a natural leader.'

The friends exchanged glances but said nothing.

'We were late for lunch and my mother came up looking for us. When she saw us on the pond she yelled, and I started skating to the side, wanting to get to her first, to blame my cousin. I can be a little manipulative.'

Brows were raised again, but nothing was said.

'My cousin hadn't seen her yet and I think his tuque must've muffled the sound of her shout. Or maybe I was just attuned to her voice. I can hear it still.'

The elderly woman cocked her head. Listening.

'I think you can guess what happened,' she said.

'He fell in?' Reine-Marie asked quietly.

'I fell in. Ice melts at the edges first, so just when you think you're safe, that's when you're in the most danger. The ice cracked. I can still remember that moment. It was like I was suspended. I stared at my mother, who was still a distance away down the path. I remember every color, every tree, the sun on the snow. The look on her face. And then, I was underwater.'

'Oh God, Ruth,' whispered Gabri.

'It was so cold it was hot, you know?' She looked around her. Everyone there had been out in minus 40, with the wind howling, their cheeks burning in the bitter cold.

But to have the whole body scald in the freezing water?

'What happened?' whispered Gabri.

'I died,' she snapped, coming back to life. 'What do you think happened, you knucklehead?'

'What happened, Ruth?' asked Reine-Marie.

'My cousin skated over to help me, and that's when he fell in. My mother could save only one of us.'

'You?' asked Olivier, and braced for the caustic retort. That never came.

Instead the old woman nodded, her eyes focused on the distance.

She took a deep breath.

'She never forgave me. *Long dead and buried in another town, / My mother hasn't finished with me yet,*' she quoted from her own poem. 'I never forgave me.'

'Alas,' said Armand.

Ruth nodded. And Rosa nodded.

'We had to move here,' said Ruth. 'Away from family and friends, who also blamed me. Blamed her. For saving the wrong one.'

Beside her, Olivier moaned and put his arm around the bony shoulder.

Ruth lowered her head. And tried to bring herself to say the next thing. The last thing.

But she couldn't speak. Neither could she forget.

'I dropped a friend when he told me he was HIV positive,' said Gabri. 'I was young and afraid.'

'I had a drug prescribed for a patient,' said Myrna. 'A young mother. Depressed. It had a bad reaction. She called me, and I told her to come in first thing in the morning. But she killed herself that night.'

Clara took her hand.

'I disobeyed you,' said Clara, looking beyond Myrna to

108

Armand. 'I went looking for you and Peter, that day in the fishing village. You told me not to, and if I hadn't ...'

Gabri took her hand.

'I've lied and cheated old men and women out of their antiques,' said Olivier. 'Giving them a fraction of what they were worth. I don't do it anymore. But I did.'

He sounded amazed, as though describing a man who was unrecognizable.

'We knew about that, *mon beau*,' said Ruth, patting his hand. 'You're an asshole.'

Olivier grunted in near amusement.

A commotion, at first dull, reached them from the village green. A raising of voices that was growing louder. And then turned into shouting.

The friends stared at each other in surprise. Armand was out of his chair. Throwing open the front door, he saw what it was.

A crowd had gathered on the village green. He could just see the top of the cobrador's head.

It was surrounded by people.

Armand ran out the door and the others followed, except Ruth, who was struggling to get up.

'Don't leave me here.'

But they had.

And once again she saw the hand of her mother, plunging into the icy water. Reaching out. Desperate. Straining.

For her cousin.

But Ruth had gripped that hand instead, and risen. Unwanted.

Then shall forgiven and forgiving meet again / or will it be, as always was, / too late?

'Alas,' she muttered.

'Come on, you old crone.'

Clara had returned, and now she reached out. Ruth looked at the hand for a moment, then gripped it.

And she was hauled out.

They rushed down the path and to the village green.

CHAPTER 9

~

'You fucker,' a large man was shouting.

He stood in the center of the circle and held up an iron rod, ready to swing.

'Stop,' Gamache shouted, breaking through the crowd and coming to a halt a few feet from the man.

He recognized him as a new member of Billy Williams's road crew, but didn't know his name.

The man either didn't hear or didn't care, so focused was he on his target. The cobrador. Who just stood there. Didn't step away. Didn't cringe. Didn't brace itself.

'Do it,' someone yelled.

The crowd had turned into a mob.

Armand had run out of the house without sweater or coat, and now he stood, in shirtsleeves, in the cold drizzle. While surrounding him, surrounding the cobrador, were young parents. Grandparents. Neighbors. Men and women he recognized. Not any he'd call hooligans or troublemakers. But who had been infected by fear. Warped by it.

Gamache approached the man from the side. Carefully. Edging his way into the bell jar.

He didn't want to surprise him, make him react. Lash out at the cobrador, easily within swinging distance.

'Get the fuck outta here,' the man screamed at the cobrador. 'Or I'll beat the crap out of you. I swear to God I will.'

The mob was egging him on, and the man tightened his grip and lifted what Armand could now see was a fireplace poker even higher.

The rod had a nasty hook, used to move logs about in the flames. It would kill someone, easily.

'Don't, don't,' Gamache said, moving forward, his voice calm but firm. 'Don't you do it.'

And then he saw movement. Someone else had come out from the crowd.

It was Lea Roux. And within a moment she'd stepped between the cobrador and the man.

The attacker, surprised, hesitated.

Gamache quickly stepped beside Lea, and in front of the cobrador.

The man pointed the rod at them and waved it. 'Get out of my way. He doesn't belong here.'

'And why not?' ask Lea. 'He's doing no harm.'

'Are you kidding,' another man shouted. 'Look at him.'

'He's terrified my kids,' someone else shouted. 'That's harm.'

'And whose fault is that?' asked Lea, turning around to look at them all. 'You taught them to be afraid. He's done nothing. He's stood here for two days and nothing bad's happened. Except this.'

'You're not even from here,' a man shouted. 'This isn't your home. Get out of the way.'

'So you can beat the shit out of him?' Lea looked at the mob. 'You want your children playing on bloodstained grass?'

'Better stained with his blood than theirs,' said a woman. But her voice was no longer so loud, so certain.

'Well, they'll have to play in my blood too,' said Lea.

'And mine,' said Armand.

'And mine.'

Someone else detached from the crowd. It was the dishwasher, Anton. He looked frightened as he took his place beside Armand and glared at the large man with the fire iron.

Clara, Myrna, Gabri and Olivier joined them. Ruth handed Rosa to a bystander and stepped forward.

'Aren't we on the wrong side?' she whispered to Clara.

'Be quiet and look resolute.'

But the best the old poet could manage was crazed.

Armand stepped forward and held out a hand for the fireplace poker.

The man lifted it again.

Behind him he heard Reine-Marie whisper, 'Armand.'

But he just stood there, his hand out. Staring at the man. Whose eyes were locked on the cobrador. Then he slowly lowered the weapon, until Gamache could take it from him.

'If anything happens,' shouted someone in the crowd, 'it's on you.'

But the mob had turned back into a crowd, and while unhappy, unsatisfied, they at least dispersed.

'Not you,' said Gamache, grabbing at the man's arm as he started to walk away. 'What's your name?'

'Paul Marchand.'

'Well, Monsieur Marchand' – Gamache patted him down for other weapons and noticed a Sûreté vehicle coming down the hill – 'you're in some trouble.'

Armand brought a small pouch out of Marchand's pocket. It had two pills in it.

Gamache recognized them.

'Where did you get these?' He held up the pouch.

'They're medicine.'

'They're fentanyl.'

'Right. For pain.'

The Sûreté agents had parked, and were walking swiftly across the village green.

Toward the cobrador.

'Over here,' called Gamache. 'This is the one you were called about.'

'In a moment, sir,' said the agent, ignoring the man in the shirtsleeves, soaked through in the rain.

There seemed an abundance of strange behavior for the Sûreté agents to choose from. Starting with the robed and masked man.

'No, I mean it,' said Gamache, his voice taking on authority.

It was almost completely dark now, and the agents turned to get a better look at the man who'd just spoken. They walked closer and then their expressions moved from scowls to astonishment.

'Crap,' muttered one.

'I'm sorry, *patron*,' said the more senior officer, saluting. 'I didn't know it was you.'

'No, and why would you?'

Gamache explained the situation. 'Keep him overnight. Watch him. I don't know if he's taken any of these.' He gave them the pouch. 'Have this sent to the lab.'

Gamache watched as the agents led Marchand away. Something had set the man off, and Gamache wondered if there'd been more pills in that pouch when the evening began.

Ruth, with Rosa back in her arms, turned to the cobrador and whispered, 'Can you leave me alone now?'

But as she walked back to the Gamache home with the others, she knew it would not.

Before he left, Armand, beginning to shiver in the cold, walked up to the cobrador and spoke to him.

'What did you say?' Reine-Marie asked as Armand got into warm, dry clothes.

'I said that I knew he was a cobrador, a conscience. I asked who he was there for.'

'What did he say?'

'Nothing.'

'A still and quiet conscience,' she said.

'I also told him to leave Three Pines. That this had gone far enough. Too far. Those were good people out there, who're frightened. And fear can make decent people do terrible things. I asked if he wanted that on his conscience.'

'He won't leave,' said Reine-Marie.

'*Non*,' her husband agreed. 'He's not done yet.'

He looked out the window. In the darkness, the cobrador looked like another pine. A fourth tree. A now permanent part of their lives setting down roots deep in their little community.

Then Gamache followed the line of the cobrador's eyes. The stare he'd held, unflinching, even while being threatened with a beating. Possibly death.

There, framed in a mullioned window, was one of the few people who hadn't come out onto the village green. To defend or attack the cobrador.

Then Jacqueline turned away, to go back to her kneading.

CHAPTER 10

'You told him to leave. You must've known then what would happen,' said the Crown Prosecutor. 'There'd even been a death threat.'

'The man was enraged and provoked,' said Chief Superintendent Gamache. 'People say things they don't mean.'

'And people do things they later regret,' said the Crown. 'When they're angry. But it's still done and can't be undone. It might be manslaughter and not murder, but still a man would have been slaughtered. Surely your experience as head of homicide taught you that.'

'It has,' Gamache admitted.

'And still you didn't act. If not then, when? What were you waiting for?'

Gamache looked into the face of the prosecutor, then at the crowd jammed into the stuffy courtroom. He knew how it sounded. How it probably would've sounded to him.

But there was nothing he could have done that would have been legal. Or effective.

What happened that November evening proved that the cobrador was having an effect.

Chief Superintendent Gamache had doubted what happened had been Marchand's idea. He was fairly new to the village and hadn't been any trouble, until that night. It seemed someone had gotten to him. Told him, either directly or through manipulation, to threaten the cobrador.

Gamache doubted that the goal was to kill the Conscience. More likely, it was to scare him away. After all, who wouldn't run when faced with a poker-wielding madman?

Despite the cliché, the dead weren't silent. They told all sorts of tales. If the cobrador had been killed, they'd have unmasked him, and found out who he was. And probably found out why he was there.

But if the cobrador had just run away, no one would ever know who he was, or why he was in Three Pines.

Or who he was there for.

Though the why was beginning to dawn on Gamache. It had come in the form of a tiny plastic bag.

The plague.

But the plan had failed. The Conscience hadn't budged. Hadn't even flinched. Had been willing to risk death, for his cause.

The Conscience knew something about someone in the village. And that someone was getting mighty rattled.

But none of this came out in court. The Crown Prosecutor didn't ask, and Armand Gamache didn't offer this information.

'Monsieur Zalmanowitz,' said the judge, and the Crown Prosecutor approached the bench. 'Monsieur Gamache is not on trial. Censor yourself.'

'Yes, Your Honor.'

But he looked like he thought Gamache should be another defendant, and not a witness for the prosecution.

Beyond Zalmanowitz's desk, reporters were madly taking notes.

There were, Judge Corriveau knew, many ways of being on trial. And different types of courts.

Chief Superintendent Gamache would be found guilty.

She turned her attention back to the Crown Prosecutor. That horse's ass.

Judge Corriveau no longer even tried to repress her private thoughts. But she fought hard to keep them from creeping into her public utterances.

Therein lay a mistrial. And this case would indeed find itself in a higher court.

'How did it strike you,' the Crown asked, 'when you saw Lea Roux come to the defense of the cobrador?'

'I would've been surprised to see anyone standing between a man swinging a fireplace poker and his target.'

'And yet, that's what you were planning to do, wasn't it?'

'I'm trained.'

'Oh yes, I keep forgetting.'

That brought a round of appreciative chuckles from the crowd and a tap of the gavel from Judge Corriveau, who wished it could have been on top of the Crown's head.

'I knew Madame Roux,' said Gamache. 'Her rise in politics. It's a fierce arena, especially in Québec.'

'Did you think it was a stunt, then? To gain political capital?'

'If it had been that, she'd have sided with the mob, don't you think?' asked Gamache. 'A populist feeding anger and fear is more likely to get elected. If that's what she was after, I doubt she'd have protected the outsider, the intruder.'

That shut the Crown up and brought a slight snort from above Gamache and to his left.

'I began to say that I knew Madame Roux by reputation. In my position I have a lot of dealings with senior government officials, elected and appointed. You hear things in the halls of the National Assembly, in the chat before committees sit down to business. Lea Roux had a reputation for being fierce, but also principled. A potent combination. She'd brought forward many progressive bills in the National Assembly, often against her leader's wishes.'

'So she would choose her principles over her career?' asked the Crown.

'It would appear so.'

Though Gamache's time in homicide had taught him something else. Appearances could not be trusted.

'That was a very brave thing you did,' said Clara, when they'd returned to the Gamaches' home.

'Can you believe it worked?' asked Lea, her eyes wide, her face flushed despite just coming in from the cold.

Reine-Marie had invited Lea and Matheo to join them for dinner.

Lea was on a high after confronting the mob. Adrenaline. Something Gamache knew a lot about.

The pounding heart. The effort to keep terror in check. Standing your ground. The body taut, the mind whirring.

And then it was over. But the adrenaline still coursed, like a drug, through the body. They were all feeling it, but none more than Lea. The first to make the stand.

'Shame Patrick and Katie can't join us,' said Reine-Marie, walking with them into the kitchen. 'I saw them driving away earlier this evening.'

'They're having dinner at Le Relais in Knowlton,' said Lea. '*Steak-frites* night. Missed all the fun.'

'Though I don't think Patrick would've been much help, do you?' asked Matheo.

It was perhaps true, thought Gamache, who'd also picked up on Patrick's timidity. But it didn't need to be said, especially by a friend.

But then, maybe Patrick wasn't really a friend. Anymore. They seemed to be spending less time together this visit than in the past.

'This looks delicious,' said Reine-Marie, ladling out the stew Olivier had brought. '*Merci.*'

'You're welcome.'

'Come on, tell them the truth,' said Gabri, taking a warm dinner roll, substituted for the baguette. 'He didn't make it. Anton did.'

'The dishwasher?' asked Matheo, looking at the stew with some suspicion.

The chicken was tender, delicately seasoned. The stew was complex. Familiar, but exotic.

'It's all things he collected in the woods,' said Myrna. 'Nouvelle Québec cuisine. That's what he wants to create.'

'The dishwasher?' Matheo repeated.

'We all have to start somewhere,' said Myrna.

'How long's he been here?' asked Lea. 'I don't remember him from our last visit.'

'And he is memorable,' said Clara, thinking of the lithe young man with the floppy hair and ready smile.

'He arrived a couple months ago,' said Gabri. 'He and Jacqueline were working together in some home and both lost their jobs.'

'Home, like seniors' home?' asked Lea.

'No,' said Olivier. 'Home like private home. She was a nanny, I think, and he was their private chef.'

'Some home,' said Matheo.

'Are you enjoying your new job, Armand?' asked Lea.

'"Enjoying" is perhaps not the word,' he said. 'I'm just trying not to be overwhelmed. Let me ask you something. When you were first elected a couple of years ago, you sponsored a bill, one you felt strongly about, if I remember.'

'That's right. Most new members have some legislation they're personally attached to. Most are defeated.'

'Was yours?' asked Clara.

'It was. A bill to end overcrowding in emergency wards.'

'Actually, it was about the war on drugs,' said Armand.

'Oh, yeah, that's right.'

'I read your bill closely,' said Gamache. 'I was head of homicide at the time and a huge percentage of the crime, of the killings, in Québec are drug-related.'

'And what did you think?'

'I thought it offered creative solutions to an obviously failing situation.'

'Then why did her bill fail?' asked Gabri.

'A number of reasons,' said Gamache.

Senior Sûreté officers on the take. Corruption in government. The cartels getting more and more powerful and calling the shots.

But he wouldn't say any of that to them. Though there was one reason that he could discuss.

'It might seem trivial, but one reason is that you named the bill after someone. I can't remember who.'

'Edouard,' said Lea. 'And why was that a problem?'

'It made it feel like a personal crusade by a member trying to make her mark, and not a sweeping solution to a growing social threat.'

'Other bills are named for people,' said Clara. 'Lots of them.'

'Absolutely, but those that succeed already have broad public support. Their sponsors have done their legwork. Gotten the media, the public and fellow politicians behind them. You' – he turned to Lea – 'did not.'

'True. If politics is an art, I was finger-painting.'

'So who was Edouard?' asked Reine-Marie.

'He was our roommate at Université de Montréal,' said Matheo.

'We all hung out,' said Lea. 'Edouard was one of the crowd.'

'A little more than that, wouldn't you say?' said Matheo.

Even in the candlelight they could see her color rise.

'I had a small crush on him,' said Lea. 'We all did. Even you, I think.'

Matheo laughed and grinned. 'He was very attractive.'

'What happened to him?' asked Myrna.

'Can't you guess?' said Matheo.

There was a lull in the conversation.

'He must've been young,' said Clara, at last.

'Not even twenty,' said Lea. 'He jumped off the roof of the residence. Fifteen stories up. Down. Stoned. It was a long time ago.'

'Not so long,' said Matheo. 'We were all very proud that the first thing Lea did when elected was propose *La loi Edouard*.'

Edouard's Law.

'It failed,' said Lea.

'But at least you tried,' said Gamache. 'And now you've learned so much more about the process. Have you considered reentering your bill? Perhaps we can work together to craft an effective one.'

'I look forward to that,' said Lea.

Gamache waited, then sat back in his chair. Considering. Lea Roux had been polite, but did not seem all that interested in working with the head of the Sûreté to stop drug trafficking.

And why would that be, he asked himself. And why would she have apparently forgotten that her very first bill, her priority, was Edouard's Law?

Appearances, again. Like the thing on the village green. They cloaked what was underneath.

CHAPTER 11

⁓

I n the morning it was gone.

Armand stood on the verandah, in his coat and cap and gloves. Henri and little Gracie on leashes. Though from their perspective, Armand was the one on the leash.

All three stared at the empty village green, shrouded in early morning mist.

He looked around. At the homes, the gardens, down the quiet dirt roads that ran into and out of Three Pines like compass points, marking the cardinal directions.

Nothing stirred. Though there was birdsong now, and a few blue jays rested on the back of the bench on the green.

'Off you go,' he said, unclipping the dogs.

Henri and Gracie took off, down the steps, along the path, over the quiet road and onto the green, where they chased each other round and round the three tall pines.

Gracie ran a little like a hare, loping at speed.

She couldn't be . . . ? Armand wondered, as he watched.

Her back feet were larger than her front, it was true. And her ears were growing longer and longer.

It was still far from clear what Gracie was. But one thing wasn't in question.

Whatever she was, she was theirs.

A slight movement off to his left caught his attention and he looked over. There, in an upper window, a large robed figure looked down on him.

Armand stared at it, his eyes sharp, his focus absolute. His body tense.

But when the figure took a step back and light fell on it, he saw that it was Myrna.

She waved and a minute later emerged wearing a wool coat, bright pink tuque with pompom, and carrying the largest mug of coffee he'd ever seen. Really, more a pail.

'Our friend has gone,' she said, her feet making a *thuck*ing sound as she yanked her rubber boots out of the mud with every step.

'*Oui.*'

'I guess Paul Marchand scared him off after all.'

'I guess so.'

He was relieved. But he was also curious, and as they walked slowly around the village green, he wondered if they'd ever know why the cobrador had appeared. And why it had disappeared.

The entire village seemed lighter, leavened. The sun was even trying to break through the chilly mist.

They'd grown almost used to the presence on the green, as one grew used to the smell of manure spread on fields. It was necessary. It might even be good. But that didn't make it pleasant.

And now the cobrador, the Conscience, was gone. The great accusation in the center of their lives had left. And they had their little village back.

Beside him, Myrna took a long, deep breath, and exhaled. A warm puff in the fresh morning air.

Armand smiled. He felt the same way. Relaxed for the first time in days.

'Do you think he got what he came for?' asked Myrna.

'He must have, otherwise why leave? If he was willing to risk a beating from Monsieur Marchand, I can't imagine what would make him suddenly give up.'

'I wonder what success for the cobrador would look like,' she said.

'I was wondering the same thing,' said Armand. 'The modern one, the one with the top hat, knows when the debt has been paid. It's a financial transaction. This debt is far different.'

Myrna nodded. 'Okay, what I really want to know is who he came for, and what that person did. There, I admit it.'

'Well now, that's not natural at all,' he said with a smile.

'You too?'

'Maybe just a little curiosity.'

They walked quietly for a moment.

'Not just curiosity, Armand. There's something else. The Conscience is gone.'

'And that leaves someone here without one. Maybe.'

Neither seemed willing to go further. They both wanted to enjoy this moment. This especially fresh November morning, with the woodsmoke from fireplaces in the air. With the soft sun and cool mist infused with the scent of the musky, muddy earth and sweet pine.

'*The children in the apple tree,*' said Myrna, watching Henri and Gracie play among the pines. '*Heard, half-heard, in the stillness.*'

'Hmmm,' hummed Armand. Her thucking steps beside him, far from being annoying, were rhythmic. Like a calming metronome. 'T. S. Eliot.'

More and more birds were returning to the village green,

and now Henri had Gracie on the wet grass, rolling her over as her tail wagged furiously and her little legs pretended to push him away.

'"Little Gidding",' said Myrna.

For a moment he thought she said 'giddy'. That Gracie was a little giddy, which she was. But then he realized Myrna was talking about the poem she'd just quoted.

'I've been there, you know,' he said.

'To Little Gidding?' asked Myrna. 'It's a real place? I thought T. S. Eliot made it up.'

'*Non*. It's not far from Cambridge. Huh,' he said, smiling.

'What is it?'

'The population of Little Gidding is about twenty-five. It reminds me a bit of here.'

They took a few more steps through the soft world.

'*And all shall be well*,' he quoted the poem. '*And all manner of thing shall be well*.'

'Do you believe it?' asked Myrna.

The poem, she knew, was about finding peace and simplicity.

'I do,' said Armand.

'Julian of Norwich said it first, you know,' said Myrna. '*All shall be well, and all shall be well, and all manner of thing shall be well*.'

Her rubber boots kept the soothing rhythm, so that the words and the world fused.

'I believe it too,' she said. 'Hard not to on a day like this.'

'The trick is to believe it in the middle of the storm,' said Armand.

And Myrna remembered that while the poem was about finding peace, it came only after a conflagration. A dreadful cleansing.

'Little Gidding' also spoke of a broken king. She looked at

her companion, and remembered their conversation the night before. About conscience.

They had a broken king. In fact, they were all broken.

'I think everyone in this village believes that all shall be well,' Armand was saying. 'That's why we're here. We all fell down. And then we all came here.'

He made it sound such a simple, reasonable, logical course of magical events.

'Ashes, ashes,' Myrna chanted under her breath, 'we all fall down.'

Gamache smiled. 'My granddaughters were playing that last time they visited. Right there.'

He pointed to the village green. And the exact spot where the cobrador had stood.

He could see Florence and her sister, Zora, dancing in a circle, holding hands with other village children, chanting the old folk song. There was something innocent but also disturbing about those old rhymes.

He could see the children laughing. And then falling to the ground. Sprawled there. Still.

He'd found it both funny and upsetting. To see those he loved lying, as though dead, on the village green. Reine-Marie said that the folk song was centuries old and originated in the Black Death. The plague.

'What is it?' Myrna asked, watching his face.

'Just thinking about the cobrador.'

But that wasn't altogether true. He was thinking of the small plastic bag he'd pulled from Marchand's pocket.

With the cobrador gone, he'd go in to work and call up the lab to see what was in the bag. But he knew the answer.

Fentanyl. The plague.

Ashes, ashes, he thought. *We all fall down.*

'All shall be well,' Myrna reassured him.

'Well, well,' said a familiar voice behind them, and both turned to see Ruth and Rosa waddling and limping down the hill, from tiny St Thomas's Church.

'You're up early,' said Armand, as the old poet joined them. 'Don't sleep much.'

Armand and Myrna exchanged glances. Their experience with Ruth was that she slept, or perhaps was passed out, most of the time. Waking up once an hour or so to hurl an insult, then back to sleep. The village cuckoo. Clock.

'Went to St Thomas's for some peace and quiet,' said Ruth.

Again, Armand and Myrna exchanged glances, wondering what riot could possibly be going on in her home, or more likely her head, that she needed to seek refuge.

'Was he gone when you came out?' asked Armand.

'Who?'

'Who do you think?' asked Myrna.

'You mean the toreador?'

'Yes,' said Myrna, not bothering to correct her, since she suspected Ruth knew perfectly well that a bullfighter hadn't descended on the village. Though, God knew, they could use help fighting all the bull.

'He was gone,' said Ruth. 'But Michael was hanging around. Making a pest of himself.'

'The archangel?' asked Armand.

'Who else? Man, that angel can talk. God this, God that. So I went to the chapel to get away.'

'From God?' asked Myrna, looking at the rumpled woman. 'What did you do there?'

'I prayed.'

'Preyed?' Myrna mouthed at Armand, making a talon gesture with her hands.

Armand flattened his lips to stop from smiling.

'What for?' he asked the old poet.

'Well, I start off praying that anyone who's pissed me off meets a horrible end. Then I pray for world peace. And then I pray for Lucifer.'

'Did you say Lucifer?' asked Myrna.

'Why so surprised?' asked Ruth, looking from one to the other. 'Who needs it more?'

'I can think of a few who deserve it more,' said Myrna.

'And who are you to judge?' asked Ruth, not completely unkindly. Though Myrna was now a little afraid she'd be added to that prayer list. 'The greatest sinner. The most lost soul. The angel who not only fell to earth, he fell so hard he broke through.'

'You pray for Satan?' Myrna asked again, still unable to get past that, and beseeching Armand for help. But he only shrugged as though to say, *She's all yours.*

'Shithead,' muttered Myrna.

Then something occurred to her. 'For him? Or to him?'

'For him. For him. For him. Jeez, and they call me demented. He was Michael's best friend. Until he got into trouble.'

'And by trouble, you mean the war in heaven where Lucifer tried to overthrow God?' asked Myrna.

'Oh, you know the story?'

'Yes, there was a movie of the week.'

'Well, none of us is perfect,' said Ruth. 'We all make mistakes.'

'That would seem bigger than most,' said Myrna. 'Especially since Lucifer hardly seems repentant.'

'And is that a reason not to forgive?' asked Ruth. She seemed genuinely perplexed by the question. Losing herself for a moment. 'Michael says Lucifer was the most beautiful, the brightest of them all. They called him the Son of the Morning. He was luminous.'

Ruth looked around, at the cottages, the gardens, the forest. The fragrant mist, and the struggling sun.

'Stupid, stupid angel,' she muttered, then turned to them. 'It's generally thought that a conscience is a good thing, but let me ask you this. How many terrible things are done in the name of conscience? It's a great excuse for appalling acts.'

'Did your friend Lucifer tell you that?' asked Myrna.

'No, the Archangel Michael told me that, just before he asked me to pray for the greatest sinner of all.'

'Who had no conscience,' Myrna pointed out.

'Or a warped one. A conscience is not necessarily a good thing. How many gays are beaten, how many abortion clinics bombed, how many blacks lynched, how many Jews murdered, by people just following their conscience?'

'And you think that's what we had here?' asked Armand. 'A conscience gone astray?'

'How should I know? I'm a crazy old woman who prays for Satan and has a duck. It would be nuts to listen to me, wouldn't it? Come on, Rosa, time for breakfast.'

The two limped and waddled over to the Gamache home.

'A conscience guides us,' Myrna called after her. 'To do the right thing. To be brave. To be selfless and courageous. To stand up to tyrants whatever the cost.'

Ruth stopped and turned back to look at them.

'You might almost say it's luminous,' she said, pausing on the steps up to the porch. Holding their eyes. 'Sometimes all is not well.'

CHAPTER 12

W ith the Conscience gone, Chief Superintendent
Gamache felt it safe to return to Montréal and work.
Driving through the November mist that persisted, he
arrived at Sûreté headquarters and went about his day, getting
caught up on the paperwork and meetings that had been put
on hold while the cobrador had occupied Three Pines.

He had lunch with the new head of Serious Crimes at a
bistro in Old Montréal. Over the soup of the day and grilled
sandwiches, they discussed organized crime, cartels, drugs,
money laundering, terrorism threats, biker gangs.

All on the rise.

Gamache pushed his sandwich aside and ordered an
espresso, while Superintendent Toussaint finished her
grilled *cubain*.

'We need more resources, *patron*,' she said.

'*Non*. We need to use what we have better.'

'We're doing the best we can,' said Toussaint, leaning forward toward the Chief Superintendent. 'But it's
overwhelming.'

'You're new to this post—'

'I've been in the Serious Crimes division for fifteen years.'

'But being in charge is different, *non*?'

She put down her sandwich, wiped her hands, and nodded.

'You've been handed a huge task. But it's also a great opportunity,' said the chief. 'You get to reinvent your entire department. Organize it, define it, put your stamp on it. Toss out all the old ideas, and begin fresh. I chose you because you stood up to the corruption and paid the price.'

Madeleine Toussaint nodded. She'd been on her way out when Armand Gamache had reached down and pulled her back.

She wasn't so sure she should thank him.

All sorts of eyes were on her.

The first woman in charge of Serious Crimes. The first Haitian to head up any department.

It was, her husband had made clear, an impossible task. It was as though a ship filled with shit was sinking in an ocean of piss.

And she'd just been promoted to captain.

'They chose you because you're a black woman,' her husband had said. 'You're expendable. If you fail, that's okay. You can do their dirty work, clean up their house, as Haitians have for decades. And you know what you'll get?'

'No, what?' Though she knew where this was heading.

'Even more shit. You'll have their *merde* all over you, and you'll be the scapegoat, the sacrificial lamb—'

'All these farm animals, André. Is there something you need to tell me?'

He'd grown angry then. But then he was often angry. Not abusive, not violent. But he was a thirty-nine-year-old black man. He'd been stopped so many times by the cops, he'd stopped counting. They'd had to train their fourteen-year-old son, from the time he could walk, how to behave when stopped by the cops. When harassed. When targeted. When pushed and provoked.

Don't react. Move slowly. Show your hands. Be polite, do as you're asked. Don't react.

André had a right to his anger, his cynicism.

She was also angry, enraged often. But she was willing to give it one last chance. As she'd been given one last chance.

'You might be right,' she said. 'But I have to try.'

'Gamache is like all the rest,' he'd said. 'Just wait. When the shit starts flying, he'll step aside and it'll hit you. That's why he chose you.'

'He chose me because I'm very, very good at what I do,' she said, getting angry herself. 'If you can't see that, then we have to have another discussion.'

She'd glared at him, her anger heightened by her suspicion he was right.

And now she sat with Chief Superintendent Gamache, at a little wooden table, surrounded by laughing, chatting diners.

And he was asking her to build the ship mid-ocean. The shit ship was taking on piss, and he wanted her not just to repair it, but to redesign it?

Madeleine Toussaint looked across the table, into his worn face. If that was all she saw, she'd think him spent and those who followed him doomed. But she saw that the creases radiating from his eyes and mouth were made more from humor than weariness. And the eyes, deep brown, were not just intelligent, they were thoughtful.

And kind.

And determined.

Far from being spent, here was a person at the height of his power. And he'd reached down, into the muck, and pulled her up. And given her power beyond imagining. And asked her to stand beside him. To stand with him.

To run Serious Crimes.

'When you feel overwhelmed, come talk to me,' he said. 'I know what it's like. I've felt like that myself.'

'And who do you talk to, sir?'

He smiled, and the lines down his face deepened. 'My wife. I tell her everything.'

'Everything?'

'Well, almost. It's important, Madeleine, not to cut people out of our lives. Isolation doesn't make us better at our job. It makes us weaker, more vulnerable.'

She nodded. She'd have to think about that.

'My husband says you've made me captain of a sinking ship. That this is an unsalvageable situation.'

Gamache nodded thoughtfully, and took a long, deep breath. 'He's right. In part. The situation as it stands is untenable, unwinnable. As I said in the meeting, the war on drugs is lost. So what do we do?'

Toussaint shook her head.

'Think,' he said, intense.

And she did. What to do when your position was unwinnable?

You either give up, or—

'We change.'

He smiled. And nodded. 'We change. But not slightly. We need a radical change, and that, unfortunately, cannot come from the old guard. It needs bold, creative new minds. And brave hearts.'

'But you're—'

She stopped herself just in time. Or perhaps, not quite in time.

Chief Superintendent Gamache looked at her with amusement.

'Old?'

'Er.'

'Er?' he asked.

'Older,' she said. *'Désolé.'*

'Don't be. It's true. But someone has to be in charge. Someone has to be expendable.'

Madeleine Toussaint knew then that her husband might've been right about many things, but he'd been wrong about one. She was not the goat tethered to the ground. To draw the predators.

Gamache was.

'We have a great advantage, Superintendent,' said Gamache, his voice crisp and businesslike again. 'Several actually. Our predecessors spent most of their energy on breaking their own laws and covering up. They also spent much of their time on internecine wars. Firing at each other, sometimes literally. Crime got out of control, partly because the attention of the top Sûreté officers was on their own corruption, and partly because the cartels paid good money for blind eyes.'

'They blinded their own eyes,' said Toussaint. 'For money and power.'

'Yes. Very Greek.' But he didn't look amused. And she wondered if that was a joke or if he really did see it as an ancient tragedy playing out in modern-day Québec.

'And now?' she asked.

'You said it yourself. We change. Everything. While appearing to change nothing.' He looked at her, studying her. 'The only reason we police as we do is because someone a century ago organized us this way. But what worked then doesn't work now. You're young. Use that to your advantage. Our adversaries are expecting the same old tactics.'

He leaned forward and lowered his voice. But it was filled with energy, awe even.

'Reinvent, Madeleine. Make it new and bold. Now's our chance. While no one thinks we can do it. While no one's looking. Your husband isn't alone. Everyone thinks that the Sûreté is irreparably damaged. Not just in reputation, but that there's rot. And the whole thing is teetering. And you know what? They're right. So we can either spend our time and energy and resources propping up a mortally damaged institution, or we can begin again.'

'And what do we do?' she asked, swept up in his excitement.

He leaned back. 'I don't know.'

She felt herself deflate, but only slightly. Part of her was pleased to hear it. It meant she could contribute rather than just implement.

'I need ideas,' Gamache said. 'From you. From the others. I've been thinking about it.'

He'd spent many autumn mornings and evenings, Henri and Gracie at his feet, sitting on the bench above Three Pines. The one inscribed *Surprised by Joy* and, above that, *A Brave Man in a Brave Country*.

He'd looked at the tiny village, going about its life, and then beyond that, the mountains and forest and ribbon of golden river. And he'd thought. And he'd thought.

He'd turned down the job of Chief Superintendent of the Sûreté, Québec's top cop, twice. Partly because he didn't want to be the one on the bridge when a ship he'd once so admired went down. And he couldn't see any way to save it.

But the third time he was asked, he again took himself up

to the bench, and he thought. About the corruption. The damage done.

He thought about the Sûreté Academy and the young recruits. He thought about a life of peace. Of quiet. Here in Three Pines. Off the map. Off the radar.

Safe.

Reine-Marie had often joined him. They'd sit side by side, quietly. Until one evening, she'd spoken.

'I was just thinking about Odysseus,' she'd said.

'Oddly' – he turned to her – 'I was not.'

She'd laughed. 'I was thinking about his retirement.'

'Odysseus retired?'

'He did. As an old man he was tired. Of war. He was even tired of the sea. And so he took an oar and walked into the woods. He walked and walked, until he found a people who had no idea what an oar was. And there he made his home. Where no one would know the name Odysseus. Where no one would have heard of the Trojan War. Where he could live out his life anonymously. In peace.'

Armand had sat very still and very silent for a long time, looking at Three Pines.

And then he'd gotten up, and returned home. And made a phone call.

Odysseus's battle was done. His war won.

Gamache's wasn't yet won. Or lost. There was at least one more battle.

And now here he was in a bistro in Old Montréal with a very young superintendent, talking about ships.

'My husband was right about the leaky ship. But he was wrong about something else. I'm not alone.'

'No, you're not.'

She nodded. She'd felt alone for so long she'd failed to

notice that was no longer the case. She had colleagues. People standing not behind her, but beside her.

'We need to commit totally,' she said. 'Burn our ships. No going back.'

Gamache stared at her, then sat back in his chair.

'*Patron?*' she asked, just a little afraid he was having a *petit mal*. Or maybe, as the moments went by, a *grand mal*.

'I'm sorry,' he said, and drew a napkin toward him.

Taking a pen from his breast pocket, he scribbled a few words, then looked up and smiled, beamed, at her. He folded the napkin and put it in his pocket. And leaned toward her.

'That's what we'll do. We won't repair the ship. We'll burn it.'

He gave one firm nod.

When Superintendent Toussaint arrived back after lunch, she was reenergized. Invigorated. By his words. And she tried not to think about the hint of madness that had played on the edges of Chief Superintendent Gamache's tone.

Madeleine Toussaint might have been the first, but before it was over she'd be far from the last person to think that the new head of the Sûreté had lost his mind.

CHAPTER 13

~

The first meeting of the afternoon was with Inspector Beauvoir, who wanted to discuss a suggestion that the Sûreté form a ceremonial drill team.

'Like in the military,' said Beauvoir. 'Those close marches.'

Chief Superintendent Gamache listened, unconvinced. 'Why would we do that?'

'Well, now, this isn't my idea, one of the senior officers came to me with it. When I stopped laughing, I started to think.'

He gave his boss a stern look of warning not to be a smart-ass. Gamache lifted his hand in surrender.

'It could start in the academy, with training,' Beauvoir continued. 'It would be, I think, a great way to bond, but it'd also be something we could take into communities. You're always saying we need to rebuild trust. We could go into schools and community centers and put on shows. Maybe as fundraisers for local food banks or rehabs.'

Now Gamache was leaning forward, nodding.

'You know, that's a terrific idea.'

They discussed it for a few minutes.

When they'd finished, Gamache got to his feet. He was

tempted to show Jean-Guy the napkin from lunch. And the words scrawled there.

But he didn't.

It wasn't time yet. He needed to sit quietly, and think.

'I'm glad that thing on the village green has gone,' said Beauvoir, walking to the door. 'But you still have no idea why he was there?'

'None. And he's taken up more than enough of my time.'

Jean-Guy adjusted his glasses. They were new to him, and the younger man found it humiliating to need them. The first sign of decrepitude.

It also didn't help that the chief, a good twenty years older than Beauvoir, only needed his for reading, whereas Jean-Guy had been told he needed to wear his all the time.

'Honoré grabbed them last night at bath time,' said Jean-Guy, taking them off and examining them again. 'Pulled them right into the water. That kid's strong.'

'Are you sure it was Honoré who threw them into the water?' asked Armand, taking the glasses from Beauvoir and quickly adjusting them.

He'd had years of experience with twisted and damaged frames.

He handed them back.

'*Merci, patron*. What are you suggesting?'

'Sabotage, sir,' said Gamache melodramatically. 'And then you have the temerity to blame your infant son. You're a scoundrel.'

'Jeez, Annie said the same thing. Are you colluding?'

'Yes. We speak endlessly about your glasses.'

That was when the very gentle *ding* was heard from Gamache's laptop.

The vast majority of his mail went through Madame

Clarke to sort and prioritize. There was a shocking amount of it, but Gina Clarke had proven up to the task, and then some. Even organizing the Chief Superintendent, as though he was just one more email to be replied to, forwarded or sometimes deleted.

Jean-Guy often sat in the chief's outer office just to watch him be bossed around by the young woman with the pierced nose and pink hair. It was as though Tinker Bell had turned.

But this email had been sent to his private work account.

Gamache got up and walked to his desk. 'Do you mind waiting for a moment?'

'Not at all, *patron*.'

Jean-Guy stood by the door and checked his own messages.

Gamache clicked on the email. It was the report from the lab on the drugs found on Paul Marchand the evening before. But the chief was interrupted by a call on his cell phone.

'*Oui, allô*,' he picked up the phone, while studying the computer screen, his face grim.

'Armand?'

It was Reine-Marie.

Something was wrong.

'So she called you first, before dialing 911?' asked the Crown.

'She did,' said Gamache. Was it getting even hotter in the courtroom? He could feel his shirt, under his jacket, sticking to his skin.

'And what did she tell you?'

Reaching out quickly, instinctively, as though for the woman herself, Armand touched the speaker button, while across the room, Jean-Guy turned toward him.

'Are you all right?' Armand asked.

'I found the cobrador.'

There was a moment's pause, just a moment, while the world shifted. Her words, and the men, felt suspended in midair.

'Tell me,' he said, getting to his feet and staring at Jean-Guy.

'He's in the church basement. I went down to the root cellar to get vases for fresh flowers, and he was there.'

'Did he hurt you?'

'*Non.* He's dead. There was blood, Armand.'

'Where are you?'

'At home. I locked the church door and came here to call.'

'Good. Stay where you are.'

'I haven't called 911 yet—'

'I'll do that now.' He looked over at Beauvoir, who was already on his phone.

'Do you have blood on you?'

'I do. My hands. I leaned over and touched his neck. He still has his mask on, but he was cold. I probably shouldn't have touched him—'

'You had to find out. I'm sorry—'

'It's not your fault.'

'*Non*, I mean I'm sorry about what I'm about to do. I'm going to have to ask you not to wash.'

There was silence as Reine-Marie took that in. She thought to ask why. She thought to argue. To beg even. For a moment, a brief spike, she was angry at him. For treating her like any other witness.

But that passed. And she knew, she was any other witness. And he was a cop.

'I understand,' she said. And she did. 'But hurry.'

He was already out the door, Beauvoir right behind him.

143

'I'm leaving now. Cancel my appointments,' he said as he hurried through the outer office, past Madame Clarke.

She didn't question, didn't hesitate. 'Yessir.'

Gamache and Beauvoir walked swiftly down the long corridor to the elevators.

'Jean-Guy has called 911, there should be agents there within minutes. Get Clara or Myrna to come over and be with you. I'll get there as quick as I can. Do you want me to stay on the phone with you?'

'No, I need to call Clara and Myrna. Hurry, Armand.'

'I am.' He hung up and said to Beauvoir. 'Call Lacoste.'

'Already done. She's sending a team.'

Beauvoir rushed to keep pace with Gamache.

He'd stood beside the older man through countless investigations. During arrests and interrogations and shootouts. During horrific events, and celebrations.

At funerals, at weddings.

Jean-Guy had seen him joyous, and devastated. Angry and worried.

But he'd never seen Armand Gamache desperate.

Until now.

And there was rage there.

That Reine-Marie should have blood on her hands.

They raced down to Three Pines with the siren on, communicating with the local Sûreté detachment. Instructing them not to enter the church, but to secure it.

'And I want an agent in front of my home,' said Gamache, describing which home it was.

Beauvoir cut the siren as they turned off the secondary road onto the small dirt road. He drove more slowly because of the potholes, and the deer that were prone to jump straight into the path of oncoming cars.

'Faster,' said Gamache.

'But *patron*—'

'Faster.'

'Madame Gamache is fine,' he said. 'She's safe. No harm will come to her.'

'And would you say that, Jean-Guy, if it was Annie who'd found a body, and had blood on her hands? Blood you told her not to wash off?'

Jean-Guy sped up. Feeling his fillings loosen and his glasses bounce as they jolted along.

'So your own wife found the body?' asked the Crown Prosecutor.

'*Oui.*'

'And she touched it.'

'*Oui.*'

'Your wife is obviously different from mine, monsieur. I can't imagine her touching a dead body, never mind one with blood all over it. It was clear, wasn't it, that this was murder?'

The already steaming courtroom grew even hotter as Gamache felt a flush rise out of his collar and up his neck, but he kept his voice and his gaze steady.

'It was. And you're right, Madame Gamache is extraordinary. She had to see if she could help. She left only when it was clear there was nothing she could do. I suspect your wife would be equally courageous and compassionate.'

The Crown continued to stare at Gamache. The judge stared. The courtroom stared. The reporters scribbled.

'You told her not to wash the blood off, is that correct?'

'It is.'

'Why is that?'

'Most people who find a murder victim inadvertently disturb the scene—'

'By doing things like touching the body?'

'Or moving something. Or trying to clean up. People aren't themselves when faced with a shock like that. Normally by the time we arrive, the damage is done.'

'Like in this case.'

'*Non*. Madame Gamache touched the body, but she had the presence of mind to do nothing else and to lock up. Then she called me.'

'Without removing the mask to see who it was?'

'That's right.'

'Wasn't she curious?'

'I don't think curiosity was her main emotion.'

'And you told her not to wash the blood from her hands, or shoes.'

'So that we could take samples and be clear about what were her traces and what belonged to someone else.'

'How magnificent,' said the Crown. 'To have your wife in such a horrible position, and still you chose your job over her comfort. Not only is she extraordinary, but you appear to be as well.'

Gamache did not respond, though his complexion did, the flush rising into his cheeks.

The two men glared at each other. The loathing no longer a matter of conjecture.

'I will, of course, be calling Madame Gamache as a witness later in the trial, but are you quite sure she didn't touch anything else? And remember, you're under oath.'

'I do remember that,' snapped Gamache, before hauling himself back. '*Merci*. And yes, I'm sure.'

At the defense desk, the lawyers stared at each other in

146

disbelief. It seemed Monsieur Zalmanowitz was doing their job for them. Destroying if not the credibility, then the likability of his main witness.

'In the meantime,' said the Crown, 'perhaps you can tell us what you found when you finally arrived.'

They passed the Sûreté car, parked by the church. And saw an agent standing at the foot of the stairs up to the door.

As Jean-Guy drove by the bistro, he noticed patrons standing at the window, staring.

Beauvoir had barely stopped the car when Gamache was out and walking swiftly, breaking into a run, down the path, past the agent, to his front door.

What had started as a misty though promising day had turned gloomy again. The clouds shutting out the tentative sun. The damp rolling down the hill and pooling in the village.

Reine-Marie was in the kitchen with Clara and Myrna. The woodstove pumping out heat. Mugs of tea in front of them.

'I'm sorry, *mon coeur*,' said Armand, as she stood and went to him and he took a step back, holding his hands up as though to ward her off. 'I can't—'

Reine-Marie stopped, her arms out for an embrace. And then she slowly lowered them.

Clara, standing a few steps behind Reine-Marie, thought she had never seen such sorrow in a man's eyes.

Jean-Guy brushed by him, moving through the gulf between husband and wife, and quickly, efficiently took samples and photographs.

No one spoke until he had finished, and stepped away.

Then Armand stepped forward, embracing Reine-Marie, holding her tight. 'Are you all right?'

'I will be,' she said.

'The police arrived about half an hour ago,' said Clara. 'Until then, Myrna stood on the porch, making sure no one approached the church.'

'Good,' said Jean-Guy. 'Did anyone?'

'No,' said Myrna.

Armand took Reine-Marie to the powder room, and together they washed the worst of the blood off her hands, his large fingers softly rubbing the now dried blood from her skin.

When they'd finished, he took her upstairs to their bedroom.

As she stripped down, he turned the shower on, making sure it wasn't too hot.

'I'll be back before you know it.'

'You're leaving? I'm sorry, of course you are. You have to.'

He held her, then stepping back he took her hands and looked down at them. There was still some blood stuck to her wedding ring. It was difficult not to see the symbolism.

This was what he'd brought into their marriage. Blood ran through their lives together. Like a river that sometimes broke its banks. Marring them. Staining them.

What would their lives have been like had he followed up his pre-law degree and not gone into the Sûreté? Had he stayed at Cambridge? Perhaps become a professor.

He was pretty sure he wouldn't be standing there trying to scrape one last bit of dried blood from his wife's hand.

'I am sorry,' he said quietly.

'Someone else did this, Armand. You're here to help.'

He kissed her and nodded toward the shower. 'Go.'

She nodded toward the door. 'Go. Oh, you'll need this.'

She took the key to the church out of her sweater pocket. It too had blood on it.

Armand grabbed a tissue and took the key.

Downstairs, Beauvoir was talking to Clara and Myrna.

'Who else knows?'

'Reine-Marie told us, of course. About the cobrador,' said Clara. 'But no one else. Obviously everyone knows something's happened, especially when the agents arrived. But not what, and the agents wouldn't tell them anything.'

'Because they don't know,' said Beauvoir. It was vital, he knew, to guard information. Sometimes from your own people.

'Everyone's gathered at the bistro,' said Myrna. 'Waiting for news. Waiting for you. Some came here, but the agent stopped them.'

'Who?'

'Gabri, of course,' said Clara. 'Honestly? Almost everyone came over.'

Joining them, Gamache asked if they'd stay with Reine-Marie until he returned.

'Of course,' said Clara.

Then he and Beauvoir walked swiftly down the path from the front porch to the dirt road, pausing briefly to speak to the agent.

'Stay here, please.'

'*Oui, patron.*' He was one of the agents who'd been called to Three Pines the evening before.

'What did you do with Monsieur Marchand, the man from last night?'

'As you asked. We kept him overnight. By morning he'd cooled down. Then drove him home.'

'What time?'

'Ten. He refused to tell us where he got the stuff in the packet. What was it?'

149

Gamache remembered the email, the lab report he'd been reading when Reine-Marie called. 'Fentanyl.'

'Ffff—' But the agent stopped himself.

Chief Superintendent Gamache nodded agreement, then continued down his walkway, noticing Gabri approaching from the bistro, taking long strides toward them. Not exactly running. Gabri did not run. He lumbered at speed.

Still holding a dish towel, he intercepted Gamache and Beauvoir.

'What's happened? The cops won't tell us anything.' He looked accusingly at the agent, who pretended not to hear.

'And neither can I,' said Gamache.

'It's something to do with Reine-Marie,' said Gabri. 'Is she all right?'

'Yes.'

'Well, thank God for that. But someone isn't . . .' He gestured toward the church, and the other agent.

Gamache shook his head and noticed more people heading their way, led by Lea Roux with Matheo close behind.

'You go. I'll take care of this,' said Gabri. He turned to head them off, allowing Armand and Jean-Guy to escape.

The agent guarding the church was waiting for them. Behind her rose the small white clapboard chapel. Pretty. Innocuous. Like thousands of others in villages throughout Québec.

Only this one held not a relic, a saint's knuckle or molar, but an entire body.

A dead creature from another time.

CHAPTER 14

I sabelle Lacoste, the head of homicide for the Sûreté, arrived just as Gamache and Beauvoir reached the church. Her car, followed by the Scene of Crime van, pulled in behind the vehicle driven by the local agents.

Investigators unloaded equipment while Gamache, Beauvoir and Lacoste quickly consulted.

'Can you swab and fingerprint this?' Gamache handed an agent the key in the tissue.

'Tell me what you know,' said Lacoste, turning to Gamache.

Beauvoir suppressed a smile and wondered if either of them realized it was exactly what Gamache used to say when he was head of homicide.

'We haven't been in yet,' said the Chief Superintendent. 'Madame Gamache found the body in the basement, then locked the church. It appears to be the cobrador.'

'The what?' asked Lacoste.

Gamache, so familiar now with the thing, had forgotten that Isabelle Lacoste knew nothing about it.

'You'll see,' he said.

'Done.' The forensics agent handed the large latchkey back to Gamache, who gave it to Lacoste.

At the top of the stairs, Gamache stepped aside while she unlocked the door and went in, followed by her Scene of Crime and forensics teams. As they streamed past him, Gamache turned and looked at the village and the villagers.

They were standing outside the bistro in a line, a semicircle. It looked, from where he stood, like a frown.

Sleet, part snow and part icy rain, was beginning to fall. And still they stood there, staring. A cluster of dark figures in the distance. Unmoving. Staring at him.

And then he went inside the church. A place that had offered peace and calm and sanctuary, even to an old woman praying for the Son of the Morning.

He went down the stairs, into near darkness.

The basement was really just one large room, with worn, scuffed linoleum floors, acoustic tile ceiling stained by water damage here and there, and fake wood siding on the walls. Chairs were stacked against the walls, and long tables, their legs folded up, leaned against one another.

Isabelle Lacoste looked around, her sharp eyes taking in the fact there was no other entrance, and while there were windows, they were covered in layers of grime. It would be easier for light, or an intruder, to enter through the walls.

But, windows aside, it was clean. Uncluttered. Didn't even smell of mildew.

There was a kitchen at one end, with avocado appliances. And a door, open, off to the side of that.

She turned as she heard the familiar tread on the stairs, and saw Gamache walk into the room.

He gestured toward the open door.

'A root cellar,' he said, as they walked across the basement.

'Madame Gamache came down looking for a vase. That's when she found him.'

'What time?'

'About one forty-five. She locked the church and called me as soon as she got home, and Inspector Beauvoir called you.'

They both, instinctively, looked at their watches. It was three fifteen. An hour and a half.

Armand was familiar with the church basement. It was where funeral receptions were held. Where wedding feasts were often prepared. Where bridge clubs and exercise classes and bake sales took place.

It was a cheerful room that time, and taste, had left behind.

He had never been into the root cellar and didn't even know it was there.

Chief Superintendent Gamache stood at the threshold, but didn't go in. There was barely room for the investigators.

A light, fluorescent, artificial, had been left on by Reine-Marie. It was the only light in the small room. There were no windows here. The floor was dirt.

The space was lined with rough wooden shelves with a few vases, and rusty old tin cans, and milky preserves in mason jars.

He took all that in, but what he focused on, what everyone focused on, was the black lump in the corner. It looked as though something had erupted from the earth, been forced out of the ground.

A big black boulder.

Isabelle Lacoste turned to him, puzzled. 'The cobrador?'

'Oui.'

Beauvoir was standing at the doorway with Gamache, throbbing. Wanting to go in, to join in. But when Gamache stepped back, so did he.

The coroner arrived, and after greeting Gamache, she looked at Beauvoir.

'Nice glasses.'

Then Dr Sharon Harris walked past them and entered the root cellar.

'What did she mean by that?' asked Jean-Guy, adjusting his glasses.

'She likes them,' said Gamache automatically. 'We all like them.'

Beauvoir stepped away. Unable to just stand idle and watch, he began pacing the periphery of the large room, like a predator in a cage. Smelling blood.

Once the videos and photos and samples were taken, Dr Harris knelt beside the body.

'He's wearing a mask,' she said, looking up into the faces.

Lacoste knelt down to get a better look, the videoing agent right beside her.

'I warn you,' said the Crown. 'This next part is pretty bad. You might want to look away.'

Everyone in the courtroom leaned forward.

The video, not particularly steady but clear, showed Isabelle Lacoste, her second-in-command, and Dr Harris bending over the dark mound.

Chief Superintendent Gamache stepped forward and knelt beside Lacoste. The shadow of another figure, Inspector Beauvoir, could be seen.

And then the camera zoomed in for a close-up of the black mass.

It was difficult to distinguish a shape, until the camera moved in even closer, on the mask.

It was cracked.

Some of the spectators in the courtroom lowered their eyes.

'I'm going to remove the mask,' Chief Inspector Isabelle Lacoste narrated.

More people dropped their gazes to their hands.

There was some difficulty getting it off, and the spectators saw glimpses of flesh.

More people lowered their eyes. Some closed them altogether.

Finally, by the time the mask was removed, no one in the courtroom was watching. Except the court officers.

Judge Corriveau forced herself to look, glancing over quickly to the jury and feeling sorry for the poor buggers. Who'd started the trial excited at being involved in a murder case. And would end it traumatized. Or, worse, numb to such horror.

The Crown, who'd seen this video often, stood at his desk, his lips pressed together and his hands made into fists at his sides.

Chief Superintendent Gamache narrowed his eyes. It was slightly easier to watch on video than in person, but not much.

Beauvoir, sitting in the courtroom, had his own mask on. Of professional detachment.

One of the defense lawyers shot a quick glance at the defendant, then looked away, hoping no one in the jury had seen the revulsion in his face as he'd stared at the person he was meant to defend.

The person he privately suspected had done this.

The camera zoomed in even more, in a merciless close-up.

At that stage, even Gamache looked away, then forced himself back, to stare at the giant face on the large screen.

*

Isabelle Lacoste handed the mask to her head of forensics, and turned to Gamache.

'You're surprised.'

He nodded.

There was a lot of damage, but the face was recognizable. Not a man, but a woman.

'You know her?' asked Lacoste.

'*Oui.* That's Katie Evans. She's staying at the B&B.'

Lacoste got up, and so did Gamache.

Isabelle Lacoste cast an experienced eye over the root cellar, then motioned toward the door.

'I'll leave you to it,' she said to the coroner and her second-in-command. At the door she paused. 'I take it the cause of death is obvious.'

They all looked at the bloody bat, propped casually against one of the shelves, next to a stained mason jar of peaches.

'I'll let you know if we find anything else,' said Dr Harris. 'But what's with . . .'

She gestured at the costume.

'I think I'm about to find out,' said Lacoste, and followed Gamache and Beauvoir into the larger room.

On the huge screen in the courtroom, the camera followed the senior officers as they left the root cellar. Just before the camera swung back to the body, it captured Chief Superintendent Gamache as he turned and looked into the room.

An expression of extreme bewilderment on his face.

CHAPTER 15

⁓

They set up one of the long tables in the center of the church basement, positioned so they could still see inside the root cellar.

'Who is Katie Evans?' Lacoste asked.

'She's a visitor,' said Gamache. 'From Montréal. An architect. Staying at the B&B with her husband and two friends.'

Lacoste took no notes. They'd get official statements later. Now she just listened. Very closely.

'And the mask and cloak she's wearing? You called it a—'

'Cobrador,' said Gamache.

He and Beauvoir looked at each other. How to explain this?

'It's Spanish. A debt collector of sorts,' said Gamache.

'We just found the body,' said Lacoste. 'How do you know this?'

'Because the cobrador has been here for a while,' he said.

'A while? How long?'

'A few days.'

'You're going to have to explain this to me,' said Lacoste. 'This Katie Evans was a debt collector? And she wore a costume?'

Again, Gamache and Beauvoir looked at each other. This

157

was going to be more difficult than they thought. Mostly because they themselves had no idea what was going on.

'No,' said Gamache. 'She wasn't a debt collector. She was an architect.'

'Then why is she in the costume?'

The men shook their heads.

Lacoste stared at them, momentarily at a loss. 'Okay, let's go back. Walk me through this.'

'The cobrador showed up the night after Halloween,' said Gamache. 'At the annual costume party here in Three Pines. We didn't know that's what it was at the time. No one knew who he was, or what he was supposed to be. There was a general feeling of unease, but nothing more. Until the next morning, when we woke up to find him on the village green.'

'Passed out?' asked Lacoste. 'Drunk?'

Gamache shook his head and reached into his pocket for his iPhone. As he brought it out, something fell to the linoleum floor.

The napkin from lunch that day.

He and Beauvoir both bent for it, Jean-Guy getting there first and handing it to Gamache. But not before noticing some words in the chief's distinctive handwriting.

'*Merci*,' said Gamache, taking the napkin. He carefully refolded and replaced it in his pocket. Then he scrolled through his iPhone.

'I took this picture Saturday morning and sent it to Jean-Guy, asking him to see what he could find out.'

He showed it to Lacoste.

She was trained not to react to sights, sounds, words. To take things in, but give nothing away. Most people watching her would not see any noticeable change as she studied the image.

But Gamache did, as did Beauvoir, being so close to her.

The very, very slight widening of her eyes. The very, very slight compression of her lips.

For a highly trained homicide investigator, it was the equivalent of a yell.

She raised her eyes from the iPhone and looked from Gamache to Beauvoir and back again.

'It looks like Death,' she said, her voice neutral, almost matter-of-fact.

'*Oui*,' said Gamache. 'That's what we thought too.'

The figure in the photograph was powerful, threatening. But there was also something almost majestic about it. There was a calm, a certainty. An inevitability about it.

A stark contrast to the rumpled mound in the root cellar. One looked like Death. The other actually was.

'What did you do?' Lacoste asked.

Gamache shifted slightly on the hard chair. It was the first time he'd have to officially answer that question, though he suspected it was far from the final. And he could already sense the expectation that the Chief Superintendent of the Sûreté should have done something. Anything. To prevent this.

'I spoke to him. Asked who he was and what he wanted. But he didn't answer. He just continued standing there. Staring.'

'At what?'

'At the shops. I wasn't sure which one.'

'And then what happened?'

'Nothing. It just stood there.'

'For two days,' said Beauvoir.

'*Pardon?*' asked Lacoste.

'It stood there for two days,' said Beauvoir.

'Dressed like that?'

'Well, not the whole time,' said Gamache. 'I stayed up that first evening, to watch. Sometime in the night it disappeared, but it was too dark to see it go. I went to bed and in the morning it was back.'

Lacoste took a deep breath, then looked behind her at the misshapen lump on the floor of the root cellar, and the coroner kneeling beside it. Him. Her.

It looked pathetic now, drained of all life and any menace it once had. Like an animal curled in a corner to die.

But there was nothing natural about this ruined creature.

'You called it a cobrador,' she said. 'I've never heard of it. Spanish, you say?' Gamache told her about the cobrador del frac. The Spanish debt collector, who followed and shamed people into paying their debts.

As Lacoste listened, her brows drew together in concern.

When he'd finished, she said, 'So the cobrador was here to shame someone into paying a debt?'

'Not exactly,' said Gamache. 'The modern cobrador does that. But what we had here was older. The ancestor. The original.'

'And what was that?'

Gamache turned to Jean-Guy, who picked up the story. Telling Lacoste what he'd found out. The island. The plague victims, lepers, babies with birth defects, the witches. And the conscience the authorities created.

'The cobradors were arrested,' said Gamache. 'And tortured, to tell them who they were and where they came from. But none talked. Those who didn't die under torture were executed. But others kept coming, taking their place. Finally the authorities figured out where they were coming from and sent soldiers to the island. They killed everyone.'

'Everyone?' asked Lacoste.

The problem with having an imagination was being able to imagine scenes like that. Men. Women. Children.

'But it seems some escaped,' said Gamache. 'Maybe even helped by soldiers sickened by what they'd been ordered to do.'

Tormented, he thought, by their own conscience.

'Now, you're not telling me what you had on the village green was some sort of ancient avenger,' said Lacoste. 'From the Dark Ages.'

'You don't believe it?' asked Gamache, then smiled slightly before Lacoste could answer. '*Non*. I'm not saying that. What I am saying is that someone knew about the ancient cobrador and decided to use it to get what they wanted.'

'That someone being Katie Evans,' said Lacoste.

'No,' said Gamache. 'It couldn't have been her. I saw her at the boulangerie and in the bookstore when the cobrador was on the village green. And Reine-Marie saw her and her husband heading for dinner in Knowlton last night.'

'So if Katie Evans wasn't the cobrador, who was?'

It was a question impossible to answer at the moment.

'And if she wasn't the cobrador,' said Lacoste, 'she must've been his target. But what's she doing in his costume?'

They shook their heads.

'Whoever did this will be long gone by now,' said Beauvoir.

'I'm afraid so,' said Gamache. 'We'll hear more from the coroner, but it must've happened sometime in the night. The cobrador wasn't there this morning when I walked Henri and Gracie.'

'What time was that?' asked Lacoste.

'Just after seven.'

'And when did you last see it?'

Gamache thought. 'Last night, but I can't tell you when it left.'

'But it wasn't there this morning,' said Lacoste. 'What did you think had happened to it?'

'I thought it left because it got what it wanted.'

'And what it wanted was Katie Evans,' said Lacoste.

'It would seem so.'

'I wonder what she did,' said Lacoste, 'that was so bad.'

Gamache was staring straight ahead of him. Not into the root cellar, but into space.

'What is it?' asked Jean-Guy.

'It doesn't make sense.'

'Really?' he said. 'A guy in a black cape and mask doesn't make sense?'

Gamache gave him a stern look, then turned to Isabelle Lacoste. 'A modern cobrador is a debt collector, not a killer. And the original cobrador, from the time of the plague, was a conscience. Not a killer. Even when provoked, even to save its own life, it didn't resort to violence. And neither did this one, last evening.'

He told them about the mob.

'So why did this one kill?' asked Beauvoir.

His question was met with silence.

CHAPTER 16

O livier stood at the window of the bistro and watched the Sûreté officers walking down the road from the church.

He wasn't alone. The rest of the village, and those from outlying farms, had gathered in the bistro, the focal point for the community, in good times and bad.

And it was very clear which one they were now in.

They watched, silently, as Armand Gamache, Jean-Guy Beauvoir and Isabelle Lacoste walked toward them through the cold November drizzle that turned, every now and then, into sleet. Then back again.

Olivier and Gabri had been handing out coffee and tea, juices, and fresh, warm cookies from Sarah's bakery. No alcohol. No need to feed already heightened emotions.

A fine mist had accompanied the drizzle so that Three Pines appeared socked in.

Both fireplaces, on either end of the bistro, were lit. And now the only sound, besides some labored breathing, was the cheery crackle of the logs.

The place smelled of woodsmoke and rich coffee. And wet wool from those who'd arrived late, hurrying through the damp afternoon.

On any other day, in any other circumstances, the bistro would've felt snug and safe and comforting. A refuge. But today, it did not.

They looked out the window, toward the trinity, and the bad news appearing out of the mist.

Then Olivier looked behind him.

At Patrick Evans. He was sitting, his legs no longer able to hold him. Lea sat beside him, holding his hand, and Matheo stood, his hand on Patrick's shoulder.

But someone was missing. The only one not there.

Katie.

Though they were fairly sure they knew where she was.

At that moment, she was still alive.

But as soon as the Sûreté officers arrived, and began to speak, she would die. They all knew that whatever had happened, however it had happened, the 'who' was not in doubt.

Patrick's breathing was fast, shallow. His hands cold. His eyes wide.

As he waited.

'When you arrived at the restaurant, Chief Superintendent, did you get the impression the people there already knew?' asked the Crown.

'I did.'

'But how? Had Madame Gamache told them?'

'No, she did not.'

'Then how did they know? All they'd seen was a bunch of patrol cars. Why automatically think it was a murder?'

He obviously doesn't know Three Pines, thought Gamache.

'When the local Sûreté agents arrived and positioned themselves at the church and my home, the villagers knew something was going on. And they knew that Madame Evans was missing. When I showed up, followed by Chief Inspector Lacoste, well, their fears were confirmed.'

'Ahhh, of course. That was stupid of me,' said the Crown, turning once again to the jury and trying to look humble. 'For a moment I'd forgotten how well the villagers know you and your work and your colleagues. They'd know Chief Inspector Lacoste was now the head of homicide. But while they know you, Chief Superintendent, you also know them. Well.'

He said it with his back to Gamache, but the insinuation was clear.

The normal, the healthy, the necessary line between cops and suspects was blurred, if not erased altogether. And that was, the Crown seemed to be suggesting, highly unprofessional, perhaps even suspicious.

'That's a good point,' said Gamache. 'And, as it turns out, a great advantage. Murder might be calculating, but it's not calculus. It isn't the sum of evidence. What tips someone over into murder?'

Now Armand Gamache was addressing the jury directly, and they'd turned their attention from the Crown Prosecutor to the Chief Superintendent.

Monsieur Zalmanowitz, sensing this shift, turned and glared at Gamache.

'What makes someone kill isn't opportunity, it's emotions.' Gamache spoke quietly, softly even. As though confiding in a good friend. 'One human kills another. Sometimes it's a flash of uncontrollable anger. Sometimes it's cold. Planned. Meticulous. But what they have in common is an emotion out of control. Often something that has been pent up. Buried. Clawing away at the person.'

The men and women on the jury were nodding.

'We've all had resentments like that,' said Gamache. 'And

most of us have felt, at least once in our lives, that we genuinely wanted to kill someone. Or, at the least, we wanted them dead. And what stops us?'

'Conscience?' mouthed a young woman in the second row of the jury box.

'Conscience,' said the Chief Superintendent, looking at her and seeing her smile just a little. 'Or maybe cowardice. Some think they're the same thing. That the only thing that stops us from doing something awful is the fear of getting caught. What would we do, after all, if we were guaranteed not to get caught? If we knew there'd be no consequences. Or if we didn't care. If we believed the act was justified. If we believed, as Gandhi did, that there's a higher court than a court of justice.'

'I object,' said the Crown.

'On what basis?' Judge Corriveau asked.

'Irrelevance.'

'He's your own witness, Monsieur Zalmanowitz,' the judge reminded him. 'And you're the one who asked the question.'

'I didn't ask for a lecture on the nature of murder and conscience.'

'Maybe you should have,' she said, and looked down at the clock embedded into the judge's desk. 'This is probably a good time to break for lunch. Back in an hour, please.'

She stood up, and in the hubbub of chairs scraping the floor, she whispered to Gamache, 'I've given you enough leeway. Watch yourself.'

He bowed very slightly to show he'd heard, and caught the eye of the Crown, who was at his desk angrily stuffing papers into his briefcase.

When the judge had gone and the jury was just being shown out, Monsieur Zalmanowitz finally erupted, striding across the courtroom to Gamache, who was just descending the steps from the witness box.

'What the hell was that about?' the Crown demanded. 'What the fuck are you doing?'

Gamache glanced over at the jury, the last few of whom were filing through the door, and had clearly heard.

'Not here,' he said to the Crown.

'Yes, here.'

Gamache turned and walked past him, but the Crown reached out and grabbed his arm.

'Oh, no, you don't.'

Gamache jerked free and swung around to face him.

The journalists, still in the room, were staring. Those on the court beat had never seen anything like this.

'Why're you sabotaging my case?' demanded Zalmanowitz.

'Not here. If you want to talk, come with me.'

He turned to Beauvoir. 'Please find—'

'I'll find a room, *patron*,' said Beauvoir, and took off, with Gamache following him, not bothering to see if the Crown was indeed behind him.

Monsieur Zalmanowitz glared after the Chief Superintendent and muttered, 'Prick,' just loud enough for the reporters to hear.

Then he grabbed his briefcase and followed.

The two men were left alone in the office.

The Chief Crown Prosecutor and the Chief Superintendent of the Sûreté. Allies by decree and bureaucratic structure. But not by nature or choice.

When the door had closed, Gamache walked over and locked it. Then turned to Zalmanowitz.

'Lunch, Barry?'

He pointed to a tray on a coffee table, with sandwiches and cold drinks.

Zalmanowitz raised his brows in surprise. Then he smiled. It was not an altogether friendly smile.

He took a salmon with dill and cream cheese on a St-Viateur bagel.

'How did you know I'd start a fight?' he asked.

'I didn't,' said Gamache, reaching for a smoked meat from Schwartz's delicatessen. 'But if you hadn't, I would've.'

He took a large bite, famished, and followed it with a long drink of iced tea.

'Well,' said Zalmanowitz after finishing half the bagel. 'You're fucking up this case nicely.'

'I think you're doing an even better job.'

'*Merci*. I am doing my worst.'

Gamache smiled tightly, and leaning back on the sofa, he crossed his legs and regarded the Crown.

'I think Judge Corriveau is beginning to suspect,' he said.

Zalmanowitz wiped his mouth with a thin paper napkin and shook his head. 'She'd never guess. It's far too outrageous. We're both lucky we have pensions. We're going to need them.'

He picked up his perspiring glass and tipped it toward the Chief Superintendent. 'To a higher court.'

Gamache lifted his glass. 'To burning ships.'

Over lunch in a nearby café, having found a shady corner of an outdoor *terrasse*, Maureen Corriveau confided in her partner.

'I think something's up.'

'Something's up?' asked Joan with amusement. 'Like the jig?'

'I wish,' said Maureen. 'That would at least mean I'd know what's going on.'

Joan's face clouded over. 'What do you mean? Are you lost? Is the case too much?'

'I can't believe you asked that,' said Maureen, genuinely hurt. 'You think I'm not up to a murder trial?'

'Not at all, but you're the one who said you didn't know what was going on. Okay, let's regroup. What's bothering you?'

'The Crown Prosecutor, who is also the head of the office for the whole province, has taken to attacking the Chief Superintendent of the Sûreté in the witness box. And, as the door was closing for the break, I heard him insult him, in front of everyone.'

'His own witness? But that doesn't make sense.'

'Worse than that, it could lead to a mistrial. I think some jury members also heard. That's what I meant. They're experienced enough to know better, and old enough to keep their personal feelings in check. They're on the same side, after all. I can't get a handle on what's happening and why. Especially in a case that should be so simple. The head of the Sûreté himself was practically a witness to the crime. His wife found the body, for God's sake.'

She shook her head and pushed her salad away.

'Maybe they just don't like each other,' said Joan. 'It happens. Two bull elephants, two alpha males. They must've butted heads before. Lots of times.'

Maureen was nodding, but in a distracted manner. 'I'd heard rumors that they don't get along. Cops and prosecutors often don't. But it's more than that. I can't explain it. They're crossing a line. One they both know is there. I just—' She ran her hand up and down the moist glass of ice water.

'What is it?'

'It's ridiculous, but the thought crossed my mind as I walked over here that they might be doing it on purpose.'

'To screw up the case?' asked Joan. 'Not only is the jig up, but they're in cahoots?'

Maureen gave one short grunt of laughter. 'You're quite a dame.'

'I'm sorry, I didn't mean to mock. It just seems unlikely, don't you think? Why would they do that? If you're right, they're actually trying to throw a murder trial. Gamache made the arrest. The Crown laid the charges. And now two men who don't even like each other are intentionally messing it up?'

Maureen shook her head, then nodded. 'I agree. It's ridiculous. Just a passing fancy.'

She fell into thought, while Joan watched the people strolling by on rue St-Paul.

They'd all started the day, she was sure, fresh and well turned out. But now most were wilted in the heat. Judge Corriveau could feel perspiration on her neck, and her underarms were clammy.

She was not looking forward to getting back into her robes, and sitting in the oven of a courtroom all afternoon. But at least she wasn't being grilled.

'Monsieur Gamache quoted Gandhi this morning,' she said. 'Something about a higher court.'

Joan tapped on her iPhone. 'Got it. *There is a higher court than courts of justice and that is the court of conscience. It supersedes all other courts.*'

Maureen Corriveau gave a short, sharp inhale. 'I just got the chills.'

'Why?'

'The head of the Sûreté proclaiming his conscience overrides our laws? Doesn't that frighten you?'

'I'm not sure he meant that,' said Joan, trying to calm

her partner. 'It seems a sort of blanket statement, not a personal credo.'

'You don't think that'll be the headline in the news? *"Head of Sûreté Follows His Conscience, Not the Law"*?'

'As long as it isn't *"Judge Goes Berserk in Courtroom".*'

Maureen laughed and got up. 'I have to get back. Thanks for lunch.'

But after taking a step away from the table, she came back.

'Do you believe it?'

'That personal conscience overrules our collective laws?' asked Joan. 'Aren't our laws based on a good conscience? The Commandments?'

'Like the law forbidding homosexuality?'

'That was years ago,' said Joan.

'Still in force in many places. That law is unconscionable.'

'Then you agree with Monsieur Gamache?' asked Joan.

'If I agreed with anyone, it would be Gandhi, not Gamache. But can a judge really believe in the court of conscience? That it supersedes all others? It sounds like anarchy.'

'It sounds like progress,' said Joan.

'It sounds like the end of a promising career on the bench,' said Maureen with a smile. She kissed Joan, then leaned down and kissed her again, whispering, 'That one's for Gandhi.'

CHAPTER 17

⁓

The two men squared off again.

While always attentive, the spectators now leaned even further forward, drawn into the square at the front of the room, like a boxing ring, where the case was being fought.

There was now an electricity in Judge Corriveau's courtroom. One she did not welcome. It was already hot enough. And as far as she was concerned, electricity and justice did not go together.

She could at least track down its source. These two men crackled with antagonism.

Bull elephants, Joan had called them.

More like rogue elephants, thought Judge Corriveau. Shitting all over her first murder trial.

But even that was wrong.

The Crown Prosecutor, Monsieur Zalmanowitz, was lithe, walking with the sinewy movement of a panther. He paced his territory, occasionally making forays past the defense table, but always keeping his eyes on the man in the witness box.

A predator sizing up his prey.

And Gamache? Sitting so calmly, as though this were his home. As though he owned the chair he sat in, the box that surrounded it, the entire room. Polite, attentive, thoughtful.

His extreme quietude was a stark contrast to the ever-pacing Crown.

Here was a patient man. Who had the good sense to wait until his attacker showed a weakness.

This was no elephant. This was no panther.

This was an apex predator, she realized. The top of the food chain.

Judge Corriveau watched as Monsieur Zalmanowitz circled closer to Gamache, and she almost gestured to the Crown, waving him away.

Warning him that the sort of composure and control Chief Superintendent Armand Gamache exhibited only came from those with no natural enemies. It would be a potentially fatal error to mistake his calm for lethargy.

An apex predator who quoted Gandhi, she marveled. And she wondered if that made Monsieur Gamache more, or less, dangerous.

And she wondered if his only real enemy was himself.

Maureen Corriveau then remembered that passing fancy, as she'd walked down the cobblestone street to meet Joan for lunch. That these two adversaries were actually allies, and only pretending to be at each other's throats.

But what could make them do such a thing?

She knew the answer, of course. There was only one reason they were acting as they were.

To trap an even bigger predator.

Judge Corriveau looked over at the defendant.

Was it possible someone who looked so very weak, so beaten, was something else entirely?

'Before we broke for lunch, you were telling us, Chief Superintendent, about bringing the news of Katie Evans's murder to her husband,' said the Crown. 'We left you in the restaurant.'

'The bistro, *oui*,' said Gamache, and saw, with satisfaction, Zalmanowitz bristle at the small correction.

For his part, Barry Zalmanowitz watched the head of the Sûreté, sitting so comfortably in the witness box, and was grateful it wasn't difficult to attack the man.

Despite their cordial lunch, he didn't have to pretend to loathe Gamache. He actually did. And had for many years. How many times had they argued about a prosecution? Sometimes the Crown refused to lay charges against a person Gamache believed was a killer. But Zalmanowitz argued there wasn't enough, or strong enough, evidence.

Your fault, Gamache, Zalmanowitz had said.

And Chief Inspector Gamache, then the head of homicide for the Sûreté, had all but called him a coward, who wouldn't risk a prosecution unless there was absolutely no chance of losing.

Yes, it was ironic that this whole plan rested on everyone believing they detested each other. The beauty of the plan was that they actually did.

As he paced the courtroom and watched the still man in the witness box, he couldn't detect any outright rancor on Gamache's part. Though there was wariness.

So great was the threat that Armand Gamache had been forced to approach a man uniquely situated to help. But one he didn't like and didn't trust.

It had been the most extraordinary meeting of Zalmanowitz's career.

Gamache had flown to Moncton and driven to Halifax, while Zalmanowitz had flown directly there.

They'd sat in a diner at the waterfront. A dive even by the questionable standards of the dockworkers and fishermen who surrounded them.

And there, in the shadow of ships bound for ports around

the world, the Chief Superintendent of the Sûreté had out-lined his plan to the Chief Crown Prosecutor.

And when he'd finished, and was completely and utterly exposed, Armand Gamache had waited. A very slight tremble in his right hand the only hint of stress.

The head of the Crown Prosecutor's office had sat there, stunned. At the hubris of the man. At the scope of the plan. At his stupidity, bordering on brilliance, to come to the last person on earth likely to help him. And ask not just for help.

'You're asking me to end my career.'

'Almost certainly. And I'll end mine.'

'Yours has barely begun,' Zalmanowitz reminded him. 'You've just come out of retirement. You've been the Chief Superintendent for a nanosecond. I doubt you even know where the toilet is on your floor. I have thirty years in the Crown's office. I'm the head of the whole fucking thing. And you want me to not only throw it all away, but risk imprison-ment? At the very least, humiliation? You want me to bring shame on my whole career and family?'

'Yes, please.'

Gamache had looked so sincere when he'd said that, before breaking into a smile. But for just a moment Zalmanowitz had wondered if this was some sort of elaborate scheme to get rid of him. Have him self-destruct. Lure him into doing something if not outright illegal then surely unethical.

And have him not simply fired, but ruined.

But looking into those eyes, searching that face, Zalmano-witz realized that Gamache was many things, but he was not cruel. And that would have been cruel.

Armand Gamache was serious.

'I need to go for a walk,' said the Crown, and when Gamache started to get up, Zalmanowitz forcefully put out his hand. 'Alone.'

He'd walked and walked and walked, up and down the pier. Past the huge container ships. He smelled the seaweed, the rust, the fish.

Up and down, Zalmanowitz paced.

If he did this, he couldn't tell anyone. Not even his wife. Not until it was over.

And who knew? Maybe people would understand. Would see that the why overrode the how.

But walk as he might, he couldn't escape the reality. If he did this thing, if he threw in with Gamache, it would be the end. He'd be pilloried. And rightly so.

It went against everything he believed in. Everything he stood for. Everything Gamache believed in too, to be fair.

So great was the threat that both men had to be willing to compromise their deepest beliefs.

Would he regret joining Gamache? Would he regret not?

What were the chances of success? Pretty low, he knew. But the chances were zero if he didn't try.

And Gamache had no other options. He was it, Zalmanowitz knew. Because of his position. Because of the respect he commanded in his profession. He would use it all up, empty the well of goodwill. In this one act.

Zalmanowitz stopped and watched the boats in Halifax Harbour, and felt the bracing sea air on his face.

Charlotte had loved going down to the old port of Montréal, to stare at the ships. Wide-eyed. She'd ask her dad where each was going and where each was from. Barry, of course, didn't know, so he made it up. Choosing the most exotic-sounding places.

Zanzibar.

Madagascar.

The North Pole.

Atlantis.

Ste-Crème-Glacée-de-Poutine.

'You made that up,' said Charlotte, laughing so hard she'd started to cry.

Well, he thought, if he could make up a story for his little girl, he could make up one for everyone else in Québec.

'Come along,' he whispered. 'We're going on a journey.'

He'd walked back to the diner, where Gamache was waiting. A tall, quivering slice of lemon meringue pie in front of each of them.

Zalmanowitz sat down.

While Armand Gamache hadn't mentioned Charlotte, Zalmanowitz suspected he knew. And he both hated the man across from him for asking this thing. And almost loved him, for asking this thing.

'I'll do it.'

Gamache had nodded, holding his eyes. 'We have to move quickly.'

And they had.

That had been months ago, in November.

Charges were laid, preliminary hearings were held.

And now it was July and they were into the second day of the murder trial.

It was almost impossible to tell if things were going their way. It seemed like such a long shot, and yet they'd made it this far. Still, the plan could fail. The ground could fall out from underneath them.

If it did, they'd go down together. But the consolation for Zalmanowitz was that at least his hands would be around Gamache's throat when they hit bottom.

'How did Patrick Evans take the news of his wife's death?' he asked the Chief Superintendent.

CHAPTER 18

'Tell me here,' said Patrick Evans, as his friends closed ranks beside him.

Not unlike, Gamache thought, what they had done the evening before, when protecting the cobrador.

'*Non, monsieur*,' said Chief Inspector Lacoste, gently but firmly. 'Please come with us.'

She pointed to what she knew was a back room, reserved for private functions. Like birthdays. And homicide investigations.

'May we?' asked Lea.

'Yes, of course,' said Lacoste, allowing Matheo and Lea to stay with their friend.

They walked into the back room and Beauvoir closed the door.

There was no fireplace here to spread both warmth and cheer. The bank of French doors looked out over a bleak back garden and the Rivière Bella Bella beyond, in full flow.

The air outside seemed to have congealed, forming a heavy mist that almost obscured the forest behind.

Beauvoir found the light switches and turned them all on, then he turned up the heat, to take the chill off the room.

Lacoste looked at Patrick Evans and saw him brace. As did

Matheo Bissonette. As did Lea Roux. As though she were the firing squad and they the target.

Without preamble, she broke the news. Quietly, softly, with compassion but also with clarity.

'I'm sorry, sir, but your wife is dead.'

Isabelle Lacoste had learned long ago that simplicity was best. A short, sharp declaration of the fact. So that there could be no doubt, no back door through which denial could slip.

There was no gentle way to break news. To break hearts. And doing it slowly simply added to the trauma.

Matheo took a step closer to his friend and, placing a hand on his arm, he squeezed.

Despite the fact Patrick Evans must've known, it still came as a shock. Apparently.

He sat down slowly, his mouth opening as his body lowered.

There was a tap on the door and Beauvoir opened it. Olivier was there with a bottle of Scotch and some glasses. And a box of tissues.

'*Merci*,' Jean-Guy whispered and, taking the tray, he closed the door.

Lacoste pulled a chair over so that she was sitting directly across from Patrick, their knees almost touching.

His hair was dark, short, cut in the manner of a much older man. He was clean-shaven and handsome, but his personality wasn't strong. Even in grief, some people emanated confidence. Or, at least, a core. This man seemed hollow. Pale in every way.

'She was found in the church,' Lacoste said, holding his blue eyes, though she wasn't sure how much he was taking in.

'How . . . ?' he asked.

'The coroner needs to investigate, but it seems she was beaten.'

'Oh, Jesus.'

Patrick lowered his eyes, then dragged them back up. But not to Lacoste.

'How could this happen?' he asked Matheo.

'I don't know.' Bissonette shook his head and looked incredulous.

Beside him, Lea looked sick. Physically ill.

Patrick's lips moved, but either there were too many words, tripping over each other to get out, or no words at all.

Just a chasm in this already empty man.

'When was the last time you saw your wife?' asked Chief Inspector Lacoste.

'Last night,' he said. 'Outside.'

'She was outside?' asked Lacoste. 'She didn't come to bed?'

'I thought she had. I went to sleep, and just assumed she'd come back.'

'But she didn't,' said Lacoste, and Patrick nodded.

'What was she doing outside?' asked Lacoste.

'Katie liked to go for walks in the evening,' said Lea.

'What time did you get back from dinner?' Lacoste asked.

'Don't know,' said Patrick.

'They were back by the time we left your place,' Matheo said to Gamache. 'About ten, right?'

Gamache nodded.

'Did you see her out for her walk?' asked Lacoste.

Matheo and Lea shook their heads.

'Was the cobrador there when you walked back to the B&B?'

'The cobrador,' said Patrick, suddenly waking up. 'Oh Christ, this's because of the cobrador, isn't it?'

He'd turned to Matheo, then looked at Lea. His eyes wide with panic.

'I don't know,' said Lea, leaning in to him. Embracing him, awkwardly. Patrick's arms didn't return the hug.

'How could this happen?' he mumbled, his voice muffled by Lea's solid body. 'I don't understand.'

But now his eyes were on Isabelle Lacoste.

There was a lot not to understand, she thought, watching them. But before this was over, she'd have answers.

She glanced at Beauvoir, who was watching Patrick Evans with those shrewd eyes of his. Then her gaze moved on to Monsieur Gamache.

His hands were clasped behind his back and he was staring out the window. A less astute observer might think he'd lost interest. But Lacoste could see, even in profile, the intense focus of the man. Listening closely to every word, every inflection.

He often said that words told them what someone was thinking, but the tone told them how they felt.

Both vital.

Yes, facts were necessary. But frankly, anyone could be trained to collect a bloodstain or find a hair. Or an affair. Or a bank balance that didn't balance.

But feelings? Only the bravest wandered into that fiery realm.

And that's what the chief explored. Elusive, volatile, unpredictable, often dangerous feelings. Searching out that one raw, wild emotion. That had led to murder.

And he'd taught her to do the same thing.

Gamache shifted his gaze now, from the dense forest, to Patrick, Matheo, Lea at the front of the room.

And the deep brown, thoughtful eyes came to rest. Not on Patrick Evans but on Matheo Bissonette.

'Where did you go for dinner last night?'

Patrick shrugged, what little energy he had seeping away.

'I think it was a place in Knowlton,' said Matheo. 'Le Relais. Right?'

But Patrick didn't react.

'Were you worried when you didn't see your wife this morning?' asked Lacoste.

He roused himself. 'Not really. I thought she was with her.' He pointed to Lea.

Her.

His words were coming slower, thicker.

'And we thought she was with Patrick,' said Matheo.

'It wasn't until the police showed up that we realized no one had seen Katie all day,' said Lea.

Lacoste leaned forward, toward Patrick Evans. 'Can you think who might have done this to your wife?'

'No.' He looked at her as a child might.

'Can you back off a little?' asked Lea. 'Can't you see he's in shock?'

She poured him a Scotch and he swallowed it in one go.

Lacoste studied Patrick for a moment. There was certainly something wrong with him. He seemed wrapped in cotton batting. Muffled. It could have been shock, compounded by a natural lassitude.

But judging by his pupils, it was more than that.

'What can you tell me about the cobrador?' she asked.

Patrick stared at her. 'Conscience. Right?'

He looked at Matheo, but his eyes weren't focusing and he was beginning to sway.

Beauvoir knelt down and looked in Patrick's eyes. Patrick stared back, his mouth slightly open. His soft lips glistening with spittle.

'Have you taken something?' Beauvoir asked, speaking

directly, slowly, clearly to Patrick, who just continued to stare.

'He did this,' slurred Patrick. 'We all know who did this.'

'Who?' asked Beauvoir.

'He means the cobrador, of course,' said Matheo, bending over Patrick. 'Right? Who else?'

'Monsieur Evans, look at me,' said Lacoste, speaking loudly, clearly. 'Why was your wife in the church?'

'No one goes to church,' he said, his words barely intelligible.

Beauvoir turned to the Sûreté agent taking notes. 'Get Dr Harris, the coroner. Quickly.'

As he said it, Patrick slumped sideways, and Beauvoir caught him, cradled him, and lowered him, with Lacoste's help, off the chair and to the floor.

'What's he on?' Beauvoir asked, not looking up as he spoke, but quickly checking Patrick's vitals.

Gamache took off his coat, rolled it, and placed it under Patrick's head.

'I gave him an Ativan,' said Lea, her eyes wide. 'Is he okay?'

'When?' asked Beauvoir.

'Just before you arrived. He was hyperventilating and beginning to panic. I wanted to calm him down.'

'Just one?' asked Beauvoir, looking from the unconscious man to his friends.

'One.' Lea rummaged through the large bag she'd dropped on the floor and found the pill bottle.

'But you also gave him a Scotch,' said Lacoste.

'Shit,' said Lea. 'Fuck, fuck, fuck. I didn't think.'

When Sharon Harris arrived, she took Beauvoir's place beside the man.

Everyone backed off while she checked him.

'Who is he?' she asked as she worked.

'Katie Evans's husband, Patrick,' said Lacoste, and got a swift glance from Dr Harris. 'We think it's Ativan and Scotch.'

The qualifier was not lost on the doctor, or the officers.

'Do you have the bottle?'

Lea handed her the pill bottle. She examined it, opening the top and pouring out a few pills. Replacing them, she handed it back to Lea. Without comment.

'He's just passed out. Probably not used to tranquilizers. And the Scotch didn't help. We should get him to bed. Monsieur Evans?' Dr Harris bent down and spoke into his ear. 'Patrick. Wake up. We're going to get you back to your bed.'

She pinched his earlobe and his eyes fluttered open, though they remained unfocused.

'Can we get him to his feet?'

Beauvoir and Matheo hauled him up and supported the man, who looked like a drunk. His head lolling, his eyes blinking. It was clear he was at least trying to come to the surface, though not quite making it.

Dr Harris led them back out through the crowd in the bistro.

Lea made to follow, but Gamache called her back.

'Is he on something?' he asked, examining her closely.

'No.'

'Now's the time to tell us.'

'I am telling you. Patrick's the straightest of all of us. Barely even drinks.' She shook her head. 'This's my fault. It was stupid to give him that Ativan.'

And Scotch, thought Gamache, studying the woman. She looked genuinely concerned.

'Everything okay?' asked Olivier, poking his head in and looking worried.

'*Oui*. Monsieur Evans is overcome,' said Gamache. 'He needs to rest.'

'Anything I can do, just ask.'

'*Merci, patron*,' said Gamache, and when Olivier had left, he indicated a seat for Lea.

She sat, and Gamache and Lacoste joined her.

'Can you think of anyone who might want to harm Katie?' asked Gamache.

'I honestly can't,' she said.

Lacoste, not the cynical sort, always felt a slight alarm go off when anyone answered 'honestly' to an interrogation question. Though Lea Roux did seem sincere, and sincerely shocked.

Though she was, Lacoste reminded herself, a politician. And politics was theater.

Now it was Lea's turn to examine them. Her sharp eyes took in the senior Sûreté officers.

'You think the cobrador killed Katie, don't you?' She looked from one to the other.

'As do Monsieur Evans and your husband. But you don't?'

'I don't see why he would,' said Lea. 'That would imply that the cobrador came here for Katie. That she was its target all along.'

'Maybe,' said Lacoste. 'What we do know is that the man in the costume disappeared and Madame Evans was murdered. It seems a bit too much of a coincidence, don't you think?'

Lea Roux thought about it. 'But that doesn't mean she was his target. Maybe he just lashed out, and she was there. On her nightly walk.'

'But she wasn't on her walk, was she?' said Lacoste. 'She was in the church. Why was that?'

Lea sat back. Considering. 'When we traveled, Katie

185

often went into churches. As an architect, they fascinated her. Flying buttresses.' She smiled. 'That's all I can remember, and only because it became a running joke. Great big buttresses.'

She brought herself out of her reminiscence. 'But that was Notre-Dame in Paris. Chartres. Mont St-Michel. Not exactly your village chapel.'

Gamache crossed his legs and nodded. There certainly were no flying buttresses in St Thomas's, though it was a nicer place to sit than Notre-Dame. It all depended, of course, on what you were looking for.

'Then why do you think she was there?' he asked, repeating Lacoste's question.

Lea shook her head. 'Maybe she just needed some quiet time. Maybe it was cold and she went in to warm up. I honestly don't know.'

Gamache noticed that Isabelle had not said that Katie was found in the basement, nor had she told them that Katie was in the cobrador costume.

A costume that was highly symbolic. It spoke of sin, of debt. Of the unconscionable and the uncollected. It spoke of revenge and shame. It was an accusation.

And it had been placed on the dead woman.

Not in error, but on purpose. With a purpose.

Yes, thought Gamache, there was a connection between Madame Evans and the cobrador.

The question was, did her friends know what it was?

'This's my fault,' said Lea. 'If I hadn't protected him last night, he might've been scared away. Or beaten. But at least Katie would be alive.' Then she turned to Gamache. 'It's your fault too. You could've done something. But all you did was talk to him. You kept saying he wasn't doing anything wrong. Well, now he has. If you'd stepped in, she'd still be alive.'

Gamache said nothing, because there was nothing to be said. He'd already explained many times to the villagers that there was nothing he could do. Though given what had happened, he knew he'd go back over it and over it. Wondering if that was really true.

He also knew that her rage was really directed at whoever had picked up that bat and killed her friend. He just happened to be a more convenient target.

So he let her have at it. Without backing away. Without defending himself. And when she'd finished, he was silent.

Lea Roux was in tears now, having opened the gates to her anger, her sorrow.

'Oh, shit,' she gasped, trying to regain control of herself, as though crying for a dead friend was shameful. 'What have we done?'

'You did nothing wrong,' said Lacoste. 'And neither did Chief Superintendent Gamache. Whoever did this is to blame.'

Lea took the tissue Lacoste offered and thanked her, wiping her face and blowing her nose. But still crying. Softer now. More sorrow. Less rage.

'You can't really think the cobrador thing came here for Katie,' said Lea.

'Do you have another theory?' Lacoste asked.

'I don't know,' she admitted. 'Maybe the cobrador did do it, but not on purpose. Maybe Katie followed him and found out who he was, and he killed her.'

Gamache nodded slowly. That had occurred to him as well.

But then, why put her in the costume?

And again, why kill her at all? It seemed an extreme overreaction to being exposed.

But that could mean that she recognized him.

Gamache returned his gaze to the fog outside. Far from being oppressive, he found it soothing. Enveloping, not smothering.

Was Katie Evans's murder premeditated? Had she been the target all along? Or was it the impulsive act of a person who'd been found out? Cornered in that church basement?

'So you can't think of anyone who might wish your friend harm?' asked Lacoste.

'Not that I know of. She was an architect. She built homes.'

'Did any project go badly wrong? An accident maybe? A collapse?'

'No, never.'

'Her marriage to Patrick,' said Gamache. 'Was it a happy one?'

'I think so. She wanted children but he didn't. You might've noticed, he's a bit of a child himself. Not in a playful way, more in a needy way. He needed mothering. Katie gives him that. She gives us all that. She's very maternal. Would've made a wonderful mother. She's godmother to our eldest. Never forgets a birthday.'

Lea looked down at the tissue, twisted into shreds in her hands.

'I think their relationship was good,' she said. 'I couldn't see it myself. Especially when—' She looked at Lacoste, then over at Gamache.

They remained silent, waiting for her to finish the sentence.

'When she could've had Edouard.'

'Your friend from college,' said Gamache. 'The one who killed himself.'

'Or just fell,' she said. It was something she had to believe. Struggled to believe. Lea gave a huge sigh. 'Love. What can you do?'

Gamache nodded. What could you do?

Beauvoir, Matheo and Dr Harris returned, having gotten Patrick to bed.

'He'll be fine,' said Sharon Harris. 'Needs sleep is all.'

'I'll walk you out,' said Gamache, putting on his coat.

Instead of going through the crowded bistro, they took the doors out onto the patio, and around the back of the shops.

In the bakery next door, through the window, they saw Anton and Jacqueline, talking.

'Monsieur Evans's friend,' said the coroner. 'The woman. Is that Lea Roux, the politician?'

'It is.'

'She said she gave him one Ativan. I've never seen a collapse like that in an adult from just one.'

'You think she gave him more?'

'Two at least. Of course, she might've been embarrassed to admit it, or maybe she gave him the bottle and he helped himself.'

'I doubt that, don't you? Is it possible it's not Ativan, but something else?'

She stopped and considered it.

Gamache could feel the mist creep down his collar and up his sleeves.

'It could be. You suspect a pharmaceutical, an opioid? Without a blood test, I can't tell. Is there a reason you suspect it?'

'Not really. There's just so much of it about.'

'You have no idea,' said the coroner, who saw victims every day on her stainless steel gurney.

Gamache didn't say anything, but he actually had a far better idea than Dr Harris.

He walked her to her car, but before she got in, she turned

to him. 'Monsieur Evans kept repeating something about a bad conscience. Is that significant, Armand?'

'The costume the victim was in was something to do with a conscience' was all he said, and she could tell it was all she was going to get.

There wasn't time, or need, to tell Dr Harris about the cobrador.

What could sound like a confession on Patrick Evans's part was simply, almost certainly, a warning. There was a bad, a very bad, conscience at work.

'*Merci*,' he said. 'Your report?'

'As soon as I can. I hope to have something to you by morning.'

When he returned to the back room of the bistro, he found Matheo and Lea sitting facing Lacoste and Beauvoir. Not exactly, explicitly, adversarial. But close.

Lines had been drawn.

He joined Lacoste and Beauvoir.

'We've been thinking, assuming, the cobrador killed Katie,' said Matheo. 'But maybe not.'

'Go on,' said Chief Inspector Lacoste.

'The cobrador came here for someone. Someone who'd done something terrible. Isn't it possible he killed Katie?'

'Why would he?' asked Lacoste. 'Wouldn't he be more likely to kill the guy in the costume?'

'Maybe he did,' said Lea. 'And maybe Katie saw it happen.'

'Then where is he?' asked Lacoste. 'The fellow in the costume? Why leave Katie's body behind, but hide his?'

'Maybe it's not hidden, really,' said Matheo. 'Maybe you just haven't found it.'

Lacoste raised her brows. She was actually a few steps ahead of them, having ordered the woods around the village searched.

'What can you tell us about Madame Evans?' asked Lacoste.

'Can't tell you much about her childhood,' said Matheo. 'I know she was raised in Montréal. Has a sister. Her parents— Oh,' he sighed, when he realized they would have to be told.

'Do you have their address?' asked Gamache, and took it down from Lea.

'We met, as we told you last night,' Matheo said to Gamache, 'at university. We were taking different courses but were in the same dorm. A wild place. My God, I can't believe we survived.'

Though, thought Gamache, not all of them did.

'Away from home for the first time,' said Matheo. 'Young. No rules. No boundaries. All the restraints were off, you know? We went wild. But Katie was calm. She was always up for stuff, but she had self-control. Not a prude, more like common sense. The rest of us had sorta lost our minds.'

'Katie was our safe harbor,' said Lea.

Gamache nodded. What they described were almost exactly the same qualities that had attracted him to Reine-Marie.

A settled warmth, a stability that wasn't staid. A calm in the maelstrom that was youth. And sometimes middle age.

'Some of the shit we did,' said Matheo, still back in those days. 'No one to tell us to stop. It was a bit like *Lord of the Flies*.'

'But who among you was Ralph and who was Jack?' asked Gamache.

'And who was the unfortunate Piggy?' asked Matheo.

'I don't understand,' said Lea.

'I'm sorry,' said Gamache. 'That was a digression. My apologies.'

But Beauvoir, who also did not understand the references,

did understand one thing. Monsieur Gamache never made an unintentional detour.

He added *Lord of the Flies* to things he needed to look up.

'There were drugs, of course,' asked Gamache.

'Oh, yes, there were drugs. Quite a lot at one stage, but that calmed down after a while. It sorta blew itself out, you know?'

Gamache did know. From his own experiences, but also from his own children. Especially Daniel, his eldest.

University was a time of education, and not all of it in a classroom. It was a time to experiment. To grab life. To consume at random, like the first time at a buffet. And then to stagger to a stop, overstuffed and nauseous. And sometimes unable to pay the bill.

They got the drugs, the booze, the random sex and the consequences out of their system. And began to make more thoughtful choices.

But some never quite managed to push away from the buffet.

What were the chances that four of them would go wild, and all four of them would find their way back to civilization?

Wasn't there a pretty good chance one of them wouldn't make it all the way back?

And then he remembered. There was one. A fifth.

'Tell us about Edouard.'

'What?' said Matheo. 'Why?'

'It was a tragedy,' said Gamache. 'And those reverberate.'

'But it wasn't Katie's fault,' said Lea. 'She wasn't even there when he fell. She and Patrick had snuck off into his dorm room. If it was anyone's fault, it was the dealer who sold Edouard the drugs.'

'And who was he?' asked Lacoste.

'You're kidding, right?' said Matheo. 'That was fifteen

years ago. I barely remember the names of my professors. And the guy took off right after Edouard died. As soon as the cops started asking questions.'

'So you don't know his name?' asked Beauvoir.

'No. Look, Edouard died years ago. It can't have anything to do with Katie today.'

'You might be surprised,' said Gamache, 'how many murders start in the distant past. They have time to fester, to grow. To become malformed and grotesque. Like those men and women abandoned on the island off Spain. But they always come back.'

He commanded the quiet room, the only sound the slight *tip-tap* of sleet on the panes.

'Where were you last night?' Lacoste asked.

'At the Gamaches' for dinner,' said Matheo. 'And then bed.'

'You didn't hear Madame Evans leave the B&B or return?'

'*Non*, I heard nothing,' said Matheo, and Lea nodded.

The Sûreté officers walked Lea and Matheo to the door.

When they'd left, Lacoste and Beauvoir turned to Gamache.

'Do you think the killer is long gone?' Lacoste asked.

'*Non*. I think whoever killed Katie Evans is still here. And is watching us.'

CHAPTER 19

'What're they doing now?' asked Jacqueline. 'They're still there.'

Anton looked out the bay window of Sarah's Boulangerie toward St Thomas's Church, while Jacqueline stood at the work-table behind the counter and kneaded. Pummeling the dough.

'They've taken her away,' said Anton, turning from the window. 'The ambulance has gone.'

He'd come in with the news that a body had been found in the chapel. That it was one of the visitors. Katie Evans.

By then, they'd known. But still, having it confirmed was a shock.

Anton tried sitting, but found he couldn't get comfortable, and so he paced the small boulangerie, while trying not to make it look like pacing.

When he'd woken up that morning and the cobrador was gone, he'd thought it would be okay. That they didn't need to tell Gamache anything. But now—

A woman had been killed and there were cops everywhere.

It was worse than ever.

'We should've told them,' said Jacqueline, pulling sticky dough off her fingers.

'That we knew it was a cobrador? You think it had something to do with what happened.'

'Of course it did,' she snapped, then scraping the dough off the counter, she threw it down with such force it flattened. The air, the life, knocked out of it. It would not rise now. 'You can't be that much of an idiot.'

He looked at her as though he'd been the one kneaded and thumped. And winded by a blow.

'Honestly, Anton. We were told about the cobrador last year. And now it's here? Didn't it occur to you that maybe it's come for us?'

'But why would it?' he asked.

'I don't know,' said Jacqueline. 'Because we worked for a madman?'

'They're the ones who left,' said Anton. 'Not us. Besides, we don't know anything.'

'We know enough. Maybe he sent the cobrador as a warning. To keep our mouths shut.'

But if the cobrador had come for them, why was Madame Evans dead?

The cops hadn't yet told them exactly what had happened, but it was obvious. Madame Evans wasn't just dead. Judging by the activity at the church, it was neither natural nor an accident.

'Is it too late to say something?' he asked.

'Maybe not.' She punched the dough. 'But it'll look bad. They'll wonder why we didn't tell them sooner.'

'Why didn't we?'

But he knew perfectly well.

He remembered that dark mask, facing the bistro. Facing him. Boring through the windows and walls, into the kitchen, where he washed dishes.

195

The Conscience. That was threatening everything Anton had built up.

Yes. That was why he hadn't wanted to say anything to that Gamache fellow. The head of the whole Sûreté. In case he figured it out. Realized who he was.

Even Jacqueline didn't know.

He looked at her. Those long fingers in the dough, once so sensuous, were now claws, ripping the life out of a baguette.

He knew why he'd wanted to keep silent about the cobrador. But he began to wonder why she did.

The door between the bakery and the bistro swung open with such force that it banged against the wall, and both Jacqueline and Anton jumped.

Lea Roux stepped in, followed by Matheo.

'We need—' began Lea, but stopped abruptly when she saw Anton.

They stared at each other. He'd seen them before, but only briefly. They were visitors, that's all he knew. But now he thought, maybe, he recognized them. Or at least her.

'There you are.' Olivier walked in behind them. He acknowledged Lea and Matheo with a sympathetic nod. He'd spoken to them in the bistro, and offered condolences.

Now his attention turned to his dishwasher. 'I've been looking all over for you.' His voice was appropriately solemn and courteous, though annoyance was poking through. 'I need you in the kitchen. It's a little busy.'

Olivier gave a strained smile and it was clear that, if not for the others present, he'd have said something else. In a whole other way.

'Sorry,' said Anton. He hurried over to the door, but paused to look at Jacqueline. 'You okay?'

When she nodded, he turned to Lea and Matheo. '*Désolé*. It's terrible.'

It was clear she'd been crying, her eyes were puffy and red.

Anton followed Olivier through the crowded bistro, filled with talk of murder, to the kitchens, filled with the scent of herbs and rich, comforting sauces, and the clatter of pots and pans and dishes.

To others it was a cacophony. To Anton it was a symphony. Operatic even. The clanging and banging of creation, of drama, of tension. Of rivalries. Of divas. Competing flavors and competing chefs. Heartbreak even. As soufflés fell. As casseroles burned.

But most of the time what rose from those noises, that grand tumult, was something wonderful. Beautiful. Exciting and comforting.

Anton had wept once, in Italy, when he'd tasted a perfect gelato. And once in Renty, France, when he'd taken a bite of baguette. A bread so sublime people traveled hours to buy one.

Yes. To others a kitchen was a convenience. Even a chore. To a precious few, it was their world. A messy, wonderful world. His world. His sanctuary. And he longed to get back into it. To hide. And hope the Sûreté didn't figure out who he was.

'Let's go,' said Olivier, holding open the swinging door to the kitchen. 'There's lots to do. Not just here, but the Sûreté agents are going to need sandwiches and drinks.'

'I'll see to it,' said Anton.

Olivier relaxed just a little. '*Merci.*'

Once back at the church, Isabelle Lacoste sent an agent into Knowlton, to interview staff at the restaurant. See if they remembered the Evanses. Another agent was sent into the village with a list of the people to be interviewed.

She invited Chief Superintendent Gamache to sit in.

He declined. 'Unless you need me, Isabelle.'

She thought for a moment. 'Well, they'd be more likely to tell the truth, since you know them and know most of their movements in the last day or so. But,' she smiled and shrugged, 'if they lie, they lie.'

It was not as cavalier as it sounded, Gamache knew.

'You'll join us for dinner and stay over, I hope,' he said. 'And perhaps we can compare notes.'

With him at the interviews, everyone would be on a short leash. Forced to tell the truth. Which, granted, was helpful in a murder investigation.

But not, perhaps, quite as helpful as a lie.

A lie didn't necessarily make someone a killer. But it hurried the sorting process. The truthful from the untruthful. Those with nothing to hide. And those with a secret.

A lie was a light. One that grew into a floodlight, that eventually illuminated the person among them with the biggest secret. The most to hide.

Jean-Guy Beauvoir made himself comfortable in the study at the Gamache home and waited for the Internet to connect.

Few could find Three Pines, hidden in the valley, and that included the satellites that provided Internet coverage for most of the planet. The village was civilization adjacent. The information superhighway zoomed overhead. And Three Pines was a pothole.

But having witnessed untold brutality in cities and towns, Jean-Guy Beauvoir had come to believe that 'civilization' might be overrated. Except for pizza delivery, of course.

But it was possible to get a book from Myrna's shop, take it into Olivier's bistro, and read it in peace, while drinking rich *café au lait* and eating a buttery croissant from Sarah's Boulangerie.

Did that make up for no iPhone or pizza delivery?

'*Non,*' he muttered as he shifted impatiently in his chair and yearned for high-speed wireless and a large all-dressed.

The dial-up, primitive, maddening, noisy and unreliable, had reached the shrieking stage, as though it was afraid to connect to the outside world.

'It's still better than what we've had in some places,' the chief always reminded Beauvoir when he grumbled about the wood-burning modem.

While Beauvoir waited, he looked out the window. He could see technicians taking equipment off vans and lugging it into St Thomas's. He marveled at Lacoste's luck. To have such an Incident Room right next to the crime scene. Warm, dry, with running water, a fridge. A toilet.

'A coffeemaker, for chrissake,' he mumbled.

She didn't even have to go outside, which, in Beauvoir's opinion, was always an advantage.

It was a far cry from some of the places he and his father-in-law had been forced to use as they'd investigated murders across Québec.

The tents, the bobbing and corkscrewing fishing boats, the shacks, the caves.

He'd told Annie about the outhouse that'd once been their headquarters, but she'd refused to believe him.

'Ask your dad,' he'd said.

'I will not.' She laughed in her easy way. 'You're just trying to set me up. Entrapment, monsieur. I'll have you up on charges.'

'You'd punish me?' he asked in a mock-hopeful voice. 'I'm a bad, bad boy.'

'No, you're a silly, silly boy. And, God help us, you're a father now. There're all sorts of new punishments I have lined up for you. I gave Honoré prunes for the first time. He liked them.'

But he'd been telling the truth. He and then-Chief Inspector Gamache had been investigating the murder of a survivalist in the Saguenay. The body had been found in a burned-out cabin, and the only structure left was the outhouse.

'A two-holer,' Gamache had pointed out, as though that was luxury.

'I'll just sit out here,' Beauvoir had said, pulling a rock up to a stump and setting out his notebook.

At two in the morning, the rains came, and Beauvoir had knocked on the outhouse door.

'Who is it?' Gamache had asked, politely.

Jean-Guy had peered through the half moon cut into the rickety door. 'Let me in.'

'It's unlocked. But wipe your feet first.'

They'd spent a day and a half there, sifting through evidence in the charred rubble. And interviewing 'neighbors' scattered through the forest. Most were trappers or fellow survivalists. The investigators were trying to find someone, anyone, who admitted to knowing the victim. But these people barely admitted to knowing themselves.

There'd been no Internet there at all. No laptops. No dial-up. No telephones. No nothing. Except, thankfully, toilet paper. And the sleeping bags, water, food packets and matches they'd marched in with.

They'd tacked up notepaper on the weathered walls of

the outhouse and made flowcharts of suspects. It became almost cozy.

'Did you catch whoever did it?' Annie had asked. She'd been seduced by the story, and her lawyer mind had reluctantly told her that he was telling the truth.

She listened, rapt. As he listened, rapt, to her stories.

'We did. Through cunning, finely honed reasoning, animal—'

'He gave himself up, didn't he?'

'No.' Though Jean-Guy couldn't help but smile at the memory. 'He came back looking for the water filtration system the dead man had. You should've seen his face when your father and I strolled out of the outhouse.'

Annie had laughed until she almost wet herself.

The Internet connected and Jean-Guy swung around, his hands hovering over the keyboard.

He had a bunch of competing priorities. But the first was obvious.

He fired off a quick email to Annie, to let her know what had happened and that he'd be spending at least the night, perhaps longer, at her parents' place.

As he wrote, he ached for her. For Honoré. For the feel and scent of them.

'Miss you,' Annie wrote back. 'Hope it's not a two-holer.'

It had become their code for big shit.

And then he typed in *Lord of the Flies*, and hit enter.

'Clara?' Myrna called.

The cottage was in near darkness, just a lamp on in the living room.

Myrna switched on the lights and the cheerful kitchen appeared. Empty.

She didn't want to disturb her friend if she was napping. But Myrna suspected after the discovery of the day, they'd all have trouble sleeping.

When Armand had returned home, they'd left. Knowing the two of them would want to be alone.

'Jesus, you woke me up, you great pile of . . . clothing.'

Myrna, once she'd returned to her skin, looked over at the doorway between the kitchen and the living room. Framed there was the demented and bedraggled old poet. And her duck. Feathers ruffled.

'Clothing?'

'Okay, I meant shit, but Michael has asked me to be more polite. So I'd appreciate it if anytime I speak to you, you replace the appropriate word with "shit".'

Myrna took a deep breath in through her nostrils, and out through her mouth. And began to worry that Ruth might actually wiggle her way into heaven with the help of a seriously deluded archangel. In which case . . .

'Where's Clara?'

'How the fuck should I know, shithead?'

'Which word would you like me to replace?'

'Hmmm, let me think about that.'

There was really only one place Clara might be. The place she always went when things went bad.

'There you are,' said Myrna, tapping softly on the door of Clara's studio.

The lights were on. Not bright. Just enough to mimic indirect morning sun.

Clara swiveled on her stool, a fine oil brush in her hand and a portrait on the easel.

Myrna could only see the edges of the painting. Clara's body blotted out the rest.

Canvases leaned against the walls of the studio. There must've been a dozen portraits. Some almost finished. Most not even close.

It looked like a roomful of abandoned people.

Myrna looked away, unable to catch their eyes. Afraid of the pleas she might see there.

'How's it coming?' she asked, nodding toward the easel.

'You tell me.'

Clara slid off the stool and stepped aside.

Myrna stared.

Normally Clara painted portraits. Extraordinary faces on canvas. Some brought smiles. Some made the viewer unaccountably melancholy, or uncomfortable, or cheerful.

Some provoked strong feelings of nostalgia for no particular reason, except that Clara was a sort of alchemist, and could render emotions, even memories, into paint. Fossilized feelings were turned into oil, then returned, framed, to the person.

But this work was different. It wasn't a portrait at all. Or, at least, not of a person.

It showed Clara's puppy, Leo, and Gracie, his littermate, the Gamaches' puppy, or something.

Leo sat, contained, magnificent, handsome and confident. While Gracie, the runt, stood beside him, cocking her head, as she often did. Quizzical. Scraggly. Ugly. Not quite meeting the eye of the observer, but looking at something beyond, behind.

Myrna almost turned to see what Gracie might be seeing.

Neither dog was adorable. Neither was cute. There was something wild about them.

Clara had captured what these two domesticated animals might have been, had they not been tamed. Had they not been captured. And civilized. She'd painted what almost certainly still lurked in their DNA.

Myrna found herself reaching out toward the canvas, then drawing her hand back.

She could almost hear the snarl.

'I'm sorry,' she said to Clara. 'I shouldn't have disturbed you. I went to the bistro, but everyone's talking about the murder, and I needed to get away but didn't want to be alone.'

'Me too. Poor Reine-Marie,' said Clara, joining Myrna on the lumpy sofa. Surrounded by the familiar and comforting scents of oil paint and old bananas.

'I tried to pump Armand,' said Myrna. 'But he just gave me that look, and walked away.'

They all knew that look. They'd seen it before. More times than you'd think possible.

There was no censure there. No suggestion they shouldn't ask. He'd be surprised if they didn't. And they'd be surprised if he answered.

More than anything, there was resolve in those eyes.

But this time there was also anger. And shock. Though he tried to hide both.

It always struck Myrna as curious that a man who'd hunted killers all his career and was now the head of the whole Sûreté should be so surprised by murder.

And yet, he was. She could see it.

He'd spoken to her about his decision not simply to return to the Sûreté, but to accept the top job.

'You think you can make a difference?' she'd asked, and seen his face break into a smile. The creases radiating from his eyes and down his cheeks.

'You sound unconvinced,' he'd said.

'I'm just trying to understand why you're doing it.'

'You're wondering if it's hubris? Pride?' he asked.

'I'm wondering, Armand, if your decision to take the top job is driven by your ego.'

This was during one of their now informal sessions, where the retired therapist listened to the retired cop, and prodded at wounds that others might ignore. Looking for infection.

'A love of power,' she'd said. 'How does that sound? Familiar?'

She spoke with only a slight smile of her own to soften the thrust.

'I don't love power,' he said, his voice still warm, but firm. 'But neither am I afraid of it when it's offered. We all have skills, things we do well. I happen to be good at finding criminals.'

'But it's more than that for you, Armand. It's as much about protecting the innocent as finding the guilty. It's good to have a mission in life, a purpose. It's not so good to have an obsession.'

He'd leaned forward then, and she'd felt the authority of the man. It wasn't smothering or threatening. If anything, it was incredibly calming.

'This isn't a hobby, this isn't a pastime. It isn't even a job. If I accept the position of Chief Superintendent of the Sûreté, it must be with complete commitment. There're big problems. Huge. I have to believe I can fix them, otherwise, why take on the task?'

He'd stared at her, his deep brown eyes thoughtful. There was no madness there. No fevered ego. But there was power there. And certainty.

The next day, he'd accepted the job. And now, months later, he was back investigating a crime. A murder. Right on his own doorstep.

Myrna sat side by side with Clara on the sofa, as though waiting for a bus, and considered.

Yes, there was reason for Armand's anger. She was angry too. She was also afraid, and she wondered if Armand was too.

Myrna glanced down at the floor, where Leo was curled on the mangy piece of rug, with his chew toy. A more adorable image would be hard to find.

Then she looked at Clara's painting of Leo. Of Gracie. Of the savagery they might be capable of. Might be hiding. And she knew that it wasn't just a portrait of the puppies.

'*Bonjour?*'

The unfamiliar voice drifted into the studio. The two women struggled out of the low sofa, and walking into the kitchen, they saw a young man in a Sûreté uniform standing there.

'There's no doorbell,' he said, slightly defensively. 'I did knock.'

'That's okay, everyone just comes in,' said Clara. 'You're here about Katie. What can we do to help?'

'Jesus, is Gamache hiring fetuses now?'

The young agent turned to the tall, thin, old piece of work framed in the doorway. Holding a duck.

'Chief Inspector Lacoste told me to find a Ruth Zardo,' he said, looking down at the wet piece of paper in his hand. 'She wasn't at her home or in the bistro. Someone said she might be here. I was told to look for a crazy old woman.'

He examined all three. From the great distance of twenty-five, they all looked old. And more than a little crazy. *But what could you expect?* he thought. Poor things. Stuck in this backwoods village. He should count their fingers and see if there were any banjos lying around.

'Fuck, fuck, fuck,' said the duck, while the three old

women stood together and stared, as though he was the strange one.

Jean-Guy called Myrna's bookshop and left a message, asking if she had a copy of *Lord of the Flies*.

Then he turned back to the synopsis online.

He read about schoolboys stranded on a deserted island. He read about happy, healthy, decent kids away from rules and authority, slowly turning into savages.

And he thought about his son, Honoré, and what he might do in a situation like that.

But mostly Jean-Guy remembered what Matheo Bissonette had said. That their first year at the Université de Montréal had been like *Lord of the Flies*.

With the cruel hunter, Jack. The rational, disciplined Ralph. The 'littluns', the youngest. Conjuring their fears. Creating beasts where none existed.

And Piggy, whose only value to the group was that his glasses made fire.

Beauvoir adjusted his own glasses and read on. Tensing, tightening up, the further he got.

He read about the boys' growing certainty that there was a beast on the island. One they needed to hunt down and kill.

Taking off his glasses, Jean-Guy rubbed his eyes.

Matheo Bissonette had likened university to *Lord of the Flies*, but he'd made it sound like fun, a wild romp.

Had those four friends, five counting the unfortunate Edouard, turned into savages? Then, in the confines of the university, turned on each other?

And what about Three Pines? It was a sort of island.

And now one among them was dead. And one of them had done it.

And the Conscience was nowhere to be found.

Beauvoir took a deep breath, chuckling at his overactive imagination.

But he decided to put reading about *Lord of the Flies* on hold and, pulling up another search, he typed in the words he'd seen that afternoon on the napkin that had fallen from Gamache's pocket.

Burn our ships.

'May I join you?' Armand asked, gesturing to the closed toilet seat as though it were an easy chair.

'Please,' said Reine-Marie, and accepted the glass of red wine he passed her, a stalactite of bubbles from the bath she was soaking in hanging from her arm. 'Nothing for you?'

'I'm afraid I'm still working,' he said, crossing his legs and making himself comfortable.

'Any closer to finding out what happened?'

'Isabelle's doing interviews. She'll join us later for dinner. I've asked her and Jean-Guy to stay overnight.'

'I should get things ready.' Reine-Marie put the glass down and made to get out of the tub, but Armand waved her to stop.

'Olivier will bring something over for dinner, and I've checked. The beds are already made and towels out.'

'Auberge Gamache is open for business?' she asked, gliding back down, deeper into the suds.

The hint of roses from the bubble bath mixed with the steam, and Armand had the strange impression that the fog from outside had permeated their home. And as he did when he walked through the mist, he had an intense feeling of comfort.

'You okay?' he asked.

'This helps,' she said. It was clear she meant the company more than the bubbles. Or even the wine.

'Would you like to talk about it?'

'It was awful, Armand. There was blood everywhere.'

She was trying not to cry, but tears streamed down her face, and he knelt beside the tub and held her hands. As she described, again, what she'd seen.

She needed to talk about it. And he needed to listen. To comfort.

'Who killed her, Armand? Was it the cobrador?'

She knew he wouldn't have the answer, but she hoped, in the extreme privacy of their own bathroom, he might have an idea he could share with her.

'I think he's at the center of it, yes. Whether he himself did it, I'm not sure.'

She looked into his eyes. 'There was nothing you could do.'

'And that's exactly what I did do. Nothing. But I'm not here to talk about me. I'm here for you.'

He caressed her skin with his thumb.

'You did do something,' she said, ignoring what he'd just said. 'You warned him. You can't arrest someone for standing on a village green. Thank God.'

'Thank God,' murmured Armand.

He knew she was right. But he could also feel his own conscience stirring. Accusing him of following the law, in lockstep. And marching right past common sense.

Katie Evans was dead. The cobrador was missing. And Reine-Marie was soaking in the bath, the blood long gone but the stain remaining.

'The law is sometimes an ass,' he said, squeezing her warm hand.

'You don't mean that.'

'I do. There are some laws that should never be upheld, enforced.'

'But you can't be the one who decides,' she said, sitting up straighter and looking at him. 'You're the head of the Sûreté. You have to follow the law, even if it's uncomfortable.' She held his eyes and spoke slowly, clearly. 'You can't kick someone off the public park in front of your home, Armand, just because you don't like it.'

She made it sound so clear, so reasonable.

'What I don't understand is how the killer knew the root cellar was there,' said Reine-Marie. 'Hardly anyone ever goes in it.'

'Why did you?'

'I had some of those Chinese lantern flowers. Long stems. I wondered if there might be a vase there, even a chipped one, I could use.' She thought for a moment. 'You think that's where the cobrador went, when he disappeared at night?'

'It's possible. Probable. The forensics report will tell us more, but it makes sense. It's a pretty good hiding spot. There's a bathroom, a kitchen. No windows in that little root cellar.'

'Did you find a weapon?'

He looked at her, confused. 'What do you mean?'

Now she looked confused. 'Do you know what killed Katie?'

'The bat, of course.'

'Of course?'

In silence he regarded her, then his eyes widened.

'Can you describe again what you saw when you found the body?'

She sat up straighter in the bath, picking up on the shift in tone. She cast her mind back. 'When I turned the light on I saw something dark, like a shadow, in the corner. It looked like a pile of black clothes. And then there was the blood.'

He squeezed her hand, and let that sit.

'What else was in the root cellar?' He hated doing this, but had to.

She frowned. 'Jars of preserves on the shelves. Some vases, mostly chipped or cracked. Some broken candlestick holders. Things we couldn't even sell in the rummage sale.'

'Anything else? On the ground?' It was as far as he could go. She had to tell him herself. Or not.

She scanned the room in her mind.

'*Non*. Why? What should I have seen? Did I miss something?'

'*Non*, but we almost did. Do you mind?' He got up.

'No, go.'

Armand bent down and he kissed her.

'It's not your fault,' she whispered.

As he left, he reflected on how many times he'd heard that from others.

It's not my fault. Though it almost always was.

CHAPTER 20

'What're you looking up?' asked Gamache, pausing in the doorway to his study.

'*Lord of the Rings*,' said Beauvoir.

He closed the search, shutting down the page.

'*Flies?*' asked Gamache.

'Right, right, *Lord of the Flies*. I just got to the part where Frodo and Ralph find the magic ring in the pig's head. But I'm not sure why the pope is on the island.'

'Wikipedia,' muttered Gamache, as he walked toward the front door. 'I need to take another look at the root cellar.'

'Why?' asked Beauvoir, following.

'Something Reine-Marie just told me.'

'What?'

Jean-Guy listened as Gamache recounted his conversation. 'You're kidding,' he said, though it was clear Gamache was not. 'I'll come with you.'

'Madame Evans's sister and parents don't know what happened, and it would be helpful to take a look at the Evanses' home in Montréal.'

Beauvoir paused, then gave a curt nod. 'I'll go. You need to stay here with Madame Gamache.'

'*Merci*, Jean-Guy. We'll probably need a court order for the home. I suspect Monsieur Evans is still asleep.'

'Don't you mean passed out?' Beauvoir asked as they put on their field coats. 'That was more than one tranquilizer. He was right out of it. Gone.'

'Dr Harris thinks it was at least two. And it might not have been Ativan.'

'An opioid?'

'Don't know.'

'Did Lea Roux give him more than he could handle on purpose? Or was it a mistake?' asked Beauvoir.

That, Gamache knew, was the real question.

The two men walked down the front path, turning up their collars against the drizzle and sleet.

'Save me some dinner,' said Jean-Guy.

As he drove toward Montréal, Jean-Guy thought about why he'd lied to Gamache just then about what he was looking at on the computer.

He'd been reading about *Lord of the Flies*, yes. But that had been earlier. The search he'd hidden from Gamache was for the words the chief had written on the napkin that had fluttered to the floor.

Burn our ships.

Beauvoir now knew what that referred to. But not why the words, the phrase, had so struck Chief Superintendent Gamache that he'd had to write them down. And keep them.

It must've been just this past lunch hour. Who did the chief have lunch with?

Toussaint. Madeleine Toussaint. The new head of Serious Crimes.

Burn our ships.

*

213

Armand Gamache walked through the late afternoon darkness. The lights from the cottages were made soft by the mist that still hung over the village. Three Pines felt slightly out of focus. Not quite of this world.

He could hear tapping, as water rolled off leaves and hit branches further down. It sounded like rain, but wasn't. It was a faux rain. Not quite real. Like so much else in this village. Like so much else in this murder. One foot in the here and now, and the other in some other world. Of a Conscience that walked. And killed.

The air smelled earthy and the cold and damp seeped through his canvas coat.

Lights were on in the church and he could see the stained-glass window, illuminated, and the village boys, the doughboys, captured there. Forever moving forward into some battle long ago won. Or lost. Moving so far forward they could never come back.

As Gamache moved forward.

Once in St Thomas's, he took the stairs to the basement.

A conference table had been set up at one end of the room, with desks filling in the middle. Technicians were working to install phone lines and computers and other equipment.

Chief Inspector Lacoste and an agent were at the conference table conducting an interview. Gamache caught her eye and she nodded imperceptibly.

'Who's there?' asked Ruth, turning stiffly in her seat.

The old poet seemed to miss the obvious but catch the imperceptible.

'Oh, it's only you.'

The agent taking notes stood, and the Sûreté technicians stopped what they were doing to stare, wide-eyed, at the new Chief Superintendent.

'*Patron*,' a few of the older ones said, nodding to the man.

The younger ones, including the agent who'd escorted Ruth up to the Incident Room, just stared.

The veteran agents knew Gamache from when he'd been head of homicide. From when he'd cleaned out the corruption, at enormous personal cost.

And now he was back, running the whole thing.

There'd been a huge sense of relief when he'd stepped up to take the job.

He could be seen walking down the corridors in Sûreté headquarters, often with people around him, briefing him on the fly between meetings.

There was a sense of urgency, of purpose, that had been missing in those corridors for many years.

But sometimes Chief Superintendent Gamache could be seen in the hallways, or an elevator, or the cafeteria, alone. Deep in some dossier. Like a college professor reading an obscure and fascinating text.

It was an oddly comforting sight, for men and women who'd been immersed in brutality. Who'd worn their guns more proudly than their badges.

Here was a man with a book, not a weapon, and no need to prove his bravery. Or descend into savagery.

It became okay to stop the swaggering, to cease the bullying that was excused as an appropriate way to treat the populace.

They could be human again.

This chief didn't hide away, plotting and dividing. Chief Superintendent Gamache was in full view, though no one expected to view him in the church basement in this obscure village.

Their GPS had warned them they were literally in the

middle of nowhere and the woman's voice had advised them, in tones their mothers once used, to recalculate.

Gamache nodded to the agents and subtly gestured to them to continue what they were doing. He'd had no intention to disrupt, but he was learning that whenever the boss appeared, disruption was inevitable.

'*S'il vous plaît.*' Isabelle Lacoste gestured to an empty chair, a hint of desperation in her voice. 'Join us. You're just in time.'

'Hello, Clouseau,' said Ruth, loudly enough for all the agents in the room to hear. 'I was telling her that I didn't kill that woman.' Then she lowered her voice and leaned toward the Sûreté officers. She spoke out of one side of her mouth like a gangster. 'But I can't vouch for the duck.'

She leaned back in her chair and gave them a meaningful look. Rosa glanced from one to the other with her beady little eyes.

They knew that, if need be, Rosa would take the fall for Ruth. Though surely Ruth didn't have that much further to fall.

'You were here this morning, I understand,' said Lacoste. Ruth nodded. 'Did you come down here?'

'No.'

'Did you notice anything different about the church?' asked Lacoste.

Ruth thought. Then slowly shook her head. 'No. Everything seemed normal. The church was unlocked, like it always is. I turned on the lights, then I sat in the pew by the boys.'

They all knew which bright, brittle boys she meant.

'No strange noises?' asked Lacoste, and braced for the caustic, sarcastic reply.

Like a murder happening downstairs?

But none came. The elderly woman just thought some more, and shook her head again.

'It was quiet. As always.'

She brought her elbows to the table and her hands to her face, and held Isabelle Lacoste's steady eyes.

'She was down here then, wasn't she? Already dead.'

Lacoste nodded. 'We think so. Did you know about the root cellar?'

'Of course. I'm one of the church wardens. It was once used by rum runners, you know. During Prohibition. To get booze across the border.'

Gamache didn't know that about the church, but it did explain why Ruth considered it an exceptionally sacred place.

Ruth looked over at the small room with the dirt floor and the crime scene tape. 'It's a terrible thing, to take another life. And somehow, it seems even worse to do it in a church. I wonder why that is?'

Her wizened face was open, genuinely seeking an answer.

'Because we feel safe here,' said Lacoste. 'We feel God, or decency, will protect us.'

'I think you're right,' said Ruth. 'And maybe He ~~did~~.'

'He didn't protect Katie Evans,' said Lacoste.

'No, but maybe He protected us from her.'

'What do you mean?' she asked.

'Look, I didn't know her, but that conscience thing was here for a reason.'

'You mean the cobrador?' asked Lacoste. 'You think the reason was Madame Evans?'

'I do. And so do you.'

Her gaze shifted to Gamache. The Chief Superintendent simply held those sharp eyes, without nodding. Imperceptibly or otherwise.

'You think the fellow in the costume killed her because of something she did?' asked Lacoste.

'It'd be ridiculous not to think that. He's gone and she's dead. Which would mean she did something so horrific she had to pay for it with her life. And he was here to collect. Now, whether she really had done something that bad or he was just crazy is another matter. I have to think someone who puts on a costume like that might not be all there.'

With great effort, Lacoste stopped herself from pointing out that Ruth might not be the best judge of 'there'.

'If Madame Evans was the target all along, why not just kill her?' Lacoste asked. 'Why the costume?'

'Have you never watched a horror film?' asked Ruth. '*Halloween*, for instance?'

'Have you?' she asked.

'Well, no,' she admitted. 'Once Vincent Price died, the fun went out of them. But I know what they're like.'

'Well, I've been investigating murders for years,' said Isabelle Lacoste. 'I've never, in real life, seen a killer actually put on a costume, draw attention to himself, and then commit the murder. Have you?'

She turned to Gamache, who shook his head.

'Maybe the idea, at first, wasn't to kill her,' said Ruth. 'What's a getup like that supposed to do? What's its purpose?'

'To humiliate,' said Lacoste.

Ruth shook her head. 'No, you're thinking of the modern cobrador. The debt collector. He humiliates. But the old one? The original? What did he do?'

Lacoste thought back to what she'd been told about the dark men from those dark days. Following their tormentors.

'They terrify,' she said.

Ruth nodded.

Terror.

The cops and even the poet, and probably the duck, knew

218

that terror wasn't the act, it was the threat. The anticipation.

The closed door. The noise in the night. The shadowy figure half seen.

The actual act of terror created horror, pain, sorrow, rage, revenge. But the terror itself came from wondering what was going to happen next.

To watch, to wait, to wonder. To anticipate. To imagine. And always the worst.

Terrorists fed off threats more than actual acts. Their weapon of choice was fear. Sometimes they were lone wolves, sometimes organized cells. Sometimes the terror came from governments.

And the Conscience was no different. It joined forces with the person's own imagination, and together they brewed dread. And if they were very successful, they took it one notch up, to terror.

'It wasn't enough to kill her,' Ruth said quietly. 'He had to torment her first. Let her know he knew. That he'd come for her.'

'And she couldn't tell anyone. Couldn't ask for help,' said Lacoste. 'If what you say is true, this is a secret she'd kept for a very long time.'

'One that had literally come back to haunt her,' said Ruth.

Gamache listened and realized, with slight amusement, that Lacoste was treating Ruth as she would a colleague. As though the demented old poet was sitting in for Beauvoir.

Jean-Guy and Ruth were much alike actually, though he'd never, ever tell his son-in-law that he resembled a drunken old woman.

Despite the apparent antagonism, there was understanding there. Affection, and perhaps even love. Certainly an odd and old kinship neither could admit to, or escape.

Gamache wondered if Ruth and Jean-Guy had also been connected, through the ages, over lifetimes. As mother and son. Father and daughter.

Ducks in the same formation.

Isabelle Lacoste rose, as did Gamache, and thanked Ruth, who looked put out that she was being kicked out. Clutching Rosa to her pilled sweater, she marched across the church basement, the agents, rookies and veterans alike scattering before her.

Lacoste and Gamache sat back down. The young agent was dispatched to get the next person on the list while the senior officers considered.

'If the cobrador was here for her, why didn't Madame Evans just leave?' asked Lacoste.

'Maybe she thought that would bring attention to herself,' said Gamache. 'And maybe she knew that if the Conscience could find her here, he'd find her anywhere.'

'How did he find her here?'

'He must've followed her.'

'That must be it.' Lacoste thought for a moment. 'How did he lure her to the church?'

'Suppose he didn't lure her,' said Gamache. 'Maybe he followed her.'

'Go on.'

'Suppose she came to the church for some peace,' said Gamache. 'Thinking she was safe.'

'There is another possibility. Another reason Katie Evans might've come here.'

'*Oui?*'

He waited, as Lacoste's eyes narrowed and she tried to see what the woman, at the end of her tether, might have done that night. Last night.

'Maybe she arranged to meet him here,' said Lacoste, seeing the thing in her mind.

The frightened woman, worn and frazzled. Realizing that someone knew her secret.

'Suppose she invited him here. Someplace private, where she knew they wouldn't be disturbed. What was it Monsieur Evans said? No one goes into a church anymore. Maybe she wanted to talk to him. Maybe even to make amends. To get him to back off, go away.'

'And failing that,' said Gamache, following her thinking, 'she'd have a plan B.'

A bat.

Lacoste leaned back in her chair and tapped a pen against her lips. Then she sat forward.

'So in this scenario, Katie Evans arranges a rendezvous here, in the church basement, last night. She hopes to give the cobrador what it wants. A full apology. And then he'd go away. But if that doesn't work, she brings along a bat. But he gets it from her, and kills her with it. Then he takes off.'

'Why did he put her in his costume?' asked Gamache.

It came back to that.

The costume. Why wear it himself, and why in the world would the killer put his victim in it?

'There's something else,' said Gamache. 'I didn't come here to listen in on your interviews. Madame Gamache told me something just now and you need to know.'

'What?'

'She says there was no bat in the root cellar when she found the body.'

Chief Inspector Lacoste absorbed that information, then she called over the photographer.

'Can you find us the pictures and video you took of the crime scene?'

'*Oui, patron*,' he said, and went to a laptop.

'Could she have just missed it?' Lacoste asked.

'It's possible,' admitted Gamache.

'But unlikely?'

'If she knelt down to make sure Katie Evans was dead, I suspect she'd have also seen the bloody bat too. Don't you? It's not a large room.'

'Here you go,' said the photographer, returning to the conference table with a laptop.

The images were clear.

Reine-Marie Gamache could not have missed the bat leaning against the wall. It looked like a bloody exclamation mark.

And yet—

And yet, Madame Gamache could not remember seeing it there.

'Which means,' said Lacoste, 'it probably wasn't there when she found the body.'

The 'probably' was not lost on Gamache, but he understood the hesitation.

'It was there when Jean-Guy and I arrived an hour and a half later.'

'Madame Gamache locked the church,' said Lacoste. 'And there's only one way in and out. The front door. Someone else must have a key.'

'I'm sure there're lots of keys floating around,' said Gamache. 'But no one went into or out of that church. Myrna stood on our porch, making sure of that, until the local Sûreté arrived.'

'But there was a small window of time,' Lacoste pointed out. 'Of what? Ten minutes? Between when Madame

Gamache locked the door and went home to call you, and when Myrna stood on the porch.'

'True. But it was broad daylight. For someone to walk a bloody murder weapon through the village, to replace it. Well, that would take—'

'A lot of balls?'

'And a pretty big bat,' said Gamache.

CHAPTER 21

⌇

Chief Superintendent Gamache had been on the witness stand all day in what had become, almost literally, a grilling.

In the stifling July heat of the Palais de Justice courtroom, it would be superhuman not to perspire. Gamache was sweating freely and willing himself not to take out his handkerchief and wipe his face. He knew the gesture could make him look nervous. He also knew they were coming to a pivotal point in the testimony.

He couldn't risk anything that suggested weakness or vulnerability.

But eventually, when the sweat trickled into his eyes, he had no choice. It was either wipe it away or appear to be crying.

He could hear a small fan humming close by, but it was under Judge Corriveau's desk and pointing uniquely at her. She needed it more than he did. Unless she was naked under her judicial robes, she'd be withering in the heat.

Still, the sound of the fan was a tease, the promise of a breeze just beyond his reach.

A single fly droned around, sluggish in the heavy air.

Spectators were fanning themselves with whatever sheets of paper they could find or borrow. Though they were longing for an ice cold beer in some air-conditioned brasserie, they refused to leave. They were stuck in place by the testimony, and the perspiration on their legs.

Even the jaded reporters listened, alert, sweat dripping onto their tablets as they took notes.

The minutes ticked by, the temperature rose, the fly sputtered along, and still the examination continued.

The guards had been given permission to sit down by the doors, and the jury had been given permission to remove any outer layers of clothes, and get down to just enough clothing to maintain modesty.

The defense attorneys sat motionless in their long black robes.

The Crown Prosecutor, Barry Zalmanowitz, had removed his jacket from beneath his own robes, though Gamache realized it would still be like a sauna under there.

His own jacket and tie remained in place.

It appeared a sort of game, a test, between the Chief Superintendent and the Chief Prosecutor. Who would wither first. The spectators and the jury watched with fascination as these two men melted, but refused to give in to the climate both had helped create.

But it was much more than a game.

Gamache wiped his eyes and brow and took a sip of the ice water, now tepid, that had been offered to him by Judge Corriveau earlier in the afternoon.

And still the examination continued.

Facing him, swaying slightly on his feet, the Crown Prosecutor swatted the fly away and gathered himself.

'The murder weapon was the bat, is that correct?'

'*Oui.*'

'This?' The Crown picked up a bat from the evidence table and took it to Gamache, who studied it for a moment.

'*Oui.*'

'I submit this into evidence,' said Zalmanowitz, showing it first to the judge then the defense attorneys before returning it to the evidence table.

In the gallery behind the Crown Prosecutor, Jean-Guy Beauvoir tensed. Never completely relaxed, he now sat stock-still, alert. Listening and glistening in the courtroom.

'It was found in the root cellar, leaning against the wall, not far from the body?' asked the Crown.

'It was.'

'Sort of casual, don't you think?'

Beauvoir wondered if everyone could hear his breathing. It sounded, in his own ears, like bellows. Rapid, raspy. Unintentionally fanning the embers of his panic.

But the bellows breathing was almost drowned out by the beating of his heart. Pounding in his chest. In his ears.

They were closing in on the moment he'd dreaded. Glancing around, he thought, not for the first time, how strange it was that the most awful events could appear completely normal. To everyone else.

This was an instant that could change everything. Could change the course of events and the lives of everyone in the courtroom, and beyond.

Some for better. Some far worse.

And they had no idea.

Deep breath in, he commanded himself. *Deep breath out*.

He now regretted not learning meditation, but he had heard that a mantra was helpful. Something to repeat over and over. To lull.

Fuck. Fuck. Fuckity, fuck, fuck, he repeated to himself. It did not help.

He was beginning to feel light-headed.

'The killer made no effort to hide the murder weapon?' asked the Crown.

'Apparently not.'

'So it was just sitting there, for all to see?'

Jean-Guy Beauvoir rose to his feet. Feeling sick to his stomach, as though he was about to throw up. He grasped the wooden railing to steady himself.

Annoyed huffs and glances were shot his way as he moved quickly out of the row, stepping on toes as he went.

'Pardon. Pardon. Désolé,' he whispered, leaving winces and grunts in his wake.

Once in the aisle, he headed to the large double doors of the courtroom. They were closed and seemed to recede into the distance, even as he moved toward them.

'Chief Superintendent, I asked you a question.'

Behind Beauvoir there was silence.

He wanted to stop. To turn around. To stand there in full view, in the middle of the aisle. In the middle of the cauldron that was the courtroom. So that the Chief Superintendent, so that Armand Gamache, could see him. And know he was not alone. Know he was supported.

Whatever he chose to do. However he chose to answer.

They all knew this question would be asked. None of the other members of the inner core at the Sûreté had dared ask what Chief Superintendent Gamache intended to do when it was.

They preferred not to know and Chief Superintendent Gamache had preferred not to tell them. And certainly not to consult any of them. So that, when the inevitable investigation was held, this decision could be proven to be his, and his alone.

But Jean-Guy had asked.

It was a sunny summer afternoon just before the trial began, and the two men were working in the back garden of the Gamaches' home in Three Pines.

The roses were in full bloom and their scent hung in the air, as did a hint of lavender, though Jean-Guy could not have named it. But it smelled nice. Familiar without being cloying. It conjured lazy days when he was very young. Weeks spent at his grandparents' home in the country. Away from bickering parents and bullying brothers and moody sisters, and teachers and tests and homework.

If safety had a smell, this would be it.

Jean-Guy was kneeling on the grass, trying to twist a thick rope through a hole in a piece of wood. He and his father-in-law were making a swing, to be hung from the branch of the oak tree at the far end of the garden.

Honoré was with them, beside his father on the grass. Every now and then, his grandfather would pick him up and bob him slightly, up and down, whispering to him.

'Really,' said Jean-Guy, 'don't feel you need to help.'

'I am helping,' said Armand. 'Aren't I?' he asked Honoré, who really didn't care.

Gamache strolled around, whispering to his grandson.

'What're you saying?' asked Jean-Guy. 'Dear God, tell me it's not Ruth's poetry.'

'*Non*. A. A. Milne.'

'Winnie the Pooh?'

Reine-Marie, *grand-maman*, read Honoré to sleep with the stories of Christopher Robin, and Pooh, and Piglet, and the Hundred Acre Wood.

'Sort of. It's a poem by A. A. Milne,' said Armand. He turned once again to the infant in his arms and whispered, *'When We Were Very Young.'*

Jean-Guy paused in his task of cramming the large rope through the too-small hole on one side of the seat, and watched.

'What're you going to say on the witness stand?'

'About?'

'You know what about.'

The lavender had made him ask. Excessive calm. Contentment. It had made him either brave or foolhardy.

Beauvoir stood up, wiped his sleeve across his forehead and picked up his lemonade from the table. When Gamache didn't answer, Beauvoir shot a quick glance back toward the house. His wife, Annie, and her mother, Reine-Marie, were sitting on the back porch with their own lemonades, talking.

Even though he knew they couldn't hear them, he lowered his voice.

'The root cellar. The bat. What we discovered.'

Armand thought for a moment, then handed Honoré back to his father.

'I'll tell them the truth,' he said.

'But you can't. That'll blow the whole thing. Not just the chance of a conviction in the murder of Katie Evans, but the entire operation of the past eight months. We've put everything into it. Everything.'

He saw Annie glance his way and realized he'd raised his voice slightly.

Modulating it again, he rasped, 'If you tell the truth, they'll know we know, and it'll be over. We're so close. It all hinges on that. All our work will be for nothing, if you tell the truth.'

Jean-Guy knew he didn't have to tell Gamache that. He was the architect of the plan, after all.

Beauvoir felt Honoré's tiny hand grasp his T-shirt, and make a fist. And he smelled the baby powder. And felt the soft, soft skin of his son. It was even more intoxicating than lavender.

And Jean-Guy knew why Armand had handed the child back to his father. So that the infant, his grandson, wouldn't be tainted by the lie he'd just been forced to tell.

'It'll be all right, Jean-Guy,' said Armand, holding his son-in-law's gaze before his eyes shifted and softened, as they rested on Honoré. He leaned toward the child. '*It isn't really / Anywhere! / It's somewhere else / Instead!* Isn't that right?'

'*And now it is now,*' came a voice over the garden fence just ahead of the head. Gray and lined, though the eyes were bright. '*And the dark thing is here.*'

'You're not kidding,' said Beauvoir, then said to Honoré, 'It's a Heffalump.'

The two men and a baby looked at the old poet.

'More like Eeyore, don't you think?' said Gamache. 'With just a hint of Pooh.'

'Depending on how you spell it,' said Jean-Guy, and saw Ruth's mouth twitch slightly into a smile.

She'd heard them talking, that much was clear. And now she stared, like some old witch in the Hundred Acre Wood who gathered secrets like honeypots.

Their apparent amusement was for Honoré's sake. The truth was, this was the worst possible turn of events. Ruth was one of the few people who might put it all together. Who might be able to work out what they'd discovered in the church basement. It was, after all, something she'd said in that first interview after the murder that had started them down this path.

Fortunately, even if she guessed, she couldn't possibly know why it was vital that it be kept a secret.

She looked from one to the other, then her eyes too came to rest on the child she called Ré-Ré. Ray-Ray.

To Jean-Guy's apparent annoyance, but actual relief, the nickname was beginning to stick, and most people in Three Pines now called him Ray-Ray. Honoré being a bit formal. A bit much for a child.

Ray-Ray fit. He was just that. A ray of bright sunshine in all their lives. The fact the nickname should come from the dark, demented old poet only seemed to add to its perfection.

'What were you talking about?' she demanded. 'Something about Katie Evans. The trial's about to begin, isn't it?'

'It is,' said Gamache, his voice light, friendly. 'Jean-Guy was just going over some strategy.'

'Ahhh,' she said. 'I thought I heard laughter. And what's to discuss? You tell the truth, don't you?'

She cocked her head to one side, and Gamache's smile froze.

'But you don't think he should,' she said to Beauvoir. 'Now, what is it we're not supposed to know? Let's see.' She cast her eyes to the sky, apparently deep in thought. 'That you arrested the wrong person? No, that's probably not it. I wouldn't put it past you, but I think you got the right person. That you don't have enough evidence to convict? Am I closer?'

'He said he wasn't going to lie,' said Jean-Guy.

'And I think that's a big fat fib, don't I, Ray-Ray,' she said in a childish voice, leaning toward the infant. 'Now, what would make your father advocate lying, and your grandfather actually do it?'

'That's enough, Ruth,' said Gamache.

She shifted her gaze back to Gamache. Sharpening, honing. Preparing to debone.

'The truth shall set you free, isn't that right? Or don't you believe it, Armand? But I think you do.' Her sharp eyes were

231

working to scrape away layers of skin. 'Did I get it right? Is it freedom that you fear? Not yours, but the murderer's? You'd lie to get a conviction?'

'Ruth,' Jean-Guy warned, but he was now on the outside of a world that contained only Armand Gamache and Ruth Zardo.

'I like you more and more,' said Ruth, staring at Gamache. 'Yes. This is definitely an improvement over Saint Armand. But you got some dirt on your wings when you fell to earth. Or is that shit?'

She sniffed.

'Ruth,' Beauvoir exclaimed.

'Sorry. Pardon my French,' she said to Ray-Ray before turning back to Gamache. 'Sounds like you're between a rock and a pile of *merde.*'

'Ruth,' said Jean-Guy. Her name now took on the complexion of an oath. It substituted for all the swear words he wanted to throw at her.

He was no longer really trying to stop her. Yet, always contrary, the old poet stopped. She considered for a moment.

'Maybe that's the dark thing. The shit show you call a trial.'

'*All shall be well,*' said Armand, and Ruth smiled.

'At least you're a good liar. That'll help.'

Then her head disappeared behind the fence, like Jack stuffed back in the box.

'When we finish this' – Jean-Guy pointed to the swing – 'we need to build a higher fence.'

'It's not the length that matters' – came the voice from the next garden – 'it's the girth.'

Jean-Guy met Armand's gaze and raised his brows.

Neither man spoke, there was nothing to say. But there was a lot to consider.

Jean-Guy handed Honoré back to his grandfather, in a gesture that was more than a gesture.

When the time came, would he lie? Beauvoir wondered, as he bent once more to the task of making the swing.

Under oath?

If he did, he'd be committing perjury. But if Chief Superintendent Gamache told the truth, their entire investigation would be blown. Putting all sorts of agents and informants in danger and ruining their one great chance of stopping the largest single trafficker in Québec. Of, in effect, crippling the drug trade. Of winning an unwinnable war.

Beauvoir was pretty sure he knew what Gamache would do.

That day, that warm afternoon as they worked together in the sunshine making a swing that would hang from the tree for generations, a swing Honoré would one day place his own children on, Jean-Guy had vowed to be in the courtroom when the question was asked. And answered.

So that everyone could see him declare his allegiance. No matter how Chief Superintendent Gamache chose to answer it. So that Armand Gamache could see. He was not alone.

But instead Jean-Guy Beauvoir found himself leaving. No, not just leaving. He was running away.

The guard stood up and opened the doors.

'We're waiting for your answer, Chief Superintendent. It's a simple question. The murder weapon, the bat, was just leaning against the wall. For all to see.'

As the heavy doors closed behind Beauvoir, something slipped out of the courtroom with him. And pursued him down the marble hallway.

The chief's voice.

Had the bat been there, the Crown had asked, in full view for all to see?

'*Oui.*'

And there it was.

Chief Superintendent Gamache had perjured himself.

Until it happened, Jean-Guy hadn't really believed the chief would do it. Lie under oath. Commit professional suicide. And worse, betray all his convictions. For a conviction.

But then, Beauvoir would never have believed he'd leave the chief and commit this act of personal treason.

Jean-Guy leaned against the wall, feeling the cool marble against his flushed face. He closed his eyes and gathered himself.

He wanted to go back in. But it was too late.

Jean-Guy took a deep breath, straightened up, and walked swiftly down the corridor, through the heavy air, batting away at the fly that had followed him.

He looked behind him, instinctively. In case something, or someone, was following. Dogging his steps. But there was no one there. The corridors were oddly empty. Not a soul in sight. All the courts were in session.

Making his way out the front door of the Palais de Justice, Beauvoir stood on the sweeping steps in the glaring sunshine and wiped his face, resting it, burying it for a moment, in the handkerchief.

Then he gave a quick scrub and, raising his head, he took a deep breath.

He felt a tickling on his arm and slapped at it, watching as the fly fell to the ground, its wings like delicate panes of stained glass in the sun. With just a bit of dirt sticking to them.

'I'm sorry,' he whispered.

He'd acted instinctively, and now something was done that could never be undone.

But there was something he could do, now that he was out here, and Gamache was in there. And that was to make sure the lie was worth it. That it achieved what they all hoped.

The Sûreté, under Chief Superintendent Gamache, would hit hard and fast and decisively. The target would never see the blow coming, shrouded as it was in lies and apparent incompetence. And all tied to a macabre murder in a tiny border village.

And a root cellar with a secret.

But as he headed along the cobbled streets of Old Montréal toward Sûreté headquarters, Jean-Guy couldn't shake the thought that they'd risked everything on this one maneuver. This *coup de grâce*. That might not work.

There was no fallback plan. No alternate route. No plan B.

Not for Gamache. Not for Beauvoir. Not for any of them.

Chief Superintendent Gamache had just set their ship aflame. There was no going back now.

CHAPTER 22

———

Chief Superintendent Gamache looked at the closed doors of the courtroom, then he wiped his eyes again, and shifted his attention back to the Crown Prosecutor.

He watched Zalmanowitz, and saw what he thought was the tiniest of acknowledgments.

Both men knew what Gamache had just done. And what Zalmanowitz had helped orchestrate.

It was, potentially, a huge step toward their goal. And it was almost certainly the end to both of their careers. And yet, the waving of papers in the courtroom continued. The hum of the little fan continued. The jury continued to listen, semi-attentively, unaware of what they'd just witnessed. Of what had just happened.

All quiet on the western front, thought Gamache.

'So the defendant was responsible for Katie Evans being in the costume?'

'Yes.'

'It was an act of revenge?'

'Yes.'

'As was her murder.'

'Yes.'

'Why?'

'Why what?'

'Why any of it. Why the costume? Why the root cellar? Why the baiting and tormenting? And why kill her? I'm sure you've heard of the concept of motive. Did you not look for one?'

'Tone, please,' said Judge Corriveau.

Had she really just seen that look of understanding pass between these men? And then just heard the unmistakable goading on the part of the Crown? Her senses were in conflict.

'My apologies.' Though Zalmanowitz did not sound contrite.

'We did,' said Gamache. 'All that you describe is accurate, and yet it's also misleading. It's all too easy in a homicide investigation to be drawn off course. To follow great screaming leads and miss the subtler, smaller clues. What seemed the stalking and eventual murder of Madame Evans only appeared macabre because we didn't understand. But once it was clear, then all that fell away. These were trappings of a murder, but the murder itself was simple. Most are. It was committed by a human being. For human reasons.'

'And what were those? And please don't recite the Seven Deadly Sins.'

Gamache smiled and rivulets of perspiration coursed into the crevices in his face.

'Oh, it was one of them.'

'All right,' said Zalmanowitz, apparently too drained to spar anymore. 'Which one? Greed? Lust? Wrath?'

Gamache raised his hand and pointed a finger.

Got it.

Wrath. That had become a wraith. That had consumed its human host, and gone out into the world. To kill.

It had started, as these things did, naturally enough. As steps in the grieving process.

But where the final step should have been toward acceptance, the person had veered off. Stepped away from the path and walked deeper and deeper into sorrow and rage. Fueled by guilt. Until they'd gotten themselves all turned around. And when they were well and truly lost, they'd found refuge. In revenge.

Comforting, consoling. They'd warmed themselves by that fire, for years.

Justifiable anger had shot right past rage, and become wrath, that became revenge. And made them do something unjustifiable. And led them all to where they were now. In this hellhole of a courtroom, trying Katie Evans's murderer.

But there was more to it than that. Gamache knew it. The melting Crown Prosecutor knew it.

Gamache looked out at the crowd. He hoped and prayed that no one in the courtroom figured out what the police had discovered. In that church basement.

And what Chief Superintendent Gamache had just done.

Though he knew that someone was listening very, very closely to his every word. And reporting back.

'We need to talk,' said Inspector Beauvoir, standing in the doorway of the office at Sûreté headquarters.

'*Bon*,' said Superintendent Toussaint, rising from her chair. Everyone else in the room also got up. 'The meeting is over.'

'But—'

'We can discuss this later, François,' she said, nodding toward her tablet and putting a sympathetic hand on his arm.

'I have your word?' he asked, then dropped his voice. 'We'll do something?'

'You have my word.'

She walked her agents to the door as Beauvoir stepped back to let them through.

'*Patron*,' they said to Beauvoir, examining him closely as they filed past for any hint as to why he was there. And why their own boss had abruptly ended their meeting to meet with him.

They knew Jean-Guy Beauvoir was second-in-command at the Sûreté. And they knew he was a formidable investigator in his own right. Not simply an adjunct to Chief Superintendent Gamache.

Inspector Beauvoir had been offered the promotion to chief inspector when he'd taken the job, but refused, saying inspector was fine with him. He was proud to be one of the troops.

All the agents and inspectors in the Sûreté, upon hearing that, turned their respect for the man into near adoration. And he became *patron*.

Though he didn't feel like one now.

These men and women, his peers, had no idea what he'd just done. And what he'd just failed to do. As each of them walked past him and said, '*Patron*,' it felt like a shot to the gut.

'*Patron*,' said the last of the inspectors.

And Beauvoir closed the door.

'Court's adjourned already?' asked Toussaint, glancing at the clock. It wasn't yet four o'clock. When Beauvoir didn't answer, she motioned to a chair. 'How's it going?'

Beauvoir sat but still didn't say anything.

'That bad?' she asked, and took a deep breath. Not so much a sigh as a sign of exhaustion. 'How's he holding up?'

'He's doing what needs to be done.'

Toussaint dropped her eyes, not wishing to meet Beauvoir's.

Giving a curt nod, she tapped her tablet and turned it around for him to read.

'I had a report on that shipment we talked about.'

'The big one.'

'Yes. My informant says it has crossed into the States. Eighty kilos of fentanyl.'

'I see.' He felt the now perpetual knot in his stomach grow and tighten. 'Where we expected?'

'Yes.' Her voice was hard, almost bitter. 'Exactly where we expected. We watched the goddamned thing.' She opened her eyes wide, with anger. 'Yes, everything was as we expected. Except, unexpectedly, we did nothing. I don't know who was more surprised. The traffickers, that it was so easy, or our informant, that we had the largest-known haul of fentanyl in our sights. In our grasp. And we did nothing. Just' – she grimaced and waved – 'let it cross into the States.'

Even as she said it, she could barely believe it was true.

Beauvoir held her eyes, his gaze steady and noncommittal.

This was what they'd hoped and feared would happen. A huge shipment had made it across the border, with the Sûreté apparently none the wiser. Because, had they known, surely they'd have stopped it.

If the Sûreté, under its new commander, was laying a trap for the cartel by simply pretending to be incompetent, this would flush them out. No police force could ignore a shipment of opioids this massive.

It was a test.

And the Sûreté, under well-meaning but burned-out Chief Superintendent Gamache, had failed.

The Québec cartel could drag a container of heroin down rue Ste-Catherine in Montréal, and the idiots at the Sûreté would still miss it.

Gamache, Beauvoir, Toussaint and the rest of the inner circle at the Sûreté had waited a long time for this. But it didn't feel like a victory. There was no celebration on the part of the senior officers. They all felt sick.

No, there was no joy in that room.

'Are you tracking it?'

'*Non*. Chief Superintendent Gamache ordered us not to, remember?'

It was impossible to hide her disgust.

'We just stepped aside. Didn't even warn the Americans. Oh, but I didn't tell you. The dealers were generous enough to leave several kilos behind. For local consumption. We've also lost track of that.'

'*Merde.*'

He did the calculation. The internal Sûreté research ordered by Gamache at the outset, so they'd all go into this with a clear understanding of the consequences, estimated that six people died for every kilo of cocaine that hit the streets. Even more for heroin.

Way more for fentanyl.

In doing nothing, they'd just killed hundreds. Perhaps thousands.

More bombs on Coventry.

'You know what that meeting was about?' She waved toward the now empty chairs around the table. 'They don't know about the shipment, but they do know that there've been no significant arrests for trafficking in almost a year. They're apoplectic, and I don't blame them. Fortunately you arrived before I had to come up with some sort of near-reasonable explanation. But I'll tell you, Jean-Guy, there're rumors. You've probably heard them.'

'I have.'

'They want to believe in Gamache. They want to trust him. But he isn't making it easy. And it's not just Gamache, it's all of us. Every superintendent, every chief inspector, is facing a possible revolt. A mutiny. You think this's funny?' she asked, on seeing his face.

'Just the word. I was imagining you with a peg leg and a parrot.'

'Those're the mutineers. I'm the one set adrift in the Pacific, drinking my own piss and eating cuticles for dinner.' She held up her hands for him to see her cuticles, which were in fact nibbled. 'There've been no significant arrests in my division in months. None. Apparently there are no more serious crimes. Most of my agents have been reassigned to community policing or prevention—'

'All important.'

'Agreed. But not at the expense of ignoring actual crime. It's like telling doctors to hand out vitamin pills and forget about treating cancer. You and I know what we're actually doing. You and I know why we're doing it. But they don't. As far as the rank and file can tell, we're sitting around with our thumbs up our asses. And that's what our supporters are saying. If Gamache knew half of what the agents and inspectors think—'

Beauvoir gave a gruff laugh. 'You think he doesn't know? Of course he does. He knows perfectly well what they're saying, and why.' Jean-Guy leaned toward her and lowered his voice, forcing her to meet him halfway. 'He was very clear. He warned us. And we all jumped on board, all excited, all pumped up at the thought of breaking the major drug ring in Québec with one shattering blow. Winning not just a skirmish here and there, or even a battle, but the war. But he warned us. There'd be hell to pay. And now that hell's here, and the bill's due, you're complaining?'

Toussaint squirmed a little in her chair. 'They won't follow him forever, you know. We're running out of time.'

'They won't or you won't?'

'There are limits.'

'Do you want out?'

The two glared at each other. Madeleine Toussaint out-ranked Jean-Guy Beauvoir. But that was more a consequence of his choice rather than his competence.

In private they treated each other as what they were. Equals.

'How do we just sit by, Jean-Guy?' she asked, softening her voice. 'It goes against all my instincts, all my training. How do we just let people die, when we can save them?'

'I know,' he said. 'I feel it too. But if we're successful . . .'

'Yes, yes, I know all that. That's what got us to support this plan. But . . . ?'

'What happens if we fail?' said Beauvoir. She nodded. 'Then we fail. But at least we tried.'

'You're not rallying the troops now, Jean-Guy. It's me you're talking to. I've been in the trenches too long to be mollified.'

'All right, I'll tell you what'll happen. In Chief Super-intendent Gamache's desk there's a notebook. And in it he's written, longhand, exactly what he sees happening, if this fails. Do you want to go look?'

'He's told us,' she said. 'He outlined it that first day, at that first meeting. The risks and rewards.'

'True, and what he said was accurate, at the time. But it was a forecast. A best guess. But things have become clearer, as the weeks and months have gone on.'

'It's worse than we thought?' She clearly didn't want to ask, but did anyway.

'As we've appeared weaker, organized crime, gangs, traffickers have grown stronger. Bolder.'

'Which is what we're counting on.'

'*Oui*. So they'll also grow reckless. That's the crack we've been looking for.'

'So to speak,' she said, and actually smiled.

He did not. Instead, his handsome, haggard face grew even more serious.

'It'll be even worse than anyone thought, Madeleine. If we fail. This will be the second catastrophe to hit the Sûreté, and by association the government of Québec, in rapid succession. First the corruption scandal, and now what would appear to be complete incompetence—'

'Bordering on criminal behavior,' Superintendent Toussaint supplied, and only Beauvoir knew that it no longer bordered on criminal behavior. Chief Superintendent Gamache's testimony in the courtroom that day had crossed that boundary.

'You likened this to the fight against cancer,' said Beauvoir. 'That's fair. That's accurate. These opiates are like a cancer. You know how doctors treat a tumor?'

'Of course I do. With chemo.'

'Yes. They poison the patient, often taking them to the edge of death, before they can be saved. Sometimes it works. Sometimes it doesn't. Do you want to know what Monsieur Gamache suspects will be the consequence of failure here?'

Superintendent Toussaint's jaw muscles tensed as they clamped down.

'I do not,' she managed to say.

Beauvoir nodded. 'I don't blame you. But I'll tell you something. If we fuck this up, we'll only be hurrying along something that was inevitable. The war on drugs was lost years ago. New designer opiates are hitting the streets every day. This really is, and always has been, our only hope. Our last great stand. But—'

'Yes?'

'The Chief Superintendent also wrote, in that notebook, what happens if we succeed.'

He smiled. 'We're almost there, Madeleine.'

Toussaint looked down at her tablet, and tapped it a few times. Then she paused.

She seemed to be weighing her options.

He'd noticed that Superintendent Toussaint hadn't asked if Gamache had lied on the witness stand, though they all knew it would come up, almost certainly that day. And Beauvoir knew why Toussaint hadn't asked.

One day soon there was sure to be an investigation, and questions would be asked of Superintendent Toussaint.

Did she know the Chief Superintendent intended to lie? And when she found out he had perjured himself, did she report it?

If she didn't ask, she could truthfully answer *non* to both questions.

Better ignorant than guilty.

She was distancing herself from the Chief Superintendent. But then, so had he.

At least hers was figurative. Beauvoir had done it literally. Fleeing from the courtroom. Retreating. Running away. Putting actual distance between himself and Gamache. And the lie.

He wasn't even sure why he'd done it. They'd stood side by side through firefights. They'd tracked down and faced down the worst killers Québec could produce. Together.

And now he'd run away?

And now it is now, he thought. *And the dark thing is here.*

He didn't turn around. Didn't need to. He knew what was standing there in the corner of the bright sunny office. Watching and staring. And when he got up, it would follow him. Forever if necessary.

The dark thing is here. Like the demon on the island in *Lord of the Flies*, the one the boys had conjured out of thin air and terror.

The demon, the dark thing, was himself.

Madeleine Toussaint wrote a word on a piece of paper, transcribing it from her tablet.

'It's bad news, I'm afraid. Another shipment.'

Beauvoir sighed. What else could he have expected?

'The inspector who brought me this information—'

'François Gaugin? I saw him say something to you when I arrived. He's a good man.'

'A loyal man. Loyal to the Sûreté,' said Toussaint.

'But not necessarily the leadership?'

'He asked me not to show it to anyone else. He begged me to let him handle this. To make an arrest. I gave him my word.'

Beauvoir met her eyes and nodded. It was that kind of day. When words and promises and oaths were broken.

It had better be worth it, he thought.

'It's a small shipment, tiny by comparison to what we just tracked.'

She pushed the scrap of paper across the table. It had a significance beyond whatever was written there. It was the canary in the coal mine. A warning that if someone like Inspector Gaugin mistrusted them, then there was real trouble.

It was possible now that Chief Superintendent Gamache would destroy the drug cartel and the Sûreté with it.

Beauvoir adjusted his glasses and read.

'Chlorocodide. Never heard of it. A new drug?'

'New to us.'

Shit, he thought. Another drug, another plague. Another bomb on poor Coventry.

'It's a codeine derivative,' Toussaint was saying. 'Popular in Russia. This shipment comes from Vladivostok. It arrived at Mirabel in a container of nesting dolls. It's just sitting in a warehouse.' She leaned toward him, her voice urgent. 'We can confiscate it. To push back, just a little. It's a tiny shipment. It won't make a dent in the cartel, but it'll make a huge difference to morale in this division. And others.'

'It's just sitting there, you say?' asked Beauvoir.

'*Oui*. Can I call Gaugin and give the word?'

'*Non*,' he said, adamant. 'Do nothing.'

'Oh, for fuck's sake. It can't matter, just let my people make some arrests. Throw them this, I'm begging you.'

'Madeleine, why do you think it's just sitting there? Big or small, wouldn't they normally try to get it on its way? What're they waiting for?'

Now she paused. Considering. 'Are you asking because you know the answer?'

'No, but I'm beginning to have an idea.'

'What?'

Beauvoir had grown very still, but his eyes darted and his mouth opened slightly.

'Tell me more about this chlorocodide.'

'Well, as far as I know, this is the first shipment into Québec, probably the first into Canada. Not sure about the

States, but if it's there it's not yet in large quantities. Its street name is Russian Magic. Also known as krokodil.'

'So this would be like an *amuse-bouche*?'

She almost smiled. 'You could say that. Something to get people started. To whet their appetite. They're sophisticated, these traffickers.'

'They're also brilliant marketers,' said Beauvoir. 'Calling something krokodil. Appeals to kids. Sounds urban. Edgy.'

'It's also called that because it makes their skin all scaly. Like a crocodile.'

'Oh, Christ,' he sighed.

He, better than Toussaint, better than most, knew the desperation of the junkie. And how detached from normal human behavior they became. They already felt and acted subhuman. Why not look it too?

They didn't care.

But he did.

'This's how it starts,' he said, taking off his glasses and tapping the paper, in an unconscious imitation of something Gamache often did. 'They bring in a small amount, to prime the pump. Build up demand. The drug is all the more desirable because it's hard to get.'

He knew the routine.

Dealers dealt in drugs, but also in human nature.

'So why leave it in a warehouse at Mirabel?' he asked. 'What're they waiting for?'

'For the big shipment of fentanyl to make it through?' Toussaint suggested.

'Yes, almost certainly. But it's crossed the border. What's stopping them now?'

They stared at each other, hoping the other might come up with an answer.

Then Beauvoir smiled. It was tiny, frail. But it was there.

'They're waiting to see what happens at the trial,' he said.

And Madeleine Toussaint's face opened in astonishment, then relaxed into a smile. 'My God, I think you're right.'

Beauvoir stood up and tilted the slip of paper toward her. 'May I?'

She stood up too, and after hesitating for just a moment, she nodded.

Beauvoir folded the paper and put it in his pocket.

'What're you going to do?' she asked as she followed him to the door.

'I'm going to show this to Chief Superintendent Gamache as soon as he gets out of court.'

'And what'll he do?'

'I don't know.'

'Push him, Jean-Guy. Make him act,' she said. 'He has to give the word.'

'Look, no one has more at stake than he does,' said Beauvoir.

'That's not true. He won't lose a son or daughter to addiction. He almost certainly isn't going to suffer a home invasion by some drug-addled crazy, or be shot on the street for drug money. You have a young son.'

'Honoré, *oui.*'

'I have a son in high school and two daughters heading there soon. We have more at stake. We have everything to lose. This cannot fail, Jean-Guy.'

'I know.'

And he did know.

'Wait.' She reached out and drew Beauvoir back into the office, and closed the door. 'Did he do it?'

'What?'

'You're going to make me say it, aren't you?'

'I am.'

'Did Chief Superintendent Gamache commit perjury today? Did he lie about the bat and the hidden door in the church basement?'

'He did.'

She grew very still, then glanced at the pocket where the slip of paper now sat.

'Then we might have a chance. But what do I tell my agents?'

'You'll think of something. This started with you, Madeleine. You can't distance yourself, even if you want to.'

'You can't possibly blame me for this,' she said, her defenses slamming back into place.

'I'm not blaming. One day you might even be given the award you deserve. You helped the Chief Superintendent come up with this plan. He kept the napkin, you know. From your lunch. It's in his desk, below the notebook.'

Toussaint nodded. Beauvoir was right. This all began that afternoon months ago, over lunch, when she'd used a cliché. And Chief Superintendent Gamache had written it down on the only thing available.

The cliché was so common that she'd failed to consider what it really meant. And she sure hadn't foreseen what it would mean to Gamache. And how he'd use it.

'Burn our ships,' she said, remembering that moment in the brasserie when Chief Superintendent Gamache had looked at her with a gleam. The ember of an idea.

'Burn our ships,' Beauvoir repeated. 'Do you know where it comes from?'

She nodded. She'd looked it up, as the days and months

had passed and things got worse and worse instead of better and better, and Madeleine Toussaint had begun to wonder what she'd done.

What she found out was no comfort.

'It was Cortés,' she said. 'Five hundred years ago. When the Spanish landed in what's now Mexico.'

Beauvoir nodded. 'They stood on the beach and Cortés ordered his men to burn their ships.'

'So there was no going back.'

The two senior Sûreté officers stood at the door and imagined that moment. What would those men have done? Would they have argued? Begged? Plotted mutiny?

Or would they have meekly done it, so conditioned were they to follow orders?

The conquistadors had traveled to the New World to conquer it. They would in a few short years destroy a great Aztec civilization. And in return they'd be given wealth beyond imagining. Except. Except.

Most would never leave those shores.

How had they felt, as they'd stood on that beach? The strange continent in front of them. Home and family and safety behind them. And in between, a smoldering ship.

Neither Beauvoir nor Toussaint had to work very hard at imagining how those conquistadors had felt.

There was no going back for them either.

They could smell the burning timbers.

'I'll let you know how it goes,' said Beauvoir, patting his pocket where the piece of paper sat. As he left, he felt the dark thing follow him out into the glaring sunshine.

Madeleine Toussaint closed the door and walked to her desk. She sat heavily in the chair, then hit the intercom and asked her assistant to call Inspector Gaugin. She stared out

251

the window, and wondered how she'd explain to him what she'd just done.

A dark thing, like some charred remain, stood quietly in the corner, and watched.

'The defendant actually came to you, is that right, Chief Superintendent?'

'It is. I was at home in Three Pines with my wife—'

'Reine-Marie Gamache,' Zalmanowitz reminded the jury. 'She's the one who found the body of Katie Evans earlier that day.'

'Exactly. Chief Inspector Isabelle Lacoste, the head of homicide, was staying with us, as was Inspector Beauvoir, my second-in-command.'

'Are they in the courtroom now?'

'*Non*.'

The Crown Prosecutor turned around, looked at the gallery, then turned back to Gamache. Surprised. A glance passed between them.

Judge Corriveau caught it, and tucked it away.

More than noting the understanding in that glance from Crown to Chief Superintendent, the judge recognized something else. Something completely unexpected.

Sympathy.

Maureen Corriveau's eyes narrowed in annoyance. She considered calling an early end to the day's testimony and dragging both men into her chambers. And forcing the truth from them.

But she was a patient woman and she knew if she gave them space and time, they'd eventually drop enough pieces for her to see what was actually happening.

'It was during dinner that the defendant arrived?'

'Actually, it was after dinner. Quite late.'

'Were you surprised by what the defendant told you?'

'I was shocked. We would have gotten there eventually, of course. The crime lab backs up the confession. By then, we were pretty sure that Madame Evans's murder was premeditated.'

'Why?'

'The cobrador costume. It speaks of a knowledge only someone close to the victim could have had. Some secret she thought she'd buried.'

'But the cobrador costume, the cobrador presence, speaks of something else,' said Zalmanowitz. 'Not just a secret, but a guilt so profound it needed to be avenged.'

Gamache shook his head. 'That's what was so strange. The original cobradors weren't intent on revenge. They didn't physically attack their targets. Their mission was to accuse and expose. To act as a conscience.'

'And leave the punishment to a higher court?' said Zalmanowitz.

'A higher court?' asked Judge Corriveau. 'That's the second time I've heard that phrase in this testimony. What's it supposed to mean?'

Barry Zalmanowitz looked like a man whose clothing had just fallen off.

'Monsieur Zalmanowitz?' she asked.

She knew she had him, and almost certainly by the tender bits. Bits that she was not at all interested in possessing, but that had now fallen into her lap.

'It's a quote,' came the deep, calm voice of Chief Superintendent Gamache.

Judge Corriveau waited. She knew the quote, of course. Gamache himself had used it earlier. And Joan had looked it up. But for the Crown to now use it meant that it hadn't been just a passing thought. It had been something the two of them had discussed.

'One of you will have to tell me,' she said.

'It's something Mahatma Gandhi said.' Gamache turned in the witness box and she could see the gleam of perspiration on his face.

'Go on,' she said.

'*There is a higher court than courts of justice and that is the court of conscience. It supersedes all other courts.*'

She could hear the now manic clicking as the press wrote that down.

'Are you quoting,' she asked. 'Or advocating?'

Because it sounded like those were his words. His thoughts. His belief.

And Maureen Corriveau knew then that this wasn't a puzzle piece. It was the key to decoding the whole damn thing. She'd been presiding over one court, while these men had been in a whole other one. A higher court.

She was both enraged and overwhelmed. And more than a little frightened. Of what she'd just unearthed. And what she still didn't know. Like what could possibly make these senior officials, both sworn to defend the law, consider breaking it.

And might have already.

'Quoting,' said Gamache. His eyes held a plea but also a warning. Let it pass.

Then he turned back to the Crown Prosecutor, while Judge Corriveau considered what she'd just heard. And seen. What had, in effect, just been admitted. And what she should do next.

'So you already suspected Katie Evans had been killed

by someone who knew her?' said Zalmanowitz, gathering himself and forging ahead. There was, after all, no going back.

'*Oui*. This was a crime that was a long time in the planning, so the killer must have known her for a long time.'

'And knew her well enough to want her dead. That must've narrowed it down.'

'It did.'

CHAPTER 23

'I have some questions,' Jean-Guy Beauvoir said, his voice quiet. But also businesslike.

He'd driven through the sleet, into Montréal, to break the news first to Katie's sister, Beth. He needed her now to focus, not to sink deeper into sorrow. That could wait. Right now he needed answers.

'Did Katie ever mention a cobrador?'

Beth looked at her husband, beside her on the sofa. From the basement they could hear the children, arguing over a laptop.

'A what? No.'

'Did she sew?'

Now they looked at him like he must be crazy. Beauvoir couldn't blame them. These questions sounded nonsensical even to him.

'Sew? Ho – wha—' Beth struggled to get a word out.

'She was wearing a sort of cloak and we wondered if she made it.'

'No, she isn't handy in that way. She cooks,' said Beth, her voice hopeful, as though that might help.

Beauvoir smiled. *'Merci.'* And making a note that he would

256

never need, he saw Beth look at her husband and give him a strained smile.

'You're close to your sister?'

'Yes. We're only a year and a half apart. She's younger. I always protected her, though she didn't really need it. It became a kind of joke. She lives just a couple streets over, and Mom and Dad are a couple blocks away. Oh, God.'

Again, Beth turned to her husband, who put his arm around her shoulder.

'Mom and Dad.'

'I'll tell them,' said Beauvoir. 'But it would help if you were there.'

'Yes, yes of course. Oh, Christ.'

'You and Katie told each other everything?' he asked.

'I think so. I told her everything.'

Beth's husband lifted his brows just a bit. Very little, but it was enough to show surprise. And some discomfort.

'I'm sorry, but you need to tell me anything she shared with you that could be compromising.'

'What do you mean?'

'Did she ever break the law? Did she ever do anything that she was ashamed of, that she never admitted to anyone? That someone could hold against her?'

'No, of course not.'

'Please, think.'

And she did.

He watched her pale, blotchy face. The rigid body, trying to contain the pain. Trying to hold it together.

'Katie used to take money from our mother's purse. So did I. I think Mom knew. It wasn't much, just a quarter or fifty cents. She once cheated on an exam. Cribbed from the girl next to her. Geography. She was never good with that.'

'Anything else?'

Beth thought, then shook her head. 'No.'

'Her marriage was good.'

'It seemed good. They work together too, Katie and Patrick.'

Again, her husband, Yvon, shifted. And Beauvoir looked at him.

Recognizing the scrutiny, Yvon said, 'We, I, never liked him. I thought he was taking advantage of her.'

'How so?'

'She was clearly the brains, the one who got things done. But she always, oh, what's the word . . . ?'

'Kowtowed?' said Beth. 'Not so much gave in to him, but whatever Patrick wanted, Patrick got.'

'He's manipulative,' said Yvon. 'Doesn't work on us.'

'Doesn't work on most people,' said Beth. 'Only Katie. It was the only sore spot. We love her, and don't really like him. But she's happy with him and so we put up with it.'

Beauvoir nodded. It wasn't unusual to find couples where one was dominant, though it was often not the one it would appear to be. From the outside, it probably looked like Katie, the architect, the successful one, had the upper hand, when in fact it was Patrick.

'The tyranny of the weak,' said Yvon. 'I read that somewhere. It described Patrick.'

'Tyranny,' wrote Beauvoir. It was a powerful word.

'Anything else?'

They thought.

It was clear Beth was just trying to hold herself together, after the initial shock and the tears. She was trying very hard to help.

Beauvoir liked her. Liked them. And he suspected he would

have liked Katie too. Except, perhaps, for whatever she'd been keeping secret.

They all had them. Secrets. But some stank more than others.

'I have a court order to get into Katie's home. Would you come with me?'

Yvon stayed behind to look after the kids, and they drove the short distance to Katie and Patrick's home.

Alone now with her, Beauvoir said, 'Is there really nothing else?'

Beth was silent, as they sat in the car, in the dark, in the cold rain outside the home. It was larger, less modest than Beth's, but hardly a trophy home. There were no lights on.

'Please, don't tell anyone.'

'I can't promise that,' said Beauvoir. 'But you need to tell me.'

'Katie had an abortion. She got pregnant in high school and had it done. I went with her.'

'Did she regret it?' Beauvoir asked. 'Was she ashamed of it?'

'No, of course not. It was the right decision for her at the time. She regretted it was necessary, but not her decision. It's just that our parents wouldn't have understood. She didn't want to hurt them.'

'You'd be surprised what parents understand,' said Beauvoir. He looked at her. 'And?'

He could sense there was one more.

'And my husband wouldn't understand.'

'Why not?'

'It was his. They went out for a few weeks in high school before breaking up. I don't think he knows that I knew they dated. And he sure doesn't know Katie was pregnant and had an abortion. He and I didn't start seeing each other until long after high school. By then Katie and Patrick were married.'

'And how would he react, if he knew?'

She thought. 'I don't know. I think enough time's gone by that it wouldn't bother him. And honestly, when he was in high school? He'd have been terrified to hear that the girlfriend he'd just dumped was pregnant. It was the right decision, and Katie didn't regret it. But neither was she proud of it. And she sure didn't feel the need to broadcast it. I think that's why after graduation she went to Pittsburgh. Fresh start.'

'Why Pittsburgh?' asked Beauvoir.

'She took a fine arts course in the summer at Carnegie Mellon University, but realized fairly quickly that she wanted to be an architect. They wouldn't let her transfer, so she applied to the Université de Montréal and got into their program.'

'How would you describe your sister? For real, now. This's important.'

Beth wiped her face and blew her nose, and thought. 'She was kind. Mothering. Maybe that's why she was attracted to Patrick. If a man ever wanted mothering, it's him. Though I'm not sure she was doing him any favors. If a man ever needed to grow up, it's him.'

'Why didn't she and Patrick have children?'

'Well, there's still time, you know,' said Beth, without thinking.

In the dark car, he heard the tapping of ice pellets, and the groaning silence. And then the sobs.

He waited until they'd passed.

'Her plan, her hope, was to get the business up and then start having children. She isn't, wasn't, even thirty-five. Plenty of time,' she said in a whisper.

They went into the home, and Beth turned on the lights.

It was a surprise. From the outside it looked like any other house on the street. Fairly nondescript. But inside it was completely redone. The colors were muted, but not washed out. Calming, warm. Almost pastel, but not quite that feminine.

'Cheerful' was the word. Homey. The bookcases had books. The closets had organizers, and were organized. The kitchen smelled of herbs and spices and he could see implements in jugs, and a coffeemaker, and a teapot. None of it placed for effect.

This kitchen was used.

It was open to the living room, and the ceiling was beamed.

It was a home, Jean-Guy knew, he could easily and happily see his own family living in.

It took half an hour to search the place. There was nothing that screamed, or even whispered, a secret, or a double life. There was some erotic literature. Some cigarettes. He sniffed them to make sure that's all they were. They smelled and felt stale.

On the dresser in the bedroom, he picked up a photo. Four of the people he recognized. The fifth he did not.

'From the Université de Montréal,' said Beth. 'First year. Lifelong friends. Hard to believe she met Patrick that long ago. So young.'

'Do you mind if I keep this?' Beauvoir asked.

He wrote out a receipt. It was the only thing he took.

They headed slowly over to Katie's parents. He was about to tell them when Beth broke in. And broke the news. And when it was over for him, but just beginning for them, he drove home. To hug Annie and kiss Honoré and read him to sleep, before returning to Three Pines.

CHAPTER 24

P atrick Evans was rocking back and forth, back and forth, on the sofa of the B&B.

What had been a chilly November day had become a cold November night.

'I don't understand,' he kept repeating. 'I don't understand.'

At first the words were said as a statement, an appeal. But as time had gone by and no explanations came, and all efforts to comfort him had failed, the words and the rocking became simply rote. A primal whisper.

Matheo had tried to comfort Patrick. His instincts were good, but his technique was lacking.

'Shove over,' Lea had said. 'He's got grief, not gas. You look like you're burping him.'

Matheo had been patting Patrick on the back and repeating, 'It'll be all right.'

'And by the way' – Lea leaned over and lowered her voice – 'it won't be all right.'

Matheo watched as his wife took Patrick's hand. Patrick looked at Lea, his focus still hazy after the pills and the sleep.

Matheo felt a pang of the old jealousy.

What was it about Patrick that brought out the mother in

women? Whatever it was, it brought out the bully in Matheo. All he wanted to do was kick the guy in the ass.

Even now. He knew it was unreasonable, even cruel, but he wanted to scream at him to get a grip. Sit up straight. Do something besides rock and cry. They had to talk. They had to work this out. And Patrick, once again, was no use at all.

Matheo got up and walked to the fireplace, taking his frustrations out on the logs. Hitting them with the poker.

This was first-year university all over again. *Lord of the Flies* all over again.

When they'd all intertwined. And never really disentangled.

That first year, when they met. When this all began. The events that had brought them to this terrible place in a beautiful spot.

'I thought you might like something,' said Gabri, standing in the archway between the dining and living room of the B&B, holding a tray with a teapot. 'I'll have dinner ready before long. I didn't think you'd want to go to the bistro.'

'*Merci*,' said Matheo, taking the tray from him and setting it on the coffee table beside the brownies he and Lea had bought at the bakery.

Gabri returned a minute later with another tray. Of booze. And put it on a sideboard by the crackling fireplace.

Then, bending over the grieving man, he whispered, 'I don't understand either, but I do know they'll find out who did this.'

But the words didn't comfort Patrick. He seemed to collapse more into himself.

'Do you think so?' Patrick mumbled.

'I do.'

As Gabri straightened up, he wondered if the lament, *I don't understand*, was about more than his wife's murder.

He also wondered why he had the insane desire to slap the man.

Gabri returned to his kitchen and poured himself a bulbous glass of red wine. And sat on a stool by the counter, looking out the back window into the darkness.

Getting up to prepare the shepherd's pie, comfort food for their dinner, Gabri suspected his guests would find very little peace in whatever Gamache discovered. And probably no comfort in the food.

As the kitchen filled with the aromas of sautéing garlic and onions and gravy and ground meat browning, he thought about the four friends and the close bond they shared. It had been obvious from that first visit, years earlier.

It had always seemed such a wonderful thing, this friendship. This camaraderie. This trust.

Until this visit.

Something had been off, from the start. And not just the timing of it. Late October instead of August, which itself was baffling. Why come when it was cold and gray and the world was going to sleep or going to die?

Why now?

The darkness and chill of November was not simply outside. It had crept into the B&B, with these guests. These friends.

They were friendly, but less friendly. They were happy. But less happy. They were enjoying being together. But less so. They spent less time together and, despite invitations, less time with Gabri and Olivier and the others in the bistro.

Then the cobrador had arrived and the chill had spread over the entire village.

And now this. Katie was dead. Someone had taken her life.

'Gone,' he said out loud, in hopes maybe it would sink in.

But more than Katie was gone. He could feel it in the living room. It was unmistakable.

They were still a close-knit circle. An old circle, that much was obvious. If the Stonehenge rocks could breathe, they'd be these friends. But now Gabri, as he drained the potatoes, found himself wondering what their relationship, through the years, over lifetimes, really had been.

Had they been comrades-in-arms in the trenches? Protecting each other? Brothers and sisters, perhaps, in the same nursery? Wives and husbands and lovers? Eternal best friends?

Or something else entirely. They were a circle, and probably always had been. But now something was clear that had been hidden before.

He had an image of the great Stonehenge rocks, leaning forward, leaning inward. Drawn to each other.

But the very force that drew them together made them fall.

And when the dust settled, they were all down. Crumbled. What was once mighty, a thing to behold, was now destroyed.

'Gone,' muttered Gabri as he poured cream onto the steaming Yukon Golds and slapped in pats of butter, then considered the potatoes.

'Oh, what the hell.'

Going to the fridge, he got out a brick of Gruyère and carved off chunks of cheese, watching them melt into the butter and cream and potatoes.

Then Gabri started to mash. Rocking back and forth, putting his considerable weight into getting every lump out.

'I don't understand,' he mumbled as he rocked. Back and forth.

*

265

'How could this have happened?' Matheo whispered to Lea as they stood warming themselves by the fire.

This had been a bad idea from the beginning. But at least it hadn't been his idea. That was some comfort and some protection.

But just now he'd begun to worry. It could be made to look like his idea. Easily.

It wouldn't be hard to convince Gamache that he'd been the instigator. And from there it was a fairly short jump to murderer.

Matheo began to wonder if that'd been the plan all along. To not just have plausible deniability, but someone plausible to hang it on.

But that would mean this had been a very long time in the planning. Longer than even he realized. And it would need the collaboration of others. Of Lea.

Was that possible?

Matheo put his glass on the mantelpiece.

'What is it?' asked Lea. She could see his anxiety.

'It'd be easy to blame one of us,' he said, lowering his head and dropping his voice.

'For Katie's murder?'

'For everything. Have you thought of that?'

The fact was, Lea was just coming to the same conclusion. That whoever got to Gamache first had the advantage of framing the story. Framing them.

There was a slight tapping on the windowpanes. Not rain. Not snow. But something in between.

The world outside was changing. And not for the better.

And they were out there. Everywhere, it seemed. Everywhere they turned. The police. Scurrying around. Crawling around. Looking in dark corners. Opening locked doors. Dragging things into the open that should remain hidden.

She and Matheo had been interviewed, while Patrick had slept. They'd been at a loss what to say, so they'd said nothing.

'They're going to find out eventually.' Lea nodded toward Patrick. 'I thought for sure he was going to tell them when they broke the news.'

'I thought so too, but I think he was just too stunned. And then there was the Ativan. That was a good idea.'

'One pill,' she said.

'Of course. Who in their right mind would give him more?'

She could hear the threat in his voice. She wasn't afraid of him. Not really. Not normally. But none of this was normal.

'So why did you?' he asked.

'I didn't.'

'I'm not Gamache. I'm not the cops,' said Matheo. 'You can't lie to me. You know what I know. Or,' he leaned closer to her, 'do you know more?'

'Don't. You. Dare,' she whispered. More a hiss.

She was his size. And while she couldn't take him physically, she could always take him intellectually. Not that Matheo was that dumb, but Lea was that smart. Clever. They all knew it. She knew it.

She had always managed to control him. Mostly, she knew, because unlike Matheo, she could control herself.

Though she felt that slipping now. It was all slipping away. It was as though they were caught in a mudslide, and going under.

They'd all lied to the police. They said they knew nothing when, in fact, they knew everything.

'We're fucked,' said Matheo.

'Katie's dead,' said Lea. 'And you're the one who's fucked?

Get your head out of your own ass. Stop thinking about yourself.'

'Oh, and you're not?'

Lea held his eyes, trying not to give him the satisfaction of knowing he was right. Lea Roux had discovered something about herself that day.

When swept away by a mudslide, all she wanted to do was save herself.

God help me, she thought. She'd always hoped she'd be like the members of the band on the *Titanic*. Or a German hiding a Jew in the attic.

But now she knew better. When the iceberg struck, she'd toss children out of the lifeboat.

When the knock came, in the middle of the night, she'd point to the hidden doorway.

Yes, she thought. More than Katie had died that day. The cold carcass of the woman Lea thought she was, hoped she was, had also been discovered.

Still, maybe it wasn't too late. Maybe there was still a heartbeat.

She'd had some time now to think.

Matheo had been right about one thing. The first person in had the advantage.

She looked at the carriage clock on the mantelpiece. Just after six. She could smell something delicious coming from the kitchen.

'I think I'll go for a walk,' she said.

'It's raining or sleeting or something out,' said Matheo. 'Or were you planning a very short walk?'

He tilted his head toward the Gamache home, just across the road from the B&B.

Hearing his tone, she could almost taste the mud.

'You're not going anywhere,' said Matheo. 'And neither am I. We stick together.'

He studied his wife. But he was under no illusions. He'd always known, from the first time they'd met at the Université de Montréal.

She was effective. She was clever and clearheaded. And she was something else.

Lea Roux was ruthless.

But then, so was he. It's what had gotten them to where they were.

CHAPTER 25

—

'Myrna just called,' said Reine-Marie. 'She's invited us over for drinks and information.'

'She has information?'

Armand was sitting on the sofa and looked at her over his reading glasses. He was surrounded by dossiers. Each file a précis of a department.

'Well, not exactly. She has the drinks, you have the information, *mon beau*.'

'Ahh,' he said, smiling.

'She seemed to think it was a fair trade, but I told her we couldn't. Isabelle and Jean-Guy will be here at some point for dinner.'

Armand looked at his watch. It was past six, though with the sun setting earlier and earlier, it felt later. He'd changed into slacks and a shirt and sweater, and now he was sitting by the fire, making notes.

He took off his glasses and put his binder down.

The notes he was making weren't about the case. Isabelle and her team were getting a handle on that. They didn't need him.

His thoughts were about something else entirely.

The napkin sat rumpled on the sofa. It was from lunch

earlier that day with Madeleine Toussaint, when they'd discussed the failure of the Sûreté, of all police forces, to control the drug trade. In fact, it seemed the more they tried to control it, the worse it got. Like ties that bound more tightly if you struggled.

But suppose . . .

He stared into the fire, mesmerized by its motion, almost liquid, certainly fluid. Letting his mind break free.

Suppose you stopped struggling? Suppose you just went with it. What would happen then?

He no longer saw the flames. At least, not those in the hearth.

Then he looked at the napkin again.

It was just too ridiculous. Impossible.

But they'd lost the war. He knew that. And yet, they went on fighting because to give up was even worse. Unthinkable.

But now, Chief Superintendent Gamache thought.

Suppose . . .

Suppose.

They did. Give up, that is.

He thought of Honoré. Just a few months old. If the cartels were this powerful now, what would it be like by the time he was thirteen? In the schoolyard. In the streets. Gamache would be over seventy by then, retired.

He thought about his granddaughters in Paris. Little Florence and Zora. Now in preschool and kindergarten.

Like some animation on the History Channel, he saw the map of Europe change color as the plague bled toward them. Encroached. Approached. Closing in on his granddaughters.

It was unstoppable. It crossed borders, it knew no boundaries. Not territorial, not of decency. Nothing would stop the opioids hitting the market.

Nothing.

Ashes, ashes, we all fall down.

He was finally in a position to do something. He was the Chief Superintendent of the Sûreté du Québec. But there was nothing to be done. Everything had been tried. And everything had failed.

Except. He glanced once more into the fire.

Burn our ships.

Putting his glasses back on, he started to write again. He wrote, and wrote.

Ten minutes later, he looked up and saw Reine-Marie sitting beside him, her hand resting on the open book on her lap. But instead of reading, she was staring straight ahead. And he knew what she was thinking. What she was feeling. What she was seeing.

The dark thing, in the root cellar.

He took her hand. It was cold to the touch.

'I'm sorry. I shouldn't be working.'

'Of course you should. I'm all right.'

'Even F.I.N.E.?'

She laughed. 'Especially that.'

Fucked-up. Insecure. Neurotic. Egotistical.

Their neighbor Ruth had named her latest book of verse *I'm FINE*. It had sold about fifty copies, mostly to friends who recognized the brilliance, and the truth.

Ruth was indeed FINE. And so were they.

'I'll call Myrna,' he said, getting up to go to the phone in his study, 'and see if the invitation is still open. We could both use that drink, and the company.'

'What about Jean-Guy and Isabelle?' she asked.

'We'll leave them a note.'

Once in the study, Armand placed the napkin and the

notebook in his desk drawer and locked it. Not against Reine-Marie or Jean-Guy, or Isabelle. But he was a cautious man, who had learned the hard way that the unexpected happened. And it would be a disaster if anyone who shouldn't saw what he'd written. Saw what he was thinking.

Before closing the drawer, he tapped the top of the notebook a couple of times. As though gently rousing something. Tapping a strange, possibly grotesque idea on the shoulder to see if it turned around. And if it did, what would it look like?

A monster? A savior? Both?

Then he closed and locked the drawer, and placed the call.

'All set,' said Armand, taking her coat off the pegs by the door.

The heavy mist had turned to drizzle, which had turned to sleet, and now was snow.

It was an ever-evolving world, thought Gamache. Adapt or die.

Jean-Guy threw himself back in the chair, took off his glasses, and stared at the screen.

After returning from Montréal, he told Lacoste about his interview with Katie's sister, and his search of the home.

'Found nothing, but I did bring this back.'

He showed her the photo.

'This other guy's Edouard?' said Lacoste. 'The one who died?'

'*Oui.*'

He looked impossibly young. Blond. A huge smile and bright eyes. His slender, tanned arm was around Katie's shoulders.

The others also smiled. Young. Powerful. Though none shone quite as brightly as Edouard.

'A shame,' said Lacoste quietly. Then paused for a moment, studying the picture more closely. 'I wonder how Patrick felt.'

'What do you mean?'

'That Katie should keep this picture of them. It's clearly from the time when she and Edouard were still close.'

That much was obvious. Even in the old photo the connection was clear.

'Well, Patrick won,' said Beauvoir. 'Maybe this reminded him. Maybe he's the one who kept it.'

'Maybe.'

They'd retreated to their desks in the Incident Room, where Beauvoir pounded another search into the keyboard.

Then he sat back and waited for the answer to appear.

Around him, other agents were tapping at keyboards, talking on phones.

Isabelle Lacoste was at her desk at the center, the hub, of the Incident Room, her feet up, legs crossed at the ankles, sucking on a pen and reading notes from the interrogations.

The agent had returned from Knowlton, reporting that it had been *steak-frites* night at the restaurant and the waitress was so overwhelmed she wouldn't know if her own mother was there for dinner the night before, never mind Patrick and Katie.

There was no credit card receipt, so if they were there, they paid cash. Which was curious, thought Beauvoir. He couldn't remember the last time he paid cash for a meal.

He turned back to his computer. Beauvoir knew he should have asked Lacoste's permission before claiming one of the desks. It wasn't, after all, his investigation. He had to get used to that fact. He was no longer second-in-command in the homicide division. Now he was the second-in-command in the whole Sûreté.

Jean-Guy had decided to take that as meaning while he belonged to no specific division, he actually belonged to all of them. It was, he was realistic enough to admit, a perception shared by almost no one else in the Sûreté. Including Gamache.

Still, until she kicked him out, he was staying. And helping. Whether Lacoste wanted it or not.

And so, he'd claimed this territory for himself and had settled in.

His laptop was plugged into the Internet. No Wi-Fi here. But a satellite dish had been put on the church steeple, and the signal boosted by the Sûreté technicians.

Beauvoir, no longer able to just sit and watch, threw his glasses on the desk, got up and began circling the room. Thinking, thinking.

As he paced, he placed one hand in the other, behind his back. And with each step, his head bobbed slightly. A walking meditation, though Jean-Guy Beauvoir would have recoiled at the description, no matter how apt.

There was a lot about the murder of Katie Evans that was bothersome. The cobrador. The motive. Where the killer had gone.

Had the cobrador done it, or was he another victim? Was the killer still in the village? Enjoying a beer or a hot chocolate by a cheerful fireplace. Finally warm. His job done.

Those were the big questions, but to get to the answers they had to first go through a pile of smaller questions.

Like what happened to the bat?

Jean-Guy still harbored the suspicion that Madame Gamache, in her understandable shock, had simply not seen it.

The root cellar was dark. And the discovery of a body would have blown everything else off the radar.

That seemed to him a much more plausible explanation than that the murder weapon had disappeared, then re-appeared, after the body was found.

His rational mind, always in control, told him that was ridiculous.

But his gut, which was growing, and a matter of some distress for Jean-Guy, made him wonder.

In his experience, Reine-Marie Gamache, who had been a chief archivist for the Bibliothèque et Archives nationales du Québec, missed almost nothing. She was calm. She was shrewd. And she was kind enough to keep most of what she noticed to herself.

His gut told him if there had been a bat in the root cellar, she'd have seen it.

Between his rational brain and his intuitive self, a lump was forming. In his throat.

He stopped his circuit and walked over to the root cellar. He stood at the crime scene tape and stared into the small, dark room.

Why hadn't the murderer, if he took the bat, simply chopped it up and burned it? In the city, not so easy perhaps. But in the country? Everyone had a fireplace. Most had woodstoves that would reduce the murder weapon to ash in minutes.

Why return it?

'What're you thinking about?'

Jean-Guy almost jumped out of his skin. 'Holy shit, Isabelle.' He brought his hand to his chest and glared at her. 'You almost killed me.'

'I've always told you,' she said, leaning closer so that no one else could hear, 'that words are worse than bullets.'

Beauvoir, who had no intention of being killed by a word, however well aimed, glared at her.

'I asked Madame Evans's sister about the cobrador. It was obviously a word she'd never heard before.'

'I think Matheo Bissonette's in the middle of this. He's the only one who came here knowing what a cobrador was. Without Bissonette, it would just be a silly man in an old Halloween costume. Darth Vader on the village green.'

'But still,' said Beauvoir. 'I don't get it. What killer, outside of comic books, actually dresses up then walks around in public? Public,' he emphasized. 'To draw attention to themselves. And then kills their victim?'

'But that's what he did,' said Lacoste. 'Unless the cobrador had nothing to do with the murder.'

'What do you mean?'

'Suppose it was here to torment someone else? Its whole purpose was as a conscience, right? Not a killer. But someone took this as a chance to murder Katie Evans—'

'And blame it on the cobrador,' said Beauvoir. 'But that would mean whoever was in the costume is also dead.'

'Dead, or frightened away,' said Lacoste. 'Knowing he'd be blamed.'

'Or next. When do you expect the analysis of the costume?'

'I've put a priority on it, but it only arrived at the lab a couple hours ago.'

Beauvoir nodded. They'd asked for DNA swabs from everyone they interviewed, and no one had refused. The samples could tell them a lot. Or could tell them nothing. What he really wanted to know was who had been in the costume before it was placed on Madame Evans. Though that person might be long gone, from the village, and perhaps from this earth.

'I've been going back over the interviews the team conducted this afternoon,' said Lacoste. 'I can't see anything helpful. Most of the villagers didn't know her, and those who did, like Lea Roux and Matheo Bissonette, couldn't come up with anything she might have wanted hidden.'

'They could be lying,' said Beauvoir.

'You think?' said Lacoste, with mock shock. 'Her sister told you about an abortion, but I can't see someone killing her over that. Can you?'

'There're a lot of crazies,' said Beauvoir. 'But no. So far we haven't found anything she'd done in the past that might've attracted the cobrador.'

'So maybe he wasn't here for her,' Lacoste repeated. 'It's possible he came for someone else. There're two people new to the village. Anton Lebrun. He's a dishwasher at the bistro. And Jacqueline Marcoux.'

'The baker,' said Beauvoir.

It did not surprise Isabelle that the man with the growing 'intuition' would know the woman who supplied the éclairs.

'As we know, they worked together before coming here. For a private family.'

'So how did they go from that to a dishwasher and an assistant in a bakery? Were they fired?'

'The family moved,' said Lacoste, reviewing the notes. 'What's interesting is that both Anton and Jacqueline refused to answer questions about their former employer. Said they'd signed a confidentiality agreement and couldn't. They seemed quite intimidated by their former boss. Afraid of lawsuits. I had to impress on them that a murder investigation takes priority over a confidentiality agreement. And that I wasn't asking what the family ate, or who they slept with. I just needed their name, to confirm everything.'

'They were that reluctant?' asked Beauvoir. 'Seems to

go beyond worry to actual fear. Intimidation. Who was the family?'

Lacoste scrolled down the page. 'Ruiz. His name is Antonio and she's Maria Celeste.'

Beauvoir had grown very still. Like a hunter who'd heard the snap of a twig.

Antonio and Maria Celeste Ruiz.

'You say they moved,' said Beauvoir. 'Where to?'

'They were transferred home. To Spain.'

He opened his mouth, slowly, and out came a 'Huh.'

'Barcelona,' she said, watching his reaction.

'It could be a coincidence,' he said. 'It must be. I can't see how the two connect.'

But he continued to be still, and quiet. Letting the skittish thing come to him.

Spain. The birthplace of the cobrador. Where they were most plentiful. The top-hatted modern version. But lately, there had been more and more sightings of the original. The Conscience.

'Did either of them admit to knowing about the cobrador? Did Ruiz ever mention it?'

'I asked about the cobrador, but both denied knowing anything about it,' said Lacoste.

'This Antonio Ruiz, what does he do?' asked Beauvoir.

'They wouldn't tell me.'

Now Beauvoir became angry. 'Come on. They wouldn't even tell you that?'

'Easy enough to find out,' said Lacoste. 'He must be in business of some sort.'

'Probably,' said Beauvoir. 'Businesspeople must be the main targets of the top-hatted cobradors in Spain. He'd be aware of them, if not because he was targeted, but he probably knows people who were. Or at least saw some in the streets.'

'Or read news reports,' agreed Lacoste. 'He probably reads the pink paper. You think he talked about it and Anton and Jacqueline overheard?'

'I think it's possible. Still,' Beauvoir admitted, 'it's a long way from that to murdering Madame Evans.'

Lacoste nodded. Murder often struck her as similar to Hannibal crossing the Alps. How does a human get from here to there? From being upset, hurt, angry. Even vengeful. To taking a life.

How do they get from a family sitting down to Sunday roast and talking about a strange phenomenon back home in Spain, to a crumpled, beaten figure in a root cellar in Québec?

And yet it happens. The Alps are crossed.

But as Gamache drilled into each of his agents when they joined homicide, a murder is always tragic and almost always simple. They were often the ones who complicated things.

And a murderer liked that. Liked to get lost in the fog.

So what was the simple answer to this?

'Let me put in a call to the Guardia Civil in Spain,' said Beauvoir. 'See if they have anything on Antonio Ruiz.'

'Good.' She turned back to her laptop, but when Beauvoir didn't leave, she swiveled back to him. 'Something else?'

'I think so.'

Beauvoir walked over to his desk, and returned with his laptop.

'This.'

'We're up here,' Myrna's voice sang down the stairs and into the bookstore.

She'd heard the bell over the door jingle and now there were footsteps on the stairs up to her loft.

Clara was already pouring a red wine for Reine-Marie and a Scotch for Armand.

'Oh my God, it's cold,' said Reine-Marie, shaking the ice pellets off her coat and laying it over the bannister. '*Merci.*'

She took the glass from Clara and followed them to the living room area. Myrna waved at the armchairs closest to the woodstove, while she and Clara sat facing it on the sofa.

'Okay,' said Clara, putting her feet up on the hassock. 'You've got your drink. Now pay for it. Information, please.'

Armand took a sip of the Scotch and exhaled.

'Isabelle's still interviewing people,' he said. 'You were interviewed, right?'

The two women nodded.

'We weren't much help, I'm afraid,' said Clara. 'At least I wasn't. I saw nothing. I didn't see Katie go up there, and I didn't see the cobrador follow her.'

'How did Katie seem to you, this visit?' he asked.

'The same as usual, I think,' said Myrna. 'Maybe a little distracted, but that could be my imagination, given what's happened.'

'Come on, Armand,' said Clara. 'Give us something. This isn't just curiosity, you know. There's a murderer out there, and honestly, I'm afraid.'

'Yes, I understand,' said Armand. 'And that's one of the reasons I'm here. I really can't tell you much, partly because we don't know much. But I can tell you that Katie Evans's murder doesn't seem to have been random.'

'What does that mean?' asked Myrna. 'She was the target all along? Did the cobrador do it? He must've.'

'It looks like it,' said Armand, and wondered if they noticed the evasion.

'But why toy with her?' asked Clara. 'That's just cruel.'

'From what you told us, the original cobradors weren't cruel,' said Myrna. 'They were almost passive. Like an act of civil disobedience.'

'Wouldn't be the first example of something good and decent twisted to suit another agenda,' said Reine-Marie.

'But still, if you look at what the cobrador actually did,' said Clara. 'He just stood there. For two days. Not hurting anyone.'

'Until he killed Katie,' Myrna pointed out. But she shook her head. 'It still doesn't add up. If you're going to try to terrify someone, why do it with some obscure Spanish creature no one knows about? And one that has a history of nonviolence.'

Armand was nodding. They were back to that. If the original cobradors were known for anything, it was extraordinary acts of bravery.

'He did nothing wrong,' said Clara, 'and we hated him.'

'You defended him,' Armand pointed out. 'When he was threatened.'

'We didn't want him killed,' said Myrna. 'But Clara's right. We wanted him gone. You too, I think.'

Armand slowly nodded. It was true. The cobrador was different, unexpected, uninvited. Not playing by the normal rules of civilized behavior.

He'd unearthed some uncomfortable, some unpleasant questions. Maybe even some truths.

'You're right,' Armand admitted. 'But for all that, it's important not to romanticize. There's a very good chance he murdered Madame Evans.'

'Maybe—' Clara began, but stopped.

'Go on,' said Myrna. 'Say it.'

'Maybe she deserved it. I'm sorry. That's an awful thing to say. No one deserves it.'

'No,' said Reine-Marie. 'But we know what you mean. Maybe Katie Evans did something to bring this on.'

'She must have,' said Myrna. 'If what you say is true. That the cobrador was a conscience.'

'But a conscience doesn't kill,' said Clara. 'Does it?'

'Of course it does,' said Myrna. 'To stop a greater evil. Yes.'

'So murder is sometimes justified?' asked Reine-Marie.

'If not justified, it's explainable, at least,' said Myrna, filling the void. 'Even atrocities. We might not like the explanation, but we can't deny it. Look at Nuremberg. Why did the Holocaust happen?'

'Because deluded, power-crazy leaders needed a common enemy,' said Clara.

'No,' said Myrna. 'It happened because no one stopped them. Not enough people stood up soon enough. And why was that?'

'Fear?' asked Clara.

'Yes, partly. And partly programming. All around them, respectable Germans saw others behaving brutally toward people they considered outsiders. The Jews, gypsies, gays. It became normal and acceptable. No one told them what was happening was wrong. In fact, just the opposite.'

'No one should have had to,' snapped Reine-Marie.

'Myrna's right,' said Armand, breaking his silence. 'We see what she describes all the time. I saw it in the Sûreté Academy. I saw it in the brutality of the Sûreté itself. We see it when bullies are in charge. It becomes part of the culture of an institution, a family, an ethnic group, a country. It becomes not just acceptable, but expected. Applauded even.'

'But what you're describing is a sort of counterfeit conscience,' said Reine-Marie. 'Something that might look "right" but is actually wrong. No one with an actual conscience would stand for it.'

'I wonder if that's true,' said Myrna. 'There was a famous psychological study, a test really. It was designed as a response to the Nazi trials, and their defense that their consciences were clear. It was war and they were just doing as they were told. It was Eichmann's defense when he was caught, years later. The public was enraged, saying that no normal person would do what the Nazis did, and no civilized society would stand by and let it happen. So the social scientists, during the Eichmann trial, put it to the test.'

'Wait,' said Clara. 'Before you tell us, I need another drink. Anyone else?'

Armand got up. 'Let me.'

He and Myrna took the glasses to the kitchen, and poured more wine.

'Nothing for you?' she asked, pointing to the Glenfiddich.

'*Non, merci.* I think there's quite a bit of work ahead tonight. That study you're referring to, is it the Milgram experiment at Yale?'

'Yes.' She looked at Reine-Marie and Clara, chatting by the woodstove. 'Would they have done it, do you think?'

'Isn't the question more, would you have done it? Would I?'

'And the answer?'

'Maybe we're doing it now, and don't realize it,' he said, and thought of the notebook locked away in his quiet home. And what it contained. And what he was considering doing.

But, unlike the Nazis, he wouldn't just be following orders. He'd be issuing them.

And hundreds, perhaps thousands, would almost certainly die.

Could he justify it?

CHAPTER 26

~

Isabelle Lacoste leaned closer to the laptop.

The fluorescent lights of the church basement were not kind to a computer screen. Or to the face reflected in it.

How did I get so old? she wondered. *And so worried. And so green?*

The photograph Beauvoir had been waiting to download had finally appeared, and he'd brought his laptop over to her desk. And now he sat beside her.

Not looking at his screen. He knew perfectly well what was there.

He was looking at Isabelle Lacoste.

She brought a manicured hand up to her face, resting her elbow on the desk and placing her fingers splayed over her mouth.

Staring at the screen. At the woman.

'That isn't Madame Evans,' she finally said.

'No. This is a picture taken eighteen months ago, in Pittsburgh. I've been researching Katie Evans. So far she appears to be what everyone says. An up-and-coming architect. She did her thesis on glass houses. Adapting them to harsh climates, like ours. She completed her studies at the Université de Montréal, as we know.'

'Where they all met.'

'*Oui*. But she spent the summer between high school and university taking a course at Carnegie Mellon—'

'In Pittsburgh,' said Lacoste, going back to staring at the screen.

The photograph was both banal and awful. Perhaps because of the extreme normalcy of ninety percent of the image. And the horror at the very edge.

'Monsieur Gamache asked me to do some research on the cobrador a couple days ago, when it first showed up here. Among the things I found was that.'

Lacoste was right. It was not Katie Evans, though the woman on the screen was the same generation. In her early thirties. Well dressed. An executive, heading to work. Or home.

Hurrying, like everyone else.

It was an ordinary moment on any crowded street.

But something had caught the woman's eye. She was just beginning to register it.

Isabelle felt the blood run cold in her veins.

The woman's expression was like all the rest who rushed around her. But her eyes had begun to change. They had that look horses got when frightened and about to buck or bolt.

There, on the very edge of the photograph. At the far reaches of her peripheral vision. Just entering her orbit. Stood a cobrador.

Busy commuters, heads down looking at their devices, flowed around it, while this apparition from a time long forgotten stood like a black rock in a river.

And stared.

Though the woman couldn't know what it was, she seemed to know that it was there for her.

'Who is she?'

'Colleen Simpson. She owned a chain of day care centers. There were allegations of abuse and she was tried. And acquitted.'

Lacoste nodded. Of course she'd been acquitted. If she'd been found guilty there'd be no need of the cobrador.

'Someone didn't believe it,' said Lacoste.

'She was acquitted on a technicality,' said Beauvoir. 'One of the cops fucked up.'

It was the dread most investigators carried. To make a mistake, and set a predator free among the prey.

Lacoste turned back to the screen. The monster had changed. It was no longer the cobrador. It was the nicely dressed woman, so much like everyone else on that street.

Lacoste's gaze shifted to the now empty root cellar.

'You're wondering if Katie Evans knew this woman,' said Lacoste. 'That maybe they met at Carnegie Mellon.'

'It's a long shot, but . . .' He lifted his hands in a 'might as well try' gesture. 'If Madame Evans knew this woman, it's possible the cobrador came for them both. First one, then the other.'

'See what you can find out.'

'*Oui, patron.*'

Chief Inspector Isabelle Lacoste returned to her laptop and the transcripts of that day's interviews. She clicked on the next interview and groaned slightly.

Ruth Zardo.

Lacoste closed that screen. Interviewing the demented old poet once was bad enough. Having to read over that mess again was too much, even for the head of homicide. Besides, there was nothing there. She went on to the next transcript, reaching for her coffee and settling in.

'Oh, *merde*,' she sighed and, closing that, she brought up Ruth Zardo, smiling slightly at the thought.

Ruth certainly resembled something brought up.

Clara and Reine-Marie were deep in conversation when Armand and Myrna returned with the wine and more sliced baguette for the cheese.

'Ahhh, *merci*,' said Reine-Marie, reaching for the bread first.

'What were you talking about?' asked Myrna. 'Nazis?'

'Pinocchio,' said Clara.

'Of course.' Myrna turned to Armand. 'I see we've returned just in time to elevate this conversation above nursery school.'

'By talking about Nazis?' asked Clara. 'That elevator is descending.'

'No, by telling you about the experiment,' said Myrna. 'Eichmann's defense was that he was just following orders, right?'

The women nodded. They'd all heard that. It was the classic defense for the indefensible.

'The prosecution, and the court of public opinion, said that was absurd. That any decent person would've refused to participate in the Holocaust. It became a talking point of the day, around water coolers and at cocktail parties. Wouldn't a person of good conscience refuse? That's what the experiment was set up to test.'

'But how can you possibly test such a thing?' asked Reine-Marie.

'Well, I know I'm forgetting all sorts of details, but the gist of it was that the subject was put in a room with two

288

other people. One was introduced as the head of the experiment. A scientist. Someone, they're told, who's very senior and very well respected. Now, the point of the experiment, they're told, is to teach the third person in the room how to better learn. It is, the subject is assured, not only a valuable experiment for that learner, but one that will help all of society.'

Armand leaned back, crossed his legs, and stared into the fire. Listening to Myrna's deep, comforting voice. Like listening to a bedtime story, but one that, he knew, was more Grimms than Milne.

'Now, the learner is strapped into a chair,' said Myrna.

'Strapped in?' said Reine-Marie.

'Yes. The subject is told that some learners want to leave when things get difficult, so they're strapped in. Like seat belts. Just a gentle restraint. They're paid for the experiment and so have to see it through, the scientist explains.'

Myrna looked at them, to see if they were following. Both Reine-Marie and Clara were nodding. So far, while a little odd perhaps, it did not sound unreasonable.

They'd probably have gone along with it. So far.

'The subject is then told that for each wrong answer the learner gives, the subject is to give him a small electric shock.'

'Like invisible fencing for dogs,' said Clara. 'They get a small shock and learn where the boundary is.'

'Right. We do it all the time. Aversion therapy,' said Myrna. 'Now, what the subject doesn't know is that both the scientist and the learner are in on it.'

'There is no electric shock?' asked Reine-Marie.

'No. He's an actor. He just pretends to get the jolt. The first time he gets a wrong answer the shock is mild and the subject easily continues on. But the shocks get stronger and stronger with each wrong answer. As the experiment goes on, and he gets more things wrong, the learner acts more and more upset. The shocks are obviously causing him real pain now. He asks that the experiment be stopped, but the scientist says it can't and orders the subject to continue on.'

'Is he upset?' Clara asked. 'The subject, I mean.'

'Now there's an interesting question,' said Myrna. 'From what I remember, he's confused and uncertain, but is reassured by the scientist that everyone else had seen this through, and he needs to as well.'

'So he continues?' asked Clara.

'Yes. Finally, the learner is crying and begging and screaming and struggling to get away. The scientist orders the subject to administer another shock. One that would, the subject knows, be excruciating. Perhaps even fatal. The scientist tells him he's doing nothing wrong. And reminds him that everyone else has done it.'

There was silence now, except for the crackling of the fire.

'And he does,' she said quietly.

Reine-Marie and Clara stared at her. Their wine and cheese forgotten. The fireplace gone. The cheerful loft in the pretty village replaced by that antiseptic room, with the scientist, the learner, the subject, and an ugly truth.

'But it was a one-off, right?' said Clara.

'No,' said Myrna. 'They conducted the experiment with hundreds of subjects. Not all of them did it, but the majority did. Far more than you'd expect.'

'Or hope,' said Reine-Marie.

'They were just following orders,' said Clara. She turned to Reine-Marie. 'Would you have given that last shock?'

'If you'd asked me five minutes ago, I'd have said absolutely not. But now?' She sighed. 'I'm not so sure.'

Armand nodded. It was a terrible admission. But it was also a brave one. The first step to not actually doing it.

Facing the monster. And recognizing it. Knowing that it was not a vile few. It wasn't 'them'. It was us.

That was one of the many horrors of the Nuremberg trials. Of the Eichmann trial. Something all but forgotten today.

The banality of evil.

It wasn't the frothing madman. It was the conscientious us.

'*Always let your conscience be your guide*,' Clara sang in a thin voice, the words drifting into the fire. 'Not so easy after all.'

'Why were you talking about Pinocchio?' Armand asked.

He was beginning to think it was more than Reine-Marie describing the nightly ritual of reading to Honoré.

'Oh, it's silly,' she said. 'Especially now, after what we just talked about. Never mind.'

'No, really,' he said.

Reine-Marie looked at Clara, who raised her brows.

'Go on,' Clara urged, and got a 'thanks a lot' look from Reine-Marie.

'Do you remember why Pinocchio wasn't a real boy?' Reine-Marie asked Myrna and Armand.

'Because he was made out of wood?' asked Myrna.

'Well, that didn't help,' she admitted. 'But what really stopped him from being human was that he had no conscience. In the film, Jiminy Cricket played that role. Teaching him right from wrong.'

'Cricket as cobrador,' said Clara. 'A singing and dancing one, but one nonetheless.'

'There's a difference between having a weak conscience or a misdirected one,' said Armand, 'and none at all.'

'You know what psychologists call it when someone has no conscience?' Myrna asked.

291

'Antisocial personality disorder?' asked Reine-Marie.

'Smart-ass,' said Myrna. 'Okay, yes, officially. But unofficially we call that person a psychopath.'

'You're not suggesting Pinocchio is a psychopath?' said Reine-Marie. She turned to Armand. 'We might have to amend Ray-Ray's nighttime reading.'

'Well, those scenes sure didn't make it into the movie,' said Clara. 'The part where Pinocchio slaughters the villagers. I wonder what Jiminy sang then.'

'You see, that's the problem,' said Myrna. 'We're used to the film versions of psychopaths. The clearly crazies. But most psychopaths are clever. They have to be. They know how to mimic human behavior. How to pretend to care, while not actually feeling anything except perhaps rage and an overwhelming and near-perpetual sense of entitlement. That they've been wronged. They get what they want mostly through manipulation. Most don't have to resort to violence.'

'We all use manipulation,' said Armand. 'We might not see it that way, but we do.'

He pointed to the wine, the lure Myrna had used to get them there. Myrna lifted her glass in acknowledgment. But without remorse.

'Unlike most of us, who tend to be transparent, people rarely see through a psychopath,' she continued. 'He's masterful. People trust and believe him. Even like him. It's his great skill. Convincing people that his point of view is legitimate and right, often when all the evidence points in the other direction. Like Iago. It's a kind of magic.'

'Okay, so I'm confused,' said Clara. 'Is the cobrador the psychopath, or was Katie Evans?'

They looked at Armand, who raised his hands. 'I wish I could tell you.'

What he was beginning to think was that this crime didn't have such a tight circle. The cobrador and Katie Evans. It was possible there was a third person, who had manipulated both of them.

And was now manipulating the investigators.

Which meant that there was someone in the village who might look it, but who was in fact not quite human.

CHAPTER 27

The gavel came down with such force that several spectators leapt in their seats.

A few had been dozing, overcome with lethargy induced by the extreme heat.

Most, though, had fought off the urge to nap, wanting to hear what the Chief Superintendent would say next.

And what the Chief Crown would do next.

To the spectators it looked like a battle of wits. Thrust. Parry. Riposte. Lunge.

But to Judge Corriveau, who was closer and could see what others could not, it had stopped being a battle and had become a relay. One man handing off to the other.

Taking turns carrying the burden.

They didn't like each other, she knew. That much had been obvious from the start. And it wasn't pretense, it was genuine. So whatever was happening, it superseded enmity.

It might even, she now knew, supersede this entire trial.

She'd had enough.

'Court is adjourned for the day,' she proclaimed. 'We'll reconvene tomorrow morning at eight.' There was grumbling among the spectators at the early hour. 'Before the day heats up.'

That seemed to make sense and as she rose, and they rose, there were nods of grudging agreement.

'Gentlemen,' she said to Gamache and Zalmanowitz. 'I'd like to see you in my chambers.'

'Yes, Your Honor,' both men said, bowing slightly as she exited.

'Oh, Christ,' said Zalmanowitz, as he finally sat and wiped the sweat from his face. He looked up and saw Gamache standing there, waiting. 'I'm sorry. I fucked up.'

'This might be a good thing,' said Gamache.

'Right.' The Chief Crown shoved his papers into his brief-case. 'A few years in prison will be just the break I need. I'd thought maybe a retirement community in Arizona, but this way I'll also get retrained. I wonder if they offer language courses in the penitentiary. I've always wanted to learn Italian.' He glanced up at Gamache. 'Do you find it at all ironic that we'll end up in jail because of Gandhi?'

Chief Superintendent Gamache smiled. But it was thin and strained.

'You did nothing wrong,' he said. 'I'm the one who perjured himself.'

'And I let you. I knew the truth and didn't call you on the lie. Which makes me equally guilty. We both know that. And I'm afraid she knows it too. Maybe not the specifics, but she smells something.'

Zalmanowitz shoved some more papers into his briefcase, then, looking up, he saw Gamache staring toward the now empty courtroom.

Though there was one man standing there.

Jean-Guy Beauvoir raised his hand in a tentative wave to Gamache.

He'd rushed over to the Palais de Justice with the news

from Toussaint. But now that he was there, he was unsure how to proceed.

Between the two men was a void where once there had been lifetimes of trust, intimacy, friendship.

All dissolved into empty space because of a single act. A simple act. Beauvoir had left the courtroom. Unable to witness, unable to watch, as Armand Gamache betrayed everything he'd believed in.

Gamache had walked right into it. And Beauvoir had run away.

'And there he was,' mumbled Zalmanowitz. 'Gone.'

Gamache turned to him, angry. 'Jean-Guy Beauvoir has stood beside me through things you can't even imagine.'

'But not today.'

It was cruel, Zalmanowitz knew. To twist the knife. But it was also true. This wasn't the day, and now wasn't the time, to hide from unpleasant facts. Besides, he was hot and tired and about to be dragged over the coals.

Barry Zalmanowitz was not in the best of moods.

'Gentlemen.' The court clerk stood at the now open door. 'Judge Corriveau will see you.'

The Chief Crown sighed, picked up his bulging briefcase, and with one more wipe of his face, he shoved the sodden tissue in his pocket and walked toward the door. A guilty man about to be condemned.

But Chief Superintendent Gamache didn't move. Caught, it seemed, between Beauvoir and Judge Corriveau's summons.

Gamache hesitated, then turned to the clerk.

'I'll be with you in just a moment.'

'Now, monsieur,' he insisted.

'In a moment,' Gamache repeated. *'S'il vous plaît.'*

He turned his back to the door and approached Beauvoir.

Behind him, Barry Zalmanowitz stopped. And waited. Trying to ignore the look of increasing annoyance on the face of the court clerk.

Oh, what the hell, he thought, putting down his briefcase. *How much worse can it possibly get?*

Charged with contempt of court, on top of everything else. It might add another couple of months to the sentence. A chance to learn the past participles of Italian.

Parlato, he mumbled, as he watched Gamache approach Beauvoir. *Amato.*

Yes, thought Zalmanowitz. *I have a lot to learn.*

'*Patron,*' said Beauvoir. Brusque. Matter-of-fact. Any other agent reporting to his superior.

Nothing unusual, Beauvoir repeated to himself. Nothing unusual has happened. Nothing has changed.

'Jean-Guy,' said Gamache.

Armand saw the face, so familiar, but he also saw the wall Jean-Guy had raised. Not stone. Not wood. But sleek sheet metal. Without purchase. Without a rivet or a crack. Unscalable.

It was a device Beauvoir didn't use often anymore. In fact, it had been years since Gamache had experienced it.

And he knew enough not to try to breach the barrier. It was unassailable. But it was also not a protection. It was, he knew, a prison. And trapped inside those walls a fine man hid. Not from Gamache, but from himself.

Jean-Guy Beauvoir had locked the enemy inside with him.

'I met just now with Superintendent Toussaint,' said Beauvoir. 'That's why I left.'

Gamache held his eyes. But said nothing.

'It's as we thought,' Beauvoir continued, stammering a

little under the steady gaze, before collecting himself. When he continued, his voice was businesslike. 'The shipment of fentanyl has crossed the border.'

'Where we expected?'

'Exactly there,' said Beauvoir. 'Our informants watched it.'

'And the DEA?'

'Know nothing about it. We've lost track of it now. As per your instructions.'

Jean-Guy had no idea why he'd said that last bit, except an infantile desire to cause pain. To drill home what this man had done, which was so much worse, surely, than anything he himself had done.

Beauvoir had thought he was beyond the childish lashing out, but apparently not. It was back, and rested, and more powerful than ever. He braced for the counterattack, hoping for some brutal response. That would justify his own attack.

He waited for the clever, cleaver word.

But there was silence.

A look, thought Beauvoir. Prayed Beauvoir. A smug little assassin glance. Something. Anything. But there was nothing. Just eyes that were thoughtful, almost gentle.

'We expected that,' Beauvoir continued. 'But there was something unexpected.'

'Go on,' said Gamache.

'They didn't take it all with them. They left some fentanyl behind. To sell here.'

Now there was a reaction. Chief Superintendent Gamache's eyes widened.

'How much?'

'At least ten kilos. We've lost track of that as well.'

Don't say it, Beauvoir warned himself. *No need to say it.*

'Of course.' He said it.

Gamache tensed and there was a quiet intake of breath, as another thrust hit home.

'Of course,' he whispered. And slowly lowered himself to the spectators' bench.

He sat there and did the calculations. According to the report he'd commissioned, there were at best fifty deaths per kilo of fentanyl. It wasn't difficult to do the math.

Seventy kilos of fentanyl now in the United States.

More than three thousand deaths.

And in Québec? Five hundred people alive today who would die. Because of what he'd decided to do. Or not do. And there could be many, many more. Deaths that Armand Gamache had just sanctioned.

'Monsieur,' the clerk called.

Gamache turned to look at him, and the man's expression changed instantly. From officious to afraid. Not of Gamache, but of what he saw in the Chief Superintendent's face.

Zalmanowitz saw it too, and guessed what Gamache was being told.

And felt both sick and elated. Relieved and appalled. Something had changed. Something had happened.

Could it be that their plan was working? God help them.

'Merci.' Gamache got up. 'I have to go. The judge wants to see Monsieur Zalmanowitz and me. It shouldn't take long.'

Beauvoir could guess what it was about.

'There's more,' he said.

'Oui?'

'A small shipment of a new drug is sitting in a warehouse at Mirabel. It was flown in two days ago in a load of nesting dolls.'

He took the paper out of his pocket and handed it to Gamache, who put on his reading glasses.

'The same cartel?' Gamache asked, without looking up.

'*Oui.*'

The chief still wore his suit jacket, and Beauvoir could see that the white shirt beneath it was soaked through with perspiration.

'Chlorocodide?' Gamache read, then looked up, meeting Beauvoir's eyes.

'Codeine derivative. Popular in Russia but not, as far as we know, over here yet. This would be the first. It's known on the street as krokodil. Very potent, very toxic.'

'And it's just sitting there?' asked Gamache. 'For two days, you say?'

'*Oui.*'

'Two days,' Gamache said softly, under his breath, his eyes narrowing as he focused on some distant target. 'Could it be?'

Then, as Beauvoir watched, Chief Superintendent Gamache closed his eyes. And dropped his head. His shoulders sagging. With a new burden? Or was it relief?

He put out an unsteady hand, touching the bench in front of him, to steady himself. Jean-Guy Beauvoir thought, just for an instant, that he might be about to pass out. From heat. From stress. From smoke inhalation.

There was a long exhale from Gamache that sounded like, 'Ohhhh.'

Then his hand closed into a fist, crushing the paper. And he looked up.

'I have to see the judge,' he said, removing his glasses and drawing a handkerchief across his eyes. To wipe away the sweat, thought Beauvoir. 'I'll text you when I'm out. Convene a meeting in the conference room.'

'Who with?'

'Everyone.' Gamache handed the paper back to Beauvoir,

then he stepped toward Zalmanowitz and the clerk. But stopped and considered Beauvoir for a moment. 'You know what that means?'

He pointed to the paper in Beauvoir's hand.

'It means we have a chance.'

Beauvoir felt the familiar flutter in his chest and rush of adrenaline.

Gamache gave a curt nod. 'We'll know soon.'

Then he headed toward the door held open by the clerk.

'*Patron*,' said Beauvoir.

But it was too soft, and Gamache was too far away. And it was, Jean-Guy knew, probably too late.

Judge Corriveau leaned back in her chair and looked at the two men.

She'd spent the past few minutes alone in her chambers and, after rubbing her armpits with a cold washcloth and throwing water on her face, she tried to work out a strategy.

She would, she decided, keep on her robes. To remind them they were in the presence not of a woman. Not even of a person. But of a position. A symbol.

Justice.

Besides, it made her feel both powerful and protected. And hid the perspiration stains. And the water that had dribbled down her blouse.

The other strategy she was putting into action, or inaction really, at that moment.

She was making them stand.

A fan had been placed in her office and it swiveled, blowing warm air over them, puffing up her robes, which had the undesired effect of lifting and flapping. Not the dignified image she'd hoped to project.

It also, when the fan swung her way, blew her now stringy hair into her face so that she was forced to constantly brush it out of her eyes and spit it out of her mouth.

The two men stood quite still, their hair rising only slightly as the breeze brushed by them.

She got up, turned off the fan, took off her robes, ran her fingers through her hair, and gestured to the two chairs in front of her desk.

'Sit.'

They sat.

'All right,' she said. 'It's just us. As far as I know the room isn't bugged.' She looked at both men and raised her brows in inquiry.

They looked at each other, and lifted their shoulders. If it was, it wasn't them.

'Good.' She paused for a moment. All the fine speeches she'd crafted, all the clever arguments, all the justified anger put into pithy phrases were thrown out when faced with Barry Zalmanowitz and Armand Gamache.

Two men who had served justice for much longer than she had. Served their province. Served their consciences. Often at great personal risk, and cost.

'What's going on?' she asked, calmly meeting their eyes. When neither spoke, she added, 'You can tell me.'

The air was heavy in the room. Humid, sticky, close. Time trickled by.

Zalmanowitz opened his mouth, his lips trying to form words, sentences, cogent thoughts. Then he glanced to his right, at Gamache.

And wished he hadn't. In the instinctive gesture, he'd given something vital away. Something the astute judge couldn't fail to see.

Whatever was happening, it had been Chief Superintendent Gamache's idea.

Gamache looked down at his hands, clasped together on his crossed legs, and spent a moment collecting his thoughts. There were so many ways to handle this badly, and maybe no way to do it right.

He didn't dare look at his watch, or even glance at the small carriage clock on the judge's desk.

But he was aware of time going by. Of the officers gathering in the conference room of Sûreté headquarters. Of the matryoshka dolls at Mirabel and what nested inside them.

They might have left already, those cheerful little ornaments, with something nasty inside.

As soon as he'd read the slip of paper Jean-Guy had handed him, he'd known that this was what they'd been working toward.

Luring the cartel into making one great, fatal mistake.

'More than fifteen thousand people died in Canada from illegal drugs,' said Gamache, meeting her eyes again. His voice calm and steady. As though he had all the time in the world. 'In a year. That statistic is a decade old and those are the ones we know about. There were almost certainly far more. We don't have a more recent report, we're working on putting one together, but we do know that opioid use has skyrocketed. As have the deaths. Heroin. Cocaine. Fentanyl. And more. Nothing is stopping these drugs from hitting the streets. From killing mostly young people. Never mind all the crime that goes with drugs.'

He leaned forward, very slightly, and dropped his voice as though inviting her into a confidence.

'We lost the war on drugs years ago and are just going through the motions, because we don't know what else to do.'

Judge Corriveau's eyes widened, just a little. But enough to register her shock at the statistic. But not at his pronouncement.

She knew he was right. They'd lost. She saw it all day, every day. In her former practice. In her current courtroom. In the halls of the grand Palais. A parade of lost youth, hauled up on charges. And they were the lucky ones. They were alive. For now.

They were also, for the most part, the victims. The ones who should be on trial were free, eating in fine restaurants and going home to large homes in respectable communities.

What Gamache had just said was true and shocking. But—

'What does that have to do with the murder trial?'

'We know that organized crime is behind the drug trade,' said Gamache.

'Cartels,' said Zalmanowitz, feeling he should contribute.

'Thank you, Monsieur Zalmanowitz,' said Judge Corriveau.

'By mutual consent, Québec has been divided into regions. Different organizations run each area. But it's become clear that one dominates all the others,' Zalmanowitz continued, ignoring the pinched look on her face. 'We've been chipping away at it, but without effect.'

'Not really chipping,' admitted Gamache. 'More like a gnat and an elephant. It didn't help that many of the top Sûreté officers were in the pay of the cartels.'

He'd said it without irony. And no one was smiling.

'But you're in charge now,' said Corriveau.

Now he did smile. 'I'm flattered you think that might help, and I am trying.' He held her gaze. 'But I came to the realization when I first took over almost a year ago that there was nothing I could do.'

'Nothing?' she asked. 'But like you said, so much of the

crime in Québec stems from drugs. Not just the gang violence, but thefts, armed robberies, beatings. Murders. Sexual assaults. Domestic violence. If you can't stop the drugs—'

'It's not a matter of stopping,' Gamache interrupted. 'We can't even keep it stable. It's growing. We're past the tipping point. Doesn't look like it, yet. People can still go about their normal lives. But—'

'What you're saying, Chief Superintendent, is that not just drug abuse is out of control, but all crime is about to get worse.'

'And worse,' said the Chief Crown.

'Thank you, Monsieur Zalmanowitz.' She turned back to Gamache. 'You said you realized there was nothing you could do. Nothing effective anyway.' She examined him more closely. 'But that's not quite true, is it? There is something you're doing, and it has something to do with the trial.'

'The Chief Crown is right,' said Gamache. 'One cartel dominates all the others. We didn't realize it for a long time. We thought they were at war, hoped they were, and that they'd do some of our job for us. But as we looked closer, we realized it was all a sham. The other organizations were satellites, circling, protecting, decoys for the main one.'

'The biggest of the cartels,' said the judge.

'*Non*, that was its brilliance and our mistake,' said Gamache. 'And why it took so long to identify it. It is, in fact, one of the smallest. It appeared to be just another organization, and not a very effective one. It was static, stale. Not growing or diversifying like all the others. It was so small it really wasn't worth our effort. We were looking for just what you said' – he gestured toward her – 'a great big powerful organization. I made the mistake of equating size with power.'

She took that in. 'The nuclear bomb,' she finally said.

305

'Smaller than a car and can wipe out a city,' said Gamache.

'And did,' said the Chief Crown.

'Thank you, Monsieur Zalmanowitz.' She was smaller than both men, and could wipe them out. And might. 'But you found it, right?' she said, returning to Gamache. 'Eventually.'

'*Oui*. Took some time. We knew we were spread too thin, trying to go after all the cartels. All the crime. We had to focus, had to find the heart. But we were looking for the wrong thing in the wrong place. We were looking for a huge organized crime syndicate in Montréal.'

She was nodding. It was a reasonable assumption.

'Where did you find it?'

'It seems so obvious now,' said Gamache, shaking his head. 'Where do most of the drugs end up?'

'Montréal,' said Judge Corriveau, though with a slightly questioning inflection.

'The stuff for Québec, certainly,' agreed Gamache. 'But this province isn't the major consumer. The problem is big enough for us, and tragic enough, but it's tiny by cartel standards. We're simply a highway. Some parcels fall off the truck, and stay here. But the vast majority is bound for the border.'

'Into the States.' She thought for a moment. 'A massive market.'

'Hundreds of millions of people. The amount of opioids consumed, the amount of money involved, the consequences in suffering and crime are almost incalculable.'

'But don't most of the illegal drugs into the States go through Mexico?' she asked.

'Used to. But more and more are coming through Canada,' said Gamache. 'With all the scrutiny on the Mexican border and so much of the DEA's attention focused on Mexico, the head of the cartel here saw an opportunity.'

'Bring it in where they aren't looking,' she said quietly. Thinking.

'The country with the longest undefended border in the world,' said Gamache. 'Thousands of miles of forest, and no guards. No witnesses. The rum runners during Prohibition knew that. Fortunes were made in Canada by getting illegal booze into the States.'

It was true, Judge Corriveau knew. Many prominent families could trace their wealth, if they had the stomach for it, back to those days.

First it was the robber barons, and then came the rum runners.

Canada had a great reputation for law and order, as long as you didn't look under the table.

'How did you discover all this?' she asked.

He opened his mouth to reply, but needed a moment to marshal his thoughts.

'The reason this one small cartel dominates all the others is because the person who runs it has made sure it's invisible. And, if spotted, is dismissed as unimportant. As we did,' he admitted. 'This is a structure that's been years in the making. Simple. Lean. It's carefully constructed and all but transparent.'

'A glass house, Chief Superintendent?' asked the judge, but he didn't smile.

'Yes. It's there, but not there. And it's almost unassailable. It's able, above all else, to hide. Not behind cigar smoke in some greasy dive, or in a fortress estate. But in plain view. Unrecognized for what it is.'

'The devil among us,' said Zalmanowitz.

Corriveau turned a jaundiced eye on him, dismissing this romantic and unhelpful statement. But then she remembered the photo, shown in her courtroom. Blown up to twice life-size.

Of the robed figure looming. Masked. Still. Staring. Standing on the pretty village green.

The devil among us. Maybe it wasn't such a ludicrous thing to say after all.

Judge Corriveau was quiet for a moment, then her brows drew together and she shook her head.

'You're still not telling me how you found it. The cartel and the person who runs it. And what this has to do with the trial.' Then her face opened in surprise. 'The defendant? You're not telling me the defendant is the head of the drug cartel?' Her mind raced. 'But the charge is murder, not trafficking. The killing of Katie Evans. Does the defendant know that you know the rest? Wait a minute . . .'

Why were the two of them in this, whatever 'this' was, together? The cop and the Crown?

It was Chief Superintendent Gamache's idea, his plan. Why did he have to involve the Crown? Why did he need Barry Zalmanowitz?

And if the defendant really was the head of the cartel, why would the Chief Superintendent of the Sûreté hide that fact? Surely arresting Québec's equivalent of a drug lord would be reason to celebrate. Especially when the government, the press, members of his own force were accusing the Sûreté, accusing Gamache, of incompetence.

The Sûreté had become a national shame. An embarrassment.

Surely this would be vindication, something to be shouted from the rooftops. A great victory.

But instead, there was this quiet conspiracy between two men who didn't even like each other.

Why?

Because ... because ... Judge Corriveau slowed down her racing mind, and stepped from logic to logic.

Chief Superintendent Gamache needed the Crown's help. His collusion.

And there was only one thing the Chief Crown could bring to the table.

The charges.

'You don't want the defendant to know that you know,' she said. 'So you trumped up these charges to buy time.' She glared at Gamache. 'You've intentionally arrested the wrong person for the murder of Katie Evans, to get them off the street while you collect evidence.' Then her eyes swung over to Zalmanowitz. 'And you're trying someone for a murder you know they didn't commit. Not this murder anyway.' She glared at them. 'Which means the person who really killed Katie Evans is still out there.'

Her eyes narrowed, studying the men.

She looked from Gamache to Zalmanowitz.

The Crown, while an effective prosecutor, would never make it as a professional poker player.

He blinked.

And she turned back to Gamache, who would have made a fortune on that circuit.

'No, no,' she murmured. 'That's not it, is it? I've missed something. There's more to it than that. Tell me, now.'

Gamache was silent.

'You came in here knowing you would, Chief Super-intendent. No more bullshit. I'm hot and tired and now I'm afraid. It's not a pleasant combination. For me. Or for you.'

Gamache gave a decisive nod, then looked toward the pitcher of water, ice now melted, on a tray on the sideboard.

'Do you mind?'

'Not at all.'

He got up and poured them each a tall glass before sitting down and drinking his all in one go. He was parched but, more than that, the gesture gave him the chance to look at his watch without being noticed.

Four fifteen. The court had adjourned early. He glanced outside. The sun was still a good way up in the sky.

And while it was up, the new shipment would remain in Québec. But he knew that as the sun approached the horizon, the opioid would approach the border.

Still, he had time. Just.

'On the day the body of Katie Evans was discovered in the root cellar, I was having lunch with Superintendent Toussaint in Montréal. She's the head of Serious Crimes.'

'I know her, *oui*,' said the judge.

'I was new to the job, and so was she,' Gamache continued. 'We were going over our notes, the mess we'd inherited. We both knew then, of course, that the drug situation was out of control. And, frankly, beyond our control. We were tossing around ideas on what to do. None of them, honestly, useful or effective. We agreed that we had to try something new. Something bold and unexpected. And then Superintendent Toussaint said something, she used an expression. A cliché, really. Burn our ships.'

He looked at Judge Corriveau to see if it meant anything to her.

She was listening closely. The phrase was familiar, but without import.

'It means doing something from which there is no return,' he said.

'I know what it means, Monsieur Gamache.'

But he let it sink in. Everyone knew what it meant. But did they really, really, know what it meant?

To her credit, he could see the judge thinking more about it. Looking beyond the cliché, beyond the words, to the action it implied.

'Tell me,' she said.

'Going after all crime, everywhere, wasn't working. That much was obvious. So if that wasn't working, what would?'

She remained still. It was clearly a question she couldn't answer, nor was he expecting her to.

'Focusing,' he said. 'Specializing. I thought about choosing two or three areas to crack down on, ones that were particularly out of control. But that would've been a half measure. It would've been like burning half our ships. We had to burn them all.'

'Which means?'

'We, I, chose one area. A single focus. From which, as you said, most other crimes spring. The fountainhead. Drugs.'

'What have you done?' she asked, almost under her breath.

'I ordered that all of our efforts, all of our resources, be focused on finding the source, and destroying it.'

'All?'

'Essentially all,' he said.

'But that would mean ...' Judge Corriveau's mind once again raced. 'The other departments were gutted. Rendered ineffective.'

'Virtually, *oui*.'

She stared at him in disbelief. 'You did this? Knowing the human cost?'

He didn't move.

'And the drug trade? Has it stopped?'

'It's grown over the past year,' he said. 'As I knew it would. As it had to. We let it.'

'You let it?' she demanded, then reined herself in. And took a couple of deep breaths. Holding her hands out in front of her as a sort of bulwark against more information. Before she dropped them and clasped one tightly inside the other. Leaning forward now.

'Why?' she asked, trying to control her voice.

'Because the cartel had to believe we were incompetent. Ineffective. That we were absolutely no threat to them. They had to be emboldened. The invisible cartel, so protected and hidden, had to know, absolutely know, it was safe to show itself. It had to get sloppy. Only then would it be vulnerable.'

'And to do that, you let them do anything they wanted?'

'But we weren't idle,' he said. 'We were working hard, with informants, undercover agents, monitoring online chatter. Following shipments, getting to know routes and routines. As the year went on, they grew bolder and bolder. The shipments grew larger and larger—'

'You make it sound like flowers or porcelain,' she said. 'These were shipments of drugs, presumably some quite large.'

'*Oui.*'

'And you just let them pass?'

'*Oui.*'

That sat in the now charged atmosphere.

Judge Corriveau's eyes narrowed and her lips thinned. And her knuckles turned white.

'You started off by quoting a statistic, Monsieur Gamache. Tens of thousands of mostly young people a year who're killed because of the drug trade. How many of those deaths can be laid at your feet?'

'Wait—' Barry Zalmanowitz began, before being silenced by her look.

She turned back to Gamache and stared. And he stared back.

Then he nodded very slowly and thought about the notebook in his desk, and the notes he'd begun making the night Katie Evans's body had been found.

Warming himself by the cheerful fire at their home in Three Pines, that November night. Sleet outside. Reine-Marie beside him. Henri and Gracie curled on the rug.

He wrote about the horror to come. About the consequences of what he was considering.

He'd pause now and then, fighting the urge to make it less appalling than it would be. If he really went through with it. If he really pulled almost all the Sûreté resources, and focused on just one crime. One battle, to win the war.

'Over the course of the past year, since I took over and issued this order, there would have been thousands of crimes and, yes, deaths,' he said to Judge Corriveau. 'Thousands more than the usual carnage. Laid, as you said, at my feet. And it's not just those here in Québec, but those across the border. The shipments we allowed to pass.'

'I should have you arrested right here and now,' she said, and looked toward the closed door, beyond which sat the clerk. And officers of the court. Who, at a word from her, would enter. And take this man away. And charge him with murder.

Because that was, they all knew, essentially what he'd committed.

Premeditated. Deliberate.

'If this works—' Zalmanowitz began.

'And if it doesn't?' demanded Corriveau. 'You've taken a

monster and fed and nurtured it over the course of a year, and let it loose. A nightmare walking.'

'*Non*,' said Gamache. 'It was already loose and growing and laying waste to everything before it. And it was getting worse and worse. It would've consumed Québec, and we were powerless to stop it. We have, over the course of a year, constructed a trap. And we've been very carefully, very gently, very quietly steering the monster toward it.'

He leaned forward. 'You can arrest me. You probably should. But know this. If you do, you'll be destroying our one chance.' He held up his finger, raised to the ceiling. Then he lowered it and closed his hand into a tight fist.

When he began speaking again, his words were measured. 'It is a huge risk. I'll grant you that. One almost certain to fail. But know this. We had no choice. I had no choice. We had lost. And don't think for a moment I'm not aware of the price that others have paid for my decision.'

'But if it works . . . ' Zalmanowitz tried once again, pausing for her interruption and surprised when she allowed him to continue. 'If it works, the cartel will be destroyed. The drug trade will be crippled, if not wiped out. We will have won.'

Judge Corriveau turned to the Chief Crown. She'd essentially dismissed him. Marginalizing him in this interview. But now she saw him with fresh eyes.

He was right.

And he was more than that. He cared so much for this province, for the men and women and children born and unborn, that he had sacrificed his career. Perhaps even his freedom.

Which was more than she had done.

The longer she stared at him, the more uncomfortable Zalmanowitz became, squirming slightly under the unrelenting gaze. Until he noticed the look in her eyes. Gentle now. Almost kindly.

Then she turned to Gamache, and before her swam the increasingly ugly headlines. The *Enquête* report on television. The questions screamed at the Chief Superintendent by reporters circling. Smelling blood and entrails. Hoping to prod him over the edge, with their sharp questions and innuendo.

The new head of the Sûreté, they proclaimed, was way out of his depth. Incompetent. A good man, perhaps, but past his prime. And maybe, they'd begun to suggest just recently, not a good man. He was allowing crime to run rampant. Maybe he, like his predecessors, was in on it.

Gamache had taken all that, and more. In fact, it was what he'd hoped would happen. He'd manufactured that image of himself and the Sûreté. The cartel had to believe he personally was no threat at all.

Québec had become Dodge City, and Marshal Dillon was napping.

But he wasn't napping. He was waiting. And waiting. And quietly gathering forces.

And it wasn't just the Chief Superintendent, she realized. It couldn't be done without the agreement of at least a handful of senior officers. A small group of men and women.

Tiny. But powerful.

'You know who it is, the head of the cartel?' Judge Corriveau studied him. 'Of course you do. Is it the defendant?' She thought for a moment and shook her head. 'But that doesn't make sense. The defendant came to you and pretty much confessed, right? Unless you're lying about that.'

She looked at Gamache, then over to Zalmanowitz.

'Oh, the defendant murdered Katie Evans,' said Gamache.

And this time Barry Zalmanowitz managed to not look at his co-conspirator. But he was surprised.

It was another lie. And one that, by now, probably didn't matter. So much crap was flying around. So why lie about that? He remembered the whispered conversation a few minutes earlier between Gamache and his second-in-command.

And he remembered Gamache sinking to the hard bench, and lowering his head.

The end wasn't close. It was here. The devil was among us.

It all, now, depended on Judge Corriveau. She knew, Zalmanowitz could tell, that she was being lied to. Not only in her chambers, but in the courtroom. It was a most serious crime. Perjury. The perversion of justice. No one knew that better than the three people in that room. Never mind her threat to arrest Gamache for murder. Though they all knew it was a charge that wouldn't stick.

His intention, misguided or not, was to save lives, not take them.

But the perjury? That would stick.

They sat in silence, as Maureen Corriveau decided what to do. Arrest them? Call a mistrial? Free the defendant? All things she should do. No one knew that better than the three people in that room.

She sat absolutely still, but they could hear her breathing. Like someone who'd just climbed a steep flight of stairs.

'I need time,' she said. 'To consider what you've told me.'

She stood, and they stood with her.

'I'll get back to you with my decision before the trial resumes tomorrow morning. At eight. I think you know what I will likely decide. Prepare yourself.'

'Yes, Your Honor,' said Gamache. 'Thank you for hearing us out.'

She held his hand, and squeezed it slightly, then her gaze widened to include the Chief Crown. 'I'm sorry.'

As the door closed, Gamache looked at his watch and hurried down the corridor, Zalmanowitz keeping up with the long strides.

'That did not sound promising,' he said. 'She's going to come for us, isn't she?'

'Yes, I think so,' said Gamache. 'She has no choice. We brought this on ourselves and knew this almost certainly would happen. But what we didn't know is that Judge Corriveau would do what she just did.'

'Haul us up?' asked Zalmanowitz.

'No.' Gamache stopped, and turned to the Crown. 'Let us go.' He put out his hand. 'This is where I leave you.'

'Can I come?'

'You, monsieur, have done more than enough. A whole lot of scorn is going to be heaped on you, no matter what happens, by people you care about. Colleagues. Friends. Family maybe. I hope you know in your heart that you did the right thing.'

Barry Zalmanowitz stood quietly, and smiled, just a little. 'I do. I might have difficulty answering to them, but I can at least answer to my big stinking conscience.'

He took Gamache's hand, and felt the slight squeeze.

'It's tonight, isn't it?'

When Gamache didn't answer, Zalmanowitz gripped tighter for an instant and said, 'Good luck.' Then added, *'Merde.'*

'Thank you, Monsieur Zalmanowitz,' said Gamache, in a surprisingly accurate imitation of Judge Corriveau. Then in his own voice, *'Merci.'*

*

In her chambers, Maureen Corriveau sat back down and stared ahead of her. Knowing what she'd just done.

It was unjustifiable, what Gamache and Zalmanowitz had confessed to. Subverting justice, and in the Palais de Justice itself. But perhaps there was, as Gandhi had said, a higher court.

What Gandhi hadn't mentioned, and what would have been helpful, was that it wasn't just the court that was high, so was the price. Almost too high to contemplate.

She thought about the original cobradors, burned at the stake for the justice they sought.

Was the cobrador who showed up in that little village of Three Pines a travesty, a mockery of that courage? Or the embodiment of it?

Were the cop and Crown a travesty, or an example of what citizenship should be?

And did it matter? Her job wasn't to write the laws, but to uphold them. And in doing that, was she keeping vigilantes and chaos at bay? Or was she just following orders?

'Oh God,' she whispered. 'Why is it so difficult to know?'

'You finished for the day, Your Honor?' the clerk asked, knocking and then poking his head into her office.

'Not just yet,' she said. 'You go. What're you up to tonight?'

'Beer and burgers, and we'll get the sprinklers going for the kids. Which reminds me. If you hear banging and swearing, they're working on the AC.'

'Perfect,' she said with a smile.

Perfect, she thought, as the door clicked shut.

She sat back and tried to make sense of what had just happened, what she'd just heard from the Chief Superintendent and the Chief Crown.

Maureen Corriveau felt as though the lies, like goblins,

were swarming. Laying siege to all that was familiar. And comfortable.

The law. The courts. Order. Justice.

She stared at the small antique carriage clock on her desk. A gift from her law offices when she'd ascended to the bench.

The fine hands were almost at the five. She'd given Gamache until the next morning. Fifteen hours.

Was it enough? Was it too much? Tomorrow at this time, would they all be arrested? Would they all still be alive?

When she left to go home to Joan that evening, would a cobrador fall into step behind her, down the long, stifling corridor? For doing too much? For doing too little?

She wished now she hadn't invited them into her chambers. Hadn't forced the truth, and the lies, from them. She wished she could hide in happy ignorance. Go home to beer and burgers.

The one question the Chief Superintendent hadn't answered was who the defendant really was. And how the murder of Katie Evans was connected to all this.

But she knew she'd find out soon enough.

CHAPTER 28

Down in Myrna's bookstore there was a sudden banging, and up the stairs to the loft came Jean-Guy, stomping and snarling and shaking snow from his boots and coat.

Isabelle Lacoste followed him, shaking her head. It was as though each November came as a surprise to him. Some investigator.

'It's awful out there,' he said, as he and Lacoste took off their coats.

Myrna smiled and watched, knowing that while Armand had two children by birth, these two were just as equally his son and daughter. Always had been. Always would be.

'How did it go in Montréal?' asked Gamache, getting up off the sofa.

'It's done,' said Beauvoir, clearly not wanting to talk about the visit to Katie's sister and parents. 'I'll tell you more over dinner. There is dinner, isn't there?'

'I asked Olivier to take over a casserole,' said Gamache. 'Let me just see where that's at.'

Beauvoir popped a slice of baguette piled with brie and ripe pear into his mouth, mumbled something that sounded like, 'I'll go,' and grabbing his coat, he disappeared.

Isabelle poured a glass of red wine and wedged herself into the sofa between Myrna and Clara.

'Long day?' asked Myrna.

'And not over yet. I'm glad you're here,' she said to the Gamaches. 'I was going to come over here anyway.'

'Really?' asked Clara. 'Why?'

'I need some information from someone who knew Madame Evans and her friends. I've been reading over the interviews. Hard at this stage to know what's important, but nothing leaps out. You know you're in trouble when the only interesting thing said was from Ruth.'

'Really?' said Gamache, who'd been present at most of that interview and couldn't remember anything at all useful.

'Well, interesting but not relevant.' She turned to Reine-Marie. 'Did you know the church was used by rum runners during Prohibition?'

'It was?' said Reine-Marie.

'Really?' said Clara. 'That's news to me.'

'I knew it,' said Myrna. 'Ruth told me.'

'Come on,' said Clara. 'When? While you were doing her dishes?'

As far as they could tell, Ruth still didn't know Myrna's name or what she did, beyond a recurring suspicion that Myrna ran a lending library and was someone's maid.

'She told me in a roundabout way,' Myrna admitted.

Since Ruth was not known for subtlety, they looked at her with disbelief.

'I prayed to be good and strong and wise,
for my daily bread and deliverance
from the sins I was told were mine from birth,
and the Guilt of an old inheritance.'

321

'One of Ruth's?' asked Reine-Marie when Myrna finished reciting. 'I don't recognize it.'

'Unpublished,' said Myrna. 'I found it in one of her note-books when I was …'

Again, they stared.

'You were what?' asked Clara. 'Snooping?'

'Worse,' admitted Myrna. 'I go over Wednesday mornings and clean her house.'

That brought whoops of laughter, which eventually died down in the face of Myrna's face. Which was bashful and uncomfortable.

'Wait a minute,' said Clara. 'You're telling the truth? You go over there every week—'

'Actually, every second week.'

'And clean?'

'She's an elderly woman on her own and needs the help,' said Myrna. 'That'll be us one day.'

'Yeah, and you know what?' said Clara. 'Ruth'll still be alive. She's indestructible. I know. I've tried. She'll bury us all.'

'But it's a bit of a leap, isn't it?' asked Reine-Marie. 'Even for one as nimble as you, *ma belle*. How did you get from those beautiful lines of poetry to Prohibition?'

'I asked her about the poem. What it meant to her. This was a couple of years ago—'

'You've been doing it for that long?' asked Clara, both astonished and annoyed that her friend hadn't told her. Then something occurred to her. 'What did you do?'

'What do you mean?'

'You must've done something awful in this life, or a past one, to have to put on that hair shirt.'

'No, not penance. I think I might be a saint.' She peered,

dewy-eyed, into the distance, a beatific look on her face. 'Saint Myrna—'

'Among the Éclairs,' said Clara.

'I'd go to that church,' said Reine-Marie.

'You were saying?' Isabelle brought the conversation back to earth. Though she agreed with Reine-Marie.

'Strangely enough, that's what Ruth and I talked about. Church. She told me she'd sit in St Thomas's as a child, and pray to be normal. Pray to fit in.'

'Sometimes the magic works . . .' said Clara.

Armand remembered Ruth's admission the evening before.

About the ice. The cousin.

The guilt of an old inheritance.

'The church warden sort of adopted her and told her all about the history of the place,' said Myrna.

'Which is how she knew about Prohibition,' said Isabelle. 'I actually assumed she was one of the rum runners.'

Myrna laughed.

'I'd love to find out more,' said Reine-Marie. 'For the archives. Not exactly the first church along the border used for that. Churches were a favorite among the bootleggers.'

'A safe place, I guess,' said Clara. 'Who'd raid God's house?'

'We think of those days with a sort of charm,' said Reine-Marie. 'Speakeasies and Keystone Kops. But they were brutal. Fortunes were made. But only by the most vicious. Prohibition might not have created the Mob, but it led to their rise and their power.'

Gamache listened and knew she was right. The drug smuggling today had, as its godparents, the bootleggers nearly a hundred years ago. The syndicates, the systems, the psyches were created back then.

'You've researched St Thomas's,' he said. 'But you've found nothing to support what Ruth says?'

'I doubt the church kept records of crates of booze in and out of the basement,' said Reine-Marie.

'True.' He lapsed into silence.

Thinking about bottles. And bats. In and out of the basement.

Beauvoir walked over to the shining wooden bar and, taking a seat, he caught Olivier's attention.

'Any chance of that casserole the chief ordered?'

'I'll check in the kitchen. Anton's in charge of that.'

'The dishwasher?'

'That's the one.'

This did not bode well, but Jean-Guy was so hungry, he didn't care if the casserole was made of old dishrags and the gunk in the sink drain.

'Can I get a hot chocolate while I wait?'

'*Bien sûr*,' said Olivier, and went into the kitchen.

Beauvoir surveyed the bistro. It was packed and, of course, all the conversation was about one subject. The discovery of Katie Evans's body just hours earlier.

He scanned the room for the dead woman's husband and friends, but they'd obviously taken refuge in the B&B.

Jean-Guy found an armchair in a quiet corner and settled in.

A couple minutes later the hot chocolate, with freshly whipped cream piled on top, and a bright pink maraschino cherry on top of that, was placed on the wooden table in front of him.

'I thought I was bringing this for a child,' said the voice that accompanied the hand, and Beauvoir looked up.

Anton stood there, in a blue apron with thin white stripes.

'The casserole's just coming out of the oven. I can take it over in about five minutes.'

'I'll be here.' Beauvoir took the cherry off the whipped cream. 'With my cocktail. Let me know when it's ready and I can help carry.'

'Thanks.' Anton hesitated. Then looked at the hot chocolate. 'Nothing stronger?'

'*Non*,' said Beauvoir, popping the cherry in his mouth.

Anton hung there, but when Beauvoir didn't offer more conversation, he left.

A few minutes later, the two men were walking carefully across the village green, their feet crunching through the layer of snow and freezing rain. Trying not to slip and drop the dinner. Beauvoir in particular was moving slowly, the precious cargo fragrant and warm in his gloved hands.

'So.' Isabelle turned to Myrna, who towered over her even in the seated position. 'Let's leave Prohibition behind. I came here to ask you about Madame Evans's friends. Your friends. I've been over the interviews, but I wanted to speak to someone who knows them well.'

'I've known them for a while, especially Lea,' said Myrna. 'But can't say I know them well. I only see them once a year. Like everyone else.'

Myrna felt slightly guilty saying that, as though she was denying them, distancing herself from them. But it was the truth. She didn't know them well. And there was a chance at least one of them she didn't know at all.

'But you've known Lea Roux since she was six.'

'Yes. And now you think she might be a murderer?'

'I don't think they're blaming you,' said Clara.

'Even killers were children once,' said Isabelle.

'Even Eichmann,' said Clara.

'Eichmann?' asked Isabelle.

'The Nazi war criminal,' said Clara.

Isabelle stared at her for a moment, far from sure why Clara would mention a Nazi war criminal.

'Yes. Even Eichmann was a child,' agreed Isabelle, baffled but vowing not to be taken off piste again. She turned back to Myrna. 'Let me start off with an easy question. They normally come in the summer. Any idea why the date for the reunion was changed?'

'I asked Lea and she said that it's tough to fit everyone's schedules. These were the only dates that worked this year.'

'Was it a last-minute decision?' she asked.

Myrna thought and shook her head. 'No. Lea wrote me back in May that they'd be coming around Halloween.'

Isabelle nodded. 'Did she ever talk about Katie?'

Myrna shifted a little. No one was comfortable giving out details of conversations that were understood to be private. But she knew this wasn't gossip, this was a murder investigation.

'She talked about all of them, but not Katie in particular.'

'Did she like Katie?'

'Ahh, well, not at first. No one did. Like we heard last night, I think they were protective of the one who died. Edouard.'

'Did they blame Katie for what happened to him?' asked Isabelle.

'A bit, at first, I think. Katie dumped Edouard for Patrick and shortly after that he took his life. They all want to think it was an accident. He lost his balance and fell off the roof, but Lea says none of them really believe it. They think he jumped. While stoned.' She shook her head. 'I doubt he really meant to kill himself. Probably momentarily overwhelmed. And the drugs took away any brakes he had. Fucking drugs.'

Off to the side, by the fire, Gamache took a breath so deep Reine-Marie looked at him. It was the sort of inhale someone takes before plunging headfirst into cold water.

'The one they really blamed was the pusher, but no one could find him after Edouard died,' said Myrna. 'He took off.'

'Lea told us last night that the family did try,' said Clara. 'Even hired a private investigator, but the guy had disappeared.'

Lacoste turned to Gamache. 'Doesn't that strike you as strange?'

'Which part?'

'Well, it always sounds so easy. To disappear,' she said. 'But we both know it isn't. And a good investigator should've been able to track him down.'

Gamache was nodding. She was right.

'Maybe he wasn't such a good investigator,' Myrna suggested.

'And maybe,' said Reine-Marie, 'it wasn't drugs and it wasn't an accident.' She turned to Armand. 'Maybe he was pushed. You wondered that last night, didn't you?'

'I always wonder that,' he said with a smile. But it didn't fool her.

It was still on his mind.

Yes, it was tragically easy to imagine a distraught and fragile young man getting high and jumping in the middle of a roof party.

But it was equally easy to imagine someone, in the middle of the dancing and laughing and chaos of a rave, giving him a little push.

'We need to contact this young man's family,' said Lacoste. 'What was his name? Edouard what?'

'Valcourt,' said Gamache. 'And I think that's a good idea.'

'But that doesn't explain the murder of Katie Evans,' said Reine-Marie.

'*Non*,' agreed Isabelle. She turned once again to Myrna. 'Did any of them ever say anything about Katie? Something she might've done that could explain—'

'Her murder?' asked Myrna.

'And the cobrador. If it really was here for her, then there must be a reason. Even one from long ago.'

'Maybe he wasn't here for her. Have you thought about that?' asked Clara. 'The only reason we think that is because she was killed.'

'A pretty good indication,' said Myrna.

She looked at Armand, but he wasn't agreeing. Or disagreeing.

He couldn't get away from the feeling that this was far simpler than it appeared, and all this other stuff was just muddying the waters.

Something happened, perhaps long ago, to create a motive. To propel someone into killing Katie Evans.

An old inheritance.

'Back up, you brute,' said Jean-Guy, trying to get past the threshold of the Gamache home while tiny Gracie tried to stop him.

'What is that?' asked Anton in a whisper, so as not to offend the creature. 'I've seen Monsieur and Madame Gamache walking the two of them.' He looked over at Henri, who was standing back and wagging his tail so furiously his entire body was swaying. 'He's a shepherd, I know that.' But even so, Anton stared at Henri for a moment. Judging by the ears, he seemed to have some satellite dish in him. Then

Anton turned back to Gracie and lowered his voice even more. 'Is it a piglet?'

'We have no idea what she is. Pup, pug, pig. Wolverine. Though we're pretty sure she's a she,' said Jean-Guy, as they took the food into the kitchen.

'Well, progress not perfection,' said Anton, and Jean-Guy paused while turning on the oven.

Anton glanced around as he unpacked the dinner, noticing the worn butcher block countertops, the open shelving with dishes and glasses.

At the far end of the kitchen, by the windows that looked onto the village green, two armchairs sat on either side of a woodstove. Books and newspapers and magazines were stacked on side tables. Not messy, but neither was it overly neat.

The room was restful and inviting. As was the living room they'd walked through.

After tossing a small piece of wood into the woodstove to get the embers going again, Beauvoir joined Anton.

'You used a phrase just now,' said Beauvoir, putting out the napkins and trying not to step on Gracie, still underfoot.

'Did I?' Anton followed him around the pine table, folding the napkins nicely.

'Progress not perfection. It's one I recognize.' He stopped and looked at Anton. 'Are you a Friend of Bill?'

'I wondered about you too,' said Anton with a smile. 'Hot chocolate in a bistro? When everyone else is drinking wine or Scotch. Six years' sobriety. You?'

'Two years and three months.'

'Well done. Booze?'

'And drugs,' said Beauvoir. 'Painkillers.'

It wasn't something he ever talked about, except to other

members, and people who knew. Like Annie, of course, and the Gamaches.

Friend of Bill was code. For a member of AA. Of which this Anton was clearly one. It was like finding a member of his tribe, unexpectedly.

The two men stood in the warm kitchen, the sleet hitting the windows, and realized that while they knew nothing about each other, they actually knew each other better than almost anyone else on earth.

'Drugs were my problem too,' said Anton. 'Pharmaceuticals. Almost killed me. I had one foot in the grave and the other on a banana peel, as they say. Ended up in treatment, and finally kicked the drugs, but took up drinking. Seemed a sensible decision.'

Jean-Guy laughed. It was, absolutely, the logic of an addict.

'Finally kicked that too,' said Anton, putting the casserole in the oven to stay warm.

'You have a moment?' Beauvoir asked, indicating the chairs by the woodstove.

One of the problems with investigations was being away from his sponsor and meetings. It was helpful to talk to another member. Someone who knew the terrain.

'When did you start?' asked Beauvoir, taking a seat. Lifting Gracie onto his lap, he wrapped her in his sweater to keep her warm.

'Using? A bit in high school but it really got out of control at university. I'm not sure I was ever cut out for higher education, but the drugs sure hurried along the inevitable.'

'Flunked out?'

'Left just before that happened.' Anton shook his head. 'You know, some kids could handle it, but some, like me, it was like putting nitro in my system.'

'Did you ever deal?' asked Beauvoir.

Anton brought his hand up to his mouth and regarded Beauvoir as he gnawed on his nails.

'I won't arrest you,' smiled Jean-Guy. 'Besides, it must've been years ago.'

'Not that long,' Anton protested, then smiled. 'Yeah, I dealt, but not as much as some. I ended up using most of it myself. Big mistake. What a shitstorm.' Anton shook his head at the memory. 'Flunking out became the least of my worries. You know what a supplier does to a dealer who becomes a junkie?'

'I've seen.'

'So have I. That's really why I left. I ran away and hid. Put shit up my nose and my head up my own ass. And hoped no one would find me.'

'So how'd you get straight?'

'Family sent me to treatment. They'd had enough.'

He glanced into the fire and put his stocking feet up on the hassock, taking a small book off it first.

Opening the book, he flipped through it, then stopped and gave a single *harrumph* and looked up at Beauvoir.

'Have you read this?'

Jean-Guy sighed. 'I have.'

'Not a fan?'

'Between us?' He leaned toward Anton. 'I am. But don't tell anyone.'

Anton went back to the book and read out loud,

> '*From the public school to the private hell*
> *of the family masquerade,*
> *where could a boy on a bicycle go*
> *when the straight road splayed?*'

331

Beauvoir smiled. He recognized those lines, and he recognized how a straight road could splay.

'Ruth Zardo,' he said, cradling Gracie as though she were Honoré.

It was a comfort, feeling the little body, the little heart, next to his.

'*Oui*. Madame Zardo,' said Anton, closing the book and looking at the back cover, where the author's photo looked like something he'd seen when his head was up his ass. 'Who'd have thought an eighty-year-old madwoman would know the heart of a little boy.'

'Pain is universal,' said Beauvoir.

Anton nodded. 'That she knows.'

'That she causes,' said Jean-Guy, and Anton laughed, one burst of genuine amusement.

'So your family put you into treatment?' asked Beauvoir.

Anton tossed the book back onto the hassock. 'Yeah. I hated them for it for a long time, but whatever their motives, they did me a huge favor. I finally got clean and sober, but something else happened. After treatment I went into a half-way house. We had to take turns doing chores. When it came my time to cook, I discovered I love it. Never knew it before. All I ate at university was Kraft Macaroni and Cheese. It was amazing, to discover that passion. And legal too.'

He grinned.

The kitchen was filling with proof of Anton's passion. The subtle scents of the casserole he'd made for them – garlic, onions, herbs, slightly musky mushrooms and beef – mixed with the fragrance of the maple logs on the fire.

If the Gamaches and Isabelle didn't return soon, thought Beauvoir, he'd start without them.

'That's how you became a chef?' he asked Anton.

'*Oui*. Couldn't get a job in a restaurant, but did find one with that family.'

'They didn't care about your history?' asked Beauvoir.

'I didn't tell 'em,' said Anton. 'If you provide a good enough service, and work for cash, people don't ask.'

'What was it like, working for the Ruizes?'

'It was okay. He was a little weird. Very guarded, like he was dealing with state secrets.'

'Was he?'

Anton guffawed dismissively. 'Please. His job was looking after plants that make cheap toys. Knockoffs, probably.'

He stopped and looked at Beauvoir. 'I shouldn't be telling you this. I signed a confidentiality agreement.'

'Toys and cooking? You can't talk about that? You met Jacqueline there, right?'

'Yes.'

'Became friends?'

'Well, kinda had to. There was no one else.'

'More than friends?' asked Jean-Guy.

Anton laughed. 'Why does everyone think that? No, she's more like a sister than anything. Great baker. Have you tried her brownies? My God.'

Poor Jacqueline, thought Beauvoir. And wondered if she realized he only loved her brownies. Though that love did seem profound.

'It was nice when Monsieur Ruiz was gone. More relaxed.'

'Did he travel a lot?' asked Beauvoir.

'Fortunately, yes. His territory was all of North America and into Central America. I think he got the job because he could speak Spanish. Couldn't have been his winning personality.'

'He was Spanish, wasn't he?'

'That's right.'

Beauvoir contemplated his companion. The fire crackled, and the cast-iron stove threw gentle heat, enveloping the two men in a sense of well-being. Of safety. Their own little world.

Beauvoir cradled Gracie, who was snoring in the crook of his arm. As he waited for his companion to speak, he tapped his fingers, counting to himself. Two, three.

Seven, eight. Then decided Anton needed help. A prod.

'You knew what it was, didn't you?' he said. 'On the village green. From your time with that family. You knew it was a cobrador.'

Anton compressed his lips. 'I promised Jacqueline I wouldn't say anything. She wanted to be the one to tell you. But we're both afraid.' He lowered his voice in a way that would have been laughable, had his eyes not looked so desperate. 'You have no idea what that man was like.'

'Ruiz? You're afraid of him? But he's back in Spain, isn't he?'

'Yeah, well . . .'

'Who is he?'

Anton looked around.

'He isn't here,' Beauvoir assured him.

'I wasn't looking for him. I was looking for a computer. Monsieur Gamache must have one.'

'He does. In the study.'

He placed Gracie carefully in the hollow of Henri's belly, as he lay curled and sleeping in front of the fire.

'Follow me.'

The two men walked through the kitchen to the living room, and into the study.

Jean-Guy woke up the computer, making sure there

was nothing private or sensitive on it, while Anton stood at the door.

Only when he'd brought up a fresh search engine did he motion Anton forward.

Anton sat, hit a few keys, clicked on a few links. Waited. Waited.

Eventually he pushed his chair back so Beauvoir could get a better look.

There on the screen was a report from a Spanish news program. A man was being scrummed on the steps of what looked like a courthouse.

'Is that Antonio Ruiz?' Beauvoir asked.

'No, that's his lawyer. Señor Ruiz is in the background. There.'

He pointed to an elegant man in a well-tailored suit. In his late forties, maybe early fifties. Looking pleased and confident.

'What're they saying?'

'I don't know, but I can guess. Señor Ruiz was arrested for money laundering. The entire company was under investigation, but exonerated.'

'They got off?'

'The verdict came with a public apology.' He stared at the screen. 'Someone got to someone.'

Beauvoir pursed his lips. Where there was dirty money, there was organized crime. And where there was the syndicate, there were drugs. Lots of them.

He wondered if Anton knew that too.

The news story continued. The lawyer answering questions and finally, waving reporters aside, he took Ruiz's arm and guided him through the melee.

And then the report was over.

'Did you see it?' Anton asked.

'What?'

Anton replayed the video. And hit pause.

Just as the image started to dissolve, as the black seeped over the screen, it appeared.

From the top of the courthouse steps.

'A cobrador,' said Beauvoir.

And not the top hat and tails, Fred Astaire type.

This was the carrier of the conscience.

'How did you find this?' Beauvoir asked.

'Someone from Spain came for dinner,' said Anton. 'A colleague of Señor Ruiz. I was serving, and the man used the word *cobrador*, before Ruiz shut him up. The man turned so pale, I decided to look it up. That's what I found.'

'Did you tell Jacqueline?'

'Yes.'

'What happened to Ruiz? Did the family really return to Spain?'

'That's what they told us, but I don't really know, and I don't really care.' He sighed. 'I'll tell you, when that cobrador showed up here, I thought I'd piss my pants. Scared the crap out of me.'

'You thought it'd come for you?'

Anton opened his mouth, then shut it and shook his head. 'I thought Ruiz had sent it, to scare us. Or worse.'

'But why would he want to scare you? Do you know something about him?'

'No.'

'About the murder of Katie Evans? If you do know something, Anton, you have to tell me.'

'I don't. I promise.'

'But there is something, isn't there,' said Jean-Guy. 'You have to tell me.'

'Just between us?'

'Depends what it is, you know that. Is it to do with Antonio Ruiz?'

'Promise you won't tell anyone.'

'I can't. Come on, Anton. Tell me. I know you want to.'

Myrna was shaking her head.

'I wish I knew Katie better and could help. But what I do know is that those friends really do like each other. They're not pretending. I just can't see one of them plotting to kill her. Katie was bright and kind. The mother hen of the group. Not the wild child she once was. We all grow up.'

Not all, thought Gamache. Some, like Edouard, fall down. And never get up. Never grow up.

His mind left the warm loft and the murmur of conversation, and traveled across the cold village green, through the snow and ice, to his home. And the book in his desk. And the notes written there, in black ink. Like charcoal.

His plague diary.

Ashes, ashes, we all fall down.

'And the cobrador?' Clara's voice cut through Gamache's wandering mind and brought him back to the loft. 'Who the hell was he? How does he fit in?'

'Well, he obviously wasn't one of them,' said Isabelle. 'Or even someone from the village. No one was missing.'

'Then who was he?' asked Reine-Marie.

'There're a couple of other possibilities,' said Lacoste. 'He could've followed Madame Evans here, playing out some old grudge. Or he was hired by someone here. Someone who knew that Matheo Bissonette had written about the cobrador phenomenon and would recognize it.'

'There is, of course, a simpler answer,' said Reine-Marie.

'Matheo Bissonette himself hired the cobrador,' said Isabelle. 'And then told everyone, including Madame Evans, what it was. Yes, we thought of that. For it to work, she had to know what the thing was. Though it doesn't answer why he, or anyone, would do it.'

They looked at Myrna.

'I don't know why. Lea didn't come to me to say Matheo was planning to kill Katie. Not that I remember, anyway.'

'Maybe he wasn't,' said Armand. 'Maybe the cobrador was just there to shame her. Murder was never part of the plan. But someone saw an opportunity, and took it. And you're right,' he said to Clara. 'It's possible the cobrador's target was someone else completely. Would you excuse me?'

He stood up and turned to Reine-Marie, who was also getting to her feet, a look of some surprise on her face at his abrupt need to leave.

'Would you ask Jean-Guy to meet us in the Incident Room, please? Isabelle, can you join me?'

They said their goodbyes to Myrna and Clara.

'Jeez,' said Clara, watching them out the window. 'It's like someone kicked him in the pants. Did we finally say something useful?'

'If we did, I can't imagine what it was.'

'Maybe we're out of cheese.' Clara turned around to look, but there was still plenty left.

Then the two women watched from the warmth of the loft as Armand, Reine-Marie and Isabelle paused on the village green, at about the spot the cobrador had stood vigil.

The evening was dire, with snow and ice pellets and freezing rain. A full English of crap.

Then Isabelle headed to the B&B. Armand put his head

down and walked straight into the driving snow while Reine-Marie went home, which by now was just a faint glow through the flurries.

'I'm heading back to my studio,' said Clara.

'To finish your painting?' asked Myrna.

'It is finished. I'm going to start a new one.'

'Clara,' Myrna began. 'Your show's coming up. I just ...'
She opened and closed her mouth.

'You're a good friend,' said Clara. 'And I know you mean well. But you're just getting me upset. Making me doubt myself. Please,' she took Myrna's large hands, 'don't say anything more. Trust me. I know when something's finished. And when it's not.'

Myrna walked her to the stairs, and heard the tiny bell tinkle as Clara left.

She wondered if Clara was right. Some things might appear done, complete. But were actually unfinished.

At the steps up to the church, Chief Superintendent Gamache paused.

Instead of hurrying inside, he made his way around the corner of the building.

Once at the back, where no one could see, he turned on the flashlight mode of his phone and examined the ground.

The snow in the beam was pristine. No tracks at all. But then, there wouldn't be. The freshly falling snow would obliterate any tracks made the night before. And Lacoste's team would have already looked.

But they wouldn't have found what he was looking for.

Playing the light over the back wall of the church illuminated the weathered white clapboard.

He stepped closer, then back, closing one eye as the snow

slapped the side of his face, then he turned to peer into the dark woods.

The guests at the B&B were just sitting down to dinner when Isabelle Lacoste arrived.

'I'm sorry to interrupt,' she said, but it did not look like she was interrupting much.

The shepherd's pie, which smelled wonderful, sat on each of their plates, practically untouched.

'Would you like to join us?' Matheo asked. 'There's plenty.'

Isabelle recognized it for what it was. A vastly insincere invitation. She wondered what would happen if she accepted.

This had been a horrible day for them. Or, at least, for most of them.

They stared at her and, as Chief Inspector Lacoste looked at them, she suspected she was seeing a killer. She just didn't know which of them it was.

'*Merci*. But I have a small question. Something we need to pursue to put to rest.' She turned to Patrick. 'I understand that you kept in touch with the family of Edouard Valcourt. Is that right?'

'Yes.'

'I'd like to speak with them, and need their address or phone number or whatever you have.'

'But why?' asked Lea.

Lacoste turned to her and smiled. 'I'd forgotten that you sponsored a bill in his name, didn't you? You must've been in touch with the family too. Do you have a way to contact them?'

'I do, absolutely,' said Lea. 'Not on me, of course, but I can contact my assistant at the National Assembly and ask him to get it for you. I have your email, I believe.'

Lacoste had given them each her card at the end of their interviews.

'*Merci*. I'd like to try to contact them tonight.' She turned back to Patrick. 'Do you have their information in your contacts list?'

'I think I probably deleted it, when I upgraded devices,' he said.

'Why would you want to speak with the Valcourts?' asked Lea again. 'You don't think they're somehow involved in Katie's death?'

'No,' she assured her. 'I don't think they were, but we do have to wonder about Madame Evans's past, and one unresolved issue seems to be the death of your friend Edouard.'

'There's nothing unresolved,' said Matheo. 'He was stoned and fell off the roof. Katie had nothing to do with it. She wasn't even there. Neither was Patrick.' He turned to him. But Patrick just stared.

Matheo suppressed the overwhelming desire to slap the back of his head and knock that pathetic puppy-dog look off his face.

'I have no problem at all giving you their phone number and address,' said Lea. 'But it'll have to wait until morning. Is that all right?'

'If you can't get it sooner, yes.'

And Lacoste left them to their dinner and headed out into the snowy evening once again.

She came away without the Valcourts' coordinates, but with something else. The certainty that whatever had happened, Lea Roux was at the center of it. She was in charge.

And Lacoste remembered the advice given to Mossad

agents. Advice Lacoste had found abhorrent, wrong on every level. Until it had been explained.

The instruction given the Israeli agents, if they met resistance during an assault, was kill the women first.

Because if a woman was ever driven so far as to pick up a weapon, she would be the most committed, the least likely to ever give up.

Kill the women first.

Lacoste still hated the advice. The simplicity of it. The baldness. But she also hated that the philosophy behind it was almost certainly true.

Gamache took a few steps through the snow, into the woods. Not far.

Then he turned around to face the back wall of the church and as he did, lights went on, illuminating the ground around him. The snowflakes, like crystals caught in the light, gleamed.

He stood for a moment, taking in the sight, so bright, then he turned and looked into the gloomy woods.

With a last puzzled glance at the back wall, Gamache retraced his steps, climbed the stairs, and entered the church, where Jean-Guy was whacking his gloves against his coat.

'Madame Gamache said you wanted to see me here.' His stomach growled and he covered it with his hand while giving Gamache an accusing look. They could be eating by now instead of standing in the chilly church. 'Why were you outside? What're you looking for?'

'Rum runners.'

'They went thataway.' He pointed toward the cemetery.

Gamache turned in that direction, his brow furrowed, thinking. Snow trickled along his scalp and down his face and the back of his neck, as though the effort of thinking was melting it. The rivulet found its way past his collar and dribbled straight down his spine, making him roll his shoulders in discomfort as he led the way downstairs to the Incident Room.

CHAPTER 29

~

A fine line of perspiration trickled down Chief Super-intendent Gamache's neck and soaked into his collar.

In the powerful air-conditioning of Sûreté headquarters, he could feel his sodden shirt growing clammy as it clung to his body.

He wished he'd had time for a quick shower and change into clean clothes, but that would have to wait until after this meeting.

The officers had stood as he entered the conference room, but he waved them to their seats and took his own chair at the head of the table.

Gamache looked at each of them, men and women of all ages, all ranks. Who'd sat around this table, in those same seats, at least once a week for almost a year.

He remembered the private interviews, as he'd decided the members of this inner circle. From the thousands of officers, he'd chosen these few, for their intelligence, their determination. Their ability to work as a team. To both lead and follow. They were chosen for their bravery and boldness and their loyalty.

Not to Gamache. Not to the Sûreté. Not even to

Québec. But to the Québécois. To protect them. Perhaps at great cost.

He'd taken the most promising, and asked them to possibly, probably, almost certainly, destroy their careers. And they'd agreed.

Not, it must be admitted, without a fight sometimes, as the long view was obscured by leaping and waving and screaming immediate needs. And by their own training and morals. To stand aside, to do nothing, as crimes were committed. It was soul-destroying.

But they'd held together. Finally.

And now here they were.

For almost a year they'd put their plan into place. As well constructed, as focused, as hidden as the cartel they were trying to bring down.

A glass house, Judge Corriveau had called it. Transparent.

That's what it was. And that's what they were. Now.

A good hunter, Gamache knew, learned from his prey. And he'd learned from the cartel to be lean. Focused. Invisible.

To appear to be weak, while actually gathering strength.

But the time had come for exposure, on both sides. By the end of this night, one would be victorious. One would be shattered.

Grabbing a tissue, he wiped the perspiration from his face, no longer concerned about how it would be perceived.

'Tell me what you know.'

His gaze moved around the table and settled on Superintendent Toussaint, who was looking uncomfortable.

'Seems we were wrong, *patron*.'

'Is that so? About what?'

He knew the importance of appearing calm and controlled, even as his heart began to pound.

'The nesting dolls. There were two shipments, we now learn. One with the chlorocodide and the other without.'

'I see. And?'

'The one with the drugs left Mirabel last night. As soon as that huge shipment of fentanyl got across the border.'

'Has it crossed the border?' Gamache asked. His voice remained steady, though all depended on the answer to that question.

The room felt like it was teetering on the edge of a cliff.

'We don't think so. We think it's in the holding area.'

'You think?' asked Beauvoir, trying, with less success than the Chief Superintendent, to sound calm.

'Yes,' said Toussaint, an edge now to her voice. 'Think.' She turned back to Gamache. 'As far as our informant knows, it's still in Québec. We have some indications that he's right.'

'Really, now this is the same informant who told us earlier today that the shit, the krokodil, was still in the warehouse?' said Beauvoir.

'It is. He made a mistake.' Superintendent Toussaint's voice was icy now. 'You've heard of those. But he went back to confirm, at great personal risk. Then he contacted me.'

Toussaint and Beauvoir stared at each other.

'We have no way to be sure?' asked Gamache.

'Not without exposure, no,' said Toussaint.

'So we don't really know where the drugs are,' said Beauvoir. 'Except that they're not in the warehouse.'

'Correct.'

'You said you have other indications, though,' said Gamache. 'What're those?'

'The head of the syndicate for the East Coast is in Vermont. Burlington.'

The officers looked at each other, then at Gamache.

'He could be there for any number of reasons,' said Toussaint. 'We don't know for sure . . .'

'It's a short drive from there to the border,' said Beauvoir, his excitement overcoming his annoyance. 'One of those reasons could be to meet the shipment.'

'And not just the shipment,' said Toussaint. She turned to look at Gamache. 'It could mean they fell for it. More completely than we dared hope.'

'Go on,' said Gamache. He was thinking the same thing, but Toussaint had had more time to consider, and he needed to hear her thoughts.

'I think the head of the East Coast syndicate is in Vermont for more than a tub of Ben and Jerry's. And more than the krokodil.'

Gamache nodded, slowly. Taking this in. Trying not to let his elation override his good sense. Trying not to race ahead to a conclusion he was desperate to arrive at.

It fell to Beauvoir to say what Gamache was thinking. What they were all thinking.

'A meeting's been set up. When the exchange is made,' his voice was low, almost a whisper. 'The heads of both the Québec and the East Coast cartels will be together, in one spot.'

'Holy shit,' said several of the officers.

'But which side of the border?' asked one. 'Would he come into Québec? Would he dare?'

'What's to stop him?' another asked. 'Not the Sûreté, that's for sure.'

That brought a round of laughter that verged on hysteria.

Chief Superintendent Gamache was relieved too, but he was also wary. It was at about this time that mistakes were made.

Just as he thought he was luring them into a trap, perhaps they were luring him. If they'd learned one thing about the cartel, it was that they were smart. They might be invisible, but that didn't mean they didn't see everything that was happening around them.

Gamache let the celebration go on. There'd been precious little to be happy about in recent months. Let them enjoy this moment. Eventually the excitement died down.

'Walk me through your thinking, Madeleine,' said Gamache.

'This's the first shipment of chlorocodide across the border. It looks poised to become a significant drug, a huge moneymaker. Cheap to produce and an easy sell to a population always looking for the next great high.'

'It turns their skin into scales,' said one of the agents, reading the briefing bullet on krokodil.

'Right, and their brains to mush and eventually kills them young,' said Toussaint. 'When has that ever stopped a junkie? These are not reasonable people making rational choices.' She turned back to Gamache. 'You want my thinking? I think they're meeting to discuss territory. Borders are for politicians, not drug runners. But I also think they're meeting to size each other up. This is an indication of just how powerful the Québec cartel has become. What else would bring the head of the largest syndicate in the US into the woods of Vermont?'

'He feels threatened?' asked Beauvoir.

'I think he might.'

'You think he's come to kill the head of the Québec cartel?' asked another agent.

Toussaint thought. 'No. I think he might be prepared to, but these are also businesspeople. It's bad business to kill your supplier, unless there's no choice. I think they want to come to an understanding.'

'The head of the Québec cartel is smart enough to figure all this out,' said Beauvoir.

'*Oui*, certainly,' said Toussaint. 'And clever enough to be prepared to strike first.'

'Hell of a tête-à-tête,' said an agent.

'I think it's time to let the DEA know,' said Toussaint. 'This meeting can get out of control real fast and we're going to need help.'

'When do you think this's going down?' asked Gamache.

'Tonight, for sure. Probably shortly after nightfall. Before midnight, I think. They'll want to get it done.'

'And you think they'll meet at the crossing point?' asked Beauvoir.

'I do. It's the safest place. We've proven to them that we have no idea it's being used. The krokodil will be given to the US syndicate. The money will come to the Québec cartel. And the heads of both syndicates will at least start the process of coming to a new understanding.'

Everyone, except Gamache, looked at the clock on the wall. He was perfectly aware of the time, but also of the folly of being pushed into a near-panicked decision.

'We do not tell the DEA,' he said.

There was a commotion, as everyone spoke at once. Objected at once. He let that die down too. And when there was silence, he spoke.

'If we told them that the heads of two of the largest syndicates in North America will be coming out into the open, that they'll be meeting tonight, when a drug deal is going through, what do you think they'd do?'

He let them think, but only briefly.

349

'They'd mobilize,' he answered his own question. 'They'd have to. We would too, if told the same thing. Even if they were willing to let us take the lead, there'd be so much activity, the syndicates couldn't help but notice. No. There're risks either way, but my decision stands. We do this alone. We stick to the plan that has brought us this far.'

'But what happens if the meeting is on the other side of the border, sir? Where we have no jurisdiction?'

'We might lose them both,' someone else jumped in.

'You let me worry about that,' said Gamache. 'Focus on your own jobs tonight, and I'll focus on mine.'

He's not going to let that happen, Jean-Guy realized. One way or another, the head of one or both cartels would be brought to justice, if Armand Gamache had to drag them back across the border by the hair.

'Chief Inspector Lacoste is on site?' Gamache asked.

'She's monitoring the head of the Québec cartel, and will let us know any movement,' said Toussaint.

'*Bon*. Inspector Beauvoir, you have the tactical plans?'

'I do.' He pointed to the ordnance maps on which he'd laid out where each of them would be positioned and what their objective would be. Plans every person in the room was very familiar with.

Their lives, and those of their comrades, depended on knowing exactly what would be expected of each of them. What each of their targets and objectives would be. Both primary and secondary.

They'd be a small force, so each agent had to be perfectly placed. Every person, every movement, precise.

The tactical team had been alerted, briefed, weeks ago, without being told the objective.

The Sûreté had two great advantages. They knew, after

months of monitoring, exactly where the drugs would cross the border. And the syndicates had been lulled into believing the Sûreté was completely useless.

There was, though, another great advantage, Beauvoir knew. One perhaps less obvious. Motivation. Desperation even. Their backs were to the wall, to the ocean. This had to work.

But now something unexpected, though not unwelcome, had been added.

The head of the East Coast syndicate would also be there, and would no doubt bring his own small army.

A series of unknowns had been thrown into their carefully constructed plan.

The stakes had just gone higher, and the rewards had become almost inconceivable. But so had the dangers.

'They might not be relevant anymore,' Beauvoir warned, gesturing toward the maps.

'The American head might change the drop-off point,' Toussaint said. 'There might be another one they prefer.'

Gamache could feel the tension rising. And he could sense the mammoth efforts each agent was making to keep their anxiety under control.

'They might. Or they might not. We can't know. All we can do is go with what we do know, and be prepared to pivot. *D'accord?*'

'*D'accord, patron,*' they said as one.

Gamache thought for a moment, going over the strategy laid out in the plans. Then he turned to Beauvoir. 'Do you think there's a better way to do this?'

Beauvoir had also been quickly reviewing the plans, now indelibly in his head.

'I'll need to adjust it,' said Beauvoir. 'With the head of the syndicate there, there'll be more security. And they'll be more alert. But' – he thought about it – 'I think the plan is still solid. As long as nothing else changes.'

'Your informant is with them?' Gamache asked, and Toussaint nodded.

'*Bon*,' said Gamache, getting to his feet. Everyone in the room rose with him. 'If we have to make changes on the fly, well, it won't be the first time, will it?'

That brought laughter and knowing nods. Though the more veteran members of the team weren't laughing so much anymore.

'I'll be in my office if anyone needs me.'

As soon as the Chief Superintendent left, Beauvoir bent over the plans he'd worked on at home, for months, hoping this day would come.

When Honoré awoke in the night, he'd fed and soothed him while Annie slept. Rocking his son gently, and poring over the map, murmuring plans of attack.

How to hunt, arrest, and if necessary kill.

Not exactly Winnie the Pooh. Or Pinocchio. Not the bedtime story he'd hoped for his child. But if they were successful, it did increase Ray-Ray's chances of growing up healthy and safe. Of never having to find out what happens when the straight road splays.

'All right.' Beauvoir got the attention of the assembled agents. 'Let's go through this.'

He glanced again at the large clock on the far wall.

Twenty to six.

Then he looked at the closed door. He had to speak to Gamache, before whatever was going to happen that night happened. There could be nothing left unsaid between them.

*

Armand Gamache loosened his tie and he pulled his damp shirt out of his slacks. Going over to his desk, his hand went to the drawer where he kept his clean shirts.

But then he hesitated and, instead, he dug into his pocket, and bringing out a key, he unlocked the top drawer. Sliding it open, he saw the notebook and napkin.

It had been a while, months in fact, since he'd looked at either.

Many lifetimes ago, many lives ago, he'd written those words on the crumpled napkin.

How many had died since then, because of them? Because of him? He hadn't turned a blind eye to the drugs and violence. He'd seen perfectly clearly what was happening. Had asked for reports every day. Had counted the cost of lives ruined, lives lost. Because of what he'd let happen.

And still, he hadn't acted.

But tonight he would.

Setting the napkin aside, Armand opened the notebook and forced himself to read what he'd written, what he'd begun, that cold November evening with Henri and Gracie curled by the fire, and Reine-Marie beside him on the sofa.

When he'd looked into that fire and considered doing the inconceivable.

He wondered if the Spanish conquistador Cortés had done the same thing, on the long journey to the New World. When had the thought first come to him? Had he considered the consequences, when he considered those fateful orders? *Burn the ships.* Did he know what slaughter lay ahead, for his soldiers and sailors and for the Aztecs, whose entire civilization was about to be wiped out?

And Gamache wondered if, when the conquerors' feet hit

the sand, and smoke filled the air, some other creature had come on shore with them.

Had the conquistadors noticed a dark figure following them? A terrible witness to the terrible deeds.

But, of course, the deeds would not be considered terrible for hundreds of years. Cortés was a hero, to everyone but the Aztecs.

In his quiet moments, later in life, as his own death approached, did Cortés wonder what he'd done? Did doubt creep into the room? Was an ageless cobrador standing at the foot of the bed?

And Churchill? Did doubt tickle him awake, the night Coventry was bombed? Or the night the great city of Dresden was firebombed, in retaliation for something that was not their fault?

Gamache picked up a pen and, turning to a blank page, he started to write.

He wrote about the huge shipment of drugs he'd let through the border the night before. When he could have stopped it.

He wrote about the lives that would be lost, because of that decision. His Coventry. His Dresden.

He wrote about Monsieur Zalmanowitz, and his career in tatters. He wrote about Judge Corriveau and the censure she would suffer, for letting them go instead of having them detained. As the law said she should have.

He wrote about the men, and women, and children who'd suffered as he'd ordered that only the minimum be done to arrest criminals. To focus their resources on the main target, but to also give the impression of complete and utter incompetence.

Armand Gamache wrote it all down. Sparing nothing. And

when he'd finished with what had already happened, he went on. To what was about to happen. That night.

And when he stopped, Gamache laid down his pen, and closed the notebook. And placed the napkin carefully on top of it.

Then he went into his bathroom and had a shower, washing away the dirt and grime, the water salty to the taste. From the sweat. And something else rolling down his face.

'*Patron?*'

Beauvoir looked into the Chief Superintendent's office. It was empty. But he heard the shower.

Jean-Guy stood there, unsure what to do. Go in. Go away?

He didn't want to see his boss, his father-in-law, coming out of the bathroom wrapped in a towel. Or worse.

But neither could he leave without saying what needed to be said.

So he stepped into the room and closed the door and was about to take a seat when he saw the notebook out on the desk.

Curious, Jean-Guy approached. The shower was still on and, emboldened, Beauvoir opened the notebook and started reading. When the shower turned off, he quickly closed the book, replaced the napkin, and sat in the chair across from the desk.

The chief came out dressed in clean clothes and rubbing his head with a towel.

He stopped instantly upon seeing Beauvoir, who'd jumped out of his seat.

'Jean-Guy.'

'*Patron.*' He stood rigid, slender shoulders squared. 'I'm sorry I left the courtroom today.' His voice was formal as though making a report, or reciting rehearsed lines. 'It was unforgivable.'

And then the formality broke down and his shoulders loosened. 'I don't even know why I did it. We've been through worse. But I just . . .'

Armand stood there, listening. Not jumping in to finish the sentence. Neither rebuking, nor saying it was all right.

He gave Jean-Guy the space he needed, to say what he needed. In his own words and time.

'I got scared.'

There it was. A grown man, a senior officer in the Sûreté du Québec. Admitting he was afraid. And that, Gamache knew, took courage.

'Of what?' he asked.

'I was afraid I'd scream, "Don't do it." Up until then, I knew we could go back. A line had been stretched, but hadn't yet been crossed. You outright lying in court, perjuring yourself, was something that could never be undone. I knew there was really no choice, but I couldn't watch.'

Gamache nodded, taking it in before he spoke. 'I think there's more to it.'

'Maybe,' admitted Beauvoir, intensely uncomfortable under the gaze.

'I think you lost some respect for me today. I don't think you believed I would actually do it. Lie under oath, under any circumstances. It breaks every law that you and I believe in. It makes me a hypocrite.'

Was that it? Beauvoir asked himself. *Did that explain it?* Because the truth was, he couldn't really explain it to himself. Even saying he couldn't watch Gamache destroy his career didn't justify his leaving. The Chief Superintendent had never put career first.

So what was it?

And he knew, at that moment, that Gamache was right.

He'd left because he couldn't watch this fall from grace. This sullying of someone who'd always been a mentor, an example. Who'd stood by his principles, stood by the law when most others were bending it to their own benefit.

But today, Gamache had done the same thing. And not just bent it, but broke it.

He never really believed this man, of all people, would lie under oath. In a courtroom. For any reason. When it came down to it, Jean-Guy had seriously thought another solution would be found. The Mounties would miraculously appear and all would be well.

But instead, in that hellhole of a courtroom, Armand Gamache had perjured himself.

Gamache watched Jean-Guy, and knew he'd hit the target. He hadn't wanted to, had hoped he was wrong. But he could see now that there was another victim, another body in the ruins.

The respect Jean-Guy had for him. Not the worst of the corpses, for sure, but there was no denying the pain it had caused. In Jean-Guy's eyes, he was now corrupt. No different from so many other senior Sûreté officers who'd sworn to uphold the law, but had broken it instead.

The fact the others had done it to amass fortunes, and Gamache had done it to bring the drug trade to its knees, did not really matter. The fact was, he'd proven himself no different from them.

Corruption starts small, often justifiable. A white lie. A minor law violated for the greater good. And then the corruption, like a virus, spreads.

'I hate to break it to you, Jean-Guy, but I crossed that line the first time I ordered that we step back and not make an arrest. I am being paid to uphold the law. It was an oath I'd taken, a duty entrusted to me. But I chose not to. Today, in court, I simply made my transgressions provable.'

'Does Judge Corriveau know? Is that why she called you into her chambers?'

'She suspects. She asked if the real murderer is still out there.'

'And what did you say?'

'I assured her that the defendant was the real murderer, but I'm not sure she believed it. She's taking the night to think and will decide what to do about Monsieur Zalmanowitz and me in the morning.'

'But she let you go,' said Beauvoir, seeing what really mattered.

His brows drew together as he considered what the chief had said. He felt a heaviness in his chest. But then something occurred to him.

'If you crossed that line when you issued the orders, then I crossed it with you when I followed them.'

Gamache knew that was true, of course, but had chosen not to say anything. This night would be long enough, hard enough, without that weighing on Jean-Guy.

But the younger man had arrived there on his own. And now Gamache saw something unexpected. Far from adding to Beauvoir's burden, he seemed lighter.

'I'm equally to blame,' Jean-Guy said, his face opening, the distress vanishing.

And Armand realized that the problem wasn't so much that he'd fallen from grace in Beauvoir's eyes, but that a chasm had opened up between them. But now they were at least in it together. The outhouse. The two-holer.

'We're both in big shit.' Jean-Guy felt almost giddy with relief.

'Up to here.' Gamache lifted his hand over his head and

returned to the bathroom to brush his hair, then came back, doing up his tie. 'Everything's ready?'

'*Oui.* Isabelle hasn't called yet, but we need to be leaving now. The rest of the team's getting their equipment together. I have your vest.'

'*Merci.*' Gamache went to his desk and, unlocking another drawer, he brought out his holster and gun and attached it to his belt before putting on his suit jacket. Rumpled, but dry at least.

The assault van would go down separately, and when it was dark the agents would get into position.

And wait.

He considered replacing the notebook and napkin in the drawer, and locking it. But realized it didn't matter. And if something happened, and it all went south, the notebook would help investigators understand. If not agree.

The two men walked down the long corridor to the elevators. The gun felt uncomfortable, foreign, on the Chief Superintendent's hip. He hated firearms. Their only purpose was to kill people. And he'd seen enough death to last many lifetimes.

'I should've stayed with you in the courtroom,' said Jean-Guy, as he punched the down button. Then he turned to Gamache. 'Are we okay?'

'We were never not okay, Jean-Guy.' The elevator came and they got in. Just the two of them. 'Did I ever tell you about my first tactical assault?'

'I don't think so. You haven't written a poem about it, have you?'

'An epic verse,' said Gamache, clearing his throat. Then he smiled. '*Non.* This is more prosaic. I was an agent, but not exactly a rookie. I'd been in the Sûreté for a couple of years.

We were going after a street gang. Heavily armed. A full assault on their bunker.'

As he spoke, he clasped his hands behind his back and stared up at the floor numbers above the elevator door.

'I passed out.'

'Pardon?'

'As soon as the first shots were fired. Woke up with a medic slapping me.'

'Pardon?' Beauvoir repeated, turning to Gamache, who continued to stare at the numbers.

'I blamed it on heat stroke. The heavy equipment, the waiting, the sun beating down. But it wasn't that. It was terror. I was so scared, I fainted.' He paused. 'Though passed out sounds a little better.'

Now he turned to look at Jean-Guy, who was staring at him, incredulous.

'Only Reine-Marie knows that story. Knows the truth.'

Jean-Guy continued to stare, openmouthed.

'That episode forced me to take a hard look at myself,' said Gamache. 'At whether I was really cut out for this, or if my fears would always get the better of me, and endanger those around me. But I loved the work and believed in it. And I realized I couldn't be afraid and do what needed to be done. And so I worked on the fear.'

'Is it gone?'

'I think you know the answer to that.'

Jean-Guy did.

It never went away completely. Not even for the Chief Superintendent.

As the elevator descended to the lowest level, Beauvoir remembered the predictions in the notebook, and the napkin laid so carefully on top of it.

360

The name of the restaurant was printed in cheerful red letters across the top.

Sans Souci. Without a care.

And below that, in black ink, *Burn our ships*.

He followed Gamache out of the elevator.

It wasn't really, he knew, about less fear. It was about more courage.

CHAPTER 30

T he bistro in Three Pines felt cool and calm to Isabelle
Lacoste, compared to the throbbing heat of the *terrasse*,
where patrons relaxed and sipped lemonade and beer.

She took off her sunglasses and waited for her eyes
to adjust. She preferred to be inside, for any number
of reasons.

'I'd love a good stiff drink,' Isabelle called to Olivier as
she made her way across the bistro toward the long wooden
bar. 'A gin and tonic, I think. Oh, make that a double. I'm
off duty.'

'Long day?' Olivier asked, as he poured Tanqueray over
the ice cubes.

Isabelle reached the bar and nodded as she opened one of
the candy jars and took out a licorice pipe. She bit off the red
candied embers first, as her kids had taught her to do, and as
Monsieur Gamache had taught them.

'How's the trial going?' he asked.

Lacoste tipped her hand back and forth. *Comme ci, comme ça.*

Olivier shook his head as he cut the lemon, the fresh scent
momentarily hanging in the air.

'So sad,' he said, pointing the paring knife toward St Thomas's chapel. 'But at least there's finally justice for Katie.'

Isabelle turned and looked through the bistro window, past the patrons on the frying pan patio, sipping their cold drinks. Past the children playing on the vivid village green, running in and out and around the three huge pine trees, as though the trees themselves were companions. Past the fieldstone and brick and clapboard cottages with their perennial beds of china blue delphiniums and old garden roses and mallow and lavender. Gardens planted by great-grandparents and tended with care.

Isabelle Lacoste's eyes traveled over the old village and came to rest on the little white clapboard church on the hill. The scene of the murder of Katie Evans, and so much else.

All of which would come to a head that night.

Justice, she thought. A few months ago she knew exactly what that meant. Now she wasn't so sure.

'Who're they?' she asked Olivier.

Two men were sitting quietly in front of the empty hearth, enjoying a meal. Anton was speaking with them, perhaps describing the food he'd made.

They looked over at her and she smiled, and raised her glass to Anton, who waved back.

'Don't know,' said Olivier. 'Just passing through, I think. Not staying at the B&B. You know Gabri. One set of guests is more than enough.'

'So there is someone at the B&B?' she asked, smelling the refreshing tonic water, and gin, and lemon.

'*Oui*. Lea and Matheo are down.'

'Really? Did they say why?' She tried to sound casual, not letting Olivier see her whirring mind.

'I didn't ask, but it's probably something to do with the trial. We're reading the reports. Seems they're giving Armand a hard time. Lea and Matheo might want to have words with him. They seem pretty tense.'

Yes, thought Lacoste. That was one explanation.

Around her there was the hum of conversation. Many patrons were now finding the *terrasse* too hot and were retreating into the cool interior. They chatted, but there was little outright laughter. The trial, so far away, was felt very keenly in the village. Some of the villagers would be called as witnesses. Thankfully the investigators had headed off the Crown's desire to call Ruth Zardo to the stand.

Lacoste's own testimony was scheduled for the next day, though she knew it would never come to that. Not after the night to come.

Chief Inspector Lacoste hadn't been in court that day and so hadn't heard Gamache's testimony. But she'd certainly heard reports. From colleagues, and on the news.

She'd heard about the increasing acrimony between the Chief Crown and the Chief Superintendent. To the point where they'd both been hauled into the judge's chambers.

What had happened there? What had Gamache said?

Had he told Judge Corriveau what had really happened that November night, when he'd returned to the basement of St Thomas's?

Had he told the judge the secret they'd been so desperate to conceal, to the point of Gamache perjuring himself?

It had started as an offhand remark by a crazy old poet and had developed, over drinks in Myrna's loft, into a suspicion. Which grew into an action.

*

Once in the church basement, Gamache took off his coat, embedded with snow, and tossed it over a chair. Then he led Beauvoir across the room to the root cellar.

'Can you get an evidence kit, please? And two sets of gloves.'

While Jean-Guy did that, Gamache turned on the industrial lamps installed that day by the Scene of Crime technicians, then he paused on the edge of the room.

All murder scenes had a solemnity, a gravity, about them, often at odds with the actual surroundings. A terrible killing in a cheerful place was especially horrible.

This little room, windowless, with a dirt floor and shelves sagging with forgotten preserves, and cobwebs made by long-dead spiders, was never going to be a cheerful place. The root cellar was meant to be cold, but the killing of Katie Evans made it all the more chilling.

It was not a place even a seasoned homicide investigator would want to spend much time in.

Gamache looked at the spot on the floor where the crumpled figure of Katie Evans, dressed in the cobrador costume, had been found. The former head of homicide for the Sûreté never forgot that this was not simply a job. A puzzle. An exercise for the reason and intellect.

A young woman had taken her last breaths, here. Lying in the dirt and dark, in the cold cellar. Not in bed, surrounded by loved ones, at the age of ninety, as she might have hoped.

'Madame Gamache didn't see a bat when she found Katie Evans's body. But it was there when Lacoste arrived. That means it was replaced, without anyone else seeing. This's the back wall of the church.' Gamache walked up to it. 'So it must be here.'

'What must?'

Gamache turned to Beauvoir. 'Bootlegged alcohol was moved in and out of the church during Prohibition. They didn't take it out the front door.'

Beauvoir's eyes widened as he realized what Gamache was saying. 'Shit.'

The two men began to carefully examine the shelving.

'Got it,' said Jean-Guy.

'Wait,' said Gamache. He picked up the Scene of Crime camera and recorded the moment Inspector Beauvoir swung out one of the shelves, then pushed on it.

A low door, built into the wall, opened.

Beauvoir got on his knees to look through it and a gust of snow blew into his face. Squinting, he saw the woods just a few steps away.

It was a fairly short haul through the forest to the American border. A smuggler's dream.

'So that's how the baseball bat got out, then back in,' said Beauvoir.

Gamache clicked off the video and handed the camera to Jean-Guy, who began documenting what they found.

'It's perfect,' Gamache said under his breath, as he looked around at the windowless room.

For the cobrador and for the killing.

'*Patron?*' came Lacoste's voice, from the Incident Room.

'We're in here,' said Jean-Guy.

'I'll just get my computer going and start downloading emails,' she called. 'Be right with you.'

Gamache looked around and saw the small door just closing. And as it did, the shelf neatly, soundlessly, fell back into place.

He bent closer and examined the hinges.

In the Incident Room, Lacoste took off her coat and

clicked on the email, then, on hearing a sound, she looked over to the stairway.

In the silence of the church, the footfalls on the stairs made an eerie sort of tattoo.

Buh-boom. Buh-boom. Like a heartbeat approaching.

And then Beauvoir appeared.

Isabelle's eyes widened and she jerked her head back in a sight so comical, Jean-Guy laughed.

'*Désolé*,' he said.

She looked over at Gamache, who was standing at the door of the root cellar. He raised his hands slightly, to indicate that he had nothing to do with this.

'He was here,' Gamache offered.

'And now I'm here,' said Beauvoir.

Lacoste stared, from Gamache to Beauvoir, then she got up and walked over to Jean-Guy.

'Tell me how you did that.'

'I'll show you.' Jean-Guy led her across the room to Gamache and the root cellar. 'It was the chief who figured it out.'

'Though I had nothing to do with ...' Gamache danced his finger toward and around Beauvoir.

Lacoste was far from sure about that. If ever two men were made for cahoots, it was these two. They were cahootites.

'Well,' she said, after being shown the hidden door. 'Well, well. You've taken samples?'

Beauvoir pointed to the evidence kit and nodded.

She walked back into the Incident Room in silence, Gamache and Beauvoir following, and when she turned around she said, 'Made by the bootleggers Myrna told us about.'

'Exactly,' said Gamache.

'And used by the murderer.'

'And the cobrador,' said Gamache.

'They're probably the same person,' said Lacoste. 'But how did he know about the hidden door? You didn't even know. No one did, except Ruth and Myrna.'

'They didn't know about the door,' Gamache pointed out. 'Only about the Prohibition story. To them it was an interesting bit of history, but nothing more.'

'Myrna or Ruth must've told someone else,' said Lacoste. 'And that person put it together and found the door. But why would anyone go looking for a hidden door in a church basement?'

Gamache was wondering the same thing.

Sometimes people stumbled onto things by accident. Like those who found Three Pines.

But most of the time something was found because they were looking, and they were looking because there was a need. Necessity drove discoveries.

It was slowly dawning on Gamache what that need might be.

When Prohibition had been repealed, those secret rooms had been abandoned. Forgotten. Those who'd created them were long dead, though the fortunes remained, as did the rooms.

On the border. Waiting. For some new need to arise.

The border was porous. Always had been. And what poured across it now was a lot more powerful, and more lucrative, than booze.

Beauvoir went to his desk to download emails.

'Antonio Ruiz is back in Spain,' Beauvoir reported. 'The Guardia Civil just confirmed it.'

He got up and took a seat at the conference table with them, bringing with him the photo he'd taken from the Evanses' home.

Gamache examined it. The smiling faces. Familiar, of course. Younger, of course. Happier.

His gaze lingered on Edouard, the ghost, the bright shadow that followed the friends.

Jean-Guy told him about his conversation with Katie's sister.

'Still nothing that would justify a cobrador,' said Gamache. His eyes went back to the photo. This time shifting from Edouard's face, to his arm, around Katie. 'I wonder why she kept this one? They look still together.'

'And I wonder why Patrick was apparently happy to keep it,' said Jean-Guy. 'There must've been other pictures of them all together. Ones less . . . '

'Intimate?' Gamache nodded. *Why this one*, he wondered.

'I had a talk with Anton, the dishwasher, just now,' said Beauvoir. 'When he brought the dinner over. He admitted that he knew about the cobrador.'

'How?' asked Lacoste.

'Antonio Ruiz had been followed by one in Spain.'

Beauvoir told them about the video and what Anton had said.

'Money laundering?' said Gamache.

That almost certainly meant organized crime. Racketeering. Gambling. Drugs.

'And Jacqueline also knew?' asked Lacoste.

'*Oui*. She made Anton promise not to say anything because then people would ask questions, want to know how they knew, and then they'd have to say something about Ruiz,' said Beauvoir. 'They seem afraid of him, and not just because of the confidentiality agreement.'

'If he's involved in organized crime, they have reason to be afraid,' said Gamache.

'Anton told me something else,' said Beauvoir. 'He thought the cobrador was here for him.'

'That's not exactly news. Everyone in the village thought the Conscience was here for them,' said Gamache. 'Including me.'

'But Anton had good reason.' Beauvoir leaned across the table, closer to them. 'He knew Katie Evans.'

'How?' asked Lacoste.

'From years ago,' said Beauvoir. 'He knew all of them. He wasn't sure at first. He only saw them at a distance since he works in the kitchens, and it'd been so long, but when he heard them talk about the Université de Montréal, he knew for sure. He was a student when they were there. Then when the cobrador showed up, he thought he was in big trouble. He thought the four of them had sent it. To collect his debt.'

'What debt?' asked Lacoste, then quickly raised her hand. 'Wait. Don't tell me.'

She thought about it for a moment, then she put her elbows on the table, her eyes bright.

'He's the one who sold Edouard the drugs,' she said, and Beauvoir nodded.

'When Edouard died and questions were asked, he took off,' said Jean-Guy. 'Ended up in treatment.'

'Did Madame Evans and the others recognize him?' Gamache asked.

'If they did, they didn't say anything to him,' said Beauvoir.

'Or to us,' said Lacoste. 'Now why would they keep that a secret?'

'Maybe they didn't realize who he was,' said Beauvoir.

'Just seems a bit of a coincidence, doesn't it?' said Gamache. 'Here we are in a tiny village few even know exists, and who arrives but the only four people on earth who can tie Anton to that death.'

Lacoste and Beauvoir nodded. Coincidences were not

uncommon in murder investigations. Just as they weren't uncommon in life. It would be foolish to read too much into it. But it would be equally foolish not to wonder.

'We need to go back to the B&B and see if they did recognize Anton,' said Lacoste.

'Though that wouldn't make them responsible for the cobrador,' said Gamache. 'The cobrador didn't just show up. It must've been months in the planning, maybe longer. Madame Evans and the others would have only just recognized Anton in the last few days.'

'And how does Katie Evans's murder fit into this?' Lacoste asked.

The cobrador, the Conscience, had rattled this secret loose from Anton, about his role in Edouard's death fifteen years earlier. But it was possible someone there had an even bigger, nastier secret.

Lacoste looked over toward the root cellar. 'We need to seal up the hidden door so no one can use it.'

Gamache, deep in thought, watched them head across the room. 'Wait,' he called and got up. 'I think we should leave it.'

'But whoever used it could come back,' said Lacoste.

'And do what?' he asked, joining them at the door to the root cellar.

'Well,' she said, feeling instinctively that an intruder must do harm, but now that she thought about it, she couldn't come up with anything, at least not anything serious.

They had all the samples, all the photos.

'Our computers,' said Beauvoir.

'You have a password,' said Gamache. 'Besides, if the murderer comes back, it probably won't be to take anything. He wouldn't risk being found with laptops stolen from the Sûreté.'

He'd met killers who were that stupid, but they were unfortunately quite rare.

'Let's at least take our notes and erase the board,' said Lacoste, pointing to the whiteboard, on which were written flowcharts and suspects and ideas.

'No, leave that too.'

'But he'll know where we're at,' said Beauvoir.

'And he'll discover that we're lost,' said Gamache.

'We're not lost.'

'No. But he wouldn't know that, would he, if he read your reports, or looked at that.' Gamache pointed to the board.

'*Non,*' she admitted.

'There's something to be said for appearing to be lost,' said Gamache, almost to himself. 'For appearing incompetent. To even appear to have given up. Puts criminals at ease. Lowers their defenses. Makes them overconfident.' He looked at them with a touch of wonderment. 'And then they make mistakes.'

'You're not suggesting we give up, *patron*?' said Lacoste.

'Just the opposite,' he said, distracted. 'I think.'

And he did appear to be thinking, hard.

Beauvoir caught Lacoste's eye with a questioning glance.

'I think,' said Gamache, turning to face them, 'that we should keep what we found tonight to ourselves. In fact, I know we should. We tell no one about the hidden door. Not even other members of the team.'

'*Pardon?*' they both asked at once. It was unprecedented, to keep a valuable piece of evidence from their own investigation team.

'Just for now,' said Gamache. 'Give me tonight. I need time.'

'I'm going to put a camera up in the corner of the room,' said Beauvoir. 'If anyone does come in, we'll at least see who it is.'

While he did that, Lacoste checked her messages.

'The lab says we won't get results from the cobrador costume until tomorrow morning. There're multiple DNA samples on it.'

'Probably rented,' came Beauvoir's voice from the root cellar. 'God knows when it was last cleaned.' His voice carried all the disgust of a well-groomed man.

'But,' said Lacoste, reading further down the report, 'we do have the results from the bat.'

She spoke slowly, reading as she went.

Gamache stood behind her, his expert eyes finding the pertinent lines buried in among the scientific jargon.

Lacoste swung around in her chair and looked up at him.

'What do you make of that?' she asked.

'What?' asked Jean-Guy, striding across the Incident Room to join them.

He read in silence, then he too straightened up, his brows deeply furrowed.

'It's not enough to make an arrest,' said Lacoste. 'Not yet. But at least now we know who handled the murder weapon, and who almost certainly killed Katie Evans.'

'But what do you make of that?' asked Gamache, pointing to another line on the report.

'That's just a trace,' said Lacoste. 'The lab says that it's probably incidental.'

'It's slightly more than a trace,' said Gamache. Though not much more. And Lacoste was right, the technicians, expert in the field, concluded it was a bit of DNA that had probably fallen from the murderer, but did not belong to the killer.

The other two results were clear. One belonged to Katie Evans. The other to her killer.

And yet.

'Why was the bat removed from the scene?' he asked. 'And then replaced? At great risk.'

It was a question that had plagued them.

There were a few reasons the murderer might do that. He was panicked. Or distracted. The way people sometimes walked out of a shop with an unpaid article in their hands. By mistake.

And when the murderer realized what he'd done, how very incriminating the bat was, he'd returned it.

That was the most likely reason.

But still, why not just burn it? Why risk returning it?

And that brought them to the other reason. The killer wanted the bat to be found.

'To manipulate the results,' said Beauvoir. 'To plant DNA evidence.'

'Maybe,' said Gamache. 'And if that's what's happened, it might be helpful to let the real murderer think he's fooled us.'

'More incompetence, *patron*?' asked Beauvoir. He smiled.

And yet Beauvoir felt a creeping concern that they weren't simply pretending to be incompetent, but that they actually were. That these decisions would lead them in the wrong direction and a killer would go free.

'We need more evidence,' he said.

Gamache was nodding. It wasn't enough to find out who'd murdered Katie Evans. They had to be able to prove it.

'Been a long day,' he said. 'We need to eat.'

There was no challenging that last statement at least.

Anton hadn't been lying about his skills as a chef.

The beef casserole, with hints of herbs, and wild garlic and succulent mushrooms he'd gathered in the fall and dried, was unlike anything they'd ever tasted.

'Does Olivier know what he has in Anton?' Reine-Marie asked.

She'd been trying to put on a cheerful face, though she was clearly exhausted, wrung out by the events of the day.

'I don't think so,' said Armand, clearing the table while Jean-Guy got out the dessert.

'Panna cotta with raspberry coulis,' Beauvoir read from the note attached to the ramekins. 'Anton told me he learned how to cook in treatment. Clearly I went into the wrong treatment program.'

'Never,' said Gamache. 'We love our macramé plant hangers.'

'That's good, because Christmas is coming up.'

'Come on,' Armand said to Reine-Marie, who had dark circles under her eyes and was fading fast. 'Time for bed. We'll save a dessert for you.'

'I'm all right,' she said.

'I know you are.'

He helped her up, and when Isabelle and Jean-Guy had said their good-nights, he walked with her upstairs, but not before taking Jean-Guy and Isabelle aside.

'Call Myrna and Ruth. See who else they told about the Prohibition story. And see what you can find out about Anton.'

The dishwasher chef had admitted to a lot, including knowing both the cobrador and the victim. But it wasn't really anything the investigators wouldn't have found out on their own eventually.

Were his admissions the act of an innocent man, clearing his conscience, or the preemptive act of a killer?

'When I come down, we'll go over to the B&B.'

'*Oui, patron.*'

After getting Reine-Marie settled in bed, he returned a

few minutes later only to find her fast asleep. Tucking the hot water bottle under the covers, he kissed her softly, so as not to wake her, and left the tea on the bedside table. The scent of chamomile, he knew, would be soothing.

As he went downstairs, he could hear Jean-Guy on the phone.

'Listen, you old hag, it's a simple question.'

He could even hear Ruth's scratchy reply.

'You call in the middle of the night to ask about Prohibition, numbnuts? Isn't it a little late, in every way?'

'It's nine thirty, and I need to know.'

'It's 2017, and Prohibition has been repealed, or hadn't you heard, asshat.'

'I'm not calling for a history lesson . . .'

Their conversation, if that's what it could be called, continued as Gamache looked into his study and saw Lacoste on his computer, entering Anton's name into the Sûreté records.

'That'll take a while. I'm going to take Henri and Gracie for a walk. Need some fresh air?' he asked, as more filth floated in from the room next door.

'Good idea.'

Once outside, they looked at the B&B. Lights were still on.

They walked, heads bowed into the wind, while the dogs played and did their business, oblivious to the driving sleet.

'*Patron*, about the cellar. Why don't you want us—' Lacoste began before Gamache stopped her by raising his hand, palm toward her, in warning.

'But we're alone,' she shouted, above the wind.

Without a word, he pointed toward the shops.

A light had gone on in the loft above Myrna's bookstore. Jean-Guy must have moved on to the next person on his list. No doubt a more pleasant conversation.

But that wasn't what Gamache was indicating.

In the bistro, patrons could be seen through the mullioned windows chatting and having dessert and coffee in front of the fireplace, before heading home.

A figure walked past the window, dark against the lights. Bundled up, so that it was impossible to see if it was a man or a woman.

Gamache and Lacoste watched as the person went directly toward the B&B.

And then kept going.

To the Gamaches' home.

Armand scooped up Gracie and walked swiftly in that direction. Henri ran right past them, straight for the dark figure, now on the Gamaches' porch.

The person stopped dead when confronted with the German shepherd. Either not noticing the furiously wagging tail and ball in his mouth, or not wanting to risk it.

Gamache arrived a moment later and, taking the visitor by the arm, he turned him to face the light.

Staring for just a moment, Gamache said, 'You have something to tell us?'

'I do,' said Jacqueline. 'I've come to confess.'

Isabelle Lacoste turned from watching Olivier, mixing a pitcher of sangria at the bar, to look out the window.

Lea Roux, in sundress and sandals, and Matheo Bissonette, in slacks and light shirt, were walking down the wide steps of the porch at the B&B, and heading in their direction.

'Were they expected?' she asked.

'*Non*. They called late this afternoon and just arrived.'

The two guests by the hearth, an older and a younger man, were again glancing in her direction. Anton had probably told them that she was the head of homicide for the Sûreté. That always brought stares.

Once again she raised her glass to them, and when they lifted theirs in a salute, she took a sip, hoping they couldn't see from across the room that the liquid only went as far as her lips. But not through them.

But Olivier saw. And frowned. And said nothing.

Lacoste turned away and leaned against the bar. Casually looking out the mullioned window at the pleasant gardens in full bloom.

Her face was placid, even slightly vacant, but her mind was racing.

When Olivier left to take the sangria to a table, she leaned across the bar and took another licorice pipe from the jar. The older man saw this and raised his brows.

Lacoste grinned and put a finger to her lips. He smiled and nodded.

Then she left the bar and walked to the bathrooms, carefully palming the handset she'd taken from behind the bar.

CHAPTER 31

⁓

G amache and Beauvoir were more than halfway to their
destination, and still no word from Lacoste.

But they had received a text from Superintendent
Toussaint.

The equipment was assembled, the van was loaded. The
assault team was ready.

'If we don't hear otherwise,' Toussaint wrote, 'we'll
leave Montréal in ten minutes and get into position before
nightfall.'

'*Merde*,' wrote Gamache. The Québécois equivalent of
'good luck', and an internal Sûreté signal that all was pro-
ceeding well.

'*Merde*,' she replied. And went silent.

They wouldn't see each other again until the action was
under way.

Gamache looked at the dashboard clock. Six thirty. It
would be dark by eight thirty. Superintendent Toussaint had
timed it perfectly.

'What's keeping her?' Jean-Guy asked, as he drove.

The 'her' he meant was obvious.

'I don't know.'

Picking up his iPhone, Gamache called home. And let it ring. And ring. Until he heard Reine-Marie's recorded voice.

He left a cheerful message, saying he was on his way and that Jean-Guy was with him.

'No answer?' said Jean-Guy. 'She's probably at Clara's or Myrna's.'

'Probably.'

Once in the bathroom, Lacoste locked the door and hit the green talk button. Hoping, hoping the old handset signal reached that far.

She heard a dial tone and quickly punched in numbers.

'Chief?' she whispered when he picked up after half a ring.

'Isabelle, where've you been?'

'I couldn't get away until now. I'm in the bistro. He's here.'

'Who is?'

'The head of the cartel. Here in Three Pines.'

'We know that,' came Beauvoir's voice over the speaker. 'That's why you're there, right? To monitor.'

'No. I mean the American cartel.'

Gamache and Beauvoir looked at each other.

'Are you sure?' asked Gamache.

From anyone else, in any other circumstances, Lacoste would have been annoyed. But she understood his need to be absolutely clear.

'Yes. The American cartel.' The insistence in her voice made it sound like a hiss.

'Shit,' said Beauvoir. 'Did he recognize you?'

'I don't know. The other man with him, his bodyguard or counselor, kept staring. I think Anton told him who I am.'

'Fucking great,' said Beauvoir.

'But I made sure to order a drink and even waved at him.'

'Waved? You waved at the head of the drug cartel?' demanded Beauvoir.

'Well, I didn't wave my gun,' she said. 'I wanted him to know I'd seen him, and clearly had absolutely no idea who he was. It was a friendly little gesture. Maybe you've heard of them.'

Gamache nodded slowly. Few people had the presence of mind, the poise of Lacoste. It was exactly the right thing to do. And if the US cartel had any doubts about the incompetence of the Sûreté, that would surely put them to rest. A senior officer not recognizing one of the top criminals in North America.

'What should we do?' she whispered.

The handle of the door rattled. Someone wanted in.

'Just a moment,' she sang out, and the handle went silent.

'How many are there?' Gamache asked.

'The Americans? None outside that I noticed. Only the two of them in the bistro.' Lacoste had dropped her voice even further. 'The head of the cartel and an older guy. He's the one watching closely.'

Yes, thought Gamache. Like in Canada. With the new opioids, the new dark economy, and new technology, there'd been a new leadership. Sometimes bloody, as in the States, sometimes generational, a passing of the torch, as in Canada.

It was a young person's game now. And few people were more vicious, in Gamache's experience, than young men. Or women. They hadn't yet grown weary, grown disgusted with all the bloodshed. In fact, they seemed to revel in it. In their ability to order a kill, and have it carried out. To kidnap and torture and deliver adversaries back in pieces.

It was their own grotesque addiction.

No one was immune. Cops, judges, prosecutors. Children, mothers, fathers. All targets for the butchers.

Unfettered by conscience, they were all-powerful. Immortal. Not godfathers, but gods.

If the Sûreté action that night didn't work, there'd be bedlam. And the payment would be in flesh and blood. Theirs. Their families'.

Gamache was under no illusion about what was at stake.

'Once you arrive we can take them,' said Lacoste. 'I'm sure of it. How far away are you?'

'Twenty minutes,' said Beauvoir, and sped up. 'Fifteen.'

'What do you want me to do?'

Gamache's mind flew over the different possibilities.

He'd expected to confront them in the woods that night, not in the bistro.

But in some ways, this was even better. It meant Toussaint was right and the cartels had fallen for it completely. They were so convinced that the Sûreté was no threat that they'd come this far into the open.

It was rare, almost unheard of, for the actual head of a syndicate to be at the site of any criminal act. They sent their lieutenants. That's what they were for.

To have not one but both exposed was exceptional.

Yes, this was far better than they dared hope.

And even worse.

Their plan was based on a meeting in the forest, surrounded by trees, not in the bistro, surrounded by friends. By family.

'We can't arrest them yet,' he said, his voice calm and steady. 'We have no proof against either of them. That's been the problem. Their soldiers, yes, but they make sure to be clean themselves. We have to catch them doing something illegal. Sitting in the bistro is not.'

'Fuck, fuck, fuckity fuck,' said Beauvoir under his breath. Once again, the mantra did not calm him down.

The chief was right.

Their entire operation depended on catching them with their hands dirty. And that meant on site when the krokodil crossed the border. Until that happened, they had no definitive proof against the heads of the cartels.

They were together, yes, but in the wrong place.

If the exchange happened in the woods, while the cartel heads were having a pleasant chat in the bistro, then they'd have failed. They'd lose them. They'd lose.

Beauvoir was staring at Gamache, his eyes wide and questioning.

Lacoste was waiting on the other end of the line. They could hear her breathing. And then the rattle of the door again.

'Hello?' came a man's voice, in English.

'*Tabernac*,' she said. 'I think that's the bodyguard. Almost done,' she sang out cheerfully.

Gamache knew once he hung up he couldn't reach her again. His orders had to be clear, definitive. And fast.

One shot.

'There's one other thing,' came Lacoste's voice, so low they could barely hear it. 'Madame Gamache is here too. With Annie and Honoré.'

The blood drained from Gamache's face and he looked at Beauvoir, whose hands tightened on the steering wheel, and the car's engine roared as he sped up even more.

'They have to get out of there,' said Jean-Guy.

'No, wait,' said Gamache. 'Wait.'

They waited a beat.

'We'll be there in fifteen minutes—'

'Ten,' said Beauvoir.

'Keep them there, and invite Ruth to join you.'

'You can't be serious,' said Beauvoir.

Lacoste flushed the toilet in case the bodyguard could hear Beauvoir's raised voice down the line.

'Honoré,' said Jean-Guy forcefully, as though Gamache hadn't taken that in. Then, more quietly, 'Honoré.'

It was as though Jean-Guy's entire world had come down to one word.

'Annie,' he whispered.

Two words.

Reine-Marie, thought Gamache.

'They have to stay. It's safe. They're there to talk, not shoot up the place.'

'How do we know?' asked Beauvoir, his voice unnaturally high. 'Wouldn't be the first time a *parlez* turned into a bloodbath.'

'*Non*. If one or both had that in mind, they'd be meeting in the woods, with their soldiers. Not in the bistro. They're brutal, but not stupid.'

He sounded more confident than he actually was. But Chief Superintendent Gamache understood that a leader could not afford to reveal his own emotions. He couldn't demand courage in others while quaking in fear himself.

'If we didn't see this coming,' said Beauvoir, 'we probably won't see what's coming next. They could do the exchange right there, in the bistro. In front of everyone. We're the ones who convinced them it'd be safe. We did this.'

'He's right,' said Lacoste, running the water now. 'What do I do then? I'd have to arrest them, or try. In a roomful of people.'

Honoré, thought Gamache. *Annie. Reine-Marie.*

Not just people.

Beauvoir's foot pressed harder on the gas. The car was going 140 kilometers an hour, and gaining speed. They'd turned off the highway and were on secondary roads. Roads not designed for speed. The car bounded off ruts, flying then bumping to the asphalt.

But Gamache didn't tell him to slow down. If anything, it was all he could do not to shout at him to hurry up. Speed up.

'Get Ruth to the bistro,' Gamache repeated, his voice low. 'And go and join Reine-Marie and Annie. The head of the American cartel probably won't know who they are, but the Canadian does. They'd never believe we'd put them in harm's way.'

There was silence.

None of them could believe it either. Especially Gamache.

But there was no choice. To have Isabelle remove Reine-Marie and Annie and Honoré would almost certainly alert the cartel, and they must already be on the lookout for anything unusual.

They might be confident that they were in no danger, but they'd still be vigilant. It was animal instinct. And these people were animals.

'Are you sure?' Lacoste whispered.

From anyone else, in any other circumstances, Gamache might have been annoyed at this questioning of his orders. But he understood her need to be absolutely clear.

'*Oui.*'

'Okay,' she said. Just before she hung up, he heard one last word. '*Merde.*'

Merde, he agreed.

But this time it wasn't the signal that all was going well. It was just *merde*.

Lacoste hid the handset in her pocket and unlocked the door.

'*Désolé*,' she said to the older man, who was examining her. 'Sorry. That time of the month.'

She put a hand over her uterus and he immediately backed up before she could tell him more. But just to be on the safe side, she mumbled, 'Cramps.'

As soon as Lacoste had hung up, Gamache called Toussaint and gave her the update. There was a long silence.

'*Bon*,' she said, her voice crisp. No sign of panic. 'What do we do? You want us in the village?'

'No, go to the border, stick to the plan. Whatever happens, the chlorocodide has to cross into the States, and the only thing we know for sure is where it'll happen. Your informant is watching the church?'

'Yes. We'll at least know when the drug is being moved. And if they don't use the established route?' Toussaint asked.

'Then you'll be in the forest for nothing, and Beauvoir, Lacoste and I will take care of it.'

He said it so calmly, as though he was talking about mending a fence.

There was silence again.

'All actions contain an element of luck,' he reminded her. 'Besides, we're all in. There's a great advantage in that.'

'Our backs to the sea. Yes, *patron*. This'll work, because it has to.' She laughed softly and wished that was actually the equation. 'Good luck,' she said, either forgetting to say *merde* or not wanting that to possibly be the last thing they ever said to each other.

'*Oui*. Good luck to you, Madeleine.'

*

386

Matheo and Lea were sitting at a table in the far corner by the time Lacoste returned. Away from the others. But close to the two Americans.

She carefully replaced the phone, making sure no one saw, and went into the kitchen to say hello to Anton. And to warn him.

'*Bonjour*,' he said, greeting her. 'I'd have thought you'd be in the city.'

'I was, but wanted to get away just for a few hours. Too hot. I'm not the only one.'

'I bet,' he said, going back to work, then looking up when she didn't speak.

'Matheo and Lea are here,' she said. 'And maybe Patrick, though I haven't seen him.'

Anton put down his knife and looked at her. 'Why?'

'I don't know, but I thought you should be warned.'

That wasn't completely true. Isabelle Lacoste had a pretty good idea why Matheo and Lea were in the bistro and she didn't want Anton to get involved.

'*Merci.*' He looked grim and took a deep breath. 'I have to testify in a few days. I've been dreading it. I hear they've been rough on Monsieur Gamache.'

'Well, they always are.'

'Even the Crown attorney and the judge? Aren't they on the same side?'

'Trials are funny things,' she said. Trying to make what had happened in the courtroom sound normal. 'It's my turn tomorrow.'

'Where're they sitting?' asked Anton. 'So I can avoid them.'

'In the corner.'

'By the two Americans?'

'You know them?'

'Never seen them before, but one considers himself a chef. After trying the soup' – Anton nodded toward a bowl – 'he asked if I'd give them the recipe.'

Lacoste looked down at the notebook and the page headed *Watermelon Gazpacho with Mint and Mango*.

She wanted to eat the paper.

'I notice that Ruth isn't out there. Do you mind if I call her?'

'Be my guest. Might be the first time her phone's ever rung. I wonder if she'll know what it is.'

Isabelle smiled, knowing that the young chef and the old poet had established a sort of friendship. Based on him giving her free food, and her giving him grief. And both knowing what happened when the straight road splayed.

Lacoste went to the phone attached to the wall and dialed. After about ten rings, during which Isabelle imagined her searching the small home for whatever was ringing, Ruth picked up.

'Hello,' she shouted into the receiver.

'Ruth, it's Isabelle Lacoste. I'm at the bistro. We're having drin—'

'Be right over,' Ruth yelled, then hung up.

Lacoste turned and saw Anton smiling. He'd obviously heard. She suspected everyone in Québec had heard.

She returned to the bistro. Clara and Myrna had joined Reine-Marie and Annie, and after greeting them, Isabelle took a seat.

Her back was to the two men at the table, and to Matheo and Lea, though she could just see their distorted reflections in the leaded-glass window.

'Not sitting with you?' Isabelle asked, tipping her head toward Matheo and Lea.

'Oh, it's not us they're avoiding.'

'It's me,' said Lacoste.

She knew why, of course. The trial. Like her, Matheo and Lea were witnesses for the prosecution. But, unlike her, they were unwilling witnesses.

Lacoste knew the first question the prosecution would ask them, and she suspected they did as well. It was pretty much the first question Chief Superintendent Gamache had asked that November night when they'd made their way through the sleet to the B&B.

'What time is it?' asked a groggy Gabri, as the knocking on the door continued. 'Did someone forget their key?'

'Everyone's in,' said Olivier, hauling himself awake. 'And what key?'

'It's one thirty?' Gabri was fully awake now, swinging his legs out of bed and reaching for his dressing gown. 'Something's happened. Something's wrong. Here, take this.'

He handed Olivier a two-by-four.

'Why?' asked Olivier.

'That's our burglar alarm.'

'Burglars don't knock.'

'Wanna risk it?'

They walked softly so as not to disturb their guests, though they were far from sure any of them would be able to sleep. Especially Patrick, who'd looked both exhausted and wide awake even as he was being led to bed by his friends.

Olivier and Gabri turned on the porch light and peered through the window. Then they quickly opened the front door.

*

Patrick heard the knocking.

Little good ever came from being aroused at that hour. Though Patrick had not been asleep.

When they'd gone to bed, Gabri had offered to put him in another room, but Patrick had wanted to go back to the one he'd shared with Katie. That had all of Katie's clothes, and her jewelry, and her toiletries.

All catalogued and photographed by the homicide team, and returned to exactly where Katie had left them, when she'd left.

Her purse on the chair. Her reading glasses on the book on the bedside table.

He'd lain in bed, listening to the creaking of the old inn. Listening as the others had settled and all human sounds died down. And he could be alone with Katie. He could close his eyes and pretend she was there, beside him, breathing so softly he couldn't even hear her.

Patrick inhaled the scent of her. And he knew she was there. How could she not be? How could she be gone?

But she wasn't gone, he told himself quickly, before he fell off the ledge. She was there. Beside him. Breathing so softly he couldn't hear.

And then, into the night, came the knock on the door. Then the tap on their bedroom door.

'Patrick?'

'*Oui?*'

'Can you come downstairs, please?' asked Gabri.

Patrick, Lea and Matheo entered the living room. And stopped.

Facing them were Chief Superintendent Gamache, Chief Inspector Lacoste and Inspector Beauvoir.

And Jacqueline. The baker.

Gabri stirred the embers in the hearth and threw on a couple of birch logs. The wood caught, and crackled, and temporarily drowned out the sound of the sleet against the windows.

'What's happening out there?' Olivier whispered when Gabri joined him in the kitchen.

'They're staring at each other.' Gabri got out the brioche and turned on the oven while Olivier brewed coffee. 'What's Jacqueline doing here?'

'She must know something,' said Olivier. 'Maybe she saw something.'

'But why do they want to speak to Patrick and the others?' asked Gabri. 'And in the middle of the night. What won't wait?'

Only one thing wouldn't wait until morning, and they both knew what it was.

'Shall we sit?' Gamache asked, gesturing toward the arm-chairs and sofa.

Beauvoir remained standing, positioning himself by the fireplace. Not coincidentally, he also blocked any way out to the door. It would be futile for any of them to try to run away, but cornered people did desperate things.

So far only Lea had spoken. She'd whispered, 'Finally,' when she'd seen the officers. Though it was Jacqueline she'd been staring at when she'd spoken.

Lacoste began.

'Jacqueline came to us tonight with an extraordinary story.' She glanced at the baker, who was sitting bolt upright and staring defiantly at the others. 'Extraordinary to us, at least, but not, I think, to you.'

And yet, Gamache thought, it shouldn't have been a complete surprise. Once said, it seemed obvious and he'd wondered how he could not have seen it sooner.

And much like Anton's confession earlier in the day to Jean-Guy, Gamache knew Jacqueline's visit to them had been preemptive. Even as she'd told her story, he knew that she wasn't telling them anything they wouldn't have discovered within hours anyway. And she knew it too.

'She told you everything?' Matheo asked, his eyes moving from Jacqueline to Lacoste and back again.

'She confessed, yes,' said Lacoste.

'To the murder?' asked Patrick, staring in shock at the baker. 'You killed Katie?'

'She told us about the cobrador,' said Lacoste. 'And now it's your turn. Tell us what you know.'

They looked at each other, and then, naturally, it was Lea who spoke.

'Jacqueline came to us with the idea.' Lea turned to her husband, who nodded agreement. 'She'd heard about the cobrador while working for that Spanish guy. At first we thought she was kidding. It sounded ridiculous. A guy stares at someone and it magically does the trick?'

'No one took Jacqueline's suggestion seriously,' said Matheo. '*Désolé*, but you know that's true.'

Jacqueline gave one crisp nod.

'But it gave me an idea for a story,' Matheo continued. 'So I wrote that piece about the cobrador del frac, the debt collector in the top hat and tails, and thanked Jacqueline for the idea. That's when she said it wasn't that cobrador she was thinking of. It was the original.'

'She sent us links from Spain,' said Lea. 'That cobrador was very different. Terrifying.'

'And yet,' said Lacoste, 'when you spoke to Monsieur Gamache about it that first time, you said the only thing you knew about the original came from that old photograph. You said sightings were rare.'

'Well, they are rare,' said Matheo. 'But—'

'But we didn't want to spoon-feed you,' Lea said, speaking frankly to Gamache. 'We knew you'd pursue it and find out what you needed. And you'd be more invested, if you came to it yourself.'

At the fireplace, Jean-Guy bristled. No one liked being manipulated, and Lea Roux had done it perfectly. She was clearly very, very seasoned at controlling, maneuvering. And he wondered how much of it was happening at that moment.

Though Gamache didn't seem upset or angry. He simply nodded agreement. But kept a thoughtful eye on her.

'That's when we began to consider what Jacqueline was suggesting,' said Matheo. 'We'd tried everything else. There seemed nothing to lose.'

'It took longer than we thought to get everything organized,' said Lea. 'For one thing, we had to find a costume. Finally, we decided to make one. Didn't Jacqueline tell you all this?'

She looked at the baker, sitting pale and contained on the sofa between Gamache and Lacoste.

'She did. But we need to hear it from you,' said Lacoste. 'Who made the costume?'

'Jacqueline,' said Lea. 'Even when it was finished, we weren't all in. It just seemed stupid. Katie was the one who convinced us. She'd been the closest to Edouard. She wanted him to pay.'

'Even after all these years?' asked Lacoste. 'Edouard died almost fifteen years ago.'

'When you see your best friend jump off the roof, it never goes away,' said Matheo. 'Especially when the person who did it hasn't paid any price. Hasn't even apologized.'

'Is that what you wanted?' asked Gamache. 'An apology?'

They looked at each other. It seemed possible they hadn't really discussed what they wanted. What would be enough.

'I think so,' said Lea. 'We'd fuck with him, scare him a bit, and then go back to our lives. What more could we do?'

'You said "him",' said Lacoste. 'Who's he?'

'Didn't she tell you?' asked Matheo.

'Again, I need to hear it from you.'

'Anton,' said Lea. 'We'd begged him to stop selling to Edouard, and he agreed, but the shit was lying to us. He kept doing it. More drugs. Stronger.'

'We didn't know,' said Matheo. 'Until—'

Matheo was staring at Lacoste, but seeing the leap.

It was no accident. No stumble. Edouard had stood on the ledge while around him everyone partied. And below him, in some dorm room, his great love, Katie, and his friend Patrick had sex.

All around him there was youth and freedom, sex and love.

But Edouard had been left on the island, with the Lord of the Flies. And the insatiable beast gnawing inside him.

Edouard had slowly spread his arms, like something magnificent. And as Matheo and Lea watched, too stunned, too far away to do anything, he'd jumped.

Beauvoir closed his eyes, and while he didn't know Edouard, he knew that despair. And the blessed release of drugs. And how easy it was to mistake falling for flying.

Edouard left the ledge, and the island. And his friends. And family. But they never left him.

Lea looked at Jacqueline, who'd sat silent through this.

'Anton killed him,' Lea said to the baker. 'He might as well have been the hand on Edouard's back. We all knew that.'

Jacqueline held Lea's eyes, and nodded a small acknowledgment.

'The cops told us Edouard's death had been ruled an accident,' Matheo continued. 'Even if they found Anton, he'd never be charged with anything other than trafficking, and even then the charges might be dropped or the sentence suspended. First offense, young university student—'

'The family hired a private investigator to find him,' said Lea. 'Took a long time. He'd bummed around, gone into rehab and later got a job with the Spanish family. Worked for cash. But the investigator finally tracked him down.'

Jean-Guy, standing by the fireplace, nodded.

Anton had told him all this. He went by Lebrun but his real name was Boucher.

Butcher.

A good name for a murderer, Beauvoir had thought. Though he also knew it was ridiculous to suspect someone because of their last name. But still . . .

'That's when Jacqueline got back in touch with us,' said Lea, looking again at the woman sitting stiffly on the sofa. 'She told us they'd found Anton, and that the family was looking for a nanny and tutor, to teach the Spanish children French.'

'She wanted to use us as references,' said Matheo. 'We agreed and when Madame Ruiz called we vouched for her.'

Beauvoir wondered, in passing, who'd vouched for Anton.

It had been a sticking point. The one thing that hadn't rung true in Anton's conversation with Jean-Guy that afternoon. He'd admitted to all this. Confessed his sins. Showed remorse.

But there was that one tiny little thing. Why the Ruiz

family, especially Antonio Ruiz, hadn't checked out Anton before hiring him. As they apparently had with Jacqueline.

Instead, Ruiz, a suspicious, perhaps even paranoid man, had hired some stranger to come live with his family.

Why was that? Beauvoir wondered. Why hadn't he placed a single call?

'What happened next?' Lacoste asked.

'After working there for a few months, Jacqueline heard about the cobrador and got back in touch with us,' said Lea. 'Once we were convinced, we just needed to work out the details. When and where to spring the cobrador on him.'

'We couldn't have it stand outside the home,' said Matheo. 'Ruiz would probably shoot it. He'd certainly think it was there for him, and so would Anton. We needed some-place else.'

'Then the family was transferred back to Spain and it looked like our plan might fall apart,' said Lea. 'But then Anton got a job here as a dishwasher. We'd been to Three Pines a few times, for reunions. It seemed perfect. It even had you.'

'Me?' asked Gamache.

'We needed to make sure the cobrador was safe,' said Matheo. 'That no one would attack him.'

'We knew you wouldn't let that happen,' said Lea.

'You played me?' asked Gamache.

'We trusted you,' said Lea. 'To uphold the law, no matter how personally upsetting the situation might be.'

Gamache took a long, deep breath. More manipulation. But, far from annoying, it was enlightening. It certainly threw a light onto Lea Roux, and her ability to strategize.

She'd come a long way from the young elected official and Edouard's Law.

'Jacqueline got a job at the bakery, and then our plan fell into place.'

'And what was your plan?' asked Lacoste.

'It was simple,' said Lea. 'The cobrador would show up and scare the crap out of Anton.'

'And then?' asked Lacoste. 'Was that it? To scare him?'

Matheo was about to answer, then he shut his mouth and looked at Lea, then Patrick, and finally Jacqueline.

They seemed confused by the question, and Isabelle thought she knew why.

What had begun as one thing, the quest for an apology, had become something else.

How often something starts off as noble, and then warps, corrupts, takes on a life of its own. Becomes a creature in a black cloak.

A body in a root cellar.

How it came to that was the question. And she intended to have the answer that night.

'This was in the spring,' said Lea. 'We were going to have the annual reunion here in the summer and it would work perfectly. Except—'

'Daylight,' said Matheo.

On hearing that, Gamache gave one small grunt.

Daylight.

That answered so many questions.

Why the reunion had been changed to late October. And how the cobrador managed to stand there all day.

And the answer was, he could do it because night was closing in.

In the summer, the sun was up for hours and hours. And the heat was relentless and merciless. No one could stand there for long.

But in late October, early November, the days were shorter, and cooler.

The cobrador could slip away when darkness fell.

Daylight. It was so simple.

But then, most crimes were. And they were now closing in on the crime.

'Myrna says she told you about the church and Prohibition,' Beauvoir said to Lea, who nodded.

'She did. That was on my first visit. Before the reunions. She even showed me the little room, the root cellar. I remembered it when we were trying to figure out some of the logistics.'

'That's where the cobrador stayed,' said Lacoste. 'Who is he? Someone you hired? What's happened to him?'

Her question was again met with confusion on their part.

Lea turned to Jacqueline. 'Didn't you tell them?'

'I told them I was responsible for the cobrador. It's all my doing.'

'And you didn't think they'd figure it out?' asked Matheo.

'Figure what out?' asked Lacoste. 'Where's the cobrador?'

'You're looking at him.'

The Sûreté officers stared at Matheo. Who pointed to Patrick. Then to Lea. Then to himself.

'We were the cobrador,' he said.

Gamache closed his eyes and lowered his head for a moment.

Just as on the island of the diseased and damned and dispossessed, the cobrador of Three Pines was not a single person. It was an idea. A community of conscience.

They were all the cobrador.

'And Katie?' he asked.

'She was it yesterday,' said Lea. 'We decided to call it quits, after the near attack last night. It was getting dangerous. So once Katie was done, we'd go home, whether Anton had broken or not. But, of course . . . '

These friends, Gamache thought, had been naïve. They thought they could threaten without consequence. In bringing the cobrador here, they'd woken up more than a conscience.

And they hadn't perhaps done quite enough research on the original cobradors.

While they'd publicly accused their tormentors of moral crimes, it hadn't been the princes of the day who'd finally paid. It was the cobradors who'd been rounded up, and killed.

As Katie had been.

He looked at Lacoste and Beauvoir. They looked at him. All thinking the same thing.

The bat. It had three dominant sets of DNA. Katie Evans's. A very small, almost certainly incidental, sample of Jacqueline's. And Anton Boucher's.

His DNA was all over it.

The bat told essentially the same story as these friends.

Anton Boucher had snapped. He'd followed the cobrador last night, through the sleet and darkness, back to the church, to the root cellar, and beaten her to death. Never removing the mask. Never knowing who he'd just killed.

Though that in itself was curious. Would Anton not want to know who it was who'd so relentlessly tracked him down?

'How did you get in and out of the root cellar?' Gamache asked.

'By the door, of course,' said Matheo.

Gamache nodded. He had to be very careful here. 'Were you not afraid of being seen?'

'Who's looking in that direction after dark?' asked Matheo.

'And no one goes into a church anymore. We figured it was the safest place. Far better than having the cobrador book a room at the B&B.'

'We'd undress,' said Lea, 'and leave the costume for the next person. And if someone saw us, then we'd just admit everything. Either way, Anton was screwed. And we'd have done nothing illegal.'

'Or even immoral,' said Matheo.

'Until last night,' said Gamache.

'But we didn't kill Katie,' said Lea. 'Surely that's obvious.'

'But we did,' said Jacqueline. 'If we hadn't done the cobrador thing, she'd be alive. If I hadn't wanted Anton to pay, she'd be alive. I knew Anton better than anyone. I knew his temper. If he didn't get his way, he became vicious. But I didn't think he'd be violent. Not like that.'

She looked at Patrick.

'I'm so sorry. I should've known he'd strike out. He killed Katie and it was my fault.'

'Why would he kill her?' asked Gamache.

'Well, he didn't know he was killing Katie,' said Matheo. 'He was killing the cobrador, who obviously knew his secret.'

'The secret being?' asked Gamache.

'Edouard, of course,' said Lea.

Gamache nodded. Then began shaking his head.

'It doesn't make sense. He recognized you all, you know. He knew you were Edouard's friends. Even if he suspected you were behind the cobrador costume, he must've known that killing one still left three others.'

'Besides,' said Beauvoir, 'he told me everything.'

'Everything?' asked Lea.

'*Oui*. About selling drugs, and Edouard's death. If Anton was willing to admit it, why kill to keep it quiet?'

Gamache turned to Jacqueline.

'The only person he didn't recognize was you. But then, he'd never met you. Not at university anyway. Your brother would never take you with him to buy drugs. He knew how you felt.'

Jacqueline, Edouard's sister, nodded.

'I'm going to have to arrest you,' he said to her, and she nodded.

'For the cobrador thing,' she said.

'For the murder of Katie Evans.'

'But that's insane,' said Lea. 'Anton killed her. You know that. If he told you all that this afternoon, it was just to cover his ass. He probably only recognized us after the murder. This afternoon, when we were all waiting in the bistro. And he only admitted the Edouard thing because he knew you'd find out anyway.'

'Manipulation?' asked Gamache, his sharp eyes on her.

'He's smart,' said Matheo. 'For God's sake, don't be fooled. You have no idea what he's like. He's not what he appears.'

'And you are?' said Gamache.

Lea Roux stared at Gamache, holding his eyes. She didn't like what she saw there.

'I'm sorry,' he said, getting to his feet. 'I think you meant well. This started off fairly innocently. No one would be hurt, not even Anton. You just wanted justice for Edouard. You wanted the drug dealer to know that you knew. But you didn't realize you were being used. Didn't see what was really happening.'

'And you do?' demanded Lea.

'What's happening?' asked Patrick, as the Sûreté officers led Jacqueline away. 'What does it mean? Did she kill Katie? I don't understand.'

Once outside, Chief Superintendent Gamache turned to Jacqueline.

'You need to put up a strong defense.'

'What're you saying? You're not really going to arrest me.'

'I am. For the murder of Katie Evans.'

Even Lacoste and Beauvoir looked surprised, but not nearly as shocked as Jacqueline.

'But you know Anton did it. You know I didn't kill Katie, but you're arresting me anyway?' she said. 'Why?'

And then her panic seemed to clear.

'I know why. Because you don't have enough to convict him. You want Anton to think he got away with it. It's my turn to be the cobrador. To stand up for what I believe in, no matter the risk. Is that what you're asking of me?'

'Is your conscience clear?' he asked.

'It is.'

And he believed her. But he wasn't so sure about his own.

Chief Inspector Isabelle Lacoste sat in the bistro, her back to Matheo Bissonette and Lea Roux. Avoiding their stares. Partly because of the accusation their glare contained. That an innocent woman was being tried for a murder she hadn't committed. And that Lacoste knew it.

Yes, there was no mistaking the ire in their eyes.

But also because she needed to concentrate on the American and his lieutenant. Sitting there so confidently, in full view.

Was he there for a friendly *parlez*? Dividing territory with his Québec counterpart, now that the Sûreté was out of the equation? Celebrating the launch of their new commodity, krokodil?

Or was he staking his claim? Why share, when he could have it all?

Was this a meeting of *confrères*, or the start of a brutal, short-lived, bloody turf war?

And they were sitting in the middle of the turf, the middle of the war.

Isabelle looked at Madame Gamache, and Annie, and Honoré. And she knew something that Chief Superintendent Gamache must've realized as soon as she'd told him the head of the American cartel was in Three Pines.

If the battle was fought in this little border village, whoever won would make an example of the villagers. And mostly of Monsieur Gamache and his family.

They would lay waste to Three Pines, so that the population of other border villages would be in no doubt what would happen to them if they didn't play along. The cartels would never rule by loyalty and affection. It would always be terror.

She could feel the long, slow progress of perspiration down her spine.

CHAPTER 32

'What're you doing?' asked Beauvoir.

Though it was obvious what Gamache was doing. The question Jean-Guy was really asking was why.

As the car slowed down to a reasonable, even leisurely, pace and descended into the village of Three Pines, Gamache twisted in his seat and came away with the automatic pistol in its leather holster, taken off his belt. Opening the glove compartment, he put it in, first removing the bullets.

'You can be seen with a gun,' said Gamache, as he locked it and put the key in the pocket of his slacks. 'I can't. Reine-Marie and Annie will notice, and ask. We can't have that.'

The sun was still up, though the unrelenting sheen of the summer day had softened. The village had never looked more beautiful. More at peace with itself. The gardens in full bloom. The children, having eaten dinner, were playing on the village green. Squeezing out every last moment of a perfect summer day.

'And what happens if the exchange is made in the bistro and you're standing there with a spoon in your hand?'

'I hope I'd at least grab a fork,' said Gamache, but Beauvoir didn't smile.

'I have this,' he said, his face serious again as he showed Jean-Guy what he'd taken out of the glove compartment, in exchange for the gun.

In his palm was what appeared to be a piece of wood. But Beauvoir knew it wasn't. It was a Swiss Army knife, for hunters. Its hidden blade designed to gut animals.

Jean-Guy looked from Gamache's steady hand into his steady eyes.

It was one thing to shoot a person. A horrific act that could never be forgotten. Nor should it be. As Beauvoir knew all too well. But it was something else altogether to stab someone. To drive the blade in.

Jean-Guy had never considered it.

But Gamache had. And was. And would. If necessary.

'Great,' said Ruth, as Gamache and Beauvoir strolled into the bistro. 'It's Rocky and Boo-Boo.'

Gamache looked at Beauvoir and shook his head in despair.

'Isn't that Rocky and Bullwinkle?' asked Gabri, putting a beer down in front of Clara, as Beauvoir kissed Annie and took Honoré in his arms.

'Moose and squirrel.' Clara nodded and took a long sip of the cold Farnham Blonde Ale.

'It's Yogi and Boo-Boo,' said Reine-Marie, greeting Armand with a hug.

'*Et tu, Brute?*' asked Gamache, and Reine-Marie laughed.

'Honoré,' Jean-Guy whispered in the little boy's ear, and smelled the scent of him. A combination of baby powder and Annie.

And Jean-Guy understood why the Chief Superintendent had asked that Ruth be there when they arrived. So she could publicly mock them. It was a tiny, telling detail. Like Clara's

405

portraits, made up of small strokes, and dabs. Deliberately placed. For effect.

To those who knew them, Ruth's insults were simply a ritual. A kind of calling card. But to strangers it would sound like the derisive mocking of two people so incompetent even an old woman could see it. And felt free to say it.

It added to the picture of Gamache as friendly, warm, easygoing. Soft. A man more suited to insults in a country inn than the cold, serrated edges of police work.

Beauvoir could see Matheo Bissonette and Lea Roux sitting in a corner. Listening. Lea's smile so tight her lips had disappeared. She looked like a viper.

The American visitors were staring at them openly. Not even bothering to pretend not to be interested.

They would know who Gamache was, of course.

This was a critical moment.

Would they get up and leave, afraid the Sûreté had bumbled onto their plans?

Would they pull out their weapons and open fire on the Sûreté officers and everyone else in the bistro? It would be far from the first time the cartel had done something like that.

But the two men just sat there, as though watching a not very interesting talk show.

'I didn't know you were here,' Jean-Guy said to Annie, surprised and relieved that his voice sounded so normal.

'I left a text on your phone,' said Annie. 'We decided to come down, to get out of the heat of the city.'

Though it wasn't much better in the country. The air was ripe with humidity. It felt one degree short of becoming water. There was no breeze and no letup in sight. People scrambled for shade, and prayed for the sun to go down.

Everyone except the children, now holding hands and

dancing in a circle on the green. Two boys were wrestling over a ball.

The bistro was filling up, many of the seats already taken.

Gamache walked over to the table with the two Americans. There was a slight scraping of wood on wood as the older man pushed his chair away from the table and dropped his hand to his lap.

Every hair on Jean-Guy's arms and the back of his neck stood on end, his skin tingling. As though a November breeze had come through the room. But he had Honoré in his arms and couldn't do anything, even if the man pulled a gun. And shot the chief.

Beauvoir forced himself to turn away. Shielding Honoré with his body, he stepped in front of Annie.

While the others had resumed their conversation, about Clara's show at the Musée des beaux-arts in Montréal, now just a week away, Ruth was watching Jean-Guy. A curious look in her curious eyes.

Gamache smiled at the two men. 'Do you mind?' he asked in French. When there was no answer, he said, '*Anglais?* English?'

'Yes.'

'Are these chairs taken?'

'No, help yourself.'

Gamache put his hands on the back of the two empty pine chairs at the table, then hesitated, staring at the men.

'You look familiar. Have we met?'

Across the room, Beauvoir thought he'd faint. He'd given Honoré to Annie, and was prepared to draw his weapon if need be.

Conversation swirled around him, words without meaning, though he did his best to appear to be following the conversation.

Jean-Guy didn't dare look at Gamache chatting amiably with the head of the drug cartel. But he could hear them.

If they don't kill him, thought Beauvoir, *I will*.

Isabelle Lacoste was seated next to Clara, a smile fixed onto her rictus face, though he could see her right hand had dropped below the level of the table.

Jean-Guy's heart was pounding so hard he could barely hear what they were saying.

'I don't think we've met,' said the younger man. 'We're just visiting.'

'Ah,' said Gamache. His English had a soft British accent. 'You're lucky. Not many people find this village, or this bistro. New chef. Try his grilled trout, it's delicious.'

'We just ate,' said the young man. 'Amazing. We'll definitely be back.'

'I hope so,' said Gamache. 'Thanks for the chairs.'

Chief Superintendent Gamache nodded to them, picked up the chairs and plunked one down for Beauvoir, then placed the other beside Reine-Marie.

'They seem nice,' said Jean-Guy, glaring at Gamache as he sat. 'Americans. Always nice.'

Armand took off his jacket and folded it carefully over the back of his chair. Showing, for anyone interested, that he had no weapon. The Chief Superintendent was unarmed, and unaware, apparently, of who he'd just given a dinner suggestion to. And what was about to happen.

Another dab for the portrait.

'What would you like, *patron*?' asked Olivier. 'A Scotch?'

'Oh, too hot, *mon vieux*.' He loosened his tie. 'I'll have a beer. Whatever's on tap.'

'We have some freshly made lemonade,' Olivier said to Jean-Guy.

'Perfect, *merci*.'

'So, how's the trial going?' asked Ruth. 'Have you lied yet?'

'Every word,' said Gamache.

The problem with Ruth, he remembered too late, was the inability to control her. Fortunately, most people thought she was either kidding or demented.

It was like playing with a jack-in-the-box. It looked like a normal box, until the crazy person popped out.

Behind Ruth, out the window, he noticed that the children had stopped their dancing and were falling to the ground. Laughing and rolling.

Ashes. Ashes.

The fight for the ball was over. One boy was bouncing it on his knee, while the other, tears staining his dirty cheeks, grabbed his bike and pedaled off.

> *Where could a boy on a bicycle go*
> *When the straight road splayed?*

In the reflection of the window, he saw the Americans. The younger man's ghostly image superimposed on the wobbly boy. Like before and after pictures.

This was where the boy on a bicycle went, Gamache knew.

Then he refocused on the children. *Go away*, he begged them. *Go home*.

But the children continued to play, and the boy on the bike continued to pump his thin legs until he'd disappeared. Leaving the ghostly man behind.

Gamache leaned back in his chair and gave a long, contented sigh. A show sigh, though he tried not to overdo it. He was careful not to scan the forest ringing the village for a mob soldier.

Even his eyes could betray him, Gamache knew. Every gesture of his was being closely watched, he suspected. Every word monitored and evaluated by the visitors. They were confident, but they'd also be vigilant.

He could not afford a misstep.

'Should we have dinner here?' he asked. 'I'm starving.'

'Well, it's time for Honoré to eat, and then bath time,' said Annie, getting up.

'And I should be getting back to the city,' said Lacoste. 'Not looking forward to tomorrow.'

'Oh, haven't had a chance to tell you, but the judge has called an early start. Eight.'

'In the morning?' asked Isabelle, and Myrna and Clara laughed at her tone.

'Sorry,' he said. 'She wants to get in as much as possible before the day heats up.'

'Then I really do need to get going. Are you staying the night?'

'Probably. Haven't decided yet,' said Gamache.

'Do you want me to help?' Jean-Guy rose with Annie.

'I'll go,' said Reine-Marie. 'You two stay here. Enjoy your drinks. Dinner in about forty-five minutes. Salmon on the grill. Would you like to come over?' she asked Myrna and Clara.

'That sounds good,' said Myrna. 'Unless you'd like to get into your studio and finish those paintings.'

'Har-dee-har-har,' said Clara, though it was obvious this needling was getting old. 'Dinner sounds great. We'll help.'

As they left, Armand hugged Reine-Marie. Not too tight, he hoped. Closing his eyes for a moment, he took in her scent of old garden roses. And Honoré.

Jean-Guy kissed Annie and Ray-Ray.

It was all he could do to not whisper to Annie to take

Honoré and go back to Montréal. But he knew if he did that, and the heads of the cartels suspected, it would be the spark that could leave them all dead.

Only Ruth and Rosa remained at their table, the old woman swilling Scotch. Rosa got up and waddled across the table to Beauvoir. He grunted as the duck hopped off the table, onto his lap. And settled down.

As he took a long pull at his beer, Armand noticed Lacoste drive away. Reine-Marie, along with Annie, Myrna and Clara, who was holding Honoré, walked the last few steps through the golden evening. Reine-Marie stopped, stooped, and picked a weed out of their front garden.

She showed it to Myrna, who clapped. It had become their running joke, from their early days in the village, when Reine-Marie and Armand had 'weeded' the spring garden, only to discover they'd left the weeds and taken out most of the perennials.

Myrna had become their gardening guru.

Armand smiled as he watched them.

'I see that politician woman and her husband are back,' said Ruth. 'She came by my place earlier this afternoon.'

'Really?' said Jean-Guy. 'Why?'

Anton had come out of the kitchen and was talking to the Americans.

He put something on the table. A piece of paper with writing.

'To tell me they're making me a Chevalier in the Ordre du Québec.'

'That's wonderful, Ruth,' said Armand. *'Félicitations.'*

The young head of the cartel was gesturing to Anton to join them. The chef looked surprised and shook his head, indicating that he had work to do in the kitchen. But a look from the American made the chef reconsider. And he sat.

411

'A Chevalier?' said Jean-Guy. 'The knight or the horse? Are you sure they didn't say *cheval*? Because you're halfway there already.'

In the back of the bistro, Gamache could see Matheo and Lea also watching the table with Anton and the Americans. Lea turned to Matheo and said something. Matheo shook his head.

Then Lea looked directly at Gamache. It was so swift he didn't have time to drop his eyes. He knew if he did it now, it would look like what it was. An effort to hide something.

Instead, he held her gaze and smiled.

She did not return his smile.

Jean-Guy and Ruth were exchanging insults, though the old poet's rheumy eyes were not on Beauvoir, but on Gamache.

Armand had settled into his chair, crossing his legs, the voices around him heard and half-heard. Nursing a cold beer after a tough day on the witness stand. Apparently at ease with himself and the world. But Beauvoir could feel what Ruth was sensing.

Something was radiating off Gamache.

Was it rage he felt from the chief? Jean-Guy wondered. It certainly wasn't fear.

It was actually, Beauvoir realized with some surprise, extreme calm.

He was like the center of gravity in the room.

Whatever the outcome, the bombing would stop, that night. The war would end, that night.

CHAPTER 33

L acoste pulled her car onto the old logging road about a kilometer from the village. The road hadn't been used in years, and the undergrowth had become over-growth. The branches of trees scraping and scratching and hiding her car.

Lacoste popped the trunk and put on her assault gear. The heavy boots and helmet with camera. She strapped the automatic pistols into their Velcro tabs and attached the belt with the cartridges. Her hands flew over the familiar gear, clicking, strapping, checking. Double-checking.

She'd called her husband in Montréal, and spoken to the children. Saying good night and telling them she loved them.

They were of an age where they were too embarrassed to say it back.

And so they didn't.

When her husband came back on the line, she told him she had to work late, but would be home before he knew it.

'Do we still have *Pinocchio*?' she asked.

'The book? Maybe. Why?'

'Do you think the kids would like to read it tonight?'

'Our children? They're a little old, aren't they? They want to watch *The Walking Dead*.'

'Don't let them,' she said, and heard him laugh.

'I'll wait up,' he said. And even though she always told him not to, he always did.

'Love you,' he said.

'I love you,' she replied. Her words clear, deliberate.

Then she hung up and locked that phone in her glove compartment, slipping her Sûreté phone into one of the Velcro pockets.

It had buzzed as soon as she'd driven over the hill, out of Three Pines.

There was a single text. From Toussaint.

They were in position.

Lacoste texted back.

G&B in bistro. Am getting in position.

As she made her way through the forest, Lacoste felt another vibration.

package left church on way to village.

Lacoste quickly typed, *village? confirm*

village

She turned and looked toward Three Pines, but all she saw were trees.

'Christ,' she whispered and stood still for a moment, her mind flashing through the options open to her.

Then Isabelle Lacoste turned and ran away. Away from the church. Away from the border.

And toward the village.

At the dirt road she paused, to make sure it was clear, then she crossed and reentered the forest. Down the hill she sprinted, clutching the assault rifle across her chest.

She slipped past the old schoolhouse. Crouched low, she

passed behind Ruth's home. At the Gamaches' back garden, she heard conversation. Madame Gamache, Myrna and Clara were talking. Someone said something, and they laughed.

And then Lacoste was gone. Running across the Old Stage Road and reentering the woods on the other side. Behind the B&B now, she rounded the corner and stopped, catching her breath and trying to catch sight of any cartel member, patrolling.

Her eyes rapidly took in the homes. The road. The village green. The children playing.

Go home, she pleaded, though no one heard. *Go home*.

She saw the door to the bistro swing shut.

Gamache watched as two large men entered the bistro, each carrying a packing crate. They lowered them to the floor next to the head of the American cartel.

Anton stood up abruptly as the American nodded to the two men.

One moved beside Anton, the other stationed himself beside the head of the American cartel.

Others in the bistro were openly watching. The boxes were stamped *Matryoshka Dolls* in English and Cyrillic. Interesting, but not interesting enough to derail drinks and conversation, which started up again.

What most couldn't see was that the words were slightly obscured by blotches, drips, of red.

Isabelle Lacoste carefully opened the internal door connecting the bookstore to the bistro.

Through the crack she saw the chief lean back in his chair, relaxed. A beer in his hand. While off to the side, the head of the American cartel gestured to Anton to sit back down.

This was a different Anton.

No longer the dishwasher. No longer the chef.

He must know now, thought Lacoste, if he didn't before, that this wasn't a friendly tête-à-tête, to divide territory. This was a hostile takeover. If nothing else, the red splashes on the boxes of toys would tell him that. They were what was left of his own couriers.

Lacoste carefully took the safety off her assault rifle.

Olivier passed in front of her and stood by the table, in direct line of sight. Direct line of fire. At the edge of her peripheral vision, she noted that Beauvoir had started to get up from the table.

The soldiers looked over at him. Lacoste lifted her rifle. Through the sights she saw the men grin.

Jean-Guy was holding a duck. The guards smiled as they watched him take the duck off his lap and give it to a woman so old she looked mummified.

It was like laying siege to Hooterville.

Ruth, clutching Rosa to her chest, got up.

'Well, fuck you too,' she said to Beauvoir, at the top of her lungs. 'Numbnuts.'

That provoked outright laughter from the enforcers, though they stopped laughing when Ruth turned her fuck-you gaze on them.

'For God's sake,' Lacoste whispered, as the old woman limped toward the two huge men. 'Get out.'

Now Ruth was also obscuring any shot she had.

'Oh, come on, Ruth,' said Gamache, getting up and ushering her to the side. 'Leave these poor men alone. They're just trying to have their dinner. And it's probably time for yours. We'll take you over.' He pushed her slightly toward the door. 'Olivier? The bill, please.'

'Of course, *patron*.' And Olivier moved to the bar.

'Jean-Guy?' said Gamache, indicating that he should look after Ruth.

The young American was watching this, amusement frozen on his face. Thrown off, slightly, by this strange turn of events. Though clearly not alarmed.

Yogi and Boo-Boo either had no idea what was going on, or the head of the Sûreté knew perfectly well, and was running away. Ceding the floor, the territory, to them.

But the head of the American cartel would have been alarmed, should have been alarmed, had he stopped watching Gamache and noticed the expression on Anton's face.

It was feral now. Savage. Not the look of an animal cornered. More the look of something that had its claws in some unfortunate creature and was about to gut it.

Lacoste, watching from the bookstore, had a clear shot thanks to the chief. But the expression on Anton's face disturbed her. How could that be? He was clearly outnumbered. Outmaneuvered. But maybe he wasn't. Maybe—

She came to it a moment too late.

'*Bonjour*,' a man's voice whispered. And she felt the thrust of a gun to the back of her ear.

Anton was not alone. Of course, he'd have his own bodyguard close by.

And now he had his weapon pressed to her head, as he twisted the rifle out of her hands.

The other thing Isabelle Lacoste knew, in that moment, was that she was dead.

There was a slight noise off to Gamache's left. As he turned to look, Isabelle Lacoste was pushed through the door from Myrna's bookstore, a man behind her with a gun to her head.

Gamache recognized the man immediately, from the attack on the cobrador. He'd been the one with the fireplace poker. Marchand. Gamache had thought he was just a drunken rowdy, but he saw now he'd been wrong. Marchand was Anton's man. A cartel soldier.

Gamache took this in in an instant.

The world seemed to stop, and everything grew very clear, very bright and colorful. Very slow.

Before Lacoste was even across the threshold, Gamache moved.

The only advantage, Isabelle realized, to already being dead, was that she had nothing to lose.

As soon as she was pushed through the door, she planted her feet and thrust herself backward, into her captor.

Beauvoir was just a millisecond behind. He could see Gamache launching himself forward toward the guard.

He could see Lacoste and the armed man behind her falling backward, suspended, it seemed to his racing senses, in mid-flight, mid-fall.

Beauvoir lowered his shoulder, and bringing his hand to his holster, he pushed off.

Gamache lunged.

Everyone else in the bistro, including Anton, including the head of the American cartel, was distracted by Lacoste. For just that instant.

That was all Gamache needed.

He couldn't see what Beauvoir was doing. Or Lacoste, though he had seen her brace, and knew what she was about to do.

All his focus now was on the nearest bodyguard, who was just turning, just noticing what Gamache was doing. A look of surprise just coming onto his face.

He had not expected an older, complacent, beer-swilling man to act so quickly. And so decisively.

The guard had just time enough to move his hand to his weapon before Gamache smashed into him, pushing him on top of Anton. Knocking them off their feet.

All three fell to the floor, a grunt escaping Anton as they landed on top of him.

Gamache brought his forearm to the throat of the first man, pushing his head back, and without hesitation he pulled the hunting knife from his pocket. Flicked it open. And plunged it in.

Gunshots were going off.

Boom. Boom. Boom. Deafening. Not the pops of a handgun but the explosions of an assault rifle. And automatic weapons. Wood was splintering, people were screaming. Chairs and tables overturned. Glass shattered.

Gamache scrambled over the dying guard trying to get at his gun, still in the holster beneath the man. Anton was struggling, writhing, trying to get out from under the heavy body.

Jean-Guy Beauvoir crashed into the table, scattering glass and china, krokodil and traffickers.

Within moments there was chaos. Screaming, shouting. Gunfire.

He couldn't see Gamache anymore, but he did see, as though in the flash of a strobe light, Lacoste crumple.

And then everything moved so quickly, it was as though frames were skipping. Unlike the chief, Beauvoir wasn't a large man, but like the chief, he had the momentary element of surprise. And he used it.

He hit and rolled, and bringing out his weapon, he shot the second guard in the chest just as the man leveled his own gun at Beauvoir.

'What's that?' asked Annie, her face white.

'Gunshots,' said Myrna. 'From the bistro.'

They looked at each other for a moment, an eternity. And then Reine-Marie got up and hustled Annie, who was feeding Honoré, from the back terrace into the house.

Myrna and Clara ran in with them.

'Call 911,' Reine-Marie said to her daughter. 'Lock the door after us.'

'I'm coming with you.'

'You're looking after Ray-Ray,' said her mother.

'Does Armand have a gun?' asked Clara, her eyes wide and hands trembling, but her voice strong.

'*Non.*' Reine-Marie looked around and grabbed the fireplace poker. Myrna and Clara did the same thing. Myrna came away with a hatchet-like thing, and Clara was left with a fireplace brush.

'Fuck,' she muttered under her breath.

The gunfire was continuing, and the dogs were barking. Annie was shouting into the phone to the 911 dispatcher. And their hearts were pounding as they left the house and ran down the path to the road.

'Oh, Christ,' said Myrna.

Half a dozen children were lying on the ground. Apparently dead.

But then they started to stir, to stand. Staring at the bistro. Arms at their sides, mouths open.

'Come here,' Clara screamed at them, waving for them to come to her. She ran over as they began to run to her. Some crying, some confused. All understanding that the safest place in the world was not safe after all.

Clara herded them down the path to where Annie was standing at the open door, frantically waving them in, just as the windows of the bistro shattered with gunfire.

Without hesitation, Reine-Marie, Myrna and Clara ran all out. Toward it.

Ruth crawled across the floor to Rosa, who was sitting, looking more stunned than usual, under an overturned table.

The air was almost unbreathable, with fieldstone and brick and plaster exploded into dust.

She reached Rosa and curled her body around the duck.

Only then did she see Isabelle Lacoste, lying on the ground, her eyes open and staring.

Gamache gripped the handle of the gun in the dying man's holster, but before he could yank it out, a boot landed in his face, stunning him.

The world went white and his vision blurred. Another blow landed.

Anton was striking out wildly. Viciously, desperately, kicking Gamache's head, his shoulders, his arms.

Anton writhed and twisted and kicked with his one free leg. Hammering away at Gamache, who hunched his shoulders against the blows, his only focus the gun in the holster.

Then his grip tightened around the handle and he yanked the gun free.

Bringing it around, he rolled and fired, bang, bang, bang. Point-blank into Marchand, who was steps away, Lacoste's assault rifle raised. Marchand looked shocked. And then was propelled backward, hitting the floor. Dead.

Gamache swung back around just in time to see Anton disappearing out the back door of the bistro.

'*Patron*,' said Jean-Guy as Gamache gripped his arm and hauled himself to his feet.

'Anton got away,' said Gamache, staggering a bit as he moved toward the open back door of the bistro.

'*Oui*. The American and his lieutenant took off after him,' said Beauvoir.

The turmoil in the bistro burst over Gamache.

Lacoste was on the floor, Ruth by her side. Holding her hand. Whispering.

Gabri was kneeling over Olivier.

Patrons, sipping drinks moments earlier, were crying and huddling and hugging and shouting. For help.

But he couldn't stop.

'Armand,' Reine-Marie shouted, as she and Myrna and Clara arrived in the mayhem.

But it was too late. He was gone.

'You get Anton,' said Gamache. 'I'll get the American.'

'There're two of them,' Beauvoir shouted after him.

He didn't know if Gamache had heard, and there was no time to make sure.

The cartels had the advantage of a head start. But Gamache and Beauvoir had the advantage of familiarity.

They knew the woods, and the paths, and the route to the border. Partly because they'd walked the trails, in preparation. Partly because they'd spent hours and hours, in the Gamache home, poring over the detailed topographical maps.

They'd talked to hunters and hikers. To geologists and campers. To those who cut wood, and those who fished in the rivers.

In the past eight months, since finding the hidden door in the root cellar, and the oiled hinge, and understanding the significance, they'd been sure to learn every inch of the terrain.

The drug smugglers had not. They'd found the most direct route through the forest, from the Prohibition bolt-hole to the border. And they'd stuck to it.

'We're studying the situation,' Gamache would reply with equanimity bordering on the dim-witted when microphones and cameras were thrust in his face. And sharp questions were asked about the rising level of crime.

Oddly enough, it was the truth. Though not the entirety of it.

He was studying the situation, just not the one the reporters were talking about.

Gamache had ordered a quiet investigation into all the cabins, barns, schools, and churches used by bootleggers almost a hundred years earlier along the long border with the United States.

There were holes that had never been plugged. All along the watchtower. His tower now. His watch now.

And then he'd ordered surveillance on them all.

And what they saw was that one by one, the Québec syndicate had used all the bolt-holes. But none more than St Thomas's, in the quiet, pretty, forgotten little village of Three Pines.

Where they could get across the border easily. And where the boss could monitor it all, from the kitchen where he worked, first as a dishwasher, then as a chef.

Anton had learned from his father, and his uncle, and apprenticed with his uncle's best friend and confidant. Antonio Ruiz. Whom he was named after.

Until he'd been ready to take over himself.

They could hear the others, up ahead. They were gaining on them, since the drug dealers were essentially running wildly. One chasing the other. The Americans needing to kill the Canadian cartel head. To take over the territory.

And Anton needing to escape, and regroup, and defend his territory.

And Gamache and Beauvoir needing to stop them both. If they failed, there would be a bloodbath.

They could not fail.

Gamache saw Jean-Guy, just up ahead, split off and head east, and Gamache, understanding what he was doing, turned west.

They were driving their quarry, herding them, toward where Toussaint and the assault team were waiting.

Madeleine Toussaint arrived at the bistro with her team, weapons drawn. They approached rapidly but carefully, not sure what they'd meet.

The krokodil heading to the village had been a surprise, but she realized that even if the exchange took place there, they'd still have to get it across the border. And so she'd ordered her team to sit tight. To stick to the plan.

Until she'd heard the shots. Then she'd changed the plan and ordered her people into the village. To help the officers down there.

Even at a run, it took precious time to get there.

They skidded and scrambled down the hills, crashing through the forest, the gunfire getting louder and longer.

And then it stopped. And there was silence.

And then they heard it. The screams. The shrieking. The cries for help.

And then even that went quiet.

Superintendent Toussaint led her team into the village. Her sharp eyes taking in everything. Her assault team in formation behind her, they crouched and swung their weapons, scanning the homes, the windows, the gardens.

Bikes were lying on the side of the village green. A ball sat there.

But there were no people. No dogs. Not cats. Not even birds.

And then a woman came out of the bistro, a fireplace poker in her hand. Behind her, Toussaint heard the familiar and unmistakable sound of assault rifles leveled.

She raised her fist. Stop.

It was Madame Gamache. Running toward them. Calling for help.

Toussaint gestured to a squad to patrol, while she went to Madame Gamache.

'Are there any targets inside?' she demanded.

'Targets? I don't know,' said Reine-Marie. 'There're people hurt. Some dead, I think. We've called for help.'

'Stay here,' said Toussaint, and led her team into the bistro, guns at the ready.

Reine-Marie did not stay there. She ran in behind them.

Toussaint saw tables and chairs overturned. She smelled the putrid scent of recently fired weapons.

But it was what she heard that she would never forget.

Nothing.

There was near total silence. As eyes, wide, turned to her.

'You have to help Armand,' Madame Gamache broke the silence.

'Where is he?'

She scanned the place and saw Lacoste on the ground, an elderly woman and two others kneeling beside her. One of the women, Toussaint noticed, was clutching a fireplace brush. Another, a duck.

Chief Superintendent Gamache wasn't there. Neither was Beauvoir.

They weren't dead. But neither were the cartel heads.

'They went through there. Into the woods.' Madame Gamache pointed toward the back of the bistro.

'How many were there?' Toussaint asked Madame Gamache, her voice urgent.

'I don't know.'

'Three.'

A slender blond man, a dishtowel tied tightly around his arm and propped against a heavyset man, spoke. His voice weak but his words clear.

'Anton and two others,' said Olivier.

Toussaint ordered her team out of the bistro.

Instead of going out the back, Toussaint led her assault team the way they came.

Past the church, up the hill, and into the woods.

If she were Gamache, she thought as she ran, she'd try to herd the cartel members toward the border. Where the Sûreté assault team would be waiting and could finish the job.

Except they were no longer there. They'd veered from the plan.

Shit, shit, shit.

Gamache's lungs were burning and he could taste blood in his mouth, but he didn't slow down. Willing his legs forward, faster.

He could see the American and his lieutenant through the trees, up ahead.

Good, good, he thought. They'd be there soon. Right into Toussaint, who'd be waiting.

But as he ran, another thought occurred to him.

What would he do, if he knew the opioid was heading to the village? And then heard shots?

Christ, he thought. He'd change the plan. Would have to. He'd take his team into the village. To help.

He'd leave the border.

Toussaint wouldn't be there. But the syndicates would. They were running right into the arms of both cartels.

But it was too late. Far too late to stop. They had to see this through, to the end.

Anton recognized this part of the forest.

The border, he knew, was just ahead. And waiting there were his people. Armed and ready.

Gamache had shocked him. The Chief Superintendent had obviously known for a long time who he was. And what he was doing. He almost certainly knew about the root cellar and the hidden door.

The Americans were gaining on him. He could hear them, like a stampede through the forest. Anton picked up speed.

But then he slowed down.

Something had occurred to him.

He wasn't running to the border. He was being herded.

The border was just up ahead, he knew. He couldn't see it. Couldn't see his men, though he knew they were there. But whether Gamache was alive or dead, he almost certainly would have positioned a Sûreté assault team

427

by the border. And the Americans would have their own people there.

He was running into a trap.

He stopped. He'd have to fight it out there. He turned and leveled his gun at the sound coming at him through the forest.

He fired.

A bullet grazed Jean-Guy's leg and he fell.

He lay there for a moment, taking in what had happened. What was happening.

For some reason, Anton had stopped and decided to take a stand. The bullets from his gun moved in an arc, away from Beauvoir, as Anton sprayed the forest.

Beauvoir edged forward, the burning in his leg ignored.

The goal had not changed. To win the war, they had to do one thing.

Get the leaders.

Anton was behind a tree, sighting on the Americans. He fired again, his automatic weapon pumping out rounds.

Jean-Guy moved to the side, any noise he made masked by the weapons fire. Then he brought his gun up, and placed it behind Anton's ear.

The syndicate soldiers, waiting at the border for their chiefs, heard the gunfire and quickly raised their weapons.

The Canadians pointing, unflinching, at the Americans.

The Americans, equally determined, held their weapons on the Canadians.

It was a standoff. Until one of the younger members panicked.

And then it was bedlam.

*

Toussaint, realizing what was happening, ordered her squad to get between the syndicates fighting it out, where she suspected Gamache and Beauvoir were running down the cartel heads.

She might not be able to help them, but at the very least she could stop whoever survived from the syndicates from going to the aid of their leaders.

The head of the American cartel heard the gunfire up ahead and guessed what it meant.

His own guard was dead. Cut down in the initial shots.

There would be no help. He'd have to find his own way across the border. Taking off like a man on fire, he ran. Racing, racing. Through the woods toward Vermont. And safety.

He could hear a noise behind him. Someone chasing him.

He could see the post marking the border just up ahead. Closer. Closer.

And then he was across.

The American was putting more and more distance between him and Gamache. Younger, swifter, the head of the cartel was getting away.

And then they were across the border. Gamache didn't pause, didn't hesitate. He raced after the man. Then he saw the man stop. Turn. And lift his weapon, even as Gamache tried to stop his own forward momentum.

He felt himself skidding, trying to stop.

He was losing his balance. Lost his balance. His feet came out from underneath him. He was falling.

*

The American stopped, turned, and saw the dark figure coming toward him out of the forest. He couldn't make out features. It was just an outline.

He raised his gun and fired.

Gamache found himself on one knee as bullets ripped into the trees millimeters over his head.

Bringing up his gun, he aimed. And fired.

CHAPTER 34

⌒

Armand Gamache and Maureen Corriveau sat together in the quiet office.

They could hear time ticking away on the clock on the desk.

It was just after eight in the morning, a week to the day after the events at the border.

A man slightly older than Gamache sat at the desk. Looking first at the judge, then at the head of the Sûreté.

Gamache's face was beaten and bruised, but the swelling had gone down.

'How is Chief Inspector Lacoste?' the Premier Ministre du Québec asked.

'We'll know soon,' said Gamache. 'They've put her in a coma. The bullet damaged her brain, but we don't know how badly.'

'I'm sorry,' said the Premier. 'And the villagers? Three Pines, is it?'

'*Oui.*'

'Funny, but I'd never heard of it. I'd like to go there, when this is all cleared up.'

'I think they'd like that, sir. They're – we're – trying to get back to normal.'

He chose not to mention that there was nothing normal about Three Pines at the best of times, and the recent events did not get it any closer. But he did know that a strange sort of peace had settled over the village. A quietude.

It had never felt more like home than it did now. And the villagers had never felt more like family, than now.

'There were injuries, I know,' said the Premier.

'The owner of the bistro, Olivier Brulé, was shot in the arm, but his partner acted quickly and stemmed the bleeding. Others were hurt by flying glass and shards of wood. Everyone's out of the hospital now. The gravest injury was to Chief Inspector Lacoste.'

'I asked you a few months ago, Armand, to tell me what was going on. You refused. You asked me to trust you. I did.' He paused to stare at the man. 'And I'm glad I did.'

Gamache nodded very slightly, his thanks.

'But it's time. Tell me what happened.'

When Gamache had finished, the Premier Ministre just stared at him.

He'd read the reports, of course. Those in the media. But also the confidential ones, stacked on his desk.

And he'd seen the video, from Lacoste's camera attached to her helmet. Her point of view, even as she'd fallen.

The video had left him ashen. He didn't think he could ever look at this man again without some part of him seeing Armand Gamache leaping forward. Throwing himself at the two men.

And the knife.

It was an image, a knowledge, the Premier could never erase. What this man, this thoughtful, calm, even kindly man, was capable of doing. What he had done.

'I'm sorry I have to ask these questions.'

'I understand.'

'Were you across the border, Armand, when you killed the American?'

'I believe I was. It's difficult to tell in the forest exactly where the border is. There's a marker that was put there during Prohibition, though I doubt the rum runners were worried about complete accuracy. But I believe I crossed the line, yes.'

The Premier Ministre du Québec shook his head slightly and gave him a wry smile.

'You choose now to tell the truth?'

He refrained from saying that Gamache had indeed crossed a line. Several, in fact. So many that the politician had stopped counting, or caring, though the Departments of Justice in both countries had not.

'And you did it knowing you had no jurisdiction?'

'I didn't even think of jurisdiction at that moment, and if I had I'd have done it anyway.'

'You're not making this easy, Armand.'

Gamache didn't say anything. Though he did sympathize with the Premier, who was, he suspected, trying to help.

He'd dragged the body of the cartel leader back past the faded old marker. Hauling the dead weight, step by step. His own body leaning forward, toward Québec, toward home.

The firefight up ahead had stopped and he heard Jean-Guy, calling him.

It was over.

But there was no celebration in his heart. He was too shattered.

When he was sure he'd crossed back into Québec, Gamache

fell to his knees in exhaustion, so that when Beauvoir found him, he saw a man covered in blood, apparently praying over the body he had created.

With Jean-Guy's help, they dragged the American back to where Toussaint was turning chaos into order.

Jean-Guy had sustained an injury to his leg, but it was minor and quickly bandaged. His was the only injury among the Sûreté team. Except, of course, for Isabelle.

The cartel members, from both sides, had almost managed to wipe each other out. Those who survived were being hand-cuffed, while paramedics sorted through the rest.

It looked, in those old-growth forests, like what it was. A battlefield. Sirens, from more ambulances and police, could be heard.

Anton had his hands secured behind his back.

'You did my job for me, Armand,' said Anton, nodding toward the body. 'You think you've won back the province, don't you? Just wait for it.'

'I should've killed him,' said Jean-Guy, as they'd made their way back to Three Pines.

Gamache wiped blood, now congealing, from his eyes. But said nothing. In that moment, he agreed with Jean-Guy. It would have been better, far better.

'It's a shame,' said the Premier Ministre du Québec, when Armand had finished his account, 'that Anton Boucher survived.'

The comment, said so dryly, so matter-of-factly, surprised Gamache. Not that the Premier would think it, but that he would say it out loud.

'There are lines,' said Gamache. 'That cannot be crossed. And once crossed, there's no going back.'

'Like murder,' said the Premier. 'Which brings me to my next question.'

Judge Corriveau shifted slightly in her chair, knowing it was her turn now. Knowing what he was about to ask.

'Tell me about the killing of Madame Kathleen Evans.'

It was much the same conversation Chief Superintendent Gamache had had with Judge Corriveau a few days after the attack.

The trial had, of course, been put on hold.

Maureen Corriveau had gone up to the Gamaches' apartment, along with Barry Zalmanowitz, to discuss the case and what should happen next.

When they knocked on the door of the second-floor walk-up in the Outremont quartier of Montréal, Gamache himself opened it.

'*Bonjour*,' he said. 'Thank you for coming to me.'

He showed them into the living room, while the two people behind him exchanged glances. They'd heard about the grave injuries to Chief Inspector Lacoste. And had read the preliminary reports, written by the senior officers. Including Chief Superintendent Gamache.

They had heard, through the information and misinformation swirling around government buildings, that Gamache himself had sustained some injuries. But they weren't prepared for the bruised face, his one eye almost swollen shut. The cuts where the boot had scraped flesh off bone.

When he'd opened the door to them, Judge Corriveau had searched his eyes, worried that they'd been hollowed out by the events in the village. In the woods.

That the warmth would be replaced by bitterness. The kindness by cruelty.

And the decency would be gone completely.

The look of pain she saw now wasn't new, and wasn't physical. It had always been there, in Gamache's eyes, like an astigmatism that meant he saw things slightly differently from the rest of them.

He saw the worst of humanity. But he also saw the best. And she was relieved to see that the decency remained. Stronger, even, than the pain. Stronger than ever.

'Thank you for your flowers,' he said, pointing to the arrangement of cheerful cut flowers on the side table.

'You're welcome,' said Judge Corriveau.

The card had simply read, *'Merci.'* And had been signed *Maureen Corriveau and Joan Blanchette.*

Judge Corriveau had never discussed her personal life, but she felt she needed to give him that much. And besides, Joan had insisted.

She took in the room around her. It was a pied-à-terre, she knew, their real home being in that little village. The one-bedroom apartment was in a classic Outremont walk-up. The ceilings were high, the room bright and airy and welcoming, with books on shelves and on side tables. *La Presse*, *Le Devoir* and *The Gazette* newspapers were scattered around. It was casual but not messy.

The sofa and armchairs were inviting, lived in. Upholstered in fresh, warm colors. It was a room she and Joan could happily occupy.

Another man was in the living room, leaning slightly on a cane.

'You know Inspector Beauvoir, I believe,' said Gamache, and they all shook hands.

'You all right?' asked Barry Zalmanowitz.

'This's for effect,' said Jean-Guy, waving it in front of

himself, as he'd seen Ruth do thousands of times. He wondered, briefly, what would happen if he called the Chief Crown numbnuts.

'How's Chief Inspector Lacoste?' asked the Crown.

'We're going to the hospital as soon as we've finished here,' said Gamache. 'I spoke to her husband this morning, and he said that there's some activity in her brain.'

The other two nodded. When that was the good news, there was nothing more that could be said.

'I don't think you've met my wife,' said Gamache, as Reine-Marie came out of the kitchen carrying a tray with cold drinks.

He took the tray and introduced her to Judge Corriveau.

'We've met, of course,' said Monsieur Zalmanowitz. 'I interviewed you as part of the witness process. You found the body of Katie Evans.'

'*Oui*,' said Reine-Marie. 'Do you mind if I join you?'

'Of course not,' said Judge Corriveau, while all the time wondering if she should mind, and if she should have brought a court reporter, to take down what was said.

But it was too late, and in the morass of unusual events, this departure from the norm would probably be forgiven if not overlooked.

Judge Corriveau turned to Chief Superintendent Gamache and Chief Crown Zalmanowitz.

'This is a meeting that had been scheduled for two days ago, in my office. But of course, it would be foolish not to realize things have changed. And yet, some things have not. A woman is still on trial for the murder of Madame Evans. I need to know if she really is guilty, in your mind, or if it was all part of what was clearly a long and detailed scheme.'

She looked from one to the other, then settled on Gamache.

The architect. The leader, who had led them all into this.

'Tell me,' said the judge, 'about the murder of Katie Evans.'

'It began,' began Gamache, 'as most murders do. Long ago. Though not far away.'

He looked to his left.

'Just a few blocks from here. At the Université de Montréal. When one of the students killed himself. Doped up, out of his mind, on drugs supplied to him by a third-year political science student. Anton Boucher.'

Judge Corriveau was very familiar with the name.

In the pretrial reports, Anton Boucher had been the dishwasher at the bistro.

In the reports she'd just read, Anton Boucher was the head of the Québec syndicate.

'His uncle is Maurice Boucher,' said Corriveau, wanting to show she'd done some homework. 'He was the head of the Hell's Angels here. In prison now for murder and trafficking.'

Beauvoir nodded. 'Right. When he was sent up, his nephew took over. He did what Mom Boucher couldn't.'

Beauvoir had used the nickname the elder Boucher went by. Apparently because he 'mothered' the members of his gang. Though that didn't stop him from slaughtering other people's children.

'Anton moved quickly,' said Jean-Guy. 'He was named after his uncle's best friend, Antonio Ruiz, who guided him in consolidating the three cartels. Anton could see where organized crime was heading.'

'And where was that?' asked Corriveau.

'It was on the verge of becoming far bigger, far wealthier, more powerful than anything anyone had known in the past,' said Gamache. 'And the catalyst was the opioids.'

'Like fentanyl,' said Zalmanowitz. 'I know all about them. My daughter was addicted. We got her treatment, but . . .'

He lifted his hands, then dropped them.

'This isn't parents overreacting to a recreational drug,' he continued. 'This's something else. It's brutal. It changes them. It changed her. And she's one of the lucky ones. She's still alive.'

'Fentanyl was the first to really explode onto the streets,' said Gamache. 'But there were others. And now they're coming in, being created faster than we can stop them. Faster than we can even get the opioids onto the banned list. A tweak of the formula, and it reads differently. It's no longer illegal. Until we catch up with it.'

'A hole in the law,' said the judge. 'The chemical compounds need to be clearly described. Even a slight change means there's nothing we can do. We have to release the traffickers.'

'It's a modern-day Black Death,' said Zalmanowitz. 'And the syndicates are the plague rats.'

'Anton Boucher saw it coming,' said Gamache. 'And he moved quickly, viciously, to take control.'

'A new generation of criminal,' said Corriveau. 'For a new generation of drug.'

'*Oui*,' said Gamache.

'Was Katie Evans part of the cartel?' asked Corriveau.

'*Non*. Her crime was that she was at school with the young man who killed himself. She was his lover for a few months, before breaking it off. His name was Edouard Valcourt. He was Jacqueline's brother.'

'I remember his name from the pretrial reports.'

'Madame Evans, her husband, Patrick, along with Matheo Bissonette and Lea Roux, were all friends with Edouard.

Classmates,' said Beauvoir. 'Lea and Matheo were at the rooftop party when he jumped.'

Maureen Corriveau didn't react, but Barry Zalmanowitz looked down at his hands.

It was his nightmare. Maybe they hadn't saved his daughter in time. Maybe they hadn't saved her at all. Maybe this chemical was in deeper than even a father could reach.

'Anton was their dealer, but he made a mistake,' said Beauvoir. 'And it was a big one. He decided to try the drugs himself. He got hooked, and then, like most addicts, he got sloppy. When Edouard killed himself and questions started to be asked, he took off. Eventually went into treatment. There he got clean, but he also met a group of other men. Some who genuinely wanted to start fresh, but some who did not. They became Anton's lieutenants. They, like him, had the advantage now of being clean. And of knowing what the drugs were capable of.'

'That was a few years ago,' said Gamache. 'As the drugs got stronger, crueler, so did the cartels.'

'So how does Madame Evans come into it?' asked Judge Corriveau. 'She knew this Edouard back at university, and presumably knew Anton Boucher.'

'She did,' said Gamache. 'They all did. He was a couple of years ahead of them. They all bought drugs off him. Mostly grass, some cocaine. Not the pharmaceuticals. Only Edouard did that.'

'Are you saying that Madame Evans was killed because of something that happened that long ago?'

'Yes,' said Gamache. 'Most murders are simple. The motive clear, though what makes them difficult to see is that they're often very old. Katie Evans was killed because of what happened at university. Because of a debt owed. And that's where the cobrador came in. Jacqueline, Edouard's sister, had the idea, but it was his friends who actually did it.'

'They took turns being the Conscience,' said Beauvoir. 'Standing on the village green. Accusing Anton. But that's as far as it was supposed to go. They'd stand there for a few days, scare the shit out of the dishwasher, then go home.'

'So what went wrong?' Maureen Corriveau asked.

She needed all the details, not simply because it was her case, but because it was her career.

She'd received a phone call that morning, summoning her to the office of the Premier Ministre in Québec City next week. It was not, she knew, to congratulate her on her role in this.

Before she went, she needed to know what 'this' was.

'Wait,' she said. 'Let me guess. They didn't realize Anton wasn't there to wash dishes. He was in Three Pines to monitor the movement of drugs.'

'They had no idea who they were dealing with,' said Zalmanowitz.

'They were focused on the suicide of their friend. Nothing more,' said Gamache. 'The private investigator hired by the family worked on it off and on for years, finally tracking him down at the home of Antonio Ruiz.'

'And this Ruiz, he's also involved in organized crime?' asked Judge Corriveau.

'In Europe. He's based in Spain,' said Gamache. 'Though the courts can't seem to convict him.'

'Another job for the cobrador,' said Zalmanowitz.

'I'll pretend I didn't hear that,' said Judge Corriveau. 'But the investigator didn't know that Anton was related to Mom Boucher? Doesn't seem possible to miss that.'

'It's a common name,' said Gamache. 'And the records

had been deliberately obscured. We knew there had been corruption in the Sûreté. Officials at all levels of the police, of government, were compromised. There was a reason we couldn't get traction on fighting organized crime.'

'They were better organized,' said Beauvoir.

Corriveau smiled, then grew serious. 'How did you know I wasn't bought?'

'We didn't. Frankly, we had to assume everyone was.'

They stared at each other, his eyes not quite so kindly.

'And the Crown?' she asked, turning to Monsieur Zalmanowitz.

'Our investigation showed the Crown's office could have been compromised,' said Gamache.

Zalmanowitz turned to him. 'You investigated me?'

'Of course we did. I had to be sure before approaching you.'

Now they were getting to it, Corriveau knew. The center, the core, of the issue.

'How did this' – she waved a finger between the two men – 'come about?'

'I needed help,' said Gamache. 'So I asked the Chief Crown for a meeting.'

'In Halifax,' said Zalmanowitz.

It took a lot to surprise Maureen Corriveau, but that did. 'Nova Scotia?'

'Yes. We took separate flights and met at some dive on the waterfront,' said Zalmanowitz. 'Though it did have great lemon meringue pie.'

'Really?' said Corriveau. 'That's what you remember?'

'It was very good,' said the Crown, smiling slightly at her annoyance. 'I've never liked Monsieur Gamache. It's not professional. It's personal.'

'And it's mutual,' said Gamache. 'I considered him a preening coward—'

'And I think he's an arrogant shithead. *Désolé*,' he said to Madame Gamache.

'But you both liked the pie,' she pointed out.

'As a matter of fact, it was the first thing we agreed on,' said Gamache, with a smile that threatened to split open his lip again. 'I outlined what I was considering, and what would be necessary, and what I would need from him.'

'What did he need from you?' the judge asked the Crown.

'I think you know,' said Zalmanowitz.

'And I think you know that I need to hear it from you.'

'He asked that I suppress vital evidence that would compromise their investigation into the cartel. He needed the time and the distraction. He needed Anton Boucher to believe he was free and clear, and that the Sûreté under Gamache's leadership was incompetent.'

Barry Zalmanowitz sat back and placed his hands on the soft arms of the chair, much like Lincoln at the stone memorial.

'And I agreed.'

There. But unlike Abraham Lincoln, his was a self-assassination. And there would be no statues commemorating his service.

Barry Zalmanowitz knew that in cataloguing so clearly what he'd done, he was possibly placing himself in prison. Definitely ruining his career. Hurting his family.

But his actions had helped bring down the cartel. They'd finally broken the back of the traffickers. There was mopping up to be done, but the war on drugs had been won.

If he, and his career, and his name were casualties, well, people had suffered worse. And the fuckers who'd sold the drugs to his daughter wouldn't ruin another young life.

Across from him, Gamache nodded, then did something that Zalmanowitz found unsettling.

He looked down at his hands, also bruised. A mark that looked like the sole of a boot clearly stamped across the swollen knuckles.

And Gamache sighed. Then he raised his eyes to Zalmanowitz and said, *'Désolé.'*

In the silence, the Crown could feel his cheeks tingling as they flushed, then went pale. As the blood rushed forward, then ran away.

'For what?' he asked quietly.

'I haven't told you everything.'

Now Barry Zalmanowitz turned to stone. 'What?'

'Anton Boucher did not kill Katie Evans.'

Zalmanowitz gripped the arms of the chair, in a sort of spasm.

'What're you saying?'

'I lied to you. I'm very sorry.'

'Tell me what you're saying.'

'You're prosecuting the right person. Jacqueline killed Katie Evans.'

Zalmanowitz's mind both froze and raced. Like a car chained to the wall. Spinning its wheels.

He was trying to understand these words. And trying to work out if this was good news, or a further disaster.

'Why didn't you tell me?' he finally got out. Not sure if that was the most pressing question, but it was the first out of the gate.

'Because I only completely trusted a small group of my own officers,' said Gamache. 'Though I'd never have approached you if I'd had serious doubts.'

'But you did have doubts,' said Zalmanowitz.

'Yes. I had no proof that you were corrupt. But neither did I have proof that you weren't.'

'So what made you approach me?'

'Beyond desperation? Your daughter.'

'What about her?' he asked, his voice, and his expression, filled with warning.

'Our son, Daniel, has had experience with hard drugs,' said Gamache, and Zalmanowitz's eyes narrowed. This was news to him.

'So have I,' said Beauvoir. 'Almost killed me. Almost destroyed the people I care most about.'

'We know what it does to a family,' said Gamache quietly. 'And I thought if anyone would do anything to stop the trafficking, it would be you. So I took the chance, and approached you. But I knew that even if you were clean, that didn't mean your department was.'

'You arrogant shithead.'

Gamache held his glare.

'If it helps, I didn't trust my own service either. That's why only a handful of officers knew what I was doing. The entire Sûreté was involved, but each department, each detachment had a very small role. So small, none could see clearly what was happening. To the extent, as you know, that there was eventually open revolt. They also felt I was incompetent and didn't flinch from saying it. But only a few saw the whole picture.'

Like Clara's paintings, thought Beauvoir. Tiny dabs that in themselves were nothing. But when combined added up to something completely unexpected.

'You think that excuses it?' said Zalmanowitz. 'Do you know what you've done? You made me betray all my training, all my beliefs. You made me lie and suppress evidence. You made me believe I was trying the wrong person for a capital crime. You know what that does to a person? To me?'

His clenched fist hit his breastbone so hard they heard the thump across the room.

'Do you regret what you did?' Gamache asked.

'That's not the issue.'

'It's the only issue, today,' said Gamache. 'Yes, I led you to believe all those things, and yes, you did it. And because you did, we have the cartels across the nation on the run. Not just here, but across the country. The head of the largest syndicate in North America is dead, the other is in prison.'

'You played me for a fool.'

'No. I realized I'd been wrong about you, and that you're not a coward. Far from it. You were and are a very brave man.'

'You think I care what you think of me?' demanded Zalmanowitz.

'No. Nor do I care, really, what you think of me. What I care about today are the results. I don't regret what I did. I wish with all my heart it hadn't been necessary. I wish there'd been another way. But if there was one, I couldn't think of it. Do you regret it?' Chief Superintendent Gamache asked again. 'Burning our ships?'

Chief Crown Prosecutor Zalmanowitz took a deep breath, and regained control of himself.

'No.'

'Neither do I.'

'That doesn't excuse you,' he said. 'That doesn't mean I forgive you. You could have told me.'

'You're right. I know that now. I made mistakes. You were brave and selfless and I treated you like an outsider. I'm sorry. I was wrong.'

'Shithead,' Zalmanowitz muttered, but his heart didn't

seem in it. 'What were you keeping from me? What was so important?'

'The bat.'

'The murder weapon?' asked the judge.

'Yes. Do you remember in the testimony, in Reine-Marie's statement, she said she hadn't seen the bat when she found the body?'

'Yes. But it was there when Chief Inspector Lacoste arrived,' said Zalmanowitz. 'You testified that Madame Gamache must've made a mistake.'

'I lied.'

He looked at Reine-Marie, who nodded.

Maureen Corriveau wished she'd chosen that moment to use the bathroom, but it was too late. She'd heard.

And, to be fair, while the specific lie was news, she already knew this trial was rife with half-truths and outright perjury.

'Well then, what did happen?' asked the Crown, slipping naturally into prosecutor mode. Cross-examining a possibly hostile witness.

'I knew Reine-Marie was describing exactly what was there when she found the body. And what was not. So how did the bat return, without anyone seeing?'

'I'd locked the church door. The only way in,' she said.

'So.' Zalmanowitz lifted his hands. 'How do you explain it?'

'I couldn't. Until a casual conversation later that day with friends. One mentioned that the root cellar already had a criminal past. It'd been used by bootleggers during Prohibition.'

Both the Crown and the judge were nodding now. It was quite a famous chapter in Québec history, one many prominent families wished would go away.

'That's when it began to come together,' said Gamache.

'The smugglers would never have hauled the contraband liquor out the front door of the church. There must be, I realized, another door. A hidden door, in the root cellar.'

'That's how the murder weapon reappeared,' said the judge. 'The murderer used the hidden door. But how did she even know about it?'

'Jacqueline followed Anton to the Ruiz home,' said Beauvoir. 'And got a job there to be close to him, to watch him. Then, when Ruiz went back to Spain, she followed Anton to Three Pines. She was watching him closely, and one night she saw him use the door.'

'But then, how did he know about it?'

'Anton grew up in a household where old war stories meant turf wars, speakeasies, bootlegging,' said Gamache. 'Stories of getting booze across the border. How they did it. Where they did it. His father, his uncle, his uncle's best friend, all saw these as part of the lore, their history, almost mythology, but not pertinent today. What separated Anton from the rest of his family, from the rest of the leadership of the cartels, is that he dismissed nothing. If something was history, it didn't make it less useful. He took everything in. Some he discarded, some he kept in his mind for later use. And some he repurposed. To others, the Prohibition stories were a way to pass cold winter nights. For Anton, they were a revelation.'

'He did his homework,' said Beauvoir. 'And discovered where all the crossing points, all the hidden rooms and passages used by the bootleggers were. He used them all, but as his main crossing point he chose a hidden room in a hidden village.'

'It was perfect,' said Gamache.

'So you discovered how the bat, the murder weapon, got

in and out, or out and in,' said Judge Corriveau. 'But how did you know it was being used for drug smuggling?'

'The hinges,' said Beauvoir. 'They'd been oiled. And not recently. The room, and the door, had been used far longer than the cobrador had been in residence.'

'And when asked, none of the friends admitted using the door. They had no idea it was there,' said Gamache. 'So the hinges must've been oiled for another purpose. I didn't know right away, of course. But I began to think maybe the smugglers were back. It had perplexed us for a while, how so many drugs were getting across the border. The traditional routes we knew about, but far more was crossing than we could account for.'

'But wait a minute,' said the Crown. 'Everything you're saying still points to Anton being the murderer. How did you figure out it was Jacqueline?'

'If Anton Boucher wanted someone killed, do you think he'd do it himself?' asked Beauvoir. 'And even if he did, would he panic, and take, then replace the murder weapon? Why not just burn it? That's when Jacqueline came to us and confessed about the cobrador.'

Jean-Guy remembered the bitterly cold November night when Gamache and Lacoste, along with the dogs, had blown back into the house, as he'd gotten off the phone with Myrna and Ruth.

Both admitted knowing about the little room. Ruth had told Myrna, and Myrna, after some thought, remembered telling Lea. Though while he'd gently probed, neither seemed to know about the hidden door.

'She didn't confess to the murder of Katie Evans,' said Gamache. 'Her confession was about the cobrador. But the bat continued to worry us. I knew the bat's only purpose, after it had killed Madame Evans, was to point to the murderer. But not, of course, the real one.'

'She wanted Anton Boucher charged with the crime,' said Zalmanowitz.

'*Oui*. That was Jacqueline's plan all along. Again, very simple. Kill Katie, and blame Anton. The two people she considered responsible for her brother's death. The Conscience had more than one debt to collect. Edouard jumped while out of his mind on drugs sold to him by Anton. But what sent him over the edge was his breakup with Katie. It broke his heart, and the drugs warped his mind. He was, by all reports, a gentle, sensitive young man, who loved her too much. And Katie Evans was a gentle, kind woman whose crime was that she didn't love him back.'

'Edouard told his sister all about it,' said Beauvoir. 'He was enraged. He painted Katie as cruel. Heartless. He didn't mean it, of course. He was insane with jealousy and the drugs had warped his thinking. I know what they can do. How we turn on the very people who care for us the most.'

'And then, having placed all his bile in his sister's head, he killed himself,' said Gamache. 'Leaving Jacqueline to despise Katie. Neither Katie, nor the drug dealer, had paid any price for her brother's death. But she would see to that.'

Barry Zalmanowitz was nodding. While others might not understand that obsession, he did. If his daughter had died, he'd have spent his lifetime getting justice. In whatever form it took.

The Premier Ministre du Québec listened to the explanation, without comment, without question.

Then he turned to Judge Corriveau.

'How much of this did you know?'

It was time. To link arms with Gamache and cross the bridge at Selma.

To stand in front of a home, and refuse entry to those who would deport, who would hang, who would beat and bully.

The knock was at the door. The Jews in the attic.

It was her time, her turn. To stand up.

'I knew none of it,' she heard herself say.

Beside her in the Premier's office, Gamache was silent.

'This was all you, Armand?' the Premier asked.

'*Oui*.'

'But your people went along with it. The Chief Crown went along with it.'

'Yes.'

It was no use saying they were just following his orders, Gamache knew. That was no defense, nor should it be.

'You know what I have to do,' said the Premier. 'Breaking the law, perjuring yourself, crossing the border and killing a citizen of another country, no matter how deserving that person was, cannot go unanswered.'

'I understand.'

'You will, of course, be—'

'I knew,' said Maureen Corriveau. She turned to Gamache. 'Forgive me, I should've admitted it earlier.'

'I understand,' he said. And then, under his breath he said to her, 'You're not alone.'

'Explain,' said the Premier Ministre.

'I didn't know the specifics, but I did know that something was happening in the trial. Something unusual. I suspected perjury and called Messieurs Gamache and Zalmanowitz into my chambers. They all but admitted it. Enough to have had them arrested, certainly detained. But I let them go.'

'Why?'

'Because I knew there must have been a very good reason. And if they were willing to risk so much, it seemed the least I could do.'

The Premier nodded. 'Thank you for that. You do know that if you had detained Monsieur Gamache, all this would have fallen apart. His plan would've collapsed, and the cartel would have really and truly won.'

'I do.'

He turned to Gamache.

'You will be relieved of duty. You'll be on suspension, pending an investigation. As will your second-in-command, Inspector Jean-Guy Beauvoir. I believe you were the leaders?'

'Yes.'

'Superintendent Madeleine Toussaint will be promoted to acting head of the Sûreté. She's certainly been implicated and will be investigated, but someone has to take over, and thanks to you, Armand, all the senior officers are now compromised. That means I either appoint Toussaint, or the janitor.'

'And Chief Inspector Lacoste?' asked Gamache.

'She will stay as head of homicide.'

Armand nodded his thanks. It was a battle he was prepared to fight, but relieved he didn't have to.

'And me?' asked Judge Corriveau.

'You're the judge,' he said. 'What do you think I should do?'

Maureen Corriveau appeared to think for a moment, then said, 'Nothing.'

The Premier lifted his hands. 'Sounds reasonable to me. Nothing it is.'

'*Pardon?*' asked Corriveau. She'd been kidding when she said 'nothing'.

'I spoke to the Chief Justice yesterday and told him what I thought might have happened. He agreed that while technically improper, you acted in the best interest of the province. Of the people. You used great judgment.'

The Premier Ministre du Québec stood up and put out his hand.

Judge Corriveau stood and shook it.

'*Merci*,' he said.

Then he turned to Gamache, also on his feet now.

'I'm sorry, my dear friend, that any punishment should come your way. We should be giving you a medal—'

Gamache leaned away from that suggestion.

'—but I can't,' continued the Premier. 'I can, though, promise you and Inspector Beauvoir a fair investigation.'

He walked them out, then the Premier Ministre closed the door, and closed his eyes. And saw again the charming bistro, and the kindly man with the knife.

CHAPTER 35

<hr>

'Well,' said Clara. 'What do you think?'

In the wake of the attacks, she'd canceled her art show. The *vernissage* would have been that very day, at the Musée des beaux-arts in Montréal. But instead, she'd hung her latest works in the bistro.

'Certainly covers up the holes,' said Gabri.

It was the best that could be said of the paintings. They couldn't cover all the huge pockmarks in the plaster walls, but the worst were now hidden behind these strange portraits.

Gabri was not completely convinced it was an improvement.

The debris had been cleaned up. The shattered glass and wood and broken furniture thrown into bins.

The injured were healing. Olivier stood beside him, his arm bandaged and in a sling.

The insurance people had been and gone. And been again, and gone again. And were returning. They could not quite believe the claim that said the damages came from automatic weapons fire. Until they saw. And still, they needed to return.

And yet, there it was. Holes blasted in the walls. The old bay window shattered, a makeshift replacement put in by a local contractor.

People from surrounding villages had come to help. And now, if you didn't look too closely, the bistro was almost back to normal.

Ruth was standing in front of a painting of Jean-Guy.

There was a light, airy quality about it. Probably because the canvas wasn't obscured by a lot of paint. In fact, there was very little.

'He's undressed,' said Ruth. 'Disgusting.'

This was not completely true. What body there was had clothes. But it was really more a suggestion of a body. A suggestion of clothing. His handsome face was detailed. But older than the man himself.

Clara had painted Jean-Guy as he might look in thirty years. There was peace in the face and something else, deep in his eyes.

They walked around, drinks in hand, staring at the walls. Staring at themselves.

Over the course of a year, Clara had painted all of them. Or most of them.

Myrna, Olivier, Sarah the baker, Jean-Guy. Leo and Gracie.

She'd even painted herself, in the long-awaited self-portrait. It looked like a middle-aged madwoman staring into a mirror. Holding a paintbrush. Trying to do a self-portrait.

Gabri had hung that near the toilets.

'But there're no holes here,' Clara had pointed out.

'And isn't that lucky?' said Gabri, hurrying away.

Clara smiled, and followed him into the body of the bistro, taking up a position at the bar and sipping a cool sangria.

She watched. And wondered. When they'd get it. When they'd see.

That the unfinished portraits were in fact finished. They

455

were not, perhaps, finished in the conventional sense, but she had captured in each the thing she most wanted.

And then, she'd stopped.

If Jean-Guy's clothes weren't perfect, did it matter?

If Myrna's hands were blurry, who cared?

If Olivier's hair was more a suggestion than actual hair, what difference did it make? And his hair, as Gabri was always happy to point out, was becoming more of a suggestion every day.

Ruth was staring at the portrait of Rosa, even as she held the duck.

The Rosa in Clara's painting was imperious. Officious. Had Napoleon been a *canard*, he'd have been Rosa. Clara had pretty much nailed her.

Ruth gave a small snort. Then she shuffled along to the next painting. Of Olivier. Then the next and the next.

By the time she'd done the circuit, everyone was watching her. Waiting for the explosion.

Instead she went up to Clara, kissed her on the cheek and then went back to the painting of Rosa and stood there for a very long time.

The friends stared at each other, then one by one they joined Ruth.

Reine-Marie was the next to see it. Then she went to the next painting, following Ruth's tour of the room, going from one canvas to the next.

Then Myrna got it. And she too followed Reine-Marie around the bistro. Then Olivier saw it.

Deep in Rosa's haughty eyes, there was another tiny perfect finished portrait. Of Ruth. She was leaning toward Rosa. Offering the nest of old flannel sheets. Offering a home.

It was a portrait of adoration. Of salvation. Of intimacy.

It was a moment so tender, so vulnerable, Reine-Marie, Myrna, Olivier felt like voyeurs. Looking into a glass home. But they didn't feel dirty. They felt lucky. To see such love.

They went from painting to painting.

There, in each of their eyes, a loved one was perfectly reflected.

Myrna turned to Clara, across the room. Across the shattered, broken bistro. Across the lifetimes of friendship.

Clara, who knew that bodies might come and go, but love was eternal.

Armand had called and spoken with Reine-Marie and then Jean-Guy, telling them what the Premier Ministre had decided.

Suspended, with pay for Beauvoir, without pay for Gamache, pending an investigation. He hoped they would take their time, because Armand had unfinished business.

He had fentanyl to find.

As for Barry Zalmanowitz, the Québec Bar Association would investigate the Crown attorney. In the meantime, his cases would be taken over by another prosecutor. But he'd remain on the job.

It was the very best they could hope for, and Gamache knew that the Premier himself would come under fire from the opposition for not doing more.

'And Isabelle?' asked Jean-Guy.

'She stays as head of homicide,' said Gamache.

There had clearly been no debate about that.

'I'm heading over to the hospital now,' said Armand. 'I'll see you soon.'

Jean-Guy hung up and went out into the back garden, where Annie was sitting with a jug of iced tea. Honoré was upstairs, napping, and everyone else was at the bistro.

They had a quiet few minutes to themselves.

His leg was doing much better and he'd put aside the cane, with some regret. He quite liked the accessory.

Jean-Guy opened the book he'd taken from his father-in-law's study, but soon lowered it to his knee, and stared in front of him.

Annie noticed, but didn't say anything. Leaving him to his thoughts. And it was clear what he was thinking about. Who he was thinking about.

He and Gamache had come down the hill, Beauvoir limping and the chief stumbling a few times.

Their bodies were screaming to stop, to rest. But they kept moving, desperate to get back to the village. To their families. To Isabelle.

Reine-Marie and Annie ran up the road to meet them.

'Oh, thank God,' Reine-Marie whispered, clutching Armand to her, as he held her tightly, resting his broken cheek on her head. Smelling the scent of old garden roses. And Honoré.

Neither wanted to let go, but he had to. He had to see Isabelle.

'You're hurt,' said Annie, drawing back from Jean-Guy and touching his leg, wrapped in a temporary bandage.

'So are you,' said Reine-Marie, when she stepped back.

The entire front of Armand's white shirt was red, and sticking to his chest. As though, in the terrible sequence of events, some transmogrification had occurred and sweat had been turned into blood.

'It's not mine,' he said.

She reached out and touched his bleeding face. Then she kissed his split and weeping lips.

'Isabelle?' Armand asked.

'They're with her now.'

'She's alive?' said Jean-Guy, holding Annie to him.

Reine-Marie nodded, then looked at Armand. And he could see the truth in her eyes.

Alive. But—

'The others?'

'Olivier was hit in the arm, but Gabri got to him. The paramedics say he'll be fine. There're lots of cuts from glass and wood, but nothing life-threatening. Only Isabelle.'

Gamache and Beauvoir walked swiftly toward the bistro, breaking into a run as they got closer.

Ambulances and emergency response vehicles were parked all around the village green. As they approached, a gurney came out the door of the bistro, piled with equipment. And in there, like a nest, was Isabelle.

Ruth walked beside her. She hadn't left Isabelle's side since crawling through the flying debris. To hold the young woman's hand. And whisper to her. That she was not alone.

Clara followed, still clutching the fireplace brush, with Myrna right behind her, holding Rosa.

They were almost at the ambulance when Gamache and Beauvoir arrived.

Lacoste's eyes were closed now, and her face was white, ashen.

Ashes. Ashes. We all fall down.

Armand touched her cheek. It was still warm.

The senior paramedic was working quickly to attend to Isabelle. He looked up briefly and, seeing Gamache, he drew back for a moment. He did not see the head of the Sûreté. What he saw was a man covered almost entirely, head to toe, in blood.

'Gamache, Sûreté,' said Armand. 'May I come?'

'Only one,' said the paramedic. 'Maybe her grandmother . . .'

Ruth drew back, her thin lips even thinner. Her rheumy eyes even more watery.

'But she's your child, Armand,' she said quietly, so that only Armand could hear. And placed Isabelle's hand in his. 'Always has been.'

'*Merci*,' he said, and climbed in quickly.

'We'll follow,' Reine-Marie shouted as the door closed and the ambulance raced off.

Armand positioned himself at Isabelle's head, making sure he wasn't in the way. As the paramedics worked, he whispered in her ear.

'You are loved. You are brave, and kind. You saved us all. Thank you, Isabelle. You are loved. Your children love you. Your husband and parents love you . . .'

All the way to the hospital.

You're brave and strong.

You're not alone.

You are loved.

You are loved.

Her lips moved, once. He leaned close, but couldn't make out what she was trying to say. Though he could guess.

'I'll tell them,' he whispered. 'And they love you too.'

When Gamache arrived at the hospital from his meeting with the Premier, he found Isabelle's husband sitting by her bed.

Breathing tubes were doing their job and machines monitored her heart and brain functions.

He was reading out loud, while music played. Ginette Reno. '*Un peu plus haut, un peu plus loin.*'

'There's been some change, Armand,' said Robert, getting

up. On seeing Gamache's alarm, he hurried on. 'For the better. Look.'

The brain waves seemed stronger. Broader. More rhythmic.

'She's responding to things,' he said, taking her hand and looking down so that Gamache couldn't see his eyes. 'The doctors say reading to her might help. Just the sound of a familiar voice, I think.' He pointed to the book on the bed. 'The children gave it to me to bring. She asked about it, that night.'

'Go get a cold drink and sandwich,' said Armand. 'Get some fresh air. I'll sit with her.'

When Robert left, Armand took the seat that had not been cold since this all happened a week earlier. Then he reached out and held her hand. And whispered in her ear.

'You are magnificent. Strong and brave. You saved our lives, Isabelle. You're safe, and you are loved. Your family loves you. We love you. You are magnificent . . .'

While in the background, Ginette Reno sang, *'Un peu plus haut.'*

A little higher.

'Un peu plus loin.'

A little further.

Then he picked up the book and started reading out loud to Isabelle. About a little wooden boy and the conscience that would make him human.

AUTHOR'S NOTE

Before I, or you, go any further, I do want to warn that if you haven't yet read the book, you might want to do that first. I believe these acknowledgments contain some spoilers, as I describe some of the things that are true, and some that are partly based on fact, and some that are completely made up (as is the nature of fiction, of course).

How I wish I could say that my next statement isn't true, but it is.

My husband, Michael, died on September 18, 2016. I'd returned from a shortened book tour, and within days it was clear he was failing. Some have suggested he waited for me. I don't know if that's true, I don't know if I want it to be true.

When the time came, Michael passed away peacefully. At home. Surrounded, as he was in life, by love.

I talked about his dementia in the acknowledgments of the previous book, *A Great Reckoning*, and many of you wrote to tell me about your own experiences with the disease. With loss. I want to thank you, sincerely and profoundly, for trusting me with those most intimate of feelings.

It is both heartbreaking and heartening to realize that Michael and I were far from alone.

*

Glass Houses was written as Michael failed, and after he died. Writing became my safe harbor, my escape in the dark hours of the morning. I could slip into Three Pines and for a few precious hours each day enter the world of Gamache, Clara, Myrna et al.

The writing and the book would not have been possible without my assistant, and great friend, Lise Desrosiers. Thank you, dear Lise. This book is dedicated to you for a reason.

Thanks as well to Lise's husband, and our friend, Del Page. To our great friends, Kirk and Walter, who kept in touch every day. For years. And who came even closer as Michael failed. That's true friendship.

Boundless thanks to Kim and Rose and Daniel, Michael's caregivers. And Dr Giannangelo. And to all the friends, astonishingly too numerous to name, who have been there for us, through the worst of times. And the best.

Thank you for supporting and, at times, carrying us.

I want to thank my amazing editors, Hope Dellon, of Minotaur Books/St Martin's Press in the US, and Lucy Malagoni, of Little, Brown in the UK, who have made this, and all the books, better with their insightful notes.

Thanks to my US publisher, Andy Martin, and the whole Minotaur team. Hope Dellon, of course, Sarah Melnyk, Paul Hochman, Martin Quinn, Sally Richardson, and Jennifer Enderlin of SMP, and Don Weisberg of Macmillan.

Thank you, too, to my agent, Teresa Chris, who always asks how I am before asking how the book is. For an agent, that is extraordinary!

Linda Lyall has been with Michael and me, managing the website and designing the newsletter and doing a million things I don't even know about since before *Still Life* was even published. Thank you, Linda!

All these people I have just named have become so much more than colleagues. We have become true friends. Many traveled to Michael's funeral.

I want to thank my brother Rob, who hurried to Knowlton from Edmonton as soon as he heard the news about Michael. He held me in his strong arms and I knew it would be okay. I would be okay. Thank you to his wife, Audi, and their children, Kim, Adam, and Sarah, who loved their Uncle Michael.

Thank you to Mary, my sister-in-law, who interrupted a vacation to hurry down with her daughter Roslyn as soon as she heard. Thanks to Doug, to Brian and Charlie.

And now, as promised, a short explanation of what is fact in the book, and what is fiction. I will, without doubt, leave out some details, but the main issue surrounds the cobrador.

I first heard about the cobrador del frac many years ago, from our great friend Richard Oliver, who was with the *Financial Times* in Madrid.

The cobrador del frac exists. Dressed in top hat and tails, he follows debtors. Shaming them into paying. It was so extraordinary, I tucked that information and that image away for years. Waiting for the time when it was right to use it. *Glass Houses* was the time.

But – what came next is fiction. The history of the cobrador. The plague, the island, the cloaked figures acting as a conscience to those without one. Forcing payment of a moral debt. I made all that up, for the sake of the story.

I think that's the big thing that isn't real. And I know if you have doubts about some issues, you will do the research yourself. That's half the fun, isn't it?

Some might argue that Three Pines itself isn't real, and they'd be right, but limited in their view. The village does not exist, physically. But I think of it as existing in ways that are far more important and powerful. Three Pines is a state of mind. When we choose tolerance over hate. Kindness over cruelty. Goodness over bullying. When we choose to be hopeful, not cynical. Then we live in Three Pines.

I don't always make those choices, but I do know when I'm in the wilderness, and when I'm in the bistro. I know where I want to be, and I know how to get there. And so do you – otherwise you would not still be with me, reading this.

The final thanks is to you, my friend. For your company. The world is brighter for your presence.

All shall be well.

Reading Group Questions
for Glass Houses

1. Most courtroom novels begin with a clear identification of the victim and the accused, but Louise Penny conceals that information for much of the book. What is the impact of this unexpected structure?

2. Gamache's relationships with multiple colleagues, from Beauvoir to Barry Zalmanowitz to the judge and others, take surprising turns in the course of the story. How do your views of those relationships change from beginning to end?

3. The weather is almost a character in many of Louise Penny's novels, and serves a particularly important function here in establishing time and place. What are some of the most striking scenes in which weather plays a significant role?

4. With the robed figure dominating the green in Three Pines, 'The villagers were pushed to the edge. Edgy.' How did the presence of that figure make you feel? By the end of the novel, how do you view the role of the *cobrador del frac*, both ancient, as conceived by Louise, and modern?

5. Gamache, Beauvoir, and the Crown Prosecutor are obviously men, but there are also many powerful women in *Glass Houses*. Who are these women, and how do their

perspectives resemble and/or stand out from those of the men?

6. Chapter 3 tells us, 'The officers in that room were the foundation upon which a whole new Sûreté du Québec was rising. Strong. Transparent. Answerable. Decent.' How does that passage and/or other elements in the story resonate with the title *Glass Houses*?

7. What do we learn about Ruth in this book, and how does it influence your view of the profane old poet?

8. When Armand, Clara, Myrna, and Reine-Marie discuss the Milgram experiment in Chapters 25 and 26, they wonder if they would have administered the final shock. What do you think they – or you – would have done in that situation?

9. There are many points at which Louise misdirects the reader about characters and plot developments in this story. What were the most shocking twists for you?

10. How do you see the significance of the lemon meringue pie (here and in earlier novels if you've read them)?

11. Early in the book, Judge Corriveau recalls that Gamache paraphrased death-row nun Sister Prejean during another trial: 'No man is as bad as the worst thing he's done.' How might that apply to the characters in *Glass Houses*?

12. How do you feel about what happens with Isabelle Lacoste?

13. 'There is a higher court than courts of justice and that is the court of conscience. It supersedes all other courts,' says Gandhi. In contrast, Ruth argues, 'It's generally thought that a conscience is a good thing. But how many terrible things are done in the name of conscience? It's a great excuse for appalling acts.' Where do you stand on the significance of conscience and its costs?

14. In her Author's Note, Louise says, 'Some might argue that Three Pines itself isn't real, and they'd be right, but limited in their view. The village does not exist, physically. But I think of it as existing in ways that are far more important and powerful. Three Pines is a state of mind.' In what ways does Three Pines exist for you, both on the page and in real life?

Now enjoy the beginning of the next Gamache case,

Kingdom of the Blind

CHAPTER 1

Armand Gamache slowed his car to a crawl, then stopped on the snow-covered secondary road.

This was it, he supposed. Pulling in, he drove between the tall pine trees until he reached the clearing.

There he parked the car and sat in the warm vehicle looking out at the cold day. Snow flurries were hitting the windshield and dissolving. They were coming down with more force now, slightly obscuring what he saw outside. Turning away, he stared at the letter he'd received the day before, lying open on the passenger seat.

Putting on his reading glasses, he rubbed his face. And read it again. It was an invitation of sorts, to this desolate place.

He turned off the car. But didn't get out.

There was no particular anxiety. It was more puzzling than worrisome.

But still, it was just odd enough to raise a small alarm. Not a siren, yet. But he was alert.

Armand Gamache was not by nature timid, but he was a cautious man. How else could he have survived in the top echelons of the Sûreté du Québec? Though it was far from certain that he had survived.

He relied on, and trusted, both his rational mind and his instincts.

And what were they telling him now?

They were certainly telling him this was strange. But then, he thought with a grin, his grandchildren could have told him that.

Bringing out his cell phone, he listened as the number he called rang once, twice, and then was answered.

'*Salut, ma belle.* I'm here,' he said.

It was an agreement between Armand and his wife, Reine-Marie, that in winter, in snow, they called each other when they'd arrived at a destination.

'How was the drive? The snow seems to be getting worse in Three Pines.'

'Here too. Drive was easy.'

'So where are you? What is the place, Armand?'

'It's sort of hard to describe.'

But he tried.

What he saw had once been a home. Then a house. And was now simply a building. And not even that for much longer.

'It's an old farmhouse,' he said. 'But it looks abandoned.'

'Are you sure you're at the right place? Remember when you came to get me at my brother's home and you went to the wrong brother? Insisting I was there.'

'That was years ago,' he said. 'And all the houses look alike in Ste-Angélique, and, honestly, all your hundred and fifty-seven brothers look alike. Besides, he didn't like me, and I was fairly sure he just wanted me to go away and leave you alone.'

'Can you blame him? You were at the wrong house. Some detective.'

Armand laughed. That had been decades ago, when they were first courting. Her family had since warmed to him, once they saw how much she loved him and, more important to them, how much he loved Reine-Marie.

'I'm at the right place. There's another car here.'

Light snow covered the other vehicle. It had been there, he guessed, for about half an hour. Not more. Then his eyes returned to the farmhouse.

'It's been a while since anyone lived here.'

It took a long time to fall into such a state. Lack of care, over the years, would do that.

It was now little more than a collection of materials.

The shutters were askew, the wooden handrail had rotted and gone its separate way from the sloping steps. One of the upper windows was boarded up, so that it looked like the place was winking at him. As though it knew something he did not.

He cocked his head. Was there a slight lean to the house? Or was his imagination turning this into one of Honoré's nursery rhymes?

> There was a crooked man, and he walked a crooked
>   mile,
> He found a crooked sixpence against a crooked stile;
> He bought a crooked cat, which caught a crooked mouse,
> And they all lived together in a little crooked house.

This was a crooked house. And Armand Gamache wondered if, inside, he'd find a crooked man.

After saying goodbye to Reine-Marie, he looked again at the other car in the yard, and the license plate with the motto of Québec stamped on it: *je me souviens*.

I remember.

When he closed his eyes, as he did now, images appeared uninvited. As vivid, as intense as the moment they'd happened. And not only the day last summer, with the slanting shafts of cheerful sunlight hitting the blood on his hands.

He saw all the days. All the nights. All the blood. His own, and others'. People whose lives he'd saved. And those he'd taken.

But to keep his sanity, his humanity, his equilibrium, he needed to recall the wonderful events as well.

Finding Reine-Marie. Having their son and daughter. Now grandchildren.

Finding their refuge in Three Pines. The quiet moments with friends. The joyful celebrations.

The father of a good friend had developed dementia and died recently. For the last year or so of his life, he no longer recognized family and friends. He was kindly to all, but he beamed at some. They were the ones he loved. He knew them instinctively and kept them safe, not in his wounded head but in his heart.

The memory of the heart was far stronger than whatever was kept in the mind. The question was, what did people keep in their heart?

Chief Superintendent Gamache had known more than a few people whose heart had been consumed by hate.

He looked at the crooked house in front of him and wondered what memory was consuming it.

After instinctively committing the license-plate number to memory, he scanned the yard.

It was dotted with large mounds of snow, under which, Gamache guessed, were rusted vehicles. A pickup picked apart. An old tractor now scrap. And something that looked like a tank but was probably an old oil tank and not a tank tank.

He hoped.

Gamache put on his tuque and was about to put on gloves when he hesitated and picked up the letter yet again. There wasn't much to it. Just a couple of clipped sentences.

Far from being threatening, they were almost comical and would've been had they not been written by a dead man.

It was from a notary, asking, almost demanding, that Gamache present himself at this remote farmhouse at 10:00 a.m. Sharp. Please. Don't be late. *Merci.*

He'd looked up the notary in the Chambre des Notaires du Québec.

Maître Laurence Mercier.

He'd died of cancer six months earlier.

And yet – here was a letter from him.

There was no email or return address, but there was a phone number, which Armand had called but no one had answered.

He'd been tempted to look up Maître Mercier in the Sûreté database but decided against it. It wasn't that Gamache was persona non grata at the Sûreté du Québec. Not exactly, anyway. Now on suspension pending the outcome of an investigation into events last summer, he felt he needed to be judicious in the favors he asked of colleagues. Even Jean-Guy Beauvoir. His second-in-command. His son-in-law.

Gamache looked again at the once-strong house and smiled. Feeling a kinship toward it.

Things sometimes fell apart unexpectedly. It was not necessarily a reflection of how much they were valued.

He folded the letter and placed it in his breast pocket. Just as he was leaving the car, his cell phone rang.

Gamache looked at the number. Stared at the number. Any sign of amusement wiped from his face.

Dare he take it?

Dare he not?

As the ringing continued, he stared out the windshield, his view obscured by the now-heavy snow, so that he saw the world imperfectly.

He wondered if, in future, whenever he saw an old farmhouse, or heard the soft tapping of snowflakes, or smelled damp wool, this moment would be conjured and, if so, would it be with a sense of relief or horror?

'*Oui, allô?*'

The man stood by the window, straining to see out.

It was distorted by frost, but he had seen the car arrive and had watched, with impatience, as the man parked, then just sat there.

After a minute or so, the new arrival got out but didn't come toward the house. He was standing beside his car, a cell phone to his ear.

This was the first of *les invités*.

The man recognized this first guest, of course. Who wouldn't? He'd seen him often enough, but only in news reports. Never in person.

And he'd been far from convinced this guest would show up.

Armand Gamache. The former head of homicide. The current Chief Superintendent of the Sûreté du Québec, on suspension.

He felt a slight frisson of excitement. Here was a celebrity of sorts. A man both highly respected and reviled. Some in the press held him up as a hero. Others as a villain. Representing the worst aspects of policing. Or the best. The abuse of power. Or a daring leader, willing to sacrifice his own reputation, and perhaps more, for the greater good.

To do what no one else wanted to do. Or could do.

Through the distorted glass, through the snow, he saw a man in his late fifties. Tall, six feet at least. And substantial. The parka made him look heavy, but parkas made everyone look heavy. The face, not pudgy, was, however, worn. With lines from his eyes, and, as he watched, two deep furrows formed between Gamache's brows.

He was not good at understanding the faces faces made. He saw the lines but couldn't read them. He thought Gamache was angry, but it could have been simply concentration. Or surprise. He supposed it could even have been joy.

But he doubted that.

It was snowing more heavily now, but Gamache had not put on his gloves. They'd fallen to the ground when he'd gotten out of the car. It was how most Québécois lost mitts and gloves and even hats. They rested on laps in the car and were forgotten when it came time to get out. In spring the land was littered with dog shit, worms, and sodden mitts and gloves and tuques.

Armand Gamache stood in the falling snow, his bare hand to his ear. Gripping a phone and listening.

And when it was his turn to talk, Gamache bowed his head, his knuckles white as he tightened his hold on the phone, or from incipient frostbite. Then, taking a few steps away from his car, he turned his back to the wind and snow, and he spoke.

The man couldn't hear what was being said, but then one phrase caught a gust and made its way across the snowy yard, past possessions once prized. And into the house. Once prized.

'You'll regret this.'

And then some other movement caught his attention. Another car was pulling in to the yard.

The second of *les invités*.

CHAPTER 2

'Armand?'

The smile of recognition and slight relief froze on her face as she took in his expression.

His movement as he'd turned to face her had been almost violent. His body tense, prepared. As though bracing for a possible attack.

While she was adept at reading faces and understood body language, she could not quite get the expression on his face. Except for the most obvious.

Surprise.

But there was more there. Far more.

And then it was gone. His body relaxed, and as she watched, Armand spoke a single word into his phone, tapped on it, then put it into his pocket.

The last expression to leave that familiar face, before the veneer of civility covered it completely, was something that surprised her even more.

Guilt.

And then the smile appeared.

'For God's sake, Myrna. What're you doing here?'

Armand tried to modulate his smile, though it was difficult. His face was numb, almost frozen.

He didn't want to look like a grinning fool, overdoing it.

Giving himself away to this very astute woman. Who was also a neighbor.

A retired psychologist, Myrna Landers owned the bookstore in Three Pines and had become good friends with Reine-Marie and Armand.

He suspected she'd seen, and understood, his initial reaction. Though he also suspected she would not grasp the depth of it. Or ever guess who he'd been speaking with.

He had been so engrossed in his conversation. In choosing his words. In listening so closely to the words being spoken to him. And the tone. And modulating his own tone. That he'd allowed someone to sneak up on him.

Granted, it was a friend. But it could just as easily have not been a friend.

As a cadet, as a Sûreté agent. As an inspector. As head of homicide, then head of the whole force, he'd had to be alert. Trained himself to be alert, so that it became second nature. First nature.

It's not that he walked through life expecting something bad to happen. His vigilance had simply become part of who he was, like his eye color. Like his scars.

Part DNA, part a consequence of his life.

Armand knew that the problem wasn't that he'd let his guard down just now. Just the opposite. It had been up so high, so thick, that for a few crucial minutes nothing else penetrated. He'd missed hearing the car approach. He'd missed the soft tread of boots on snow.

Gamache, not a fearful man, felt a small lick of concern. This time the consequences were benign. But next?

The threat didn't have to be monumental. If it were, it wouldn't be missed. It was almost always something tiny.

A signal missed or misunderstood. A blind spot. A moment

of distraction. A focus so sharp that everything around it blurred. A false assumption mistaken for fact.

And then—

'You okay?' Myrna Landers asked as Armand approached and kissed her on both cheeks.

'I'm fine.'

She could feel the cold on his face and the damp from the snow that had hit and melted. And she could feel the tension in the man, rumbling below the cheerful surface.

His smile created deep lines from the corners of his eyes. But it did not actually reach those brown eyes. They remained sharp, wary. Watchful. Though the warmth was still there.

'Fine,' he'd said, and despite her disquiet she smiled.

They both understood that code. It was a reference to their neighbor in the village of Three Pines. Ruth Zardo. A gifted poet. One of the most distinguished in the nation. But that gift had come wrapped in more than a dollop of crazy. The name Ruth Zardo was uttered with equal parts admiration and dread. Like conjuring a magical creature that was both creative and destructive.

Ruth's last book of poetry was called I'm F.I.N.E. Which sounded good until you realized, often too late, that 'F.I.N.E.' stood for 'Fucked-Up, Insecure, Neurotic, and Egotistical'.

Yes, Ruth Zardo was many things. Fortunately for them, one of the things she was not was there.

Armand stooped and picked up the mitts that had fallen off Myrna's substantial lap, into the snow. He whacked them against his parka before handing them back to her. Then, realizing he was also missing his own, he went to his car and found them almost buried in the new snow.

*

The man watched all this from the questionable protection of the house.

He'd never met the woman who'd just arrived, but already he didn't like her. She was large and black and a 'she'. None of those things he found attractive. But worse still, Myrna Landers had arrived five minutes late, and instead of hurrying inside, spouting apologies, she was standing around chatting. As though he wasn't waiting for them. As though he hadn't been clear about the time of the appointment.

Which he had.

Though his annoyance was slightly mitigated by relief that she'd shown up at all.

He watched the two of them closely. It was a game he played. Watching. Trying to guess what people might do next.

He was almost always wrong.

Both Myrna and Armand pulled the letters from their pockets.

They compared them. Exactly the same.

'This is' – she looked around – 'a bit odd, don't you think?'

He nodded and followed her eyes to the ramshackle house.

'Do you know these people?' he asked.

'What people?'

'Well, whoever lives here. Lived here.'

'No. You?'

'*Non*. I haven't a clue who they are or why we're here.'

'I called the number,' said Myrna. 'But there was no answer. No way to get in touch with this Laurence Mercier. He's a notary. Do you know him?'

'*Non*. But I do know one thing.'

'What?' Myrna could tell that something unpleasant was about to come her way.

'He died six months ago. Cancer.'

'Then what—'

She had no idea how to continue, and so stopped. She looked over at the house, then turned to Armand. She was almost his height, and while her parka made her look heavy, in her case it was no illusion.

'You knew that the guy who sent you the letter died months ago, and still you came,' she said. 'Why?'

'Curiosity,' he said. 'You?'

'Well, I didn't know he was dead.'

'But you did know it was strange. So why did you come?'

'Same. Curiosity. What's the worst that could happen?'

It was, even Myrna recognized, a fairly stupid thing to say.

'If we start hearing organ music, Armand, we run. Right?'

He laughed. He, of course, knew the worst that could happen. He'd knelt beside it hundreds of times.

Myrna tipped her head back to stare at the roof, sagging under the weight of months of snow. She saw the cracked and missing windows and blinked as snowflakes, large and gentle and relentless, landed on her face and fell into her eyes.

'It's not really dangerous, is it?' she asked.

'I doubt it.'

'Doubt?' Her eyes widened slightly. 'There is a chance?'

'I think the only danger will come from the building itself.' He nodded to the slumping roof and sloping walls, 'and not from whoever is inside.'

They'd walked over, and now he put his foot on the first step and it broke. He raised his brows at her, and she smiled.

'I think that's more the amount of croissants than amount of wood rot,' she said, and he laughed.

'I agree.'

He paused for a moment, looking at the steps, then the house.

'You're not sure if it's dangerous, are you?' she said. 'Either the house or whoever's inside.'

'*Non*,' he admitted. 'I'm not sure. Would you prefer to wait out here?'

Yes, she thought.

'No,' she said, and followed him in.

'Maître Mercier.' The man introduced himself, walking forward, his hand extended.

'*Bonjour*,' said Gamache, who'd gone in first. 'Armand Gamache.'

He swiftly took in his surroundings, beginning with the man.

Short, slight, white. In his mid-forties.

Alive.

The electricity had been turned off in the house and with it the heat, leaving the air cold and stale. Like a walk-in freezer.

The notary had kept his coat on, and Armand could see it was smudged with dirt. Though Armand's was too. It was near impossible to get into and out of a vehicle in a Québec winter without getting smeared by dirt and salt.

But Maître Mercier's coat wasn't just dirty, it was stained. And worn.

There was an air of neglect about him. The man, like his clothing, appeared threadbare. But there was also a dignity there, bordering on haughtiness.

'Myrna Landers,' said Myrna, stepping forward and offering her hand.

Maître Mercier took it but dropped it quickly. More a touch than a handshake.

Gamache noticed that Myrna's attitude had changed slightly. No longer fearful, she looked at their host with what appeared to be pity.

There were some creatures who naturally evoked that reaction. Not given armor, or a poison bite, or the ability to fly or even run, what they had was equally powerful.

The ability to look so helpless, so pathetic, that they could not possibly be a threat. Some even adopted them. Protected them. Nurtured them. Took them in.

And almost always regretted it.

It was far too early to tell if Maître Mercier was just such a creature, but he did have that immediate effect, even on someone as experienced and astute as Myrna Landers.

Even on himself, Gamache realized. He could feel his defenses lowering in the presence of this sad little man.

Though they did not drop completely.

Gamache took off his tuque and, smoothing his graying hair, he looked around.

The outside door opened directly into the kitchen, as they often did in farmhouses. It looked unchanged since the sixties. Maybe even fifties. The cabinets were made of plywood and painted a cheery blue the color of cornflowers, the counters of chipped yellow laminate and the floors of scuffed linoleum.

Anything of value had been taken. The appliances were gone, the walls were stripped clean except for a mint-green clock above the sink that had long since stopped.

For a moment he imagined the room as it might once have been. Shiny, not new but clean and cared for. People moving about, preparing a Thanksgiving or Christmas dinner. Children chasing one another around like wild colts, with parents trying to tame them. Then giving up.

He noticed lines on the doorjamb. Marking heights. Before time had stopped.

Yes, he thought, this room, this home, was happy once. Cheerful once.

He looked again at their host. The notary who did and did not exist. Had this been his home? Had he been happy, cheerful, once? If so, there was no sign of it. It had all been stripped away.